JAN 1 2 2024

D1155886

PRAISE FOR LUANNE RICE

The Shadow Box

"Rice's compelling heroine and crisp prose lift her brisk thriller . . ."
—*Kirkus Reviews*

"[A] gripping psychological thriller . . . Prepare to be up all night reading."
—*Publishers Weekly*

"Decades-old crimes lead to current murder in a case unwound through the efforts of strong women. With a core of appealing characters, bestselling author Rice—known for domestic fiction and romance—has the makings of a promising mystery series here."
—*Booklist*

"*The Shadow Box* is a heart-stopping yet enthralling breath of sea air, with as much dark beauty as one of Claire Beaudry Chase's own shadow boxes. It's also a resolute testimonial of inner strength, no matter how far from our plots and plans life takes us."
—*The Big Thrill*

"*The Shadow Box* is a captivating read as much for its illuminating portrayal of domestic disenchantment as for its requisite, and robustly handled, mystery elements. Ultimately, Luanne Rice has given us a deeply affecting meditation on how we both lose and find ourselves, proving once again that she's a luminary in any, and all, literary realms of her choosing."
—*Criminal Element*

"*The Shadow Box* is Luanne Rice at her dazzling best. Filled with dark family secrets and wells of deep emotion, this novel will stick with you long after you've finished reading."
—Harlan Coben, #1 *New York Times* bestselling author of *The Match*

"As always, Luanne Rice gives us characters so real they feel like family and families so flawed they give us chills. Shocking, compassionate, and told with the unerring eye of a true and gifted observer, *The Shadow Box* will keep you turning the pages long past your bedtime."
—Tami Hoag, #1 *New York Times* bestselling author of *The Boy*

"A clever protagonist in extreme danger pitted against a cruel and powerful circle made the stakes in *The Shadow Box* so high I could barely stop reading for a drink of water. Luanne Rice creates a thrillingly compelling tale of common cruelty, high ambition, and the courage it takes to oppose them. Well done!"
—Barbara O'Neal, *Wall Street Journal* and *USA Today* bestselling author of *When We Believed in Mermaids*

"Every family has secrets, but in Luanne Rice's clever thriller *The Shadow Box*, the truth won't set you free—it will put you in a shallow grave . . . particularly if you live in the posh Connecticut enclave of Catamount Bluffs, where corruption, kidnapping, and murder are only a few of the community's hidden sins."
—Lee Goldberg, #1 *New York Times* bestselling author

Last Day

"In a family drama that is as suspenseful as it is empathetic, Rice again displays her ability to portray female friendship and the pain of loss."
—*Booklist* (starred review)

"Rice keeps the reader guessing as she gradually doles out long-hidden family secrets. Fans of intense family dramas will be rewarded."

—*Publishers Weekly*

"Strong love overcomes pain in this latest from Rice (*Pretend She's Here*), which combines suspense with stories of survivors, sisterhood, best friends, and small communities shaken by violence or death."

—*Library Journal*

"A riveting story of a seaside community shaken by a violent crime and a tragic loss."

—*Brooklyn Digest*

"From the exquisite opening, through twists and torment, this domestic thriller weaves an irresistible story of family and friends, trust and betrayal, love and murder."

—*Suspense Magazine*

"Luanne Rice's opening pages of *Last Day* illustrate elegant writing at its finest. Twist after twist is guaranteed to keep readers guessing all the way to the surprises in the final pages . . . a sheer pleasure to read. Rice, the author of more than 30 books, is a master at writing descriptions and portraying story settings, a skill other writers admire and strive to acquire."

—*New York Journal of Books*

"The themes of love, loss, sisterly devotion, betrayals, and family ties are skillfully interwoven. [Rice] provides just enough intriguing detail to make the reader want to learn more . . . She once again doesn't disappoint in this novel."

—*LymeLine.com*

"*Last Day* by Luanne Rice is a gripping psychological suspense story. It starts out with an intensity from page one that never lets up."

—*Crimespree Magazine*

"If you're a fan of Shari Lapena or Ruth Ware, order this book and get ready to be sucked in. It's one of the best books of the year so far."

—*GQ* magazine

"A compulsive thriller . . ."

—*The Patriot Ledger*

"Lovely, lyrical—and lethal. Luanne Rice turns her talents in a new direction and succeeds completely."

—Lee Child, #1 *New York Times* bestselling author

"Luanne Rice is the master of small towns with big secrets. With a deft touch, she draws us into a picture-postcard New England village, behind the closed doors of a well-loved home with its beautiful gardens and perfect family, only to expose the truths within. Surprising, powerful, a total page-turner."

—Lisa Scottoline, *New York Times* bestselling author of *Someone Knows*

"In *Last Day*, Luanne Rice shows once again her unique gift for portraying the emotional landscape of a family. By adding a riveting thread of suspense, she proves beyond the shadow of a doubt that love and murder make brilliant bedfellows."

—Tess Gerritsen, *New York Times* bestselling author of *The Shape of Night*

"*Last Day*, by Luanne Rice, shines with its brilliant plot about four women friends, their families and loves, and, shockingly, a murder. Rice's writing is flawless and fast, her characters are like the women I have coffee with, and the desire, violence, and betrayals shock me and remind me of Liane Moriarty's *Big Little Lies*."
—Nancy Thayer, *New York Times* bestselling author of *Surfside Sisters*

"A dark family history. A deeply flawed marriage. The complicated tangle of the ties that bind. Luanne Rice writes with authenticity and empathy, unflinchingly exploring her characters and diving into the shadowy spaces where they hide their secrets. Like all great stories, *Last Day* is a compulsive, twisting mystery dwelling inside a searing portrait of what drives us, as riveting as it is human and true."
—Lisa Unger, *New York Times* bestselling author of *The Stranger Inside*

"A brutal murder, a failed marriage, secret lovers, and enough suspects to fill a room. The truth lies somewhere between betrayal and love. A compelling mystery you won't put down or solve until the final pages."
—Robert Dugoni, *New York Times* and Amazon Charts bestselling author of the Tracy Crosswhite series

"I've long loved Luanne Rice for her trademark elegant style and her deep understanding of familial relationships, and she brings these superpowers with her as she delves into suspense. *Last Day* is a true page-turner, peopled by characters I care deeply about, with an ending I never saw coming."
—Joshilyn Jackson, *New York Times* and *USA Today* bestselling author of *Never Have I Ever*

LAST NIGHT

OTHER TITLES BY LUANNE RICE

LAST NIGHT

LUANNE RICE

THOMAS & MERCER

This is a work of fiction. Names, characters, organizations, places, events, and incidents are either products of the author's imagination or are used fictitiously. Otherwise, any resemblance to actual persons, living or dead, is purely coincidental.

Text copyright © 2024 by Luanne Rice
All rights reserved.

No part of this book may be reproduced, or stored in a retrieval system, or transmitted in any form or by any means, electronic, mechanical, photocopying, recording, or otherwise, without express written permission of the publisher.

Published by Thomas & Mercer, Seattle

www.apub.com

Amazon, the Amazon logo, and Thomas & Mercer are trademarks of Amazon.com, Inc., or its affiliates.

ISBN-13: 9781542030199 (hardcover)
ISBN-13: 9781542030205 (paperback)
ISBN-13: 9781542030212 (digital)

Cover design by Kimberly Glyder
Cover image: © DenisTangneyJr, © Walter Bibikow, © Adrian Zurbriggen / 500px / Getty Images

Printed in the United States of America

First edition

To Andrea Cirillo
and the spirit of Agnes Martin
With love

1

The path to the beach was deep with snow. It covered the thickets on both sides, creating rounded shapes that looked like sea animals, like the white beluga whales at the aquarium. It softened everything and turned the world cold. The shape in the middle of the path was buried, and no matter how she tried to dig the snow away, it just kept falling and falling, so the face wasn't a face anymore; it was just a lump.

The snow was white except for the pink, but even that little bit of color went away as the storm got stronger and the evening got darker.

Her fingers were frozen in her mittens. She squeezed and squeezed her hands, but that didn't work. Her chest was full of tears. Screams were trapped in her throat. She wanted to let them out because they might bring help, but she was more afraid they might bring the bad person back.

Her feet had been the warmest part of her body because when they were in the yellow hotel where they lived, her mommy had put thermal socks on her and laced up her boots for a walk on the beach. They always walked in the rain here in Rhode Island, and in the snow this winter, but tonight was extra exciting because the wind was howling, the flakes were falling fine and fast, and there were big waves.

"We're having a blizzard, CeCe!" her mother had said.

"What's a blizzard?" CeCe had asked. She was six, and this was new to her.

"A gigantic snowstorm that we'll talk about forever. When you're grown up and I'm old, we'll say, 'Remember the blizzard, when we went to the beach?'"

"And built a snowman!" CeCe had said. "Can we?"

"Not sure about that," Mommy said. "We're just going to make a quick trip down there to see my friend and take some pictures. We want to get back before it gets really dark."

"Papa?" CeCe asked.

Mommy didn't answer. She had said she wasn't sure if they could build a snowman, but just in case, CeCe ran around the hotel room and filled her pockets with things to decorate one with: grapes from the cheese platter for eyes, a red Christmas tree bulb for a nose, and a length of gold ribbon to make a smile. She had Star, too. Star was all that was left of her baby blanket, and even though she was six, she carried it with her everywhere.

Then Mommy finished tying CeCe's laces, and they walked out of their pretty new home with the big windows overlooking the ocean. They had moved to the big yellow hotel during the summer, when the sand was hot and the sea was blue, and they had stayed there all autumn, when the leaves were the color of sunshine and fire.

That first night in the suite where they were going to live from now on, Mommy had shown her the five towers with blinking red lights, far away across the sea, behind a low line of land that she said was Block Island. Mommy had said the lights were on windmills standing in the ocean. CeCe counted them: one, two, three, four, five. A little later she fell asleep.

As the drifts piled up around her on the beach path, CeCe thought of the red windmill lights and the warm hotel. She thought of how happy she felt going down in the hotel elevator. It was made of wood, with a fancy black grate, and it felt like a little room. Mommy had said it was very old; she remembered it from when she was a little girl. CeCe loved that she was allowed to push the button that took them to the lobby—all full of Christmas trees and tiny sparkling lights, millions of them like stars when the sky was black and clear—and the dining room, where she got to order whatever she wanted for breakfast. Today it had been chocolate chip pancakes.

Mommy had said Aunt Hadley would arrive that night. In case she got there before they returned from their walk, Mommy would leave a note for her and tell Isabel, CeCe's favorite front desk lady, to let Aunt Hadley into the suite. Isabel was nice, and funny. She said there were twinkling lights on whales and swans, and the lights in the lobby were stars.

Now, in the snow, CeCe's teeth chattered so hard she bit her tongue. Instead of going to the beach the special way, just for people staying in the hotel, her mother had taken her along the road, past the big houses to this narrow path that Mommy had said was a better place to meet her friend, where people from the hotel couldn't see. She told CeCe to hide because it was a big secret, just between Mommy and the person she was going to meet, and nobody was supposed to know, at least not yet.

"But where do I hide?" CeCe had asked.

"Here in this little hollow," Mommy had said, clearing out a space between two bayberry bushes. "You go in there now, and don't make a peep. Pretend you're a baby beluga diving under the ice for fish, okay?"

"Okay," CeCe said and giggled, because she loved whales at the aquarium; it was her favorite place to go, except maybe now the hotel, because it was their home and they were happy there.

"I'll tell you when to come out," Mommy said, and when she kissed her, CeCe saw that she had snowflakes on her hat and in her eyebrows, and it made CeCe laugh.

The little snow cave was nice and cozy and even a little warm, or at least warmer than out on the path in the December wind. CeCe hugged her arms around her knees, knowing that belugas lived in the Arctic, a very cold place, so this was part of pretending.

She heard a voice. It was a very low voice, as deep as Papa's, and that would be a wonderful surprise. She nearly burst out of the cave and into his arms, but she had promised Mommy that she would stay inside and be quiet, no matter what. So she did. The voice kept talking.

Although she wasn't supposed to go out, she hadn't been told not to look, so she peeked. There was someone standing beside Mommy. Was it a man? She couldn't tell because of the thick jacket and wool hat, but the person was taller than Mommy, just like Papa. She didn't think it was him, though, because if it were, he would find her and pick her up in his arms. The wind was howling so loudly she couldn't hear what Mommy and the person were saying.

The person shoved Mommy. That's when CeCe was ready to break her promise and rush out, because no one should push her mother. Then there was a loud bang that frightened and startled CeCe so much that she squeezed her eyes tight and covered her ears.

The wind rose, and the person was gone. When CeCe's mother didn't call her, CeCe went out of the snow cave onto the path and saw red ribbons streaming from a black hole in her mommy's head. CeCe knelt down, tried to push the ribbons back into the hole, but they wouldn't go; they made her mittens wet.

"Open your eyes," CeCe commanded. "*Now*, Mommy!"

Her mother's fist was closed tight. CeCe decided to hold that hand, to keep Mommy warm, but when she did, Mommy's fingers were as limp as yarn. That sent a quick, scary shiver all through CeCe's whole body and gave her a horrible feeling. CeCe felt something hard inside her mother's glove. She wriggled her hand inside and pulled out a key.

A funny-looking key. It didn't look like the kind that went in doors to unlock houses. CeCe knew she should put it back in her mother's glove, but her mother couldn't hold it right now, so instead she put it in her own pocket.

The snow fell harder. The red ribbons turned pink. Then they weren't ribbons at all, just pale streaks, and then they disappeared. Mommy was a snowdrift, and so were all the bushes, and now so was CeCe. She closed her eyes, put her head down on the snowbank where Mommy's shoulder should have been.

But Mommy had told her to hide in the snow cave, and she didn't want to disobey, so she crawled back inside. She reached into her pocket to hold the key and Star, but they weren't enough to calm her. A huge shudder shook her entire body. She needed to be with Mommy, even if she was disobeying, so she flung herself out of the hollow. She pressed her cheek to her Mommy's cold face, and she couldn't hold it in anymore. She just couldn't, and she began to cry, louder than anyone has ever cried before.

2

After a harrowing drive from Providence, Hadley Cooke pulled into the circular drive in front of the Ocean House and felt grateful for her good old reliable truck. Four-wheel drive had gotten her here safely in the wild storm, even though the highway was down to one lane, and cars had skidded into guardrails and barriers all along the way, a version of vehicular pinball. Twenty miles per hour with ten-foot visibility all the way from her studio on Fox Point, and now her hands were cramped from holding the wheel in a death grip.

"Hello, Ms. Cooke. You made it through the storm! So glad to see you again," Dermot, the familiar valet said, opening her door and beaming at her as if she were visiting royalty instead of an itinerant artist in a rusty old Dodge. "Here to visit your sister! They told me you'd be arriving."

"Oh, good. Thanks, Dermot."

Hadley felt the tension leave her body, just as if she had come home. She and Maddie had stayed here as children and knew every inch of the property. Later, as teenagers, they would drive down to Watch Hill for the day—to go to the beach and have lemonade on the porch after swimming. The salty old Ocean House, built in 1868 and buffeted by over a hundred years of storms like this one, had been torn down and lovingly rebuilt with meticulous attention to every detail, making it the regal seaside retreat it was now. The owners treasured the hotel's history, and it showed in every aspect of the architecture and decor.

The Ocean House was the perfect sanctuary for Maddie. She had bought Sea Garden, one of the Signature Suites, and it would be home for her and CeCe. Both Hadley and Maddie thought it was pretty great that CeCe could pretend to be Eloise, the little girl who grew up in a hotel. Only instead of the Plaza in New York, it was the Ocean House in Watch Hill.

"Ms. Cooke," Dermot said, "let me walk you inside to reception, and then I will deliver your bags to Ms. Morrison's suite. Are all of these going up?" He gestured at the overflowing passenger seat.

"Yes, thank you," she said. One duffel held a change of clothes, her sketchpad, and her laptop. The others were shopping bags packed with Christmas gifts for Maddie and CeCe, 90 percent of them for her niece. She knew Maddie would scold her for spending so much money, but Hadley couldn't resist spoiling CeCe.

Hadley texted Maddie: I'm here!

Then she preceded Dermot up the sweeping staircase to the grand yellow hotel. It had wings and turrets, and it was adorned for the season with wreaths, towering Christmas trees, pine-and-laurel garlands draped around the tall columns and the verandah's ornate white railings. Twinkling white lights were everywhere. She walked inside to the sound of harp music. The lobby was decorated with evergreens and tiny lights. If a hotel could greet someone with a warm embrace, she decided it would be the Ocean House. Dermot walked her to the reception desk and told the friendly, chic young woman who Hadley was visiting. Hadley knew her from past visits.

"Hello, Isabel," she said.

"Welcome, Ms. Cooke," Isabel said. "How was your drive?"

"Intense," Hadley said. "Especially when I got into Westerly."

"Nor'easters come in off the ocean, so we get pretty fierce winter storms. Especially this blizzard. We won't have as many guests in-house as we'd expected. I'm so glad you made it safely. May I get you a glass of champagne or sparkling water?"

"Oh, champagne, please!" Hadley said. They offered a glass to everyone who checked in, and although she was just visiting, she knew they treated Maddie like family and therefore Hadley, too. As beautiful as Maddie's other homes were, Hadley thought she had finally found a place to be truly happy. She looked at her phone, but Maddie hadn't replied to her text yet.

Isabel handed her a flute of bubbles. Hadley felt a little self-conscious in her down jacket and paint-flecked Joan of Arctic Sorel boots. But Isabel's smile and graciousness reassured her that she was welcome and fit right in.

"Your sister stepped out, and I haven't seen her come back yet," Isabel said.

"Out in this storm?" Hadley asked, surprised.

"Perhaps she returned and I didn't see. I'll ring her now," Isabel said and lifted a telephone receiver. Hadley looked around at the blazing fire in the massive stone fireplace, the harpist in her long black dress, the cozy seating nooks with sofas and armchairs, and the beautiful paintings in gilded frames on the walls. Some of the Christmas tree decorations were inspired by the sea: scallop shells, starfish, and sand dollars. The taste of champagne and the sense of being nurtured helped her relax even more.

"She's not answering," Isabel said. She slid an envelope across the highly polished desk. "She told me that if she wasn't back when you arrived, I was to give you this."

Hadley accepted it, wondering why Maddie hadn't just texted her instead of leaving a note. She would read it when she was alone.

"You can wait in her suite until she and her daughter return." Isabel's eyes crinkled with a smile. "CeCe is the sweetest little girl."

"Best niece in the world," Hadley said.

"Dermot has already taken your bags upstairs. I know you know the way, but would you like me to walk up with you?"

Hadley looked around. The lobby was so festive. Even though the blizzard had no doubt kept many guests from arriving, there was a buzz of conversation, a sense of anticipation as the dinner hour approached.

"I think I'll wait down here by the fire," Hadley said.

"Of course," Isabel said. "Please let me know if you need anything at all."

"I will," Hadley said, checking her phone again. Still no word from Maddie.

She sat on a window seat just in front of the fireplace. It was vast and made of round fieldstones, with an antique iron anchor set just above the wide mantel. She knew that when the owners had taken down the old hotel, they had dismantled the fireplace stone by stone, numbered and stored them in a bucket, and then put them back exactly as they had been. It threw good heat, warming her fingers and toes. She leaned into plush pillows. The sound of crashing waves came up the hill and harmonized with the harp's gentle strings.

It was obvious why Maddie had chosen this hotel—it felt like a soothing oasis in the midst of the aggression and insanity of her perpetually ongoing divorce. Another sip of champagne and Hadley checked her phone. Still no word, so she opened the envelope, pulled out a folded piece of heavy-bond stationery, and read Maddie's note:

Hi, H! I'm not going to text because you are driving and I don't want you spinning out in the storm. I have a little errand to run, a very quick meeting on our favorite path. Sorry to be mysterious—I'll explain when I get back. I'm taking CeCe, hoping a walk in the snow will tucker her out so you and I can have a good talk while she sleeps. Lots to tell you. Heading out now, be back in no time. XXXX M.

Hadley reread the note. How long ago had Maddie written it? The weather was getting worse—shouldn't she be back by now? What meeting could possibly be worth heading into this storm?

She walked back to the front desk, waited for Isabel to finish helping a man and a woman, about Hadley's age. She wanted to be patient, but the ferocity of the storm, and the fact that Maddie hadn't returned yet, was making her uneasy. She shifted from one foot to the other, wishing Isabel would hurry up and send the couple on their way.

Conor Reid stood at the front desk of the Ocean House, his arm around his longtime girlfriend, Kate Woodward. The receptionist was telling them that dinner reservations were wide open; there'd been cancellations due to the storm, and they could have their choice of times.

"How about seven o'clock?" Kate asked Conor. "Is that okay with you?"

"That would be great," Conor said. "Whatever you want."

He had his hand in his right pocket, fingers closed around a small blue velvet box. Tonight was going to be the night. After they had been together for years, he had arranged the getaway he thought would make the stars align for him and Kate.

They were on vacation until after Christmas. They'd checked into the hotel earlier that day, before the gale cranked up into a blizzard. They both loved the beach, and he'd envisioned proposing on the sand, by the water's edge. He had pictured constellations in the sky, or possibly moonlight glowing through clear, green waves. But with this snowfall, that wasn't happening.

"Would you prefer to dine in Coast or the Bistro?" the receptionist asked. He heard her describing the offerings of the two different dining rooms, but he was distracted by a woman standing behind him. He sensed her anxiety—the way she was inching forward, wanting service right away.

"Let's see," Kate was saying. "Coast is lovely, but it's more formal. I remember that from taking an artist to dinner last summer." She glanced at Conor and didn't even have to ask which he would prefer. "The Bistro," she said, knowing he favored the more casual of the two.

He squeezed her shoulders. He was thinking that since the storm-swept beach might be too rugged tonight for what he had in mind, she deserved the second-most special setting he could come up with.

"How about Coast?" he asked, looking into Kate's eyes. He saw her big smile, and that's all he needed.

"Really?" Kate asked.

"Yeah," he said. "Seven p.m. in Coast."

He saw the receptionist note the reservation, and he took Kate's hand. The woman standing behind them was edging forward, seeming impatient. He wanted to let her have her turn. Even more, he wanted to go outside and stand on the hotel's verandah, his arms around Kate, feeling the storm's energy.

As fierce as the weather might be, it was no match for his emotions. Did she have any idea why he had brought her here? They were so close they could sometimes read each other's minds. But his years in law enforcement had honed his talent for keeping a poker face. He wanted tonight to be a surprise for her, and he hoped he could hold back until they were sitting at the table.

"Excuse me," Hadley said to Isabel when the couple finally stepped away from the desk and headed outside. "What time did my sister leave?"

"Let's see," Isabel said, tilting her head and calculating time. "It was getting dark . . . maybe about four thirty?"

Hadley checked her phone. Now it was five thirty. Maddie and CeCe had been out for an hour. She felt a flutter inside as worry crept in. But she told herself to knock it off and thought of times when she and Maddie had gone out adventuring in storms. Ever since they were kids, they had loved wild weather, swum in hurricanes, skied in driving snow. It made sense to Hadley that Maddie would take advantage of being right on the ocean, to feel the force of the wind.

But would she stay out this long with CeCe?

Hadley knew there were two beach paths—the private one in front of the hotel and the public one a short walk away. The latter ran from Bluff Avenue down to the sea, right next to a storied white mansion on the highest point of land.

She pulled on her down jacket, zipped it all the way up, tugged on her black wool watch cap, and headed out the front door. Dermot asked if she needed her truck, but she said no.

The couple in front of her at the front desk were standing on the verandah, gazing out. She wondered what they could possibly be seeing through the curtain of snow, but then she saw: the beam of the light-house. It flashed almost imperceptibly through the snow, red alternating with white, every five seconds. The foghorn sounded beneath the wind, and she could barely hear the bell buoy's mournful toll. Hadley felt the couple watching her as she ran down the steps onto Bluff Avenue. She slipped on a slick patch, lost her balance, went down hard.

She heard the woman ask: "Are you okay?"

"I'm fine," Hadley called over her shoulder. She brushed herself off and kept going. Faster. Snow stung her eyes, blinded her. She passed a driveway, then another. She had to slow down to make sure she didn't miss the path. Here it was, adjacent to the majestic Holiday House, marked with a tidy sign:

WELCOME TO THE EAST BEACH!
YOU ARE ENTERING ONE OF THE MOST BEAUTIFUL BEACHES ON THE
EASTERN SEABOARD!

The streetlights had illuminated Bluff Avenue, at least a little, but their glow was no help here as Hadley began to make her way down the narrow path. She pulled out her iPhone to turn on the flashlight. She looked for footprints, but the deep snow was smooth and pristine, like a ski trail before the first run. Gorse hedges lined the way, heavy with snow. A tree branch overhead creaked under the weight of it.

Hadley was about to turn around. Maddie must have met whomever she'd come to see and gone somewhere warm. Was the Olympia Tea Room, just down the hill on Bay Street, open for the holiday season? She doubted it, because the town basically closed at the end of October.

Could they be having hot chocolate somewhere? Was it possible Maddie and CeCe had been heading back to the hotel and Hadley had missed them, stumbled right past them in the thick snow? *Two ships—I mean sisters—who passed in the night,* she'd say when they finally met.

Then her foot caught something under a high drift, and for the second time, Hadley fell. She'd tripped over a rock, perhaps. Maybe one of the tree limbs had fallen and gotten covered again. Brushing snow off her boot, she uncovered whatever lay beneath. It wasn't a rock or a log. She caught sight of a black sleeve. There was a patch on the shoulder: Moncler, the fancy brand of winter coat that Maddie wore.

Hadley tugged at the arm in the sleeve. It was stiffer than a branch. She began to dig madly. She heard sounds coming out of her own mouth. When she got to the person's head, to the face, when she saw the blue eyes and the hole in the forehead, the sounds became screams. She threw her arms around her sister. "No, no, Maddie, no! MADDIE!"

She rocked back and forth, then felt arms around her from behind. She half turned, tears already frozen to her cheeks.

"My sister," Hadley said to the woman standing there, the woman who had been at the hotel. "Help my sister!"

"We will," the woman said. The man stood beside her. He reached out a hand. Hadley hesitated. She couldn't let him pull her up; she couldn't leave Maddie.

"Where is CeCe?" Hadley asked.

"Who is CeCe?" the man asked.

"My niece," Hadley said. "Where is she?"

3

Conor held the woman's hand and helped her to her feet. She strained against him, obviously wanting to stay crouched down beside the body under the snow. Kate put her arms around the woman's shoulders, helped to ease her away, just a few steps. The woman wailed, staring down at the body. A question tumbled out, her voice shaking so hard Conor could barely understand: "Tell me, oh God, is my niece under there, too?" she asked.

"Your niece?" Kate asked.

"She's only six," the woman said, the words tearing out of her.

Conor didn't want to disturb the victim, but he knew that if there were a chance a child was buried there as well, he had to. He knelt down and, as carefully as he could, felt under the snow. The woman's body was cold and stiff, and there was no sign of a girl. He saw the bullet wound in the center of the woman's forehead.

"Tell me your name," Kate said to the woman's sister. "I'm Kate, and this is Conor."

"Hadley."

"Okay, Hadley. Let's go back to the hotel," Kate said. "In case CeCe is there."

"CeCe wouldn't have left her mother."

"Maybe she would have if she thought she could get help," Kate said.

Hadley's expression changed. She nodded. "Yes," she said. "She might have." She began walking, then running, up the path.

"I'll go with her," Kate said to Conor.

"Good," Conor said. "I'll stay here. I'll call this in."

Kate hurried away, after Hadley. Conor pulled his cell phone from his jacket pocket and dialed 911. He identified himself to the Westerly, Rhode Island, emergency dispatcher and gave the location. He had to repeat himself to be heard over the wind. Then he hung up and waited.

The snow was falling so fast and heavy it had already covered the body. He realized that he didn't know the victim's name. He texted Kate to request that she ask Hadley for it, as well as a description of CeCe and Hadley's last name.

The response came quickly: Hadley Cooke. Her sister is Madeleine ("Maddie") Morrison. And CeCe isn't here. Six years old, about three feet tall, light brownish-blonde hair, blue eyes. Full name is Cecelia Lafond.

So a missing child with a different last name than her mother. Conor immediately called the dispatcher back and told her that information, along with CeCe's description, so they could initiate an Amber Alert right away. Conor was a detective with the Major Crime Squad of the Connecticut State Police. Although he was out of his jurisdiction, he often worked closely with detectives in the neighboring state of Rhode Island, so he made a direct call to his friend Detective Joe Harrigan.

"Already got the word, and I'm on my way, Conor," Joe said as soon as he answered. "Stick around."

"I will," Conor said.

Conor waited, standing still so he wouldn't disturb the crime scene more than he, Kate, and Hadley already had. It was pitch dark. He heard the foghorn and the clang of the bell buoy marking the treacherous shoals of Watch Hill Passage.

Within minutes he heard sirens and saw blue-and-red strobe lights. Two uniformed officers came down the path. Conor told them what he knew. Together they waited until a four-wheel drive state police vehicle pulled up and Joe Harrigan joined them.

"Hey, Conor," Joe said, walking over, looking past Conor toward the spot where Maddie lay. "Tell me what you know."

"Her name is Madeleine Morrison, according to her sister, Hadley Cooke, who found her. One bullet wound, forehead. All I could see, anyway," Conor said.

"You dug around?" Joe said, and Conor heard apprehension. Joe wouldn't want anyone tromping on evidence.

"Only to make sure her daughter wasn't there, too. CeCe, age six."

"No sign of her?"

"None."

"Where's the father?"

"No idea. We didn't get that far. Kate took Hadley back to the hotel."

Joe wore glasses. He took them off to wipe snow from the outside of the lenses and steam from the inside. "You know these people?"

"No," Conor said. "We just met Hadley—the victim's sister—right here, half an hour ago."

"What made you decide to take a walk down the beach path in the middle of a blizzard?" Joe asked.

"Kate and I were on the Ocean House porch when Hadley— though we didn't know her name then—went running out. She looked frantic, as if something was wrong, and she slipped. Kate said we should follow her, to make sure she was okay. We came upon her here."

"She had just found her sister's body?"

"Yes."

"How did she seem?"

"Hysterical. Worried about CeCe."

"Okay, thanks. We'll question her at the hotel. And I'll come find you there, too," Joe said.

"You mean I'm dismissed?" Conor asked. He sounded sarcastic, but he understood. This was Joe's turf.

"Tricky, isn't it?" Joe asked.

"Yes," Conor said. "But I'm here if you need me. Unofficially."

"Thanks," Joe said. "Unofficially."

Conor stood there, watching Joe approach the body. He had offered his help if Joe wanted it, but he knew he was already personally involved. Another detective arrived, along with an investigator from the Rhode Island State Crime Lab.

Conor and Kate had been second on the scene. They had seen the body of a young woman who'd been alive just hours ago. They had witnessed Hadley's shock and grief—just the beginning of a lifetime of missing her sister. Conor wasn't going to be able to let go easily. Or at all.

The uniformed officers had closed Bluff Avenue—the short stretch of road that ran from the Ocean House to the lane that led to the lighthouse—and they had set up a perimeter from Maddie's body to the sidewalk. Conor assumed they would be placing crime-scene tape as far down as the beach, but he didn't wait to watch. He hiked up his collar and kept his head down as he hurried through the roaring storm toward the hotel.

He liked working parallel cases, across state lines, especially with Joe. Harrigan was smart, thorough, and not above bending the rules when he needed to. Conor had the feeling Joe wanted him to stay, but he understood why Joe had sent him away; Conor would have done the same, if their roles were reversed. Conor was a witness in this situation, not a police detective.

A mother murdered, her child missing. This was going to be a big case, and optics were going to matter. Joe would want to keep the press away for as long as possible. In that regard, the blizzard would work in his favor.

Conor walked into the hotel's circular drive. There was a black Chevrolet Suburban parked in the turnaround. Considering that a child was missing, he knew that the FBI would be called in, and he wondered if this vehicle belonged to an agent. The bellmen watched Conor pass, and one of them held the door for him.

The same front desk attendant who had helped him and Kate make dinner reservations greeted him, her solemn tone letting him know that she was aware of at least some of what was going on.

He started through the lobby, on his way to the room. He spent two seconds reflecting on how he had brought Kate to the Ocean House for what he'd expected to be one of the most important weekends of their lives. He wouldn't say his plan had gone out the window, exactly, but right now his focus had shifted to murder.

"Mr. Reid!"

At the sound of his name, he turned to see the receptionist hurrying toward him. He hadn't paid attention to her name before, so he glanced at her name tag.

"Yes, Isabel?" he asked.

"They've gone to Ms. Morrison's suite. Would you like me to take you there?" she asked.

"Yes, please," Conor said.

He followed Isabel past the bar and restaurant to the ornamented oak-paneled elevator and up two stories. She had concern in her eyes, but she discreetly didn't ask any questions and left him at a door marked Sea Garden. He thanked her and knocked.

Kate answered, letting him in. He stopped just inside, holding her. He whispered, in case Hadley was within earshot.

"How are you?" he asked. It wasn't a casual question.

"I'm fine."

"This is part of the crime scene," he said.

"I know," she said. "I thought of it too late, after we'd already come inside."

19

Conor knew that Kate knew. He would have done anything to shield her from this—the killing of a sister. He had met her five years earlier while investigating her sister Beth's murder. She'd been traumatized—beyond healing, it seemed at times. She had been withdrawn, even from him, even after they'd started living together. But things had changed recently, and it was why he had chosen this time to take her here.

"We'd better move her to a different room, until the police can process this suite," Conor said.

"It's called Sea Garden," Kate said. She stared down the short hallway at the wall of windows facing east. "It looks out at the ocean, like our room does. When the sky is clear, the view must be spectacular. Maddie must have seen the sunrise this morning, before the storm."

"Yes," Conor said, his arms around her, never taking his eyes off her face.

"I can't stand to think of her that way," Kate said, tears spilling out. "To have watched the sunrise from this room, to have found this beautiful place and thought it was safe—and then to have been murdered. I wish I hadn't seen her—Maddie, under all that snow. And to think of Hadley, having to find her. Seeing her, wanting her to be okay, now out of her mind over CeCe . . ."

Conor knew it was all coming back to Kate: how she had discovered Beth's body, strangled and posed, on her own bed in the house she had shared with her husband, Pete, and their daughter, Samantha. Of course Kate would be thinking of Hadley and her niece. She had gone through the aftermath of violence with Sam.

"Where is Hadley now?" Conor asked.

"In one of the bedrooms," Kate said. "There are three in here."

"Can you go downstairs and see if the hotel has a place for her while the police work in here? We've got to clear out, and she's going to need somewhere to stay."

"I will," Kate said. "And thanks."

"For what?"

"Giving me something to do. So I can stop picturing Maddie lying there. It takes me back to Beth . . ." She kissed Conor and closed the door behind her.

Conor stood in the foyer, looking around. This might not have been his case, but being a detective remained his true nature, and he couldn't just leave it at the door. He walked slowly down the corridor, a half bath on the right. The pale-yellow walls were covered with framed black-and-white photographs of Watch Hill in the 1800s. He noticed that one was askew, and considering the attention to detail throughout the hotel, he wondered about it, and whether it might indicate that a struggle had taken place here. He stood close to the frame, looking it over, but he didn't touch it.

The living room was vast, extending to the tall windows Kate had referenced. A set of french doors led to a wide terrace that ran the length of the suite. There was a stone fireplace with shells and glass lanterns arranged on the mantel. It was flanked by bookcases. Every shelf was full of novels and books of nonfiction about the sea and the history of the Ocean House and Watch Hill.

He saw that one book had been taken down, placed on the writing desk. It was a novel—*Reef Road* by Deborah Goodrich Royce. He read the cover copy and saw it was a thriller based on a true crime. That piqued his interest.

A sheet of stationery had been folded and placed inside to mark a page. Conor removed a pen from his pocket and used it to open the book. The paper was blank, so he figured Maddie had been in the midst of reading and had used it to save her place. He was intrigued and decided he'd get a copy of the book and read it.

There were two distinct seating areas, one in front of the fireplace, the other by the windows. They were gracious, flanked by lamps that gave off soft light, with a sofa, armchairs, and a coffee table in each. Toys and children's books were strewn around the sofa by the fire. Crayons, colored pencils, and drawing paper covered the low table.

Some of that artwork was obviously done by a child, but there was one sketch clearly made by an adult. It depicted a carousel, with a woman buckling her little girl onto one of the horses, and there was a phrase written in pencil: *Together Forever.*

A key had been drawn, and it looked too real to be sketched. Conor leaned down and saw an impression, as if an actual key had been pressed into the paper and traced with charcoal. There was a faint imprint of numbers. He took photos of the drawings, including the ones most likely done by CeCe, and he wrote down the numbers from the key in a pad he always carried.

The kitchen had new, high-end stainless-steel appliances. Conor had worked many cases in affluent Connecticut towns, and he recognized the brands. The stove was embossed with classical marine motifs: dolphins and a sailing ship. There was a sleek stainless-steel Italian coffee maker that could make cappuccino and espresso, with a design that looked like it belonged in the Museum of Modern Art.

He saw three glasses and two bone-china coffee cups in the sink. There were also three plates at the dining table. At first, he figured Maddie must have put out three place settings in anticipation of Hadley's arrival, but he reminded himself not to make assumptions. Who was the third person? He took photos of the table and the rest of the room, as well as of the kitchen.

A hallway led to the bedrooms. He found Hadley in the master bedroom, sitting on the edge of the king-size bed. She was going through a large black leather purse.

"Is that yours?" Conor asked.

"No, it's Maddie's."

"You need to put it down, Hadley. It's evidence."

"I know," she said. "That's why I'm looking—I want to know who she met! I thought maybe she'd written it down."

"Wouldn't she have just put it in her phone? If she wrote it down at all?"

"No, she used a day planner. A red leather Hermès agenda." Hadley looked up. "She got it in Paris. She took me there last June to celebrate."

"Celebrate what?"

"My birthday and her separation."

That filled Conor's mind with questions, but his phone buzzed, and when he looked, there was a message from Kate: Isabel has arranged for Hadley to wait in room 200 until Sea Garden is ready again. I'll meet you there.

"Come on now, Hadley," Conor said. "We've got to leave here so the detectives can do their work."

He knew she didn't want to put down her sister's purse. She didn't want to leave her sister's suite. This was the last place Maddie had stayed. Leaving now would be walking away from another part of her sister's life. Conor knew that there would be much more leaving to come. It wouldn't get easier.

Finally, Hadley set the bag down on a chaise longue beside a second set of french doors leading to the same terrace that curved around the living room.

"This is where I found it," she said.

"Good," Conor said. "It will be helpful to leave everything just the way it was."

"The way she left it."

"Yes," he said.

She walked out ahead of him, and he took a moment to photograph the room and walk-in closet. There was a small safe tucked between two shelves. Maddie's suitcase was open on a folding luggage caddy, and he snapped a photo of that, too.

Photographing the victim's room was habit, whether it was his investigation or not. But this was about sisters, Maddie and Hadley.

He thought about Kate and Beth and felt the electricity he always did when a case grabbed hold of him.

Conor and Hadley arrived at room 200 where Kate was waiting. She led Hadley to a small sofa by the window. A few minutes later, Conor answered a knock at the door and greeted Joe Harrigan and the detective Conor had seen at the crime scene.

"This is my partner, Garrett Milne," Joe said to Conor. "Garrett, this is Conor Reid. Conor heads up Major Crimes, closest district to us, over in Connecticut."

"Hey, Conor," Garrett said. As they shook hands, Conor was pretty sure he had encountered him at New England police seminars, but they had never actually met. The small world of regional law enforcement.

Conor and the two Rhode Island detectives walked over to Kate and Hadley. Joe said hello to Kate and introduced himself and Garrett to Hadley.

"Ms. Cooke, we've asked the FBI to join the investigation," Joe said. "Special Agent Patrick O'Rourke is on his way upstairs now."

Conor knew that Joe's statement was not, strictly speaking, correct. The FBI automatically worked child abduction cases and would not have to be invited in by state or local police. It was a misconception to believe that the agency entered a case only when it involved a victim being taken across state lines. Under the Violent Crimes Against Children program, the FBI investigated all disappearances of children of "tender years"—under twelve years old.

"We'd like to talk to you now, Ms. Cooke, and Special Agent O'Rourke will have his own questions," Joe said.

"Okay," Hadley said. "You need to find CeCe. Please tell me she's alive. She must be so scared—she needs us." Then, as if hearing that last word made her realize Maddie was gone, Hadley corrected herself. "She needs me."

"Do you have a recent photo of her?" Joe asked.

Hadley nodded and pulled out her phone. She held it up; the wall-paper on her lock screen was a close-up of CeCe's face. Conor saw a beautiful, happy-looking little girl with bright-blue eyes and a big smile.

"Can you send it to me?" Joe asked, giving her a number.

"Hadley," Conor said, "you can believe that every officer in New England is looking for her right now."

"The FBI will be posting billboards all up and down 95 and other highways, with that photo and the offer of a reward," Garrett said.

Conor knew that Pat O'Rourke was out of the FBI's New Haven field office. He had worked with him in the past, on kidnapping and other cases in Connecticut. He was very good, an agent who worked well with local cops.

Joe said that they would like to interview Hadley in private and question Conor and Kate next. Conor completely understood. He and Joe respected each other, and he was pretty sure Joe would blur the lines when it came to Conor's input, but at the moment, procedure took precedence. It didn't matter how invested Conor felt; the investigation belonged to Rhode Island. He was just a shadow for now.

4

CeCe sat next to the boy. He looked angry. She had screamed when he had pulled her away from her mother, picked her up, and carried her to the car, but now she was silent. Her fingers and toes were frozen, and the heat from the radiator was making them hurt so much she thought they might fall off; what would she do if they did? Why wasn't her mother here with her? Her heart beat with the question, not the answer, because the answer was too terrible. She wanted her mother.

"This sucks," the boy said.

Don't say "suck," CeCe wanted to tell him. Her mother had told her not to use bad words, and she didn't like them; they scared her. Another thing that scared her was wondering if the boy was the one who had made the red ribbons in the snow, streaming from her mother's head.

"Did you see those fucking cop cars?" the boy asked. "I should have let you stay there. I shouldn't have gone back for you. You know how much trouble I'll be in if they catch me with you?"

"Then let me go," CeCe said. "I won't get you in trouble."

"Yeah, sure. You'll tell."

"Tell what?" CeCe asked. Her mother sometimes said "he meant well" or "she meant well" when someone did something in a way that wasn't very nice. Maybe the boy thought he was helping her, rescuing her, by carrying her to his car. It was dry, warmer than the snowbank. She thought of her mother on the beach path.

"Tell—what do you think?" he asked. "I'm basically a kidnapper now. And worse." He reached down between the seats and pulled out a gun. "See this? Now you understand? You weren't supposed to be with her!"

CeCe hunched her shoulders.

"Can we go back and get her?" she asked.

"Are you serious?" he asked. "Don't you get it?"

CeCe was shaking, trying to erase her mind. She only wanted to sit and hold Star, rub the cloth on her cheek and smell its familiar scent. She didn't want to "get it."

"Didn't your parents teach you to be afraid of strangers?" he asked. "I'm a stranger."

"Star," she whispered. "Star, Star, Star."

"Fuck it," he said. "Never mind." He rubbed his sleeve on the window next to him to clear the fog. He looked out into the storm. CeCe knew where they were. They were parked just down the hill from the hotel and the beach path. She and her mother had walked around the pretty little town almost every day since they had moved into the suite.

The carousel was close by. The flying-horse merry-go-round. She had taken so many rides on it during the summer. Her favorite horse was brown with a red-fringed saddle blanket. Older kids grabbed for the brass ring, and her mother had told her she could do that when she was bigger, maybe even next summer.

The water on this side was the harbor, and it was calmer than the ocean. During the summer and fall, it had been full of boats. She and her mother had walked out on the big, curving beach called Napatree Point, and her mother had told her that this part of the harbor was called "the Kitchen" because almost a hundred years ago there had been a hurricane and many houses were wrecked, their things dashed into the water, and people still sometimes found forks and knives and plates from those long-ago families.

There were lots of shops, and her mother had bought things in them, presents for CeCe. The dark-brown building by the dock was the yacht club. Her mother had said that maybe they would get a sailboat next year and join so they could sail through the harbor and around Sandy Point, and meet people and make friends. But now it was closed for the winter.

"Why are we sitting in the car?" she asked the boy.

"Because we're waiting for my dad's boat, and it's not here yet. And we can't drive to it. Check it out. I mean, can't you see the freaking snow? They'd stop us if we drove anywhere. Besides, this piece-of-shit car has shitty tires because we don't have enough money to fix stuff."

CeCe closed her eyes tight. After the boy had grabbed her away from her mother and put her in the car, they'd had a scary ride. It wasn't very far, just down an icy hill, and the car had spun around in a circle, like a ride at the Santa Monica Pier when her father had taken her there on one of his weekends, and the boy had steered the car into the alleyway just behind the row of shops. There were other cars here, too, lumpy under the snow in the dark.

"Nobody is going to see us back here unless you do something dumb," he said. "Like try to escape."

How would that be dumb? CeCe wondered. Running away from him would be smart, and she would, but she was afraid to make him even madder.

"Because if you got out of this car, you could die in the snow. They wouldn't find you till spring. Like your . . ."

CeCe didn't want to know what he was talking about, but she sort of did anyway, and that thought stabbed her in the heart so hard she wrapped her arms around herself and bent over double in her seat.

"What's the matter?" he said. "You still crying about your frozen fingers?"

"I didn't cry about them," she said.

"It's not my fault if you got frostbite. I didn't know you'd be there with your mother. I am going to get in so much trouble."

She didn't know what any of that meant.

"You should thank me for going back for you," he said. "I could have left you there, but I was feeling bad; you're just a little kid."

"Who are you?" she asked instead of thanking him. She would never thank him for anything.

"I'm my father's son," he said. "And my uncle's nephew. They taught me, you know? Oh yeah, that's the truth. I do what they tell me."

That was a weird thing to say. She gazed at him long and hard. He was skinny, and his dark-blue jacket was dirty, stained with black smudges. There was a patch on his chest embroidered with red script and a lobster. He smelled like fish, or like the beach when it was covered with seaweed. The letters *RG* were above the lobster.

"Stop staring at me," he said. "I should've blindfolded you. No, forget that—I should have left you there."

"I thought you had to be a grown-up to drive," she said. "You don't look very old."

"Yeah, well, I'm fifteen," he said. "So what if it's not legal? A lot of things aren't legal. I should know. But don't think it was my idea!"

What was he talking about? What wasn't his idea?

"You weren't supposed to be there," he said again.

Why did he keep saying it?

"You were supposed to be in the stupid hotel," he said, banging the palm of his hand hard on the steering wheel. "Waiting for her in your nice warm room. What kind of mother would take her kid out in a blizzard?"

"Don't say that about her," she said.

She wouldn't say another word to him. She curled up in a ball on the seat, trying to stay warm. He kept turning the car on and off. It would heat up, then get cold right away. Every time the car got cold again, he swore. She wondered how long they had been there and how long they would stay there.

"It will be warmer on the boat," he said.

A boat? In the winter? What was he talking about?

"Once my damn father gets here. Where are your mother's paintings, anyway? They're worth a fortune, aren't they?"

He sounded crazy. Why was he asking about her mother's paintings? CeCe scrunched down in her seat, leaning against the cold door, as far away from him as possible.

She wanted to reach inside her pocket to hold the key. She kept thinking of how it had been in her mother's hand. If she could touch the key, it would be as if her mother were in the car with her.

Maybe CeCe had dreamed the bad things. It had been a terrible dream, and it was still going on. An endless dream—she just hadn't woken up yet. She would wake up and be in their suite in the hotel, with the fireplace burning and a good dinner in her tummy and her mother watching TV on the sofa beside her.

It was night, dark and late, so that meant she really was asleep; her mother never would have let her stay up this late. She didn't have to be upset, because this wasn't real. She was in Sea Garden, leaning against her mother by the fire.

But deep down, she knew it wasn't a dream, no matter how much she wanted it to be. It was something else; she just didn't know what. At least she was near the yellow hotel, the place she and her mother loved and where they were happy. It was just up the hill. That made her feel better. Her mother wasn't in her body anymore, under the snow. She was here with CeCe.

She had to be sure she had the key. She wriggled her fingers into her pocket, but it wasn't there. Her pocket was empty. No snowman decorations, no key, and no Star. She must have dropped them in the snow cave. She thought of Star alone in that horrible place, and she had to bite her fist to keep from making a terrible sound, from wailing louder than the wind.

5

Conor and Kate sat in their room, a peaceful refuge amid the chaos. She had a book open, but he could tell she wasn't reading it. She was lost in her own visions; he was, too. He wondered if she was seeing Maddie's body, and if that was giving her flashbacks to finding Beth. He felt a surprising emptiness, stuck in the room while the investigation went on without him. He was in the middle of a crime, with no assigned role to solve it or help. He scrolled through the photos on his phone, the ones he had taken in Maddie's suite. He wasn't sure what he was looking for, but that was always the way in the early hours after a murder.

"Are you okay?" he asked, glancing over at Kate.

"Yes, are you?" she asked.

"Yes."

She smiled. "We're both lying."

"This getaway isn't turning out the way I'd planned," he said. He still had the ring in his pocket. Watching her, he had the feeling she might know, or at least suspect it. They never had taken that walk on the beach; they never had gotten to Coast for dinner.

"Coming here was the perfect idea," she said. "I've always wanted to stay in the Ocean House and to be here during a blizzard—I love the wild weather. I mean, you couldn't have planned it better."

"Except . . . ," he said.

"Yes. A young mother being murdered," she said. She inched closer to him on the love seat. He put his arm around her. He almost wished she would cry so he could comfort her, but except for that quick burst of tears when they'd first returned to the hotel, that wasn't Kate. She held it all in. Her way was to pull back, harden her shell, shut him out.

"I am glad we are here," she said. "I wouldn't trade being here right now for anything."

He nodded. He knew what she meant.

"We need to be here," she said. "Hadley needs us. Maddie does . . ."

"I feel that way, too," Conor said. "But part of me wishes we'd never come. I don't want to put you through it. Reliving it all. As soon as the roads open, we can check out. We can come back another time."

"As if you would," Kate said. "No, we belong here right now. It's meant to be."

Meant to be. Was this Kate? Sometimes, during murder investigations, he had heard victims' families try to make sense of the unthinkable act: if only their mother/daughter/brother/sister/friend had left the house ten minutes later, or if she had never fallen in love with the man who turned out to be her killer, or if the victim had remembered to turn on the house alarm before going to bed. "It must've been part of God's plan," he had heard the families say. "God needed her in heaven. It was meant to be."

But not Kate. She wasn't religious. She was an inveterate pragmatist. She had never sought refuge in what she would consider easy sentiment—she hated it. She was a pilot and owned her own Cessna. She kept it at Westerly State Airport, just five miles from here. She tended to go flying when things got rough—temporary escapes that helped clear her head and push the world away. She relied on her own inner toughness, never platitudes. She wasn't a "meant to be" kind of person, so the words, coming from her, were alarming.

"You look worried," she said. "Don't be; I'm not losing my mind."

"I don't think you are," he said.

"Yes, you do. I can read it in your face."

That was probably true. They'd been able to do that with each other, almost since the beginning.

"I know you want to protect me from—what did you say?—'reliving it all.' I do anyway," Kate said. "I think about Beth every day. I think about finding her—I see how she looked; I picture her on the bed. That's not going away."

Conor felt the same way—not just about Beth but about all the murder victims. He had seen them in death, and to solve their murders, he'd had to get to know them as they had been in life.

"So I don't want you to protect me, okay? But there is something I want."

"What's that?"

"I want you to work the case."

"We're in Rhode Island," he said.

"So what? Just because you're not assigned to it? It's still yours."

"It's Joe's."

"Then what are all those photos on your phone that you keep staring at?"

She had noticed. Kate was an astute observer of life—especially of Conor. Even when she seemed emotionally detached, nothing escaped her. She ran an art gallery, and it wasn't just a business to her. She saw clues in paintings: about the artists, about the subjects, about the world.

"Just habit," he said.

"Right," she said. "Conor, we fell into this. From the minute we followed Hadley to the path. You know why we did, right? We saw something was wrong. The way she ran into the storm—we wanted to make sure she was okay. And she wasn't."

"How could she be?"

"Exactly. No one understands what she's going through more than we do. It doesn't matter whether this is a Connecticut State Police case or not. You can help her."

"Joe Harrigan's a good detective. He's got a whole team . . ."

Kate shook her head. "It's different."

He stared at his phone. She knew how badly he wanted to examine each shot, let the images sift through his brain, come up with questions that might assist with the case.

"Do you think they're finished questioning Hadley yet?" Kate asked.

"Maybe," he said, checking his watch.

"And going through the suite?"

"That could take a little longer."

"Should we go see?" Kate asked.

Conor didn't want to get in their way, but the answer was yes. "We should. Let's go see," he said.

He'd call the front desk and make sure they could keep their room. The hotel had been fully booked, but because of the storm, there had been cancellations, and there was availability. Conor extended the reservation.

He and Kate were going to stay and see this through.

6

Hadley felt the detectives' eyes on her. The questions they were asking made her feel like a suspect. She knew they were trying to read her, to look beneath the answers she was giving to their questions. Joe Harrigan was the senior detective, Garrett Milne obviously his subordinate. Harrigan sat in the chair opposite Hadley, and Milne stood behind him. Neither of them took notes. She had the feeling that what she said mattered less than how she said it. She was ready to jump out of her skin. All she wanted was for them to get out there and find CeCe.

They asked for the note Maddie had left for her.

"When will I get it back?" Hadley asked, not wanting to let go of it.

"I'm not sure. The lab has to examine it," Detective Harrigan said.

Before Hadley handed the note to them, she gazed at it long and hard. These were the last words Maddie would ever write to her. She couldn't stand to hand it over.

"I'm going to take a picture of it, just in case," she said.

"Of course," Detective Harrigan said.

She took photos of the front and back. But Maddie had held the actual note in her hand; her pen had touched the paper, this beautiful stationery. Photographs weren't the same. After a few moments, Hadley let Detective Milne take the note, and the two detectives left.

Just past eleven o'clock that night, the police finished with Maddie's suite. Martyn, the hotel's hospitality manager, had sent housekeeping to clean, and by midnight they had helped Hadley move in. Her things were already there, from when she had first arrived. She changed into her pajamas. They were ridiculous—green silk imprinted all over with the face of Tigger, the gray tiger cat she and Maddie had had as children. Maddie had given them to Hadley for Christmas last year. She had sent a picture of Tigger to the pajama company, and they silk-screened it onto the fabric. She had gotten a pair for herself and one for CeCe, too.

When she heard the knock on the door, Hadley went running—she had the quick, insane thought that Maddie had forgotten her key. But it was Kate and Conor, the couple who had walked her back from the path. She saw Kate notice her pajamas.

"From my sister," she said.

"They're great," Kate said.

Hadley felt embarrassed. She opened the coat closet by the front door and reached for Maddie's long black cashmere dress coat. She pulled it on over the pajamas, tied the belt tight, and turned back to Kate and Conor.

"We were wondering if you'd like some company," Kate said.

Hadley had thought that was the last thing she wanted, but now she was glad they were here. She nodded and invited them in. They all sat around the fireplace. As soon as Hadley had been allowed back, she'd turned on the gas flame to try to warm up. She had gotten so cold out in the snow that every bit of her was still chilled. Maddie's soft, warm coat felt good.

"Hadley, I'm a detective with the Connecticut State Police," Conor said. "I don't want to intrude, but if there's any way I can help, I'd like to."

"I just want to find CeCe," Hadley said. "Did someone take her? Or what if she's lost in the snow?"

"The police are searching," Kate said. "See their lights?"

Hadley looked out the window, and it was true—through the screen of driving snow, the beach was illuminated.

"I'm sure Detective Harrigan went over everything with you," Conor said. "But maybe something different will come to you. A detail, a memory you might not have thought was important. Do you mind if I ask you some questions?"

"No, if it will help find her," Hadley said.

"Tell me what you can about the family," he said.

"No one in the family would hurt her," she said.

"It's not to blame anyone," he said. "It's just, the more we know about Maddie and CeCe's background, the better the chance of figuring out who did this."

"Someone knows the truth," Kate said. "I don't want to say I know what you're going through—no one can—but my sister was murdered. Talking about it was so hard at the beginning; I just wanted it to go away. I wanted to hide from what had happened. But you'd be surprised how the smallest things, the ones you think couldn't possibly matter at all, can turn out to be incredibly important."

"Did they find her killer?" Hadley asked.

"Yes," Kate said. "Conor did." Hadley saw her glance at him. "He solved the case; it's how I met him. You can trust him, Hadley."

Something about the look in Kate's eyes, the sorrow in her bearing, made Hadley believe it was true. Kate had said she couldn't know what Hadley was going through, but Hadley thought that maybe she did.

"A good place to start would be CeCe," Conor said. "Does she have any brothers or sisters?"

"She's Maddie's only child," Hadley said.

"Are Maddie and her father together?"

"No," Hadley said. "They're getting divorced."

"Where is he now?" Conor asked.

"That's a good question," Hadley said. "I've tried calling and texting him, and I've left messages with his office. Now the police have his information, and they'll follow up."

"The way you said 'they're getting divorced' . . . ," Kate said. "Is it contentious?"

Kate's tone of voice made Hadley believe that she knew something about bad divorces.

"Did you go through one?" Hadley asked.

"No, but my sister had a . . . difficult marriage."

"So did Maddie. And the divorce is even worse."

"Where does he live?" Conor asked.

"California," Hadley said. She wanted to hold on to the next part as long as she could. The minute she said his name, Conor and Kate would see everything differently. The police had. Everyone did. "Her husband is Bernard Lafond."

She could see on their faces that it registered in a hazy way, a big name from years past. A film star and director with a lifetime of award-winning movies and a long list of lovers and ex-wives.

"I thought he lived in France," Kate said.

"Well, he's French, and they have places there, but long ago he decided that Los Angeles was where the work was. The kind he wanted to do, anyway."

"Is that where Maddie lived before she moved here into the Ocean House?" Conor asked.

"In Malibu," Hadley said. "After they separated, Bernard stayed in an apartment they had on Wilshire."

"I feel bad saying this, but I love his movies," Kate said. "Or loved—I haven't seen one in a long time."

"Don't feel bad," Hadley said. "I love them, too. And at the beginning, I used to love him as well. He seemed wonderful at first, but that changed. Even though I completely get why Maddie left him, I can't believe he would do this. The divorce is terrible, but I think it's mostly the lawyers. They're making a fortune off it, and it just keeps getting worse."

"I guess with all those movies, there's a lot to fight over," Kate said.

Hadley gave a sad smile. "It wasn't that at all. Bernard spent most of his money on alimony and child support for his previous wives. He was a wild man who bought vineyards and castles that dried up and crumbled. He has a weakness for yachts and vintage Porsches. He trusted the wrong advisers. No, he's going after Maddie's money. He's broke. Maddie has a fortune."

"An actual fortune?" Kate asked.

Hadley knew the word was sometimes thrown around, but in this case it was warranted. "Oh yes," she said.

"Inherited from your family?" Kate asked.

"No."

"How did she acquire it?" Conor asked.

"From her art."

"She made art?" Kate asked. "What kind?"

"Her paintings. Early in her career, she did large installations. For a while it seemed that every big-name architect had to have one in the lobby of the newest and tallest glass tower, every brokerage house and top law firm wanted them in their boardrooms." Hadley paused, thinking of how art ran in their family but Maddie's had taken her into the stratosphere.

"That's quite an accomplishment," Kate said. "It's a challenge for artists to make a living, much less attain that kind of success."

"Well, it wasn't until she began to license her work that things really took off. Reproductions, T-shirts, mugs, even a limited-edition Fiat. Then a line of clothing. A perfume company launched a fragrance based on one of her paintings. Almost all of these products came from her two most famous designs."

"What designs?" Kate asked.

"The upside-down tiger and the swan on the back of the white whale."

"MC!" Kate said, with shock and a burst of obvious delight. "Your sister is MC?"

"Yes. MC, Maddie Cooke—her maiden name." Hadley turned up the cuff of Maddie's coat; just inside, on the black silk lining, a tiny inverted tiger was embroidered in orange and black, bright-green thread for its emerald eyes. The swan and whale were inside the other sleeve, both images hidden from the world.

"Oh God," Kate said. "What a brilliant artist. So many layers to her work—the sheer beauty of it, the way every painting was a poem. I've seen her exhibitions in New York and Paris. It made me sad when she stopped showing original work."

"So many people say that. They think she turned commercial, just concentrated on making money. And she did make plenty—she's a billionaire—but she had managers for that. She barely paid attention to it." Hadley had to close her eyes.

"I can't believe it," Kate said. "Maddie is MC!"

"It's so hard talking about Maddie this way. Kate, you said Maddie is MC—but it's *was* now. She *was* MC," Hadley said.

"No," Kate said, putting her arm around Hadley. "She will always be MC. That work lives forever. It's indelible, part of the world now. And Hadley, you will never lose her, I promise. Sisters are present tense, whether they are here or not. That's how I still think of Beth."

Hadley tried to let that in. She did feel it in her heart, but would it wear off? This time yesterday, Maddie had been alive. She had been sitting right here in Sea Garden, maybe even in the same chair where Hadley was now. She'd been dead for barely a few hours.

"Why did she stop showing new work?" Conor asked.

"Well, she had all that tremendous success when she was younger. She was only thirty when the licensing began. It scared her to think of her art becoming a commodity, so she stopped exhibiting."

Kate's eyes widened, and Hadley could see she got it. "But she kept painting?"

"In secret, yes," Hadley said.

"How did she get the name Morrison?" Conor asked.

"It's funny how Kate is all about the art, and you are all about the rest," Hadley said.

"He's just being a detective," Kate said.

"Maddie was married twice," Hadley said. "First to Johnny Morrison, right after art school. It only lasted about a year—they were really too young to know what they were doing—and it was about a year after that that she hit the big time. So he had no right to her money—not that he would have gone after it. It was an amicable split. She never legally changed her name back to Cooke."

"And what about Bernard Lafond? I thought California had community property laws, that the couple automatically split the assets," Conor said. "Why would their divorce be so contentious?"

"From what Maddie told me, community property only covers the money made or property bought during the marriage. They've been together for seven years, married for six. She made most of her money before they even met. She told me he has a right to some of her investments and a share of the real estate—she paid for the Malibu house, among others. She was happy to give him that. She felt it was fair, and she just wanted out."

"Bernard is CeCe's father?" Kate asked.

"Yes, they got married after she got pregnant. CeCe is named for his mother, who lives in France."

"There's an age difference," Conor said.

"He's old enough to be CeCe's grandfather, but for the most part, he's been a good dad. Even Maddie thought that, at least before things turned so vicious. Whether he turned it into a war or his lawyers did, it didn't matter. It really tore Maddie up, and as much as she tried to shield CeCe from the worst, it has affected both of them." Hadley sighed. "The crazy thing is, they had a prenup. Supposedly ironclad."

"But you said Maddie was willing to give Bernard what sounds like a generous settlement," Conor said.

"That wasn't enough for him. He wanted to go after both past and future earnings. His lawyers are working overtime to get the prenup overturned. Because Bernard claims he got used to a way of life, being married to her. The lawyers maintain he should be able to continue it."

"Lawyers are good at finding loopholes," Kate said.

"What happened between them, to cause the breakup?" Conor asked.

"He was envious of her success and jealous of anyone who came into her life."

"Possessive?"

"Very. She never cheated on him, but he saw it everywhere—with old friends, new friends, even Johnny. He got to the point when he'd be upset when she and I spent time on the phone. He hated the time she took me to Paris—he felt that Paris was 'their' city, that she shouldn't go there with anyone else, even me."

"You said he envied her success," Conor said.

"Yes, and that seemed crazy. It's not as if he wasn't incredibly successful, too. And famous. At first I really liked him, and I was overjoyed for Maddie—she'd found a partner who seemed equal to her, in terms of a big career," Hadley said. She pictured her sister on the day she'd told Hadley she was getting married. Maddie had been full of light. She had beamed at Hadley, at everyone, as if she had discovered how to illuminate the world.

"It must have been hard for her to find someone who wasn't threatened by her art and money," Kate said.

"Yes," Hadley said.

"But Bernard did feel threatened?" Conor asked.

"Very much so. Even though she was paying the bills and was always generous to him and his children," Hadley said and closed her eyes. She knew that that was a big part of the problem. "Ultimately, Bernard wanted everything Maddie had yet resented her for giving it."

"How many children does he have?" Kate asked.

"Seven," Hadley said. "All grown with kids of their own. I never met them—they didn't approve of him marrying Maddie, so they didn't go to the wedding. They never accepted her into the family."

"But she was generous to them?"

"She wanted to make Bernard happy—or to make him look good. He didn't want them to know he had blown all the money. And I think Maddie hoped that if she opened her heart to them, they might soften toward her."

"Did they?"

"No. They all live in Europe. I guess there were occasional visits to California, and at first, Maddie and Bernard saw two of his daughters when they stayed in France. But the last few times she was there, they couldn't seem to get together. She felt as if his kids wrote him off, just because he loved her."

"You said Bernard was jealous of her first husband. Was Maddie still in touch with him?"

"Oh yes," Hadley said. "She and Johnny stayed friends after they split up. He was always part of our family. He and I work together."

"What do you do?"

"We're muralists," Hadley said. "Maybe you've seen those big murals in seaside New England towns, with sailing ships and scenes from the waterfront history. New London, New Bedford, Rockport . . . a lot of them are by me and Johnny."

"Art talent runs in your family," Kate said.

"I'm nothing like Maddie. She was the true talent," Hadley said.

"I know exactly the murals you're talking about. I love them," Kate said.

"Did Maddie mind you working with her ex-husband?" Conor asked.

"Not at all," Hadley said. "There is nothing romantic between us. Johnny is almost like a brother—I've known him so long, know how much he loved Hadley, watched him with girlfriends along the way."

"Is he with someone now?" Conor asked.

"Yes," Hadley said.

Conor seemed to pick up on what she was thinking. "You don't like her?"

"It's not that; I've never even met her. It's just that she seems insecure, from what he tells me. She wants him all to herself. And I say, 'Go for it!' As long as he finishes our murals, he's all hers."

"Kind of like Bernard with Maddie," Kate said.

"Yes," Hadley said. "Seems that way." And that was probably the reason she felt guarded when it came to Johnny's latest. She'd seen how destructive being possessive could be.

"How did Johnny feel about CeCe?" Conor asked.

"Everyone loves CeCe. Johnny had only met her recently, when Maddie bought this suite and moved back east to live."

"Did he come here?" Conor asked.

"Not that I know of. Maddie brought CeCe to Newport a few times, where Johnny and I were doing a mural on a building on Creighton's Wharf."

"How did everyone seem?" Conor asked.

Hadley looked at the tall window, the balcony drifted with snow, police lights still glowing on the beach. She remembered handing CeCe her paintbrush, letting her paint a starfish on the seafloor. She could hear CeCe's delighted squeals, see Maddie's pride, and see Johnny as he exclaimed about what an excellent addition to the painting CeCe had made.

"It was all fine until Bernard called Maddie's mobile," Hadley said.

"What happened then?"

"We were having such a great time, but Maddie's phone rang, and it was Bernard. He had called to talk to CeCe—Maddie never kept her from him, encouraged him to call whenever he wanted."

"Was custody part of the fight?"

"No. Maddie had sole custody; he was clear that he wanted that. He said it was because it was best for CeCe, but Maddie thought it was also because he was too selfish to take care of her. Even though he wanted to keep the family intact, he also wanted to have his fun."

"Other women?" Conor asked.

"That didn't seem to be his thing," Hadley said. "He was too obsessed with Maddie. But he liked being a movie star. Celebrity golf tournaments, playing poker with his own version of the Hollywood Rat Pack, driving his cars on Mulholland Highway—around 'the Snake,' a curve where he knows the photographers wait to snap fast cars. He loves having lunch at Nobu, hanging out at Malibu Kitchen with other Porsche owners. Coffee at Malibu Country Mart. Places he knows he'd be seen and photographed. He's invited to every big premiere, and Maddie said he never missed one."

"She didn't like to go with him?" Conor asked.

"Sometimes she did," Hadley said. "They had a nanny, and she could have gone out every night. But that wasn't Maddie. She loved being home with CeCe." Hadley could hear her sister's voice. At first it had been full of longing and loneliness for her husband, but then it was angry. Bernard wanted to keep constant track of her, to judge and limit her activities with other people while he did whatever he desired.

"No wonder he wasn't fighting for custody. He doesn't leave lots of time to spend with CeCe," Kate said.

"It's true," Hadley said. "But I believe he really does love her, and he does dote on her when they're together. Before things went really bad, Maddie gave him generous visitation. She wanted CeCe to have a good relationship with her father."

"So Bernard called when they were at the wharf with you. When was that?" Conor asked.

"October sometime. I remember we were all planning to go to a farm in Stonington when I finished work that day, to pick apples and pumpkins. Later we were going to carve jack-o'-lanterns."

"How did the call go?"

"At first it seemed fine. I wasn't paying attention, but all of a sudden CeCe began to cry, and Maddie grabbed the phone. I could tell the conversation was heated. Later she told me it was because Bernard had asked CeCe what she was doing, and she'd told him she was painting with us. Hearing that Johnny was there set him off. I guess he went nuts and said some terrible things to CeCe." Hadley pictured her niece crying, dropping the phone, running to Maddie. And Maddie picking her up, trying to comfort her.

Conor nodded. "Did Maddie and CeCe see Bernard at any point after that?"

"No," Hadley said. "In fact, the fight was so bad, and what Bernard said to CeCe was so traumatic, Maddie wouldn't let him see CeCe. She had her lawyer file a motion for a restraining order and to suspend visitation."

"And the outcome?" Conor asked.

"The motion was granted. Bernard was out. A hearing to restore his rights was scheduled for after the holidays."

"Do you know what he said that made Maddie react that way?" Conor asked.

Hadley shivered just thinking about it. "Oh yes. She told me. He told CeCe that Maddie was exactly like Désirée, and she would end up just like her."

"Who is that?" Conor asked.

"Désirée," Kate said. "The title character of one of Bernard's most famous movies."

"I never saw it," Conor said. "What happened to her?"

"It's not so much the character," Kate said, "but the actress who played her. Nathalie Guyard. The character cheated on Bernard's character. There were rumors of a romance between them in real life."

"Bernard claimed that wasn't true," Hadley said. "Besides, it was years before he met Maddie. The film won the Palme d'Or at Cannes—he and Nathalie were there for the ceremony—and the next morning she was found with her throat slit. In her hotel bed. With her two-year-old daughter in her crib beside the bed."

"It was horrific," Kate said. "I remember—it was all over the news. The stabbing was so savage, Nathalie's blood splashed onto her daughter."

"But would CeCe have known about it?" Conor asked. "It happened before she was born, and would anyone even have told her? How could she grasp what her father meant by mentioning Désirée? How would she know it was a threat?"

"He said, 'Your mother will die like Désirée,'" Hadley said. She remembered how Maddie had been livid. Before Maddie had gotten the chance to tell her what Bernard had said, she'd bundled CeCe into the car and driven back home to the hotel. It wasn't until later that she'd called Hadley.

"Well, that's definitely a threat," Kate said.

"That's how I took it," Hadley said, "when Maddie told me. He had basically hinted that her throat would be slit. That CeCe would be there to see it and left in her blood."

"Hadley," Kate said, "considering all that, you really don't think he was capable of killing her?"

"Maddie didn't believe he meant it. She said he was dramatic, that he'd only said it for effect. She said he was a wild artist. They were alike in that way—incredibly passionate people who didn't always do a good job of controlling their emotions."

"Still, he said it," Kate said.

"I know. He is very theatrical—he likes shocking people," Hadley said.

"But to not have the sense to keep it from CeCe . . . ," Kate said.

"I hate him for what he said, but I can't bring myself to believe he would have attacked Maddie—done *that* to her," Hadley said, picturing the black hole in her sister's head. "It's unthinkable that he would have left CeCe without a mother. Someone else did this."

"When did Maddie last see Johnny?" Conor asked.

"It's not him, either," Hadley said. "Don't waste your time thinking that."

"Still, when did she last see him?"

"I don't know for sure. I didn't keep tabs on her—and definitely not on him. He took us all for a sail, right before he hauled his boat for the winter, end of October, not long after that call. She brought CeCe to our worksite a couple more times, and they visited us in the studio. We have a space in Providence, in a big warehouse with other artists. I think she and Johnny made plans to have a drink, but I don't know if it happened."

"Bernard wouldn't have liked that," Kate said.

"He couldn't have found out," Hadley said. "Maddie obviously thought his jealousy was insane, nothing to do with her actual behavior, and even though she thought the Désirée comment was just heat of the moment, she wasn't going to let him scare CeCe again. She never even told him she'd moved into the Ocean House. He had no clue whatsoever."

"Where did he think she was living?" Conor asked.

"In our family home, in Connecticut," Maddie said. "We still own it and rent it out. She had all her mail sent to our local post office, and Steve, our postmaster, forwarded it here. She hired security for a while. This hotel was the perfect place for her to hide. They're so discreet here. They take such good care of her. Other than me, they don't let people up to the suite. If anyone calls, the switchboard operator says there's no such guest. She only took calls on her mobile."

"Divorce lawyers follow the money and dig into real estate transactions. He might have hired someone to track her down," Conor said.

"I don't know, but I don't think so. He really is broke. She's been paying him temporary alimony, but it barely covers his expenses. I doubt he could have afforded to fly out here to visit CeCe."

"And how did CeCe feel about that?" Conor asked.

"She misses him, I'm sure," Hadley said, her voice catching in her throat.

Conor and Kate sat there quietly. They all did. Hadley's heart was pounding. *How did CeCe feel about that?* Conor had asked. How would CeCe feel when she learned her mother was dead? Was she feeling *anything* right now? Was she still alive?

"Where is she?" Hadley asked, wrapping her arms around her body as if she could hold herself together, as if she could stop the river of icy worry and grief flooding through her. "Where is CeCe?"

7

Conor could see how troubled Kate felt by everything Hadley had just told them. "What do you think of all that?" she asked Conor when they returned to their room.

"Maddie led a complicated life. Was she really a great artist?" Conor asked. "Or, should I say, was MC?"

Kate stared into the middle distance to think about it. She took her time. Conor knew how discerning she was, how carefully she assessed the art that she represented at the Woodward-Lathrop Gallery and that she saw when they visited museums and other galleries.

"She almost was," Kate said. "Her paintings were extraordinary. They were technically brilliant. Her brushstrokes were exquisite. As I said to Hadley, her work was poetic. Every painting held worlds of meaning. Secrets and mysteries in each one."

"What does that mean?" Conor asked, partly because he still, after years with or at least around Kate, didn't know much about art, but mostly because he loved to hear her talk about it.

"Think of Claire's shadow boxes," Kate said.

Claire Beaudry Chase was an artist in Black Hall. She had been the victim of a violent crime, and Conor had worked the case. Much of it was connected to Claire's work—deep frames separated into compartments, each filled with treasures Claire had found in nature: sea glass, crab claws, fallen leaves, a mouse skull, a shard of old pottery, a silver button. The effect was to give the viewer the feeling they had entered a private world. Kate had told him that together the elements contained the key to the artist's soul.

"MC's art is like that—but she does paintings on linen, not shadow boxes. She incorporates dreams, myths, legends, talismans, spells into each one. They're woven together. Often disparate things you wouldn't expect to see together."

"Like a swan riding on a whale?" Conor asked.

"Yes. Hadley mentioned that particular image. It's one of the two that took off. They were beautiful, they seemed to be out of a dream, and they captured people's imaginations."

"The whale and swan," Conor said. "And the upside-down tiger? Like the one Hadley showed us, embroidered inside Maddie's coat sleeve?"

"Yes, exactly. MC became a phenomenon, and you can't imagine how unheard of that is, in the world of serious art. To bypass the gallery world on the way to a larger marketplace. Andy Warhol did it, obviously, with soup cans and images of Jackie Kennedy and Marilyn Monroe. Georgia O'Keeffe's *Ladder to the Moon*. Jeff Koons's balloon dogs. Edward Hopper's *Nighthawks*. Monet's water lilies have wound up on everything from coffee mugs to mouse pads to shower curtains. Prints that kids hang on dormitory walls. But for a contemporary young artist known for making fine art as opposed to the deliberately mass-produced work of a commercial artist, it doesn't happen."

"But it did for Maddie. So . . . to go back to my question, you're saying she—MC—was great?" Conor asked.

"What I said is, she almost was. There was truly a Georgia O'Keeffe quality to her—the way she used color and light, archetypes and symbols. Her inspiration was the Northeast, not the Southwest. Whaling ships, anchors, breakwaters, swans, ospreys, white church spires filled her work."

"Sounds like the murals Hadley says she does with Johnny Morrison."

"Similar elements. All except the tiger. That never fit. What did a jungle cat have to do with the rest of her themes, mostly set in New England?" Kate paused, considering her own question. "She was already larger than life when she just stopped showing. And suddenly she went from exhibits at the best galleries here and in Europe, with whisperings of a major exhibition at the Whitney and the Grand Palais, to front-of-store displays at Target and Walmart and in airport gift shops. And then . . . nothing. She went silent."

"Hadley explained it, but it still seems strange," Conor said.

"A letdown," Kate said. "Everyone wanted to know what she would do next, other than print money for those mass-produced reproductions. And the clothing line and the perfume." She shook her head. "She had haters, as brilliant people often do. Envy over her financial success, but even more because of her talent. Some claimed her disappearance was a publicity stunt."

"Maybe she just stepped away. Hadley said she continued to paint but kept it to herself."

"That is an exciting idea," Kate said. "If there is a body of work that she's hidden from the public, I would love to see it."

Conor kissed her. He could tell by the way she'd talked about MC that she was caught up in the fascination that art held for her. For his part, he was gripped by an investigation he hadn't been invited to pursue. He put on his snow boots and parka and told Kate he was going to look at the path again. He made sure he had his room key card and left Kate at her laptop. She was searching the archives of *ARTnews* and *Artforum* for stories about MC and barely looked up when he left.

As Conor walked through the lobby, he heard other guests talking about the blizzard, calling it a "bombogenesis." Three feet of snow had already fallen, power was out throughout the region, and with high tide still an hour away, coastal storm-surge flooding was guaranteed. When he stepped outside, he noticed that the neighborhood was dark, but the Ocean House was glowing like a beacon. He told the valet he needed to access his car, and Dermot seemed relieved when Conor said he would do it himself. He went to the parking lot and grabbed his big flashlight.

The weather energized him. In a storm like this, it was all hands on deck for the Connecticut State Police. Whether the roadways were officially closed or not, there were always accidents on the interstate highways and secondary roads. House fires were more prevalent, as people used badly wired space heaters or fireplaces with chimneys that hadn't been cleaned in years. Cheap landlords kept the thermostats low, and some residents used their gas ovens for heat, with deadly potential for explosions or asphyxiation. Homeless people froze to death.

Head down, Conor trudged along Bluff Avenue into the wind. He thought of how domestic violence calls skyrocketed during blizzards or other severe weather. He considered the possibility that Maddie had been attacked by a partner Hadley was unaware of. In most storm-centric domestics, the violence seemed to erupt when the couple was trapped inside, with no way to escape each other. A partner prone to anger could find any number of reasons to blow up. It could happen anywhere but usually happened inside the home. And clearly Maddie had been outdoors.

Conor had no idea what he'd expected to see here, revisiting the scene where Maddie had been found. The crime-scene tape had, for the most part, been blown down in the gale, but a few scraps of yellow, tied to branches, blew straight out in the wind. The body had been removed; he saw packed sled marks in the snow. He wouldn't disturb the marked-off section; he knew that once the blizzard abated, investigators would be back to search for more evidence.

Still, he wanted a closer look. Hedges lined both sides of the path, which began at Bluff Avenue and meandered downward toward the ocean. It had some elevation at the road end—Conor estimated about fifty feet above the beach. He could see that the area was somewhat protected from the blowing snow. The thicket to the north abutted private property. He backtracked to a stately stone wall and found the driveway. He cut through it, through thigh-high snow, over to the hedge. He had been right—there was less snow accumulation in the bushes, where the tangled branches had blocked the worst of the snowfall.

The hedges ran from Bluff Avenue all the way down the length of the snow-covered sandy path. They were mostly made up of coastal scrubs, but there were also oak and pine saplings. This was outside the perimeter marked by the police, so he walked slowly toward the beach, shining his flashlight into the gorse, stopping when he drew even with the place where Maddie had lain. That spot was just on the other side of the bushes.

He shouldered his way into the shrubbery, but he didn't get far before he noticed a small hollow. It was the size and shape of a pup tent, a place where branches had either broken or had never knit together at all. The ground was nearly bare inside, other than a thin layer of snow, but the wind had changed direction, and now the snow was blowing sideways, straight into the hollow.

Lying there were a handful of objects: some grapes, a red glass bulb, a gold ribbon, and a square of flannel. Did these things have anything to do with Maddie or CeCe, or had someone else dropped them? Had they been here long? He reached in, dislodging a clump of snow from a pine bough. It went into his collar, but he barely felt it.

His hand, gloved in black leather, closed around the flannel, and when he pulled it out of the hedge, he saw that it was wrapped around a silver key. The key looked like the kind that went to a safe-deposit box.

Because he was wearing gloves, he wouldn't be destroying fingerprints. He photographed both items as well as everything else. He made sure to capture the spot where the key and flannel had been. Blowing snow was filling the indentations, covering the entire space. He rang Joe's number.

"What's up?" Joe asked.

"I found something," Conor said. "Might be connected to Maddie, or might not. Can you meet me on the path?"

"Can't right now," Joe said. "What have you got?"

"A collection of little objects, including a key."

"A key to what?"

"I don't know. The snow's coming down hard, and this space is a little hard to locate. I'd like to show you. Or I can secure the items for you before they get buried."

Conor waited for Joe to tell him what to do. The line was silent, and after a minute he realized the call had dropped. He figured cell service had been interrupted by the storm; it usually was along the coast when winds hit these velocities.

His hands were frozen, and snow blew straight into his eyes. He hadn't heard Joe's response to his question about whether or not to secure the items, so he did what he would have wanted a colleague to do if the situation were reversed. He removed evidence bags from his jacket pocket—he seemed to never leave home without them—and slipped the key and flannel into them. Then, one by one, he collected the grapes, bulb, and ribbon. When he was finished, he backed out of the small hollow, turned into the wind, and hurried along Bluff Avenue the way he had come.

He walked into the Ocean House and felt instant warmth. The lobby fireplace was going strong. He knew he should head straight upstairs to the room. Take off his boots and jacket, sit down with Kate to go over the notes about Maddie's case that he had made so far. But the bar, just behind the fireplace, looked awfully inviting.

The barroom was mostly empty. He thought he'd take a seat right there at the bar, text Kate and ask her to come downstairs to join him. But the bartender smiled and nodded his head toward another fireplace. There were three tables with deep leather chairs and a wrap-around window seat.

"Hello," Kate said, smiling. She sat at the window seat, her laptop on the table in front of her. "I was waiting for you. I thought you might come in here."

Conor didn't reply. He dropped his jacket on an empty chair, slid next to her, and put his arms around her. He kissed her, glad no one was at the nearby tables.

"Mr. Reid has arrived, so on cue, here's the Jameson," the bartender said, placing two glasses of whiskey in front of them.

"Thank you," he said.

He and Kate clinked glasses and drank. He reached across for his jacket, pulled the evidence bags out, and placed them on the table. The key and fabric scrap were visible through the clear plastic, and the key glinted in the firelight.

"What are they?" she asked.

"I don't know," he said. "I found them under the bushes close to where we found Maddie. I'm not sure whether they were there before or if they were dropped by her or CeCe during the attack."

"Do you think the killer might have torn the fabric?" she asked.

Conor leaned forward. The bar was cozy and the light was dim, but even so, he could see that the flannel was worn almost threadbare. It had once been pale blue, but it had faded to gray. It was printed with a pattern of tiny white whales, each with a swan balanced on its back.

Conor and Kate were so absorbed by what they were seeing that they hadn't heard Hadley come up behind them.

"That's Star," she said, grabbing the plastic bag. Before Conor could stop her, she pulled out the square of well-worn flannel. Eyes closed, she squeezed it in her hand.

"Hadley, that's evidence," Conor said, trying to take it from her. But she held on tight, half turning away to protect it from him getting it.

"Star?" Kate asked.

"All that's left of CeCe's baby blanket. She had started to outgrow it, but during the separation, when everything was so tense, she needed it again. She took it everywhere, never put it down. To bed, on the plane, to the beach, to school. She wouldn't let Maddie wash it." Hadley held it to her face. "It smells like CeCe."

"I recognize the whales and swans," Kate said. "MC's design."

"Yes, they were printed on baby things," Hadley said.

"So this means CeCe was definitely with Maddie, there on the path," Conor said. He had assumed it—everyone had—but this discovery made the theory more likely to be true.

"It means she saw her mother killed," Hadley said, her voice rising.

Conor was silent. He thought Hadley was probably right.

Kate turned her laptop slightly so that Hadley and Conor could see the screen. She had her browser open to an article with photographs of Maddie's paintings. The largest showed a detail of one titled *The Whale and the Swan*. It depicted a white whale with a swan on its back. In this context, it was possible to see that the creatures were flying through the night sky, surrounded by constellations.

"Is this why CeCe called her blanket Star?" Kate asked.

"Yes, exactly. Maddie was so inspired by nature, and she was very precise about the things she painted. The constellation you see here is Cygnus—the Swan. It's visible from our childhood home in summer and fall, and it was Maddie's favorite. Deneb is one of the brightest stars in the sky . . ."

"Deneb is in Cygnus?" Kate asked.

"Yes. It is the most distant first-magnitude star that we can see from Earth. There's so much meaning to it, especially for me and Maddie. We grew up loving astronomy, oceanography, anything to do with nature. We dreamed of having an observatory and a marine biology lab."

"Sister dreams," Kate said quietly. "I had them with Beth."

Hadley nodded, as if she knew exactly what Kate meant, as if sister dreams were part of their language.

"We took sailing lessons," Hadley continued. "And our parents let us take a semester at sea, on a schooner out of Woods Hole. We did whale research. Our cruise track took us into the Gulf of St. Lawrence, and we studied humpback whales—feeding behaviors and migratory routes. We filled sketchbooks with watercolors of everything we saw, especially the whales. We learned celestial navigation."

"To steer by the stars," Conor said, thinking of his brother Tom and how, even though Tom was a commander in the United States Coast Guard and had the most sophisticated navigational equipment on his ships, he still knew how to use a sextant, how to shoot sun lines and navigate by the stars.

"Yes," Hadley said. "We loved the Summer Triangle—an imaginary triangle in the sky with three stars as defining vertices. Deneb is one; Altair and Vega are the others. Maddie claimed Deneb as her favorite. Mine was Vega, in the constellation of Lyra."

"Who was the third in the triangle?" Kate asked.

"A friend we met on the schooner," Hadley said. "A girl from Maine. Her star was Altair, from the constellation Aquila." She folded her arms across her chest. She was still wearing the black cashmere coat she had put on in the suite upstairs, and the soft wool shimmered in the firelight.

Conor had done plenty of profiling in his day, and he recognized her arm crossing as a self-protective gesture indicating she wanted to end the conversation.

"Was that Genevieve Dickinson?" Kate asked.

"How do you know about her?" Hadley asked, sounding shocked.

"I read about the lawsuit," Kate said, gesturing at the laptop.

"The suit was completely unfounded," Hadley said.

"But Maddie settled it," Kate said.

Conor had no idea what they were talking about, but he paid attention to Hadley's body language, and he saw her pupils enlarge with what he knew from countless interrogations to be rage.

"She settled because she wanted peace. We only knew Genevieve from that single semester aboard the ship. She wasn't even a close friend, but she latched on to us, especially Maddie. She wanted to be an artist, but that was laughable. All she ever did was copy what Maddie was doing."

"Yet Genevieve claimed Maddie had stolen her idea about the whale and the swan and the stars."

"That was such a lie."

"Where did the idea come from?" Kate asked.

Hadley bowed her head, buried her face in CeCe's blanket scrap, looked up again. When she did, her eyes looked calm. The anger had left.

"Maddie and I saw the most amazing thing," Hadley said. "We were on watch just before dawn one day, the two of us alone on the bow. The ship was anchored just off the shore of Newfoundland. Several swans were close to the boat; they appeared to be asleep, heads tucked under their wings. It was still dark."

"Sounds magical," Kate said.

"It was. And then we heard a loud whoosh—we'd been on board long enough to know it was a whale surfacing for air. We saw its glossy black back, illuminated by starlight. But the amazing thing was, it came up right beneath one of the swans. And when it did, the swan stayed balanced on the whale's back."

She closed her eyes, as if picturing the moment.

"Only you and Maddie saw that?" Conor asked.

"Yes. And once we were relieved by the next watch, Maddie ran below and immediately painted the scene. It was just a watercolor, about four by six inches. Years later she did it as an oil, and it became her iconic image."

"Genevieve wasn't on deck?" Kate asked.

"She was on the watch that took over—we saw her as we left the deck."

"And was the swan still on the whale's back?" Conor asked.

"No—that lasted only a few seconds before the whale sounded and the swan flew away. No one else saw it, just me and Maddie."

"Did Genevieve see the watercolor?"

"Maybe," Hadley said. "Maddie was never sure. Genevieve was so obsessed with being an artist like Maddie; we had the feeling she spied on her, maybe even went through her things."

"Could she have been spying on you that night, seen the whale and swan at the same time you did?"

"I'm sure not," Hadley said. "She didn't see them."

"The article says that Genevieve produced sketches and watercolors of the whale and the swan and claimed that she had done the original painting that became so famous," Kate said.

"Did you and Maddie tell your shipmates about what you'd seen?" Conor asked. "Even if Genevieve wasn't actually there, could she have heard the story and truly made the work on her own?"

Hadley shook her head. "Maddie and I kept it to ourselves, just for us. We never told anyone, not even our parents. Talking about it could never have done justice to what it was like." She closed her eyes, as if seeing the scene, reliving that moment.

"How did Genevieve know the details? During the lawsuit, she described exactly what you just told us—about dawn, and the stars, and being on watch on the ship's bow," Kate said.

"We never knew how she found out," Hadley said.

"Unless she was stalking Maddie and went through her things. Saw the little painting she did," Kate said.

Hadley nodded. "That's one possibility. Also, I kept a journal. It was like a private ship's log, an account of everything I did and saw on that cruise. We wondered if she might have read it."

"That sounds possible," Kate said. "If she was so obsessed."

"What is your relationship with Genevieve now?" Conor asked. "And what was Maddie's?"

"She disappeared after the settlement and sank into the muck she came from. I guess she's still living in Maine. She grew up there, and she had an address in Wiscasset when she brought the lawsuit."

"There was a nondisclosure clause in the agreement," Kate said. "So she can't discuss anything about the suit. The documents are public, and the reporter who wrote this piece took all her information from them."

"A lot of journalists came around Maddie during the suit and just after she settled with Genevieve, but she never spoke to any of them. She was a very private person. Most people who knew her personally had no idea she was MC."

"I wonder if Genevieve has held a grudge all this time," Kate said.

Conor thought of the little hollow where he had found Star, and of Maddie lying dead under the thick blanket of snow, and he wondered the same thing.

8

Hadley was restless. After she'd said goodnight to Kate and Conor, she'd wandered around the hotel. It was past midnight now, and she saw no other guests. She'd kept her phone with her and checked it constantly. The hotel corridors were filled with art. Grand landscapes in museum-quality gilded frames, but also two collections that fascinated Hadley: work by Ludwig Bemelmans—the author of the Madeline books—and drawings by the French artist Sem. A caricaturist of the Belle Époque, Sem had drawn the upper classes in Paris, Deauville, Monte Carlo, and other playgrounds of the rich.

Along with the art that filled the lobby and every hallway, there was a little jewel box of a gallery down the grand staircase. The Bemelmans Gallery had walls painted Buxton Blue, an oceanic blue-gray that perfectly set off the owners' extensive collection of Bemelmans's work.

One wall featured "Adieu to the Old Ritz," an array of pen-and-ink drawings Bemelmans had done to illustrate essays inspired by his fifteen years of working at the post-Depression New York Ritz. They were charming and comforting—chefs and the maître d' and sommeliers and diners. Hadley gazed at them, reading the note that said the collector had acquired them all at once after seeing them displayed in a window at Bergdorf Goodman, on Fifth Avenue.

She took the beautiful old elevator upstairs and continued wandering. Seeing art calmed her. It seemed uncanny to see so much of Sem's work here; she wondered how Maddie had felt about it. Hadley could understand how she would love the Bemelmans pieces, especially those of Madeline, but Sem was another story. Bernard owned a folio of his work focusing on theater and horse racing. It was bound in red leather with gold print, and Hadley remembered seeing it when she had visited their house in Malibu. Bernard was incredibly proud of it and shared how Sem's real name was Georges Goursat, and he had been born in Périgueux, in Nouvelle-Aquitaine. Bernard came from that region as well; he'd been born and raised in a small town outside Bordeaux.

"He relates to Sem," Maddie had said during Hadley's last visit, before the separation. It was late afternoon, and they were sitting on the deck of Maddie and Bernard's house in eastern Malibu, just above the mouth of Topanga Canyon, where it met the Pacific.

"What is it about Sem?" Hadley had asked.

"They both came from upper-middle-class families and had family money that gave them an advantage in life. Bernard feels he had it almost too easy—or at least that's the perception of the public. Of his peers. That it would have been more impressive if he hadn't had that leg up."

"You can't buy talent," Hadley had said. "And Bernard obviously has it. He wouldn't have made it the way he did if that wasn't the case." She watched her sister. Bernard may have been born with money, but he had lost it, and now he was relying on his wife for support—not just of their lifestyle but of some of his film projects.

"I know he comes off as confident, and even brash," Maddie had said. "But his financial position is his Achilles' heel. He started out with too much, and now, when he should be at the top, he's completely out of money. The other day he said to me he feels like a kept man."

"Do you feel that way?" Hadley had asked. "That you're 'keeping' him?"

"Of course not," Maddie had said. "It would be different if he sat around all day, but he's constantly working. He still has a very good agent, and he gets offered wonderful roles. The problem, he says, is that they're all 'prestige'—they might get him a nomination, but what he really wants is an action film."

"Can't he do both?" Hadley had asked.

"Maybe when he was younger, when he was too snobby to take anything like that. Now he looks at Liam Neeson and can't figure out why he can't have the same roles. He's angling to be the villain in the next James Bond, but it will most likely go to Dirk Von Briels."

"Isn't that the guy with the patch over one eye? He did some dystopian space movies?"

"Yep," Maddie had said. "Bernard's archrival, or at least that's what he thinks. It's true, they're the same age and often up for the same parts. Different styles, though." She paused. "He's mad at me because I wanted him to do a guestie."

"A what?"

"Guest spot on a TV series. He hates to do anything where he's not one of the main stars, but this would have been a great chance for him. Top-rated show, brilliant cast, and last year Dirk did it and won the Emmy for Outstanding Guest Actor."

"Maybe that's what turned Bernard off," Hadley had said. "He wouldn't want to follow in Dirk's footsteps. It would be like coming in second."

"That's exactly right," Maddie had said. "But it would have brought him a lot of attention and possibly a nomination. Maybe even an award. Casting directors would have started seeing him differently. Bernard is old school and still looks down on television. It used to be that actors like him only did feature films—forget TV—but now streaming series are everything. His agent barely even puts him up for TV because he knows what Bernard will say."

The sisters had sat quietly as evening began to fall. The mountains were in shadow, and the Pacific gleamed rose gold in the last light. It was January, chilly even in Southern California.

CeCe had been at a play group, but she had just gotten home, and her nanny brought her out to the deck. She was dressed in a navy UCLA sweatshirt, a pink tulle skirt, high-top red sneakers, and a necklace strung with what looked like real pearls. She beamed at the sight of her mother and Hadley.

"Auntie," she had said, slinging one arm around Hadley's neck.

"I've been waiting all day for you," Hadley had said. "I was about to hop on the back of one of those whales and go flying to see you."

"Whales do fly, you know," CeCe had said solemnly.

"They do?"

"Haven't you seen Mommy's painting?"

"I sure have," Hadley had said. "*The Whale and the Swan*."

"I always watch the stars," CeCe had said, pointing down the mountainside at the ocean. "And I wait for them to rise into the sky."

Hadley had followed her gaze. The northern migration of the California gray whales was underway, from their winter calving grounds at Laguna San Ignacio on the Baja Peninsula back to the Bering Sea. Mothers and babies swam close to shore, where the shallow water provided safety from killer whales and great white sharks, and Hadley watched spouts, the spray iridescent in the last light.

"What these whales need," Hadley had said, "are a few swans. To ride on their backs and spread their wings. Then they could fly."

"Let's go in for dinner," Maddie had said, abruptly changing the subject, "and see if Papa is home yet."

"Yes!" CeCe had said, running through the garden toward the house.

Hadley remembered that now as she walked the corridors of the Ocean House in the middle of the night, feeling the presence of the Lafond family in all the art, and thinking of the conversation she'd had with Conor and Kate, how she had told them about Maddie's painting, how it had been inspired by a real whale. And how Genevieve Dickinson had reacted with such fury.

Art and rage, art and identity.

She wasn't sure where one ended and the other began.

9

USCG Commander Tom Reid was at Station Point Judith when the blizzard hit. He was normally the command duty officer in New London, but a temporary assignment had taken him to Sector Southeastern New England. Point Judith was under his command, and he'd wanted to visit the station. His command was at Woods Hole for the next few months, but this was much closer to his home in Connecticut, and to his wife, Jackie, and her daughters. To his brother, Conor, and his brother's girlfriend, Kate. Family.

The station was located beside the Point Judith Lighthouse, a structure built of wood in 1806, battered and leveled by storms and rebuilt several times since then. It was old and crumbling. The wind was howling, blowing shingles off the roof, and causing the power to go out. Everyone on duty was busy trying to keep it all going, and Tom did his part, too, by making rounds.

The generators were in the building at the foot of the lighthouse, and they needed to be filled with diesel. Same with the ones at the boathouse in Galilee. Tom walked through the dark corridor, feeling the icy cold and hearing the howling of the wind and the ghosts. He had no problem believing this place was haunted by mariners they'd been unable to save, in nor'easters just like this one.

He heard the echo of footsteps and saw Sam Walker—the station's senior coxswain—hurrying toward him.

"Sir, we have a distress call."

In the radio room, Tom heard the caller on channel sixteen identify himself as Zane Garson aboard the *Anna G*, a forty-five-foot Novi lobster boat out of the Port of Galilee. The radio transmission was terrible, and it was hard to make out words over the crackle.

"I'm icing really bad," Zane said. "Taking on water, swamping on the starboard side."

"What's your location?" the radio operator, Irving Jenkins, asked.

"Block Island Sound, running west. I was trying to beach, but the wind is too strong. Can't see shit, but I'm near Charlestown Breachway."

"How many aboard?"

"Just me."

"I advise you to put on your survival suit and launch your life raft," Irving said.

"I don't have a fucking survival suit!" Zane said.

As the captain, he was in violation of the Fishing Vessel Safety Act, but he wasn't the only one trying to save money at the expense of crew lives. Zane advised that he did have a four-person inflatable life raft with an ACR GlobalFix EPIRB—a marine distress beacon—and a weatherproof canopy for shelter. The internal GPS would pinpoint and transmit his location.

Tom was calculating. The wind was fifty knots sustained, gusting to sixty, with twelve-foot seas. Parameters for Station Point Judith were thirty knots sustained and ten-foot seas. Normally a rescue in these conditions would be done by Station Montauk—their forty-seven-foot boat was better equipped than the forty-five-foot RB-M used by this crew—but Zane was in danger of sinking, with imminent threat to life, and Tom knew response time was critical.

"Can we have a waiver, sir?" Sam asked.

As Sector Commander, Tom had the responsibility to decide whether the risk of sending this crew—given the parameters—into the blizzard was worth it. It was up to him to issue the waiver and permit this station to take the mission instead of calling in Montauk. He knew what a fine and experienced crew he had on watch. Stone Crawford was an excellent senior engineer. Tom had had Machinery Technician Petty Officer Second Class Crawford aboard his ships, and he valued Stone's experience greatly—MK2 Crawford was superb at his job—so he granted the waiver without hesitation.

"Will we get air support?" Stone asked.

Tom was on it. He radioed air station Joint Base Cape Cod. They had the ability to supply an MH-60T Jayhawk helicopter or an HC-144A Ocean Sentry fixed-wing aircraft, and Tom spoke directly to his friend and fellow commander Paul Bristol and requested the helo. Normally it would be up to the pilots, but Paul didn't even ask.

"Tom, we've got zero ceiling, zero visibility. I can't send them up," Paul said.

"I figured," Tom said. He'd already known that would be the answer, but he had to ask.

"I'm sorry," Paul said. "Be safe."

The crew put on dry suits, and so did Tom. All five of them—coxswain, engineer, two crew members, and Tom—crammed into the crew cab of the Ford F-450 pickup. The road from the lighthouse to the dock was deep with snow, but the F-450 was equipped with a plow, and they cleared their own way.

Galilee was home to the largest fishing fleet in Rhode Island and to the Block Island Ferry. The ferry hadn't gone out since the night before the blizzard started, and most fishing boats were in their slips. There were plenty of Novi boats like the *Anna G*; Tom wondered what had possibly caused Zane to go out in weather like this.

Tom and the crew climbed aboard RB-M 45738. It was a forty-five-foot response boat medium, all aluminum, powered by twin diesels. It had replaced the forty-one-foot utility boats and was much better able to right itself in high seas. That kept the crew safe, which was what mattered most to Tom. As COD—commander on duty—he normally wouldn't go out on a mission like this, but he didn't want to send the guys without going himself.

Sam Walker, the senior-most coxswain, drove the boat. They left the fishing village via a channel between the two stone jetties, the salt spray turning instantly to ice. Tom knew this was what had happened to the *Anna G*; with twelve-foot seas and a fifty-knot wind roaring out of the north, the Novi would quickly ice up. The ice was heavy, and blowing snow would stick to it and make it exponentially heavier, and the boat would start to list.

Tom felt confident with this crew. They knew heavy weather, none more than engineer Stone Crawford. He had been at Station Golden Gate in Sausalito, California, a designated Coast Guard surf station, where twelve-foot seas were not uncommon. He had surfed pretty much every storm in Point Judith. They were nothing compared to the fifty-foot waves he had surfed at Mavericks, in Half Moon Bay, on his days off from duty under the Golden Gate Bridge. He stood at the console, peering into the murk—a combination of total darkness and the wall of falling snow.

Zane's EPIRB indicated that he was less than a mile away. The RB-M was taking a pounding but rode the waves fine. When they neared the source of the rescue beacon, they encountered the *Anna G* with her starboard rail underwater. Her mast, her winches, and every inch of her fiberglass were coated with ice and snow, salt-crystal icicles dripping from the rigging. About a hundred yards off the bow, the life raft's strobe blinked and reflected off the flakes. They approached the raft, its rounded, snow-covered canopy giving it the appearance of a storm-tossed igloo.

Sam slowed the engines and drew along the raft's windward side. Zane was not visible at first, but he unzipped the viewing and ventilation port, and his hand shot out. The wave action was fierce. The raft and rescue vessel bounced up and down on cresting waves, completely out of sync with each other. Timing was critical. One wrong move would send Zane or a crew member overboard.

There wasn't time to lose when Stone—the Golden Gate surf-station veteran, the big-wave surfer—turned to him and grinned.

"I got this," Stone said.

And Tom knew he did, and Stone did what he had to do, and Zane Garson was safely brought aboard USCG RB-M 45738. Tom was relieved to see that he was alone. Often Zane took his teenage son, Ronnie, out lobstering; it reassured Tom, slightly, that Zane's judgment had been good enough to leave the kid on shore today. He gave the order, and they turned and headed back to their home port.

10

Conor woke up at dawn. Gray light filtered into the bedroom. His mind had swum with dreams—as often happened when he first got a case, his dreamworld had been all about the victim, the crime, the scene. He got dressed and left Kate sleeping under the down comforter. He went down to the gym.

He did half an hour on the treadmill, then a circuit on the weight machines. Kate joined him then—she'd brought his swim trunks down, so he changed and they went into the pool. They had it to themselves. The sun had no doubt risen, but the snow was still falling, and that was all he could see. There was something about swimming in warm water with a blizzard raging outside the wall of windows. He felt the tension leave his muscles, but last night's dreams were still with him.

"Do you think the storm will ever stop?" he asked Kate after they had showered and changed and had had coffee in the lobby.

"Do you want it to?" she asked. "I like being trapped here."

He smiled at her. She was amazing to say so. They had both taken vacation time to be here. Her plane was a ten-minute ride away, and he knew that she had hoped to take him up in it, fly out to Block Island, and walk or cross-country ski the trails in Rodman's Hollow. He'd wanted to take her to Newport, have clam chowder at the Black

Pearl and drinks while overlooking Narragansett Bay from the Inn at Castle Hill.

"I like being trapped here, too," he said. "With you."

"But there's a lot to do on this case," she said.

"You're right about that," he said. "Not so much me, but Joe and Garrett. They're really constrained by the weather. The crime scene is a mess—no way for them to get useful tracks or prints."

"What did Joe say about you taking the things you found under the bush?"

"He thanked me. I'm sure he'd rather his guys had retrieved them, but under the circumstances . . ."

"At least they were found by a cop," Kate said.

"Yeah," Conor said. "At least that."

Conor was glad to have been able to examine the evidence he'd found in the snow cave before Joe picked it up, after Kate was asleep. Conor had spread the objects out on the desk: the key, the now-defrosted grapes, the red Christmas tree bulb, the piece of ribbon, and the square of baby blanket. Star.

That was valuable evidence for Joe's investigation. Conor and Joe now knew almost conclusively that since CeCe never went anywhere without her security blanket, she had been present at the time her mother was murdered.

Conor imagined her hiding in the hollow. Had Maddie put her in there, anticipating the arrival of someone dangerous? Or had CeCe crawled in on her own, after seeing her mother get shot? Either way, he was sure that she had been there during the attack. Why had the killer let her live? She was a witness, and Conor would have expected her body to have been found beside Maddie's. He believed that someone who would shoot a mother in front of her child wouldn't hesitate to kill the child as well.

Unless the murderer hadn't known she was there. Or knew and cared about her. Loved her.

Unless taking CeCe had been the reason for Maddie's murder. A custody kidnapping couldn't be ruled out, but there was another category that Conor feared more. Child disappearances and kidnappings were the worst cases. He knew there were monsters out there. He was certain that Joe Harrigan and Pat O'Rourke were combing through the Connecticut, Rhode Island, and southeastern Massachusetts sex-offender registries. That would be their focus, but they would also be questioning anyone in the region with a history of violent crimes.

He opened the photo file on his laptop. His pictures were stored in the cloud, so they had migrated from his phone, and he looked through the most recent until he found the shots he had taken in Maddie's suite.

He noticed the Christmas tree covered with bright bulbs, and he figured that's where CeCe had gotten the red one. There was a stash of wrapping paper in the corner, along with rolls of ribbon, including gold. On the kitchen's marble counter was a charcuterie platter, including small bowls of fruit—the grapes.

He flipped through until he got to the photos that he had taken of Maddie and CeCe's drawings. The one of the carousel and the key made him lean closer. The key was the same shape as the one he'd found at the scene. He noticed, again, how Maddie seemed to have pressed it down into the paper, and he studied the faint impressions of numbers.

Last night Conor had snapped on gloves, removed the silver key from the evidence bag, and set it on the desk. There were nine digits imprinted into the metal. He had compared them with the ones from the drawing, which he had documented in his notebook. They were the same, and that's when he realized they were a routing number. This was a safe-deposit key, and the routing number would identify the bank where the safe-deposit box was located. He had taken close-up photos of both sides of the key.

He had worked on many investigations that involved financial issues, and he had access to several databases of bank information. In a recent case, he had downloaded files to use while offline. They were stored in a folder on his computer, so he opened it now and began to run through the list. He hoped to compare the routing number on the key with those in the document, but nothing matched.

He called Hadley's cell phone.

"Do you know where Maddie did her banking?" he asked.

"I don't," Hadley said. "Why?"

"Just wondering." Conor knew that the police would have taken Maddie's purse, and he wished he'd had the chance to examine it before.

"What is it?" Hadley asked after he'd been silent for a few seconds.

"I was thinking her checks would have the bank's name printed on them."

"Oh," Hadley said. "I have a copy of one of hers from when we paid the property tax on the house in Connecticut."

"Could you look?" Conor asked.

After a minute, Hadley came back on the line. "The bank is BSNE."

Bank of Southern New England, Conor thought. He recognized the abbreviation and had most recently encountered it during the investigation of a murder-suicide of a couple in Silver Bay. BSNE was known for its private-wealth division, located in branch offices throughout the region.

"Can you read the routing number to me?" he asked. "It's on the lower left."

She did, and it matched the one on the key.

"Now, can you tell me which office? Is that printed on the check?"

"It just says 'Resource Management Account' with a phone number." She read it to him, and he wrote it down.

"Thanks, Hadley," he said. The thought of a custody kidnapping was still on his mind. "Have you heard back from Bernard?"

"No, I've been trying him nonstop."

"Let me know when he calls back."

"I will," Hadley said.

Next, Conor rang the BSNE number she had given him and got a recording. *You have reached the Bank of Southern New England, Hartford, Connecticut, office. If you know your party's extension, you may dial it at any time . . .*

Conor hung up, then did an internet search and got the bank's address. He assumed they had safe-deposit boxes and that the key went to one of them. Even though the branch was in Connecticut, the key had been found at a Rhode Island murder scene, so this would be a matter for Joe Harrigan. It was time to hand over everything he had. Conor texted Joe's cell.

Joe didn't text back.

So this part of the case still belonged to Conor, at least for now.

11

CeCe was hungry and thirsty. It was daytime now, and she and the boy were still in the freezing-cold car. Snow kept falling hard. She had to go to the bathroom. He got out of the car and was gone for a few minutes, and she wanted to run, but he came back looking like a snowman, and she was stuck.

"Where's the boat?" he asked, as if she knew. "I just checked, and it's not there."

She didn't answer. She hadn't said a word to him since last night, when he had said the terrible thing about Mommy.

"It's supposed to be in the harbor," he said. "Where the hell is it? I mean, what if I missed him, didn't see him through the snow? But he was going to wait. If he came and didn't see us and left . . ."

CeCe heard a rumbling sound. Smashing and crashing. Bright lights shone through the snow as the noise got louder.

"Duck down!" the boy said.

CeCe didn't do what he said. She stretched her neck as far as it would go so she could see. When she saw a big huge snowplow going by and dropping sand, with fountains of snow and slush shooting into the air from the blade, she screamed.

"They can't hear you," he said.

She thought the boy was going to yell at her for disobeying, but he actually sounded happy.

"Finally," he said. "We're supposed to wait here, but screw that. Forget the boat and the plan. Now that the road is plowed, I'm driving us home to Galilee."

My home is the yellow hotel, CeCe thought.

But she didn't say it out loud. She sat very still as he backed the car out of the alley, wheels spinning. He steered onto the road, the narrow strip just cleared by the snowplow, and with the window wipers going, he drove slowly out of town, away from the yellow hotel, away from where she had been happy with Mommy.

12

Conor assumed that when Bernard Lafond called Hadley, it would be from California. But the origin was much more local—from across the lobby in the Ocean House, where Conor and Kate sat with Hadley.

"Hadley! You're here? Impossible!" Bernard said. He was about Conor's height—six two—and was dressed as if he had just come in from the cold. He wore a black Moncler parka—the same label as the one Maddie had been wearing. His silver hair curled over his collar. He leaned down to kiss Hadley on both cheeks, and he smiled as if very happy to see her.

"Bernard, I've been calling you!" Hadley said. "Have you gotten my messages? Is that why you're here?"

"Here because of your messages? What are you talking about? I turned my phone off. I haven't checked my voice mail. I need quiet."

"Why are you here, then?" Hadley asked.

"Scouting a location for my next film," he said. "At least I was, before this insane storm." He spoke directly to Hadley, but then his eyes flicked toward Conor, then Kate. His gaze lingered on Kate for a moment. "Excuse me for interrupting."

"This is Conor Reid and Kate Woodward," Hadley said. She sounded nervous, and Conor imagined her trying to formulate how to give him the news. He seemed relaxed. Was it possible he had no idea about the crime?

"I'm Bernard," he said, giving no last name, as if he assumed everyone knew exactly who he was.

Conor stared at Bernard, taking in his affect. He hadn't mentioned Maddie or CeCe. The murder and kidnapping had occurred less than twenty-four hours ago. One benefit of the weather was that it had kept the news trucks away. The Amber Alert for CeCe was attracting attention, though, and soon it would be worldwide news. If Bernard was not answering his phone and hadn't been watching TV, he could have missed it. But wouldn't he have seen the police in the lobby, on the beach? Seeing Bernard seemed to break a dam in Hadley; tears began to flow, and she let out a sob.

"What's wrong, Hadley?" Bernard asked, seemingly taken aback. "Is it so hard to see me? Has Madeleine so thoroughly poisoned you against me?"

Kate put her hand on Hadley's arm. It was enough to urge Hadley to get up and follow her out of the lobby. Kate had seen Conor's investigative style firsthand; she knew that he hoped to avoid Hadley saying too much. Conor wanted to observe Bernard's reactions to a few questions.

"Merde," Bernard said. "The divorce is destroying everything. She is a lovely person, ma belle-soeur. She was always kind to me."

"Excuse me, belle-what?"

"*Belle-soeur.* My sister-in-law," Bernard said.

"Well, it's probably a shock to see you here," Conor said. "She thought you were in California."

"Did she say that?" he asked.

"It was mentioned," Conor said.

"I should be pleased, maybe even relieved, that she spoke of me—I know Madeleine has told her terrible things to turn her against me. We were a good family; I always welcomed her visits to us."

"The separation must be hard," Conor said.

"I miss my wife and daughter terribly. So yes, you could say that," Bernard said in a scoffing tone.

"When did you last talk to them?" Conor asked.

Bernard laughed. "What are you, a cop?"

"Why would you ask that?" Conor asked.

"Because I've played them, and that's how they speak. 'When did you last talk to them?' Come on!"

"You got me. I'm a cop."

"No wonder you have the delivery," Bernard said. "Let me give you some advice. Change it up. You'll be more effective."

"Thanks for the tip," Conor said.

Bernard smiled and pushed his silver hair out of his eyes. "Sorry. I was rude. I'm just fucking frustrated about the weather."

"When did you land?" Conor asked.

"The day before this mess."

"Funny, we haven't seen you around the hotel."

"Jet lag, working on my movie, good room service. No need to leave the room. How do you know Hadley?" Bernard asked.

"Just fellow hotel guests."

"I get that," Bernard said. "Trapped in the blizzard. Survivors of the storm. It's like being marooned on a desert island; you get to know people quick."

"Hello, Conor."

Conor looked over his shoulder and saw Joe Harrigan and Garrett Milne coming through the lobby. Conor had called Joe an hour ago and made arrangements to hand over the things he had found at the murder scene.

"Hi, Joe," Conor said. "This is . . ."

He was about to introduce the men, but he saw the recognition in Joe's eyes.

"Bernard Lafond?" Joe asked.

"Yes," Bernard said, with the same self-assured smile he'd given Kate and Conor when they'd first laid eyes on him.

"We've been trying to contact you," Joe said. "I'm Detective Harrigan, and this is Detective Milne."

"Wow, cops everywhere," Bernard said. "Why would you want to contact me?"

"How long have you been here?" Garrett asked.

Bernard looked annoyed. "What is it to you?"

"I'm sorry to inform you that your wife is deceased," Joe said, his gaze boring into Bernard's eyes.

Conor stared at Bernard, watched the blood leave his face. Bernard shook his head, held it in his hands. "No," he said softly once, then again.

He didn't ask how she had died; he didn't ask where she had been found. He just stood there, in the circle of detectives, his eyes shut tight and his head shaking as if he could dislodge the news he had just received.

"Where is my daughter?" he asked, opening his eyes. His voice trembled.

"CeCe is missing," Joe said.

"No!" Bernard said for a third time, but this time he didn't say it softly.

Conor had seen many suspects lie, pretend to be surprised when given bad news. He could have sworn that Bernard's reaction was honest and spontaneous.

But, then again, Bernard Lafond was widely considered throughout the world to be a very fine actor.

13

Hadley felt calmer, after the shock of seeing Bernard. By the time she and Kate had returned to the bar, Conor was alone.

"Where's Bernard?" Hadley asked.

"The police are questioning him."

"Why is he here at the Ocean House?" Hadley asked. "It seems too crazy to think it's a coincidence. Scouting locations? Really?"

"He said he had a fantasy of Maddie walking through the door. He knew she came east, and I suppose he knew she loved this hotel."

"Yes, but she absolutely didn't tell him she had bought a suite here. The whole point was to hide from him—she was scared. That's why there was so much secrecy and security, the reason why no one could know she was here. It was because of Bernard," Hadley said.

Hadley stepped away from Kate and Conor, stood at the door that led to the verandah. She glanced at the ship model in the glass case. The classic yacht was sleek and streamlined, with a glossy black hull and a varnished cabin top. It was a replica of *Aphrodite*, the real yacht that lived in Watch Hill Harbor during the summer. Hadley wished she could step aboard with her sister and niece and go out to sea, get away from all of this, have life be beautiful again.

The pain of that thought was too much. She looked out the window. Incredibly, the snow had stopped, and there were breaks in the clouds. The ocean was actually visible, for the first time since she had arrived. It was silver green, filled with whitecaps, and spread out as far as she could see. Past Block Island, all the way to Portugal.

The blizzard was over. She'd thought it would never end. Claustrophobia had settled upon her, but it wasn't about being trapped in the hotel—it was about being held hostage by her mind and emotions.

She checked with the front desk, and they said that Westerly town crews had cleared most local roads and that state plows were working on the interstate. Hadley asked for her truck, and Dermot brought it around. He gave her an insulated bottle full of spring water.

"You're not leaving, are you?" Dermot asked.

"No, I'll be back in a few hours."

"Ms. Cooke, I am so sorry about your sister. I don't even know what to say. We're all so sad. What a terrible thing. If there's anything we can do, don't hesitate. We are all here for you," Dermot said.

"Thank you, Dermot," Hadley said. "That means a lot."

She glanced at the seat beside her, where Maddie and CeCe's presents had been. Now they were up in the suite, and she tried not to think about how some of them—maybe all of them—would never be opened.

The roads had been plowed. There hadn't been much traffic yet, so the banks and trees glistened white with pristine snow. Ice crunched under her tires. She fishtailed once, but when she hit I-95 north, the highway was sanded and clear, and she made good time up to Providence.

She lived in a Victorian house on College Hill, two blocks from the Brown campus. It was a two-unit condo, and Hadley had the top floor. She started to drive there, but she didn't have the heart to go inside. There were photos of Maddie and CeCe everywhere; she had paintings by Maddie, a plaster-of-paris paperweight with CeCe's handprint that she had made in preschool, and a small drawing by Sem that Bernard had given her before the wedding, when Hadley was Maddie's maid of honor. She couldn't bear the idea of seeing all that.

The studio she shared with Johnny was on Fox Point, where the city of Providence met Narragansett Bay. The candy-colored houses used to be inhabited mainly by Portuguese fishing families, but the last decade had brought gentrification to many streets, with properties being snapped up by Brown and Rhode Island School of Design professors and students, by lawyers and businesspeople who worked downtown.

Hadley pulled into the parking lot just across the Point Street Bridge. She and Johnny had their studio in the vast brick mill where, in the 1800s, hosiery had been produced. Now the building was called Silk Stocking Square. It was full of artists and small manufacturing companies; she and Johnny had their studio on the third floor.

She took the freight elevator up. It opened directly into their studio, so she inserted her key in the panel and slid open the metal gate. She smelled paint and turpentine, linseed oil and fixative. Her workbench was on the far side; Johnny's was just inside the door. The Bose sound system was playing "Sing Sweetly" by Rosa Pullman. It was one of Hadley's favorite songs, on a playlist Maddie had shared with her.

There was a small bedroom behind a partition, where either she or Johnny could sleep if they worked into the night, and Johnny walked out of it now. He looked ashen and walked straight to Hadley.

"Why are you playing this song?" Hadley asked.

"Because she loved it."

Loved. Past tense.

"How did you hear?" Hadley asked.

"The police were here, questioning me, just an hour ago. I heard an Amber Alert in the background, but it was for 'Cecelia Lafond'—I only knew her as CeCe. Maddie doesn't use 'Lafond,' so it went over my head. And there was nothing about a murder—just a missing child."

Johnny's eyes were full of sorrow. He looked the way Hadley felt, so she walked straight to him, and they hugged. She was shaking.

"Oh my God," she said, crying. "I can't believe it. Oh, Maddie . . ."

Hadley had been holding it together the best she could, but here in her studio with Johnny, she could finally let go. She cried for a long time without saying anything, and when she broke away from him, she could see that his eyes were wet with tears, too.

"What did the police say to you?" she asked.

"They didn't say anything—they just asked questions. I'm her first husband; I guess I'm second on the list, after Bernard. Why didn't you call me, Hads? Why did I have to hear about it from cops?"

"I should have called you," she said. "I just couldn't stand the idea of saying it out loud. I'm sorry."

"When did you find out?" he asked.

"I found her body, Johnny," Hadley said. "Not even twenty-four hours ago. Didn't they tell you that?"

"They didn't really tell me anything," he said. "CeCe's gone? And no one can find her. Are there any leads at all?"

"No," Hadley said. "I can't stop thinking about her—how terrified she must be, what whoever took her is doing to her . . ."

"Jesus, Hadley. The person must have left some trace."

"In a blizzard? In three feet of snow? Any tracks were blown away. If anything was left behind, it hasn't been uncovered yet. I'm sure the police are there now, looking for evidence." She paused. "Conor found a key."

"Who is Conor?"

"A detective staying at the hotel with his girlfriend. They were right behind me when I found Maddie. After we gave our statements, he went back to look. Johnny, he also found Star."

"Star? CeCe's blanket?" he asked.

"Yes," Hadley said, feeling a wave of emotion so strong she thought her knees would give out.

"She always has it with her," Johnny said. He saw that Hadley was ready to collapse, so he put his arm around her and led her to the daybed behind the partition and eased her down so she was sitting on the side. "Put your head down, between your knees." He had his hand on the back of her neck. "Breathe. Are you going to faint?"

"I'm okay," she said, but she felt as if every part of her was trembling. Her bones felt as if they had turned to ice.

"No one's okay," Johnny said.

"Who did this, Johnny? Who in Maddie's life could have done it?"

"Bernard," Johnny said.

Hadley didn't reply.

"Love and money are the biggest motives there are," Johnny said. "Besides, he didn't love her, not really. He wanted to *own* her. She was his possession. It tortured him when she left. His ego couldn't take it."

"You don't know that. You've never even met him."

"She told me," Johnny said.

"Really?" Hadley asked. Had he and Maddie had that drink after all? She was surprised that he would know anything about Bernard. "You and she talked about her marriage?"

"Some," he said. "Since she got back to Rhode Island. She'd call late at night, once in a while, when she couldn't sleep. She was wrecked about what the split was doing to CeCe."

"I know," Hadley said. "She did her best to shield her, but CeCe is smart. Bernard said some awful things over the phone that day when they came to Newport. She knew her parents were fighting."

"Not just fighting. They were at war," Johnny said.

Hadley's antennae were up. He knew that? How often had he and Maddie spoken? How close had they become? She felt like an idiot for feeling hurt.

"Did you meet with her?" Hadley asked.

"Just the times she and CeCe came here, and to the site," he said. "No, these were phone calls. And honestly, it wasn't that often. I just know her well, Hadley. We were married."

"A long time ago."

"And I'm with someone now. You know that. I wouldn't have seen Maddie, even if she wanted me to, out of respect for Donna."

"But I thought she told me you and she might meet for a drink," Hadley said. She had the impression that Donna was clingy.

"It never happened. That's just something we said, being polite, I guess."

"For old times' sake?"

"Old times are in the past," he said. "That's why they call them old times. But now she's gone, and that's just wrong, Hads. I'm sad, just the way you are."

He sat beside her on the bed, put his arm around her shoulder. He was the only person who called her Hads. He had said he was sad, and Hadley could feel the grief pouring out of him. She could only wish she were sad; that would be a huge step up—she felt eviscerated, as if someone had cut her heart out. As if the bullet that had murdered her sister had killed a part of her, too.

"What can I do for you?" Johnny asked.

"Nothing," she said. "We just have to wait until they find CeCe."

"They will," he said. "They have to. What about arrangements? You know, for Maddie?"

"I haven't thought about that," Hadley said. "She never told me what she wanted."

Johnny smiled a little wickedly. "Well, maybe her wishes changed along the way, but I know what she wanted back when we were together."

"What?"

"To be cremated and have her ashes scattered in museums. She wanted me to take a little of her to the Louvre, some to the Prado, some to the Frick, enough to the Mystic Museum of Art to fertilize the roses, some in Venice—during the Biennale, of course—and split the rest between the Whitney and the Met. She told me, 'This is the only way I'll ever get into a museum as an artist.' That was before she became MC."

"Leave it to her to come up with a plan like that," Hadley said, smiling. "She'd probably see it as performance art. Or an installation."

"She totally did. She wanted me to document it on video and in still shots, and to publish a book about it, about her."

"What about us, the people who loved her? If that was to be her memorial, where would we be? Wouldn't she want me there?"

"You more than anyone, Hadley. You were going to be the lookout while I strewed her about. Then we were supposed to dance on her grave. Right in the middle of the museums."

"Seriously, she said that?"

"Actually, I did. She made the whole thing sound like an art project, but I thought it was morbid. I guess it was my feeble attempt at humor."

"*Feeble*, good word—that's about what it is," Hadley said, and Johnny fake-elbowed her in the ribs.

"What are we going to do?" Johnny asked.

"You mean about her memorial?"

"I mean without her in the world."

"I don't know," Hadley said. She saw that his eyes were wet, and she felt like telling him that he sounded, for all the world, like someone in love. They held each other for a long time and didn't break away until his phone rang. He gave her an apologetic look and answered.

"Hey, Donna," he said, listened, then spoke. "Yes, I know. The police were here; they told me. I should have called you—I'm so sorry, baby. How did you hear?"

When he hung up, he turned back to Hadley. "It's all over the news," he said.

14

Conor wasn't used to being off to the side on an investigation, but he felt that way now. Joe and Garrett had dropped Bernard off after questioning him, and Joe found Conor in the bar, looking up MC on the internet and drinking club soda.

"Okay, so tell me everything," Joe said.

"Well, it was snowing like crazy. The items were under the hedge opposite Maddie's body. Your guys had left—nobody was processing the scene. Understandable, given the conditions. With CeCe missing, I thought it was important to secure everything and get it all to you as soon as possible."

"Well, thanks for that," Joe said. "We don't know what any of them mean. A strange collection. The blankie, I get that. But the Christmas decoration? And the ribbon? What's that about?"

"Things little girls put in their pockets," Conor said, thinking of Tom's stepdaughters, Hunter and Riley. How they had loved to collect odd, random objects when they were younger. Maybe they still did. He thought of Claire Beaudry Chase, the subject of a recent case, and how she had filled shadow boxes with things she had found—picked up on the beach, in the woods. "Maddie was an artist. Maybe CeCe had her mother's eye, was taking after her."

"That's not art," Joe said. "It's just a jumble."

Conor wasn't going to argue with him. People either saw it or they didn't, and maybe Joe was right.

"Here," Conor said. "I'm texting you photos I took under the hedge."

He opened his phone and texted Joe the pictures he had taken. Joe's phone buzzed, and he looked.

"Kind of blurry," he said.

"The snow was blowing," Conor said.

The two men peered at the same image on their separate phones.

"What does it look like to you?" Joe asked. "How did those things get there? Are you saying you think someone did some artistic whatever and placed them in that pile? The mother, the child, who?"

"I think CeCe was in that hollow under the shrubbery," Conor said. "The fact that Star—her name for the square of baby blanket—was there. Hadley says CeCe took it with her everywhere. So it wouldn't have been Maddie."

"What's your theory on why CeCe was in there?" Joe asked.

"You have to see the spot, to put it in context," Conor said.

"Let's go. You can show me," Joe said.

They bundled up and walked the short distance to the crime scene. It felt like a different world with the sky clearing. Conor assumed the forensics team would be back, now that the blizzard had passed. It was still frigid. The wind whipped fallen snow and ice crystals up from the ground and off the trees. It stung his face, so he kept his head down, chin tucked into his jacket collar.

Conor led Joe toward the beach on the far side of the hedge that abutted the path where Maddie had been shot. When he got to the break in the shrubbery, he motioned for Joe to crouch down beside him. They both studied the enclosure without speaking for a few minutes. Conor saw things he had missed the first time: two broken branches, a bittersweet vine that had become disentangled from the brambles.

"Okay, tell me your theory," Joe said.

"I think Maddie and CeCe walked down the path together. And I think Maddie had plans to meet someone."

"Out here? In a blizzard?" Joe asked. "Why not in the hotel?"

"Because she didn't want to be seen with the person—or the other way around. It was a secret meeting. And the timing must have been critical, or they could have waited for the storm to let up," Conor said.

"Well, we're thinking alike," Joe said. "That's what Garrett and I came up with, too. Now show me exactly where you picked up the trinkets."

"There," Conor said, pointing. Even though the hollow was protected, snow had drifted inside, most likely obliterating any trace evidence.

"How did they get there?"

"I think Maddie told CeCe to hide. Or CeCe heard someone coming and was afraid."

"So, before Maddie was shot?" Joe asked.

"Yeah. Maddie obviously wasn't expecting an attack, but the meeting may have been with someone she didn't want CeCe to see."

"Or someone who had an interest in CeCe."

"The father?" Conor asked.

"I don't know about that," Joe said. "He seemed genuinely shocked to hear that Maddie was dead. We'll polygraph him, of course. He claims he didn't even know she was staying in the hotel."

Conor thought about that. While his first impression had been that Bernard had no clue, he'd started thinking about acting skills, how Bernard could probably conceal his emotions better than anyone.

"He told us he's staying in Watch Hill to scout locations for a film," Conor said. "But seriously—he ends up at the Ocean House at the same time his wife and daughter are staying there? Hiding out from him?"

"Wicked coincidence," Joe said. "But he did agree to take the polygraph, and we're setting it up for this afternoon. In fact, I'd better get back so I can be there when he's in the hot seat."

They stood up and began walking back toward the Ocean House. The great yellow hotel rose out of the snowy landscape, the majestic tower looking out at a three-state view, promising shelter that Maddie would never have again. Conor wondered if CeCe would.

"Are there any leads on CeCe?" Conor asked.

"No sightings have been reported, and the storm obviously covered any tracks out of here."

"Maddie had sole custody," Conor said. "Could Bernard have come here to grab his daughter?"

"Everything is on the table. What about the aunt?" Joe asked.

"My instinct is no. But like you said, everything is on the table."

"Where is she now? I had a few more questions, but she wasn't in the suite. And the valet said he brought her truck and she drove off."

"Not sure. She was talking with me and Kate, then she left rather abruptly. Kate thought she was just overwhelmed with everything that's happening. Maybe she needed to shake the cobwebs out."

"If it was my niece missing and my sister murdered, I'd stay at ground zero to keep track of what's going on," Joe said.

Conor had felt the same way—he'd been critical about Hadley leaving. But Kate had said he was wrong. When her sister, Beth, was found strangled and her niece, Sam, was far away, at camp on an island off the Maine coast, Kate had gotten into her Cessna and flown north to Maine to pick up Sam. Conor trusted Kate—she had incredible intuition about people, and her experience as a woman dealing with a sister's murder made her ideas invaluable.

Halfway between the hedge and the hotel, Conor spotted something shiny in the snow. He bent down and saw a key chain. One key dangled from it; the fob was made of foam, shaped like a buoy, striped red and white. The letter *G* was scratched into the soft material. Conor had been out on the water often enough to know that this was the kind of thing boaters carried. If it fell overboard, it would float.

"Check that out," Conor said.

"Huh, some poor yachtsman lost his key. In the middle of winter. He's a long way from the Bahamas."

"Could be connected to your case," Conor said.

"Wouldn't you or any of my cops have seen it if it was dropped that night? How many times have you walked this street since then?" Joe asked.

Conor knew that Joe had a point, but the snowdrifts kept shifting and re-forming in the strong wind. "Maybe the killer dropped it in the street, and a snowplow turned it up," Conor said.

"Not sure about that, but I'll take it just in case, have it examined," Joe said. He used a pen to pick the key up by the chain. He dropped it into an evidence bag. "But, hey, it reminds me—that other key. The one you found with the other stuff, in the hedge. With CeCe's blanket thing."

"Yes, reminds me, too," Conor said.

"It obviously goes to a safe-deposit box. What's a kid doing with something like that?"

"That I don't know," Conor said. "But I can tell you it's from the Bank of Southern New England. Hartford office."

"Don't tell me you talked to them," Joe said.

"Of course not, Joe," Conor said. "I know better than to meddle in your investigation."

"Yeah right," Joe said, rolling his eyes as they walked up the wide steps to the Ocean House.

15

That floating boat key stuck in Conor's mind. Even if Joe doubted its connection to Maddie's murder and CeCe's disappearance, Conor wasn't so sure. He knew it would be a good idea to check with someone who knew about boats, and there was only one person he wanted to call.

"Reid," Tom said when he answered the phone.

"Hey, Reid," Conor said.

Static on the line.

"You there?" Conor asked.

"I'm here," Tom said. "The storm is messing up cell reception. Can't tell if it's you or me."

"Wait, you're the Coast Guard," Conor said. "You're supposed to have failproof communications."

"Uh, you're the state police, so back at you."

"Blizzards will be blizzards," Conor said. "Are you home or at the station?"

The call dropped before Tom could answer. Conor tried him back; the line went dead again, so he waited for Tom to return his call. His brother had been moving around the region lately. He was commander at Sector Southeastern New England in Woods Hole, and Station Point Judith was under his command. Being stationed in Rhode Island made it much easier for him and Jackie to see each other. When it came to marriage, Conor looked to his brother as an example of how to do it right. Tom and Jackie had the kind of closeness Conor wanted for himself and Kate.

Finally the phone rang again, and Conor picked up.

"I'd call you on the station landline," Tom said, "but I'm down at the dock. I just moved to the other side of the lot, and I think reception is better. Let's hope. Where are you?"

"I'm on vacation," Conor said. "I brought Kate to the Ocean House . . ."

"Oh really," Tom said, and Conor could hear the smile in his voice. "I approve."

"Of what?" Conor asked.

"You picked a good spot to propose. Am I right? I better be—it's about time."

"That was the plan," Conor said, not surprised by Tom's guess. It was a reflection of how well his brother knew him. "Have you been following the news?"

"Wait," Tom said. "Watch Hill. The murder and the missing girl. Are you on that case?"

"Unofficially," Conor said. "It's why I'm calling you."

"How can I help?" Tom asked.

The line crackled, and Conor waited for the noise to stop. Tom being stationed in Massachusetts put him just far enough away that Conor hadn't seen him much lately. He missed getting together regularly. The sound of Tom's voice, the possibility of his counsel and collaboration, felt very good.

"You there?" Conor asked.

"I'm here. Can you hear me?" Tom asked.

"Yes," Conor said. "There's a piece of evidence I'd like to tell you about."

"Hey, Point Jude is just down the road from Watch Hill. Why don't I head over and we can talk. This phone thing is ridiculous."

"That would be great," Conor said. And it was clearly the right decision, because the phone went dead again. He stuck it in his pocket and headed down the curving walkway from the hotel to the beach. He wanted to check on the searchers working there, but he could see that all the police vehicles had left.

The white cottage with a gingerbread roof served meals on the beach in summer, but it was locked tight now. He passed it, walking onto the sand where the wind had flattened the snowfall. Cutting between snow fences put in place to protect against blowing sand and erosion, he finally got to the hard sand below the high-tide line.

The waves were still enormous, ten feet at least. They had washed all the snow off the beach in the intertidal zone. He stayed at the edge of the tide line, head down, and looked for anything possibly related to the case. It was unlikely that he would find anything, but the elements kept sand moving, potentially uncovering evidence. Although the sun was out, the temperature had actually dropped since the storm. Ice crystals sparkled on the snow and sand. The beach was beautiful but deadly cold.

Conor thought of CeCe. He didn't know who had taken her, or where, but he found himself hoping she was warm. That whoever killed her mother hadn't left CeCe out in this cold. She wouldn't survive long, if she had survived at all. He walked a little farther and then turned back toward the hotel, heading across the beach to meet his brother.

16

The boy took CeCe to a house next to a dock. She saw a small building with a lobster-shaped sign that looked exactly like the lobster on the boy's jacket patch. Next to the door was a big stack of logs. Rectangular cages made of green wire were piled on top of each other. She didn't like the look of them. They seemed too small to fit a girl her size, but what if he was going to put her in one? Coils of dirty rope lay on the dock beside them. Seagulls cried and swooped.

"What are the cages?" she asked. She had told herself she would not open her mouth to him, but she was really scared he might make her get in one, and that fear won out.

"Huh?" he asked, following her gaze. "Oh, those are lobster pots."

"What are they for?"

"We drop them in the ocean with bait, and they sink to the bottom, where lobsters crawl in. Then we haul them up with those ropes and sell them."

"Oh," she said. "Not for people?"

"No," he said, laughing as if she had just said something funny.

They stood outside the door of a very small house with paint peeling off the side, and the boy patted the pockets of his jacket. Wind swirled off the water, stinging CeCe's cheeks. There were icicles stabbing down from the roof.

"Where is it?" he asked.

She didn't know what he was talking about. He went back to the car, checked inside, and retraced his steps to the house, staring at his feet as if he were looking for something he dropped.

"That's great," he said, his face red, and gave her an angry look. "Did you take it?"

"Take what?" CeCe said, and she froze as he patted the sides of her jacket, then reached into her pockets.

"Shit," he said when he realized they were empty.

He stomped to the building a little farther out on the dock. There were more lobster pots there. They were stacked high, taller than he was. There were also big blue barrels. He reached under one and came back with a key, and without saying anything to CeCe, he used it to unlock the door.

"Yeah, we live here. What about it?" he asked, glaring at her when they stepped inside.

She didn't know what he meant.

"It's a fish shack. We'll be moving soon, when we get the money," he said. "We'll be getting a real house."

Inside, the little house, the shack, was a mess, and that made CeCe feel strange. It gave her the feeling that the people who lived here didn't take care of each other and didn't care about anything. There were dirty dishes on a counter, a bunch of mud-crusted rubber boots by the door. Some fishing rods leaned against the wall, and on one table there was a pile of feathers. CeCe was afraid to look at them, in case there were dead birds. The room was almost as cold as the outdoors.

"My dad probably didn't pay the oil bill," the boy said. "It will warm up, though. I'll build a fire."

He went outside and returned with an armload of the logs she had seen piled next to the door.

"What happened to the birds?" CeCe asked, mesmerized and terrified by the feathers.

"We shot 'em. My dad and I go hunting and collect the feathers to tie flies, and then we sell them," he said.

She couldn't imagine killing a bird. She pictured a fly buzzing around. "How do you make flies out of birds and feathers?"

"We tie the feathers to hooks, and that's how some people catch fish. Fly fishermen. Haven't you ever gone fishing before?"

CeCe shook her head. Once on the pier in Malibu, she and her papa had watched a fisherman haul in a gigantic manta ray. It took a long time, and CeCe had felt so sad because even though the big ray looked frightening, and she wouldn't want to swim with it, she thought it was beautiful and knew it was going to die.

"You sell flies? I thought you sold lobsters."

"Both," he said, sounding mean. "We're not rich like you."

CeCe closed her eyes, wishing she had Star. *I want my mommy,* she said inside her head.

"Are you hungry?" the boy asked.

"No," CeCe said, even though she was.

"You better eat something," he said. "I am in so much trouble. The last thing I need is you passing out from starvation. He's going to kill me."

She wondered whom the boy meant, but she didn't ask. It was time to stop talking again. Everything felt confusing, and in a way, she felt as if she were drifting. Hovering overhead like a bird, seeing things and people on the ground, including herself. How could she be up here and down there at the same time? Was she alive or dead? Had she turned into a bird?

"Stay here," he said and went outside again. He was gone for more than a minute. She looked out the window and saw him open the car door.

This would be a good time to run away, but she didn't know where she was. It wasn't like during the snowstorm, when they were in the car just down the hill from the yellow hotel. So she stayed still.

When he came back in, he was carrying the gun he had shown her. She curled up into a ball, like a sleeping kitten, so she wouldn't feel it when he shot her. But he didn't shoot her. He went into another room. She heard a drawer open and close. When he returned, he wasn't holding the gun.

There was a fireplace, and he moved the screen from in front of it. He crumpled up some newspaper and put little sticks on a grate, then three logs. On top of the mantel were some wooden matches, and he lit one and touched it to a corner of the paper. The kindling flamed, then caught the sticks, and within a few minutes, there was a blazing fire.

It began to heat up the room, because the room was getting to be warmer than the outdoors. The boy came close and stared down at her. He still smelled like fish and seaweed. When she looked into his eyes, they looked sad.

"You're not that bad," he said. "You're a pretty brave kid."

She wasn't at all. She was scared. But she didn't cry; she didn't say a word. If she pretended to be brave, maybe she really would be.

"I fucked up taking you," he said. "We're both going to pay for it."

She wondered: *Pay what?*

"Promise me you won't run or yell when he comes home," he said. "That would just make things worse."

She just kept looking into his brown eyes. She didn't believe she looked brave or scared or anything. She was just air. She was invisible. She was floating up to the ceiling. She wasn't going to promise him anything.

17

Tom was on his way along Route 1 from Point Judith to see Conor in Watch Hill, and he registered how good it had felt to speak with his brother. They had worked together on a few cases, and even though he couldn't quite figure out how the Coast Guard could help in a murder that had occurred on land, he was all in. Just as he was passing the exit for Moonstone Beach, he got a call.

"Reid," he answered.

"Hey, Tom," Stone Crawford said. "Just got word about Garson's boat. It's drifting onto the jetty."

One of the Charlestown Breachway jetties, Tom knew. After Zane's distress call, he and the crew had located the *Anna G* just off the Charlestown Breachway. Rescuing Zane had been their mission; because of the conditions, they had left the boat where it was. Now it had floated free and been carried by the tide and currents toward shore.

"I'm just about at that exit."

"Sea Tow is already on it," Stone said. Sea Tow was a marine-assistance company that provided towing and salvage services. Its fleet of yellow-hulled boats was familiar to any sailor up and down the coast.

"Okay, good," Tom said. "Any fuel seepage?"

"None reported," Stone said.

"We'd better check it out," Tom said. "Meet you at the dock."

"Yes, sir," Stone said.

Tom pulled off Route 1. Hauling the lobster boat to safety would be the owner's responsibility—the cost of being towed off the beach belonged to Zane, but the Coast Guard would be there. Tom texted Conor and said he had to postpone getting together. Then he made a U-turn and headed back to the Coast Guard dock in Narrow River, Galilee, where he had started from after talking to Conor.

He was eager to see his brother and learn what he needed help with, but first he had to deal with the *Anna G.*

18

Conor was disappointed that Tom had to postpone their meeting, but he was used to it. They both were. As close as they were, they each had jobs that called for last-minute changes of plans. He knew Tom would come when he could. Just as he was about to get into the elevator and head up to his room, he caught sight of Bernard Lafond coming through the lobby. He let the elevator go and headed toward him.

"Detective Reid," Bernard said. "I was just about to call you."

Conor waited.

"Can we talk?" Bernard asked.

"Sure."

Bernard said a few words to someone at the desk, and they were led through the lobby to a door marked THE CLUB ROOM, MEMBERS ONLY. Conor had seen the sign earlier and wondered what was inside. They stepped into what felt to him like an exclusive club in London or somewhere. There were red leather chairs, highly polished dining tables, bookcases flanking a large fireplace, art everywhere, and a wall of windows and french doors facing the beach.

A tall man stood behind the bar and greeted them warmly. Bernard introduced him as Brian and ordered a Grey Goose martini. Conor said he'd have coffee.

"But it's cocktail hour," Bernard said.

"Coffee's fine for me," Conor said. "What did you want to discuss?"

Bernard ran his hand through his shaggy hair and exhaled long and hard. He looked more haggard than he had when Joe Harrigan had led him away. "You would need vodka, too, if you had just been hooked up to that machine and grilled as if they already believed you to be a murderer."

"The polygraph?"

"Exactement. When I play cops in films, I'm the one standing in the corner while the technician measures the murderer's lies. I've stood on the other side of the mirrored window, studying the suspect. Does he blink too fast? Do his eyes shift left when he answers the questions? But to be the one hooked up, for real, not fiction . . . Give me that martini."

They heard the ice being shaken as Brian mixed it. Conor watched him pour it into the chilled glass and felt the urge to ditch the coffee and join Bernard. But instead he directed his gaze at Bernard and watched for tells. Bernard's face was red, his brow furrowed. Conor read anger.

"Here you are, Mr. Lafond," Brian said, setting the glass down on a coaster.

"À votre santé," Bernard said, taking a large slug of his drink.

"To your health, too," Brian said.

"You speak French?" Bernard asked.

"When it comes to toasts," Brian said, smiling. He walked away and returned a few moments later with coffee for Conor. Conor warmed his hands on the cup, watching Bernard. He sensed Bernard was working his way up to whatever it was he really wanted to talk about.

"You know, of course, that they suspect me of killing Madeleine," Bernard said.

"I do not know that," Conor said.

"I saw you talking to Detective Harrigan." His French accent was more intense than it had been earlier, and he pronounced the name "Arrigan."

"Yes, but he didn't tell me his theory of the case."

"Two detectives? I assume you share information."

"Only to some extent," Conor said. "I work in Connecticut. That's another jurisdiction."

"Well, surely, wherever you work, you share the opinion that the husband is always the number-one suspect," Bernard said. "Whether justified or not."

"It's common to question everyone who is close to the victim," Conor said.

Bernard shook his head. "You cops stick together. They are making a mistake, focusing on me. And the longer they do, the more time my daughter is missing."

"They are very aware of the fact CeCe is missing, and they are doing everything possible to find her."

"They are not doing enough," Bernard said. "That is why I want to talk to you."

"What can I do for you, Mr. Lafond?"

"I need help. I want to hire an outside investigator. A private eye, if you will. To find my daughter, to learn who killed my wife," Bernard said.

"Detectives Harrigan and Milne and the Rhode Island police will do that, Mr. Lafond."

"Bernard, please. And perhaps they will, but I can't bear to let things unfold as slowly as bureaucracy demands. Harrigan is a detective, yes, but he is a fonctionnaire."

"A what?"

"A civil servant. An employee of the government. He doesn't have the same urgency that I do. That her family does."

"I'm sure that's not true," Conor said, thinking of his own cases as a Major Crime Squad detective, how the victims of violent crime became very much his own family. How he came to care about them, even love them, to need to get justice for them.

"You can't convince me," Bernard said, finishing his drink and signaling for another. "I told you, they treat me with suspicion, and meanwhile, nothing of substance is being done . . ." He trailed off.

"They have to conduct their investigation the way they see fit," Conor said. "They'll get to the truth."

"Not fast enough. I want to hire the best. Who is that? You know, I am sure. Someone local but with excellent credentials, who might have insight into suspects, or ideas of where my daughter might be hidden," Bernard said. "Tell me, please, who would that be?"

"I don't have a name for you," Conor said.

"That's not acceptable," Bernard said, raising his voice. "What would you do if your daughter was missing? Wouldn't this slow pace be driving you out of your mind?"

Conor didn't have children, but during crimes in which kids were at risk, he always asked himself the same question that Bernard had just posed. "I would be as upset as you are," Conor said.

"C'est ça," Bernard said, with apparent relief at being understood. He took a long drink. "That's it. Exactly. So, will you help me?"

"In what way?" Conor asked.

"Since you don't have a recommendation of an outside investigator, I would like to hire you."

As a member of the state police, Conor would never take a private case, and he suspected that Bernard knew that. He studied Bernard's face. He saw desperation, but he questioned what lay beneath it. He knew from Hadley that Bernard was broke; he assumed that there were no funds available to pay a detective. So was this behavior performative? Was this an attempt to convince Conor of his innocence?

"I want *you* to solve this," Bernard said. "I don't care so much about being treated like a criminal." He paused, peering at Conor. "I see you don't believe that. The husband always did it? What lazy thinking. I love—loved—Madeleine. To know what was done to her, and to not know where my daughter is, is torture for me. I want you to find the killer, the kidnapper. Is my daughter alive? What the fuck are they doing to her?"

Conor could see he was roiling with emotion. His face was scarlet, and his bloodshot eyes were wet with tears. Conor knew that powerful feelings shook everyone touched by violent crime. It wasn't a barometer of guilt or innocence.

"What do you charge? I don't care. I will give everything I have in the world to get my daughter back," Bernard said.

"I don't charge because I don't take private clients," Conor said. "I'm a state police detective—just not in this state," Conor said.

"Everyone has a price," Bernard said.

"I guess you didn't hear me," Conor said. "You're not my client."

"You don't care about what happened to them?"

"I do," Conor said. "And I have some questions."

"Like what? Ask me anything."

"Start with what you're doing here. And why you weren't answering your phone."

"I told you—I needed quiet. And I came here to find the right location for my next film. It is a very atmospheric part of the world, we need a setting by the Atlantic Ocean . . ."

"Bullshit, Bernard," Conor said. "That answer alone guarantees you failed the polygraph. You're not only on the East Coast when your wife is murdered, you're staying in the same hotel. And you were completely unreachable for hours after she was killed and CeCe taken."

"Why should I tell you anything if you don't trust me?" Bernard asked, raking his fingers through his long hair. "Do you want to help find CeCe or not?"

"Do *you* want to?" Conor asked. "Think carefully before you tell more lies, because no one can do anything without the truth."

"I knew that Madeleine loved this hotel when she was a young girl," Bernard said, and he paused, looking at the ceiling.

Conor knew he was about to ease his way out of the outright lie. He had come into first the police interrogation and now Conor's questioning leaning heavily on his charm and fame, assuming that he could convince people of what he wanted them to believe. Did he know how obvious he was?

"So, no, it wasn't a complete coincidence," Bernard continued, "that I chose the Ocean House as my home base while being here. The truth is, I dreamed of Madeleine walking through the door."

"Did you see her? Did your paths cross?" Conor asked.

"No, absolutely not. But I told you—I needed privacy, and I tend to be a hermit when working. I barely left my room."

"What about 'scouting'? How were you supposed to find the perfect location without actually going out to look for it?"

"The weather changed my plans. My assistant always makes the initial visits—consults with local film boards, real estate agents, you know."

"Is your assistant here with you?" Conor asked.

"No," Bernard said. "Marie-Laure sometimes travels with me, but not this time. She visited Watch Hill in advance. She gave me plenty of places to consider."

"Where is she now?"

"I assume in Los Angeles." Bernard stared at Conor. "There is nothing romantic between us. Rien du tout."

Interesting statement, Conor thought. Considering he hadn't asked.

"Back to you, being a hermit and staying in your room," Conor said. "Didn't you come down for meals?"

"No. I happen to love room service. I will confess, I did walk around the hotel late at night, when people were presumably asleep. I am a fan of some of the artists represented here. I wanted time to examine their work."

"Why late at night?"

"Because I didn't want to be seen. To be recognized. One good thing about being here is that TMZ isn't camped outside at all times.

My divorce—Madeleine's and mine—has given the tabloids a great gift. They can't get enough of it. In LA I can't leave my house or office without some asshole shoving a camera into my face."

"But you said they're not here."

"Conor, on social media everyone can have their own private TMZ. Before the divorce, the worst that would happen would be someone with a cell phone bothering me in a restaurant. I tend to get angry, Conor. The rudeness, the lack of respect. People with cell phones catch me in the moment and post the photos. I want to rip their phones right out of their hands, shove them into the street. But I never do."

Conor took note—angry rant, and the kind of fury that made him want to grab someone's phone and throw it away. Bernard was minimizing it, but it was a thought of violence.

"Listen," Bernard said, seeming to read Conor's thoughts. "I wouldn't actually do it. And you know why? Because some other idiot with another cell phone would catch me throwing punches, and that would be the story: 'Bernard Lafond and his rage problem.' It's been a headline before; I don't need to see it again."

"Were you very angry at Maddie?"

Bernard shrugged. "Of course. Some of the time. But mostly just very sad. You know, in therapy I'm told that anger is a cover-up for sorrow. Fury is less painful to feel than grief or sadness. I use it in my work." He looked up at the ceiling. "I am known for my seething. And then I break down and the tears come."

"You can cry on cue?"

Bernard shrugged. "That's acting."

"Were you furious at John Morrison?" Conor asked.

"You mean *Johnny*?" Bernard asked, glaring at Conor. "He's a flea. Not worth a second of my emotion. She divorced him so long ago; he's not in our lives."

That didn't square with what Hadley had told Conor, and if Bernard truly didn't care, why did Johnny's name set him off? Didn't fleas bite, and did that mean Johnny had gotten to him?

"But Maddie and Johnny remained friends," Conor said. "Isn't that true?"

"I don't waste my thoughts on that. Madeleine was polite to him, I'm sure. She's kind. That is just how she is."

"I hear you weren't happy about Maddie and CeCe visiting him and Hadley at the dock," Conor said. "The things you said caused Maddie to get a restraining order against you, to stop your visitation. You made threats, saying Maddie would end up like Désirée? You said that to CeCe?"

"Yes, I lost control. But not because of Johnny. I was upset by the fact my wife and daughter were a continent away from me. It was too much to take. Nothing to do with him. I regret saying what I said about Désirée, especially to CeCe. I didn't mean to scare my daughter."

"Okay," Conor said, knowing there was much more there.

"I hope the police are questioning *Johnny*," Bernard said, again putting the name in invisible italics. Conor felt his loathing come through. "He is pathetic. I'm sure he resents Madeleine for her success, while he's stuck painting tacky little municipal advertisements on walls."

"He works closely with your sister-in-law," Conor said. "Is that how you see Hadley, too?"

"No," Bernard said. "Look, Hadley isn't as talented as Madeleine, but no one is. Still, Hadley has vision; her wall murals have much more soul than his. It kills me that Hadley has lost Madeleine—she loved her as much as I do. We were all very close. The divorce is hard on her, too."

"She told me that you have other children," Conor said. "How do they feel about Maddie?"

Bernard exhaled. "Depends on which one you ask. You know, I have several ex-wives, and I've noticed that the children's reactions mirror exactly their mothers'. My second ex-wife is halfway decent. Others hate when I am happy and loved, which means, therefore, they hate Madeleine. That is just a fact."

"Where do they live?"

"The ex-wives? Paris and Bordeaux. One might be in London. I can't keep track; she is peripatetic."

"And your kids?"

"Paris, London, Saint Paul de Vence, Venice. Venice, Italy, not California." He sighed. "Look, it's been years, and the dust has settled. They have their own lives. They had nothing to do with this; I don't want them harassed. I told Detective Harrigan the same thing. Leave them alone."

Conor was pretty sure Joe was already tracking down the Lafond offspring, but he held that inside.

"Tell me about Genevieve Dickinson," Conor said. He figured that he might as well cover as many bases as possible as long as Bernard was talking.

"Madeleine rarely spoke of her. I know that it hurt her deeply at the beginning, to be sued by someone she thought was a friend. To have her name dragged through the mud because this person made a false claim," Bernard said.

"Did you ever meet her?" Conor asked.

"Funny you should ask," Bernard said. "Yes, our paths did cross once, but in a most peculiar way."

"What way?"

"I was shooting a film in Quebec. A ridiculous but brilliant surrealist director was trying to tell a story based on Paul Éluard's poetry. Do you know it?"

"The film or the poetry? Either way, no," Conor said.

"Well, Éluard was known for his explorations of love. Very beautiful and heartbreaking. But he also wrote about war, the disaster of it, and he was passionately antifascist. The love of his life was Gala, and when I played him in that film, I drew on my love for Madeleine."

"Tell me about meeting Genevieve."

"Oh yes. On the film set. It was supposed to be a small town outside Paris, but the producers decided to be cheap and shoot in Canada instead of doing it properly. A 'prestige production' they called it—what a joke. No wonder the film died a quick death. She was working for the local production company as the continuity editor."

"What's that?"

"You know, to make sure things stay consistent from shot to shot. Like, if I am smoking a cigarette in one take, it has to be the same length in the next one. Or if my shirt is buttoned to the top, or if my hair is falling into my right eye—these things must stay the same way throughout the scene. Genevieve sat behind the second AD with her notepad, keeping track of those details."

"How did you put it together?" Conor asked. "That she was the woman who sued Maddie?"

"Because Madeleine and CeCe came to visit me on set," Bernard said. "And there was Genevieve. Madeleine was certain Genevieve was there to ambush her—confront her. Because of course she knew who I was, and who I was married to."

"Was there a big confrontation?" Conor asked.

"No. Madeleine kept her cool and stayed away from Genevieve. She handled it very well, with great equanimity."

"And Genevieve?"

"It was all very civil," Bernard said.

Brian came to ask if they would like another drink or to order food. Bernard said yes, one more martini. Conor declined.

"Of course, now there is no more privacy, even here," Bernard said. "After these hours in the blizzard. The news trucks have arrived, I've been forced to speak with a lawyer, and I am going to make a statement. I am going to beg for Cecelia to come home. Do you think she is still alive?"

His question was blunt, matter of fact. There seemed to be no emotion behind it. He might have been asking about the weather.

"We have to believe she is," Conor said.

"I didn't ask you what we *have* to believe—that sounds like phony hope, cheap spirituality. I asked what you think."

"Why don't you tell me what *you* think?" Conor asked.

And now there was emotion. There were tears. Bernard broke down. "I think she is dead," he said. "Whoever murdered her mother killed her as well. Murdered my little daughter."

Conor sat still, watching Bernard sob, his head in his hands. It went on for a long time. The tears were real. The question was: What was he really crying for? The loss of his wife and daughter, or the regret he felt for having discovered a need to kill them?

Brian delivered the martini. Without looking up, Bernard reached for the glass. His hand closed around the stem, and he drained the drink in one gulp. Then he glanced up at Conor, as if to make sure Conor had seen, registered the hard-drinking desperation of a worried father.

19

Hadley stayed at her studio until late that night. Nothing comforted her more than making art, so she put on her painting clothes and stood at her easel, letting dreams flow from her paintbrush. Images of whales and swans, of two sisters in a sailboat, of a tiny child swimming through the stars overhead filled the canvas. On the other side of the room, Johnny sat at the workbench, sketching out plans for their latest commission.

Around eleven, Hadley heard the freight elevator creak and begin its ascent. When the grate rattled open, a tall dark-haired woman bearing grocery bags stepped out.

"I thought you might be hungry," the woman said.

"Wow, perfect timing, I'm starving," Johnny said, walking over to kiss the woman, to carry the bags to the kitchen area.

"Hello," the woman said, approaching Hadley. She put out her hand to shake, then saw that Hadley's were covered in paint and withdrew it. "I'm Donna Almeida. I've been wanting to meet you, Hadley. I am so sorry about Maddie and CeCe."

"Thank you," Hadley said.

"She was lovely, your sister," Donna said. "I am very happy we had the chance to spend time together."

"I'm glad you met her."

"Do the police have any idea of who did this?" Donna asked.

"Not that they have told me."

"Johnny, I haven't seen you since they questioned you," Donna said. "It must have been so upsetting."

"Not the questioning part," Johnny said. "Just the fact of what happened to Maddie. I still can't believe it."

Hadley followed Donna into the kitchen area. She saw that the bags were from Penguins, a café on Thayer Street that stayed open late. Donna set out plates and sandwiches. Johnny opened a bottle of pinot noir. The three of them sat on stools at the counter. Hadley couldn't eat.

"You were really close to Maddie, weren't you?" Donna asked.

Hadley nodded.

"I apologize," Donna said. "I don't mean to pry. It's probably too painful for you to talk about . . ."

"No, I like to talk about her," Hadley said.

"You must have been so happy when she came to Rhode Island to stay," Donna said.

"I was. Over the moon. After all those years of her being in California, so far away, it was heaven to have her here, just a short drive away."

"I'm sure she missed you, with all that distance. And then, here she was. Close to two people who meant so much to her—probably more than anyone."

"Two people?" Hadley asked.

"You and Johnny," Donna said.

Hadley wouldn't let her eyes meet Johnny's. If she did, she had the feeling she'd see humor in them—he wouldn't kid himself that Maddie considered herself to be in any way as close to him as she was to Hadley.

"No offense to Johnny," Hadley said, "but I don't think it was that way."

Donna rested her head on his shoulder, staring at Hadley with a small smile. She had wavy dark hair and almond-shaped eyes, topaz flecked with green. It was too hard for Hadley to talk about Maddie and her feelings for her, so she changed the subject.

"You're a lawyer, right?" Hadley asked finally.

"No, a paralegal. I work at a firm in Connecticut."

"Are you from there originally?" Hadley asked.

"No, I'm from South County, right here in Rhode Island," Donna said. "Narragansett. My family still lives there."

"I love that area," Hadley said. "So many beautiful beaches."

"And the best clam shacks anywhere," Johnny said. "Her parents own the Binnacle—you've been there, right, Hads?"

"Of course—it's a classic," Hadley said, picturing the salty restaurant with the bright-red awnings on Ocean Road.

"They would love me to run it eventually, but we have a big family— plenty of people to step in when the time comes. Meanwhile, I like what I do," Donna said. "Trust and estates, working with absolutely awesome people, helping them plan for their futures, and . . ."

Hadley nodded. She was getting tired. Donna obviously saw, because she stopped in the middle of her sentence. "Hadley, I'm just so sorry for what you're going through. I can't imagine. I know we just met, but please, if there's anything I can do . . ."

"Thank you," Hadley said. She was done talking about it; she just wanted to leave. "I'm going to take off."

"To your apartment?" Johnny asked.

"No, heading down to Watch Hill. I want to be there for CeCe. She's coming back, I know it. And I'll be waiting for her."

"I'm sure you're right," Donna said, reaching across the counter to touch Hadley's hand. "The power of love. It's going to pull her back to you. I'm an aunt, too. I'd do anything for my nieces and nephews."

Hadley nodded. Her gaze met Donna's and held. They were two aunts who understood that particular kind of unconditional love. In that moment, Hadley believed Donna knew exactly what she was feeling.

20

The next day dawned bright but still cold. Conor looked out the window at the ocean and saw that the snow on the beach and all around the Ocean House was still coated with ice that glinted in the sunlight. A room-service tray sat on the table by the window. It held the morning's second pot of Dave's Coffee. Kate lay on the bed with her laptop, and Conor sat at the desk with his.

"I think Genevieve should be your next call," Kate said. "That lawsuit between her and Maddie was really ugly. Did Bernard say anything about it?"

"He did," Conor said. "And he mentioned a weird situation on a film set in Quebec, when both Maddie and Genevieve were there. He said it was civil. But I agree—I'm going to contact her."

The room phone rang, and Kate answered.

Conor figured it was housekeeping asking when they could clean the room, but when Kate hung up, she was grinning.

"We have a visitor," she said.

"Who?"

"Your brother," Kate said. "He's on the way up."

Two minutes later, Tom knocked on the door. Kate opened it, and they gave each other a big hug. Conor walked over and shook his brother's hand.

"You made it," Conor said. "Got a lot going on?"

"Sure do," Tom said, glancing around. "Nice place you have here. I've gone past this hotel on boats hundreds of times but never been inside. Plenty of sailors use it as a landmark when they're navigating this stretch of coast. You can see the yellow hotel—the tower, at least—all the way from Block Island and Montauk."

"We were so excited to be here," Kate said. "And then this terrible thing happened."

"I heard a little about it," Tom said, turning to Conor. "Like all other law enforcement, we received a bulletin about Cecelia. Everyone is looking for her. Any leads at all?"

"I spoke to Joe Harrigan first thing, and no—nothing substantial. The billboards are getting attention, people are calling in, and the FBI is weeding through tips," Conor said.

"I know Joe," Tom said. "Good cop."

"You've worked cases with him?" Conor asked.

"We've overlapped at times. I know him mostly from seeing him on the water. He's a sailor, keeps his boat in Avondale," Tom said. "What else is going on with the investigation?"

"I met with CeCe's father," Conor said. "He's here in the hotel, and so is Hadley Cooke, Maddie's sister."

"The father is Bernard Lafond, the actor?" Tom asked. "It came through in the briefing."

"That's him," Conor said.

"Jackie likes his movies."

"But you don't?" Kate asked.

"Not that I don't like them," Tom said. "It's just that I haven't seen many of them." He smiled. "Come on, you know what I mean," he said to Conor. "We were raised on action movies and comedies."

"It's true," Conor said. "We didn't spend a lot of time reading subtitles."

"So, what did you want to talk to me about?" Tom asked. "You mentioned a piece of evidence?"

"A key," Conor said. "It might have nothing whatsoever to do with Maddie and CeCe, but I found it on the side of Bluff Avenue, between the hotel and the spot where Maddie was killed."

"How can I help you with it?" Tom asked. "Is there some kind of maritime connection?"

"The key chain looked like something that might belong to a boater," Conor said. "Made of foam."

"Floatable," Tom said. "Boat owners use them so the key won't sink if it falls overboard."

"That's what I thought, but seems like a strange time of year to be thinking about boating," Conor said. "And for someone to lose a boat key during a blizzard."

"Some people don't go by the weather reports," Tom said. "We rescued someone two days ago—when the storm was at its worst. And the reason I had to cancel yesterday is that I was dealing with the aftermath."

"Tom! You were out in that?" Kate asked.

"Yep. We got a distress call from a fishing boat—top heavy with ice and taking on water. Just down the beach from here. My guys did a great job, and we saved the captain—the only one on board—but it was tricky."

"Who goes fishing in a blizzard?" Conor asked. "Why was he out?"

"It was a moronic thing to do," Tom said. "He put himself and us in danger. But people are struggling. He fishes for lobster, and the fishery is diminished. That plus a whole lot of new regulations have been hell on the captains. They're taking a lot more chances. More time on the water equals more catch."

"Understandable but crazy," Kate said.

"That's right," Tom said. "Okay, you have a key that belongs to someone who most likely owns a boat. You found it near the murder site. So, what are you thinking?"

"Who dropped it?" Conor said. "People weren't exactly out enjoying a stroll along Bluff Avenue. You know what the weather was better than anyone. According to the note Maddie left her sister, she went to the beach path to meet someone. Hadley went looking for her, and Kate and I followed."

"The storm was insane," Kate said. "Conor and I wouldn't have gone to the path, but we could tell Hadley was upset. It seemed dangerous for her to be heading into the blizzard alone, and we wanted to make sure she was okay."

"And no one else would have been out there, considering the weather conditions," Tom said, nodding and getting their point.

"Except the murderer," Conor said.

"Are you thinking Bernard did it?" Tom asked.

"He's in the mix," Conor said, "but my gut says no. Besides, what would he be doing with a boat key?"

"Doesn't have to go to a boat—lots of people put their house and car keys on the same ring. They're sold at marine supply houses but also in souvenir shops. Tourists who want a little nautical action to rub off from the old salts. Could you tell by looking at the key what it might be?"

"Looked like a standard house key," Conor said. "But I don't know."

"Let me see it," Tom said.

"The detectives took it," Conor said. "I was walking with Joe Harrigan when I saw it in the snow."

"So, tell me what the foam looked like. Some of them are printed with logos, vessel names, custom details like that."

"It was oval, buoy shaped, red-and-white striped," Conor said. He saw something register in his brother's eyes.

"Huh," Tom said. "Could belong to a lobsterman. A lot of them will get merchandise that look like their buoys, holding the traplines. Every captain has a signature color or stripe pattern to identify their equipment out at sea—red and white is a common combination. I can think of several locals who use it. It would depend on the width of the stripes."

"These were wide," Conor said. "Three of them—white, red, white." He pictured the foam—scuffed and discolored, cracked from being in the sun and other elements.

"Any logo?" Tom asked. "Or vessel name?"

"Nothing professionally printed, other than the stripes, but there was a letter scratched into the foam. The letter *G*."

"Holy shit," Tom said. "That's a pretty big coincidence."

"What?" Conor asked.

"You know that boat I was telling you about?"

"The one that almost sank in the blizzard?"

"Yes," Tom said. "The *Anna G*. Belongs to Zane Garson."

"*G*," Conor said.

"And Garson's buoys are red and white—wide striped," Tom said.

"Well, if he was going aground on his boat, he couldn't have also been walking down Bluff Avenue."

"True, but he does have a crew. Family members—his brother and his son. They might have the same key ring, if he had a few made," Tom said.

"What's Zane Garson like? Has he or the others been in trouble?" Conor asked.

"I can't speak to specifics; I'm not aware of details. You'd have to ask the police, but Zane and his brother are known for drinking and brawling. The kid has had some issues, too, since his mother died. When he was about twelve, he lit some fireworks and tossed them down the dock. Fourth of July and supposedly a prank, but they damaged a powerboat and gave a deckhand second-degree burns."

"Start 'em young," Conor said. "How about Zane?"

"He changed, too, after Anna—his wife—died. The market for lobsters crashed around the same time. That didn't help. He lost his house, wound up moving into a shack owned by his older brother. Grub is a surly SOB, and ever since Anna died, Zane's been taking after him. There have been allegations of the Garson brothers messing with other fishermen's gear. Serious business with bad repercussions."

"Well, you just saved Zane's life," Conor said.

"Yeah, and all he could really do was complain that we didn't save his boat at the same time. I tried telling him that a full-blown blizzard, with sixty-knot gusts, wasn't the time."

Conor nodded. "The grateful type. What about guns? Any issues with firearms that you know of?"

"He has them—a lot of captains do—but I haven't heard of any trouble. I should put you in touch with Dick Brady, the local police chief. He'd know more details about the family," Tom said.

"Where's Zane now?" Conor asked.

"Home, maybe," Tom said. "Counting his lucky stars, I hope. It could have gone a whole lot worse. He's talking to insurance people, I'm sure."

"Where is his home?"

"Galilee," Tom said. "Half an hour down Route 1."

"Can you give me an address?" Conor asked. "I know it's a long shot, but finding that key chain so close to our murder victim makes me want to talk to him."

"I can do better than telling you his address," Tom said. "I'll drive you there. I have some questions for him, too, about his boat salvage."

"Great," Conor said. "Let's go."

21

CeCe and the boy had stayed in his house all night. She had tried to sleep, but even though he had given her a scratchy blanket, the room was still so cold that she couldn't stop shivering. The boy had kept trying to call someone on his phone, but the person wasn't answering, so he had kept swearing.

Now she watched him sitting in front of his computer, his face nearly touching the screen. She could hear the low drone of voices, so she knew he was watching a movie or TV show. But when she tried to look, he blocked her. So instead, she stood by the window, looking out at the dock. A man pulled up in a dark-blue truck with a lobster printed on the side, the same as the one on the sign and on the boy's jacket.

The man wore overalls and a yellow jacket, and he had a cap with the lobster on it, and his face was whiskery, like her father's face got when he needed to shave but didn't because he had to look a certain way for the movie he was in. He wore tall black rubber boots, like the ones standing by the door, and CeCe watched him walk toward the house. She heard the doorknob turn. Her heart pounded because maybe he was here to rescue her.

"Help," CeCe said. Ronnie had told her not to yell, so she barely whispered it. The man acted like he didn't hear.

"Ronnie!" the man shouted, even though he was just a few feet away.

The boy jumped up from his chair. Now CeCe knew that his name was Ronnie.

"Dad!" he said. "Where were you?"

The man glared at Ronnie, then at CeCe.

"What. The. Fuck?" the man asked.

"I waited and waited where you said, but you never came into the dock. And where did you stay last night?"

"She sank," the man said. "My beautiful *Anna G* went down in the goddamn storm. I was up all night trying to straighten things out. She let me down, just like everyone else. Just like my fucking brother, just like you."

"Dad, I didn't let you down!"

"Could we reschedule the operation?" the man asked, looking up at the ceiling. "No, we could not. It had to be right then, that very hour. And now my boat has a broken mast, and a big hole in her side, and I've got to pay a big fat salvage fee, and I'm sure I'll get fined a shitload for environmental cleanup; they'll lie about my fuel tank leaking. And now *this*?" He pointed straight at CeCe.

"I was waiting for the boat," Ronnie said. "If the boat came . . ."

"Well, dickhead, I just told you why the boat didn't come. Open your ears. I give you a job to do—I trust you with the most important part—and you fuck it up. What about the other part? Tell me you didn't fuck that up, too."

"I didn't," Ronnie said. "I'm watching it on the news right now. It's done, just watch the news! And you can see it on social media. They're talking about it."

CeCe's head tingled, as if her hair were standing straight up, the way it sometimes did when her mom pulled a sweater off over her head and it made electricity. She had an electric feeling in her heart and down her legs, too, because somehow she knew that the news Ronnie was talking about had to do with her and her mother.

"What am I supposed to do with her?" the man asked, turning around to point at CeCe. "Did you think of that?"

"Dad, it was only gonna be the lady. I didn't know Cecelia would be there, too!"

"Don't say her name," the man said. "It will only make the next part harder."

Ronnie and his father had their backs to her as they looked at the computer screen. She didn't want to stand near them, but she needed to see what they were watching. She inched toward them, but then she had a better idea. If they weren't looking at her, maybe she could disappear. The door looked heavy, but she was strong, and if she pulled really hard, she could open it and run away.

"Well, that part's okay," the man said, eyes on the computer. "We'll get paid. Good job, son."

"Thanks, Dad. When will this all be over?"

The father didn't answer that question. He was still intent on the news story. "And you got clean away. Ha, listen to that! That's what they're saying—good, music to my ears. 'We have no suspects.' Ha, that is good; that is excellent. You really did a great job in that. You did that right."

"Yeah," Ronnie said.

"Maybe we should be glad of the freaking storm. I was pissed about the timing, and my goddamn boat, but it did cover your tracks. Wrecked evidence—that works for us. And believe me, I will be compensated for the boat. We have a new Novi in our future, son. It will be loaded, too, I tell you that. The best electronics on the market."

"Yeah, Dad. Way to go," Ronnie said.

"Remodel this house, too. Everything's gonna work; it will be beautiful."

"Or a real house, Dad. Not a dump we rent from Uncle Grub. A place like we used to live when Mom was alive. Only bigger, right? With a garage and a workshop."

"Maybe. Who's the best?" the man asked. "What father-and-son team is the best?"

"We are," Ronnie said.

"It ain't my fault the bottom fell out of the lobster market after your mom passed. But thank God she never had to move into this shithole," the man said.

CeCe had been walking backward very slowly, a tiny step at a time. She kept her eyes on Ronnie and his father, and she sent magical thoughts their way, casting a spell on them so they wouldn't turn around and see her.

"We still got to be careful," the man said. "Check out the Amber Alert; that means we got to be extra, extra careful. And look—billboards on the highway! CeCe's face everywhere. They want everyone to know her nickname. They're making her Rhode Island's little sweetheart. The FBI is here; they're putting her on electronic billboards up and down ·95."

"Those ones that flash about 'Drive Sober or Get Pulled Over'?" Ronnie asked. "'Click It or Ticket'?"

"Yeah. Wow, they are not fooling around. This is about money, it's a kid with money. If there's a reward, I'm telling you, that will be bad. That will be a disaster. Even Uncle Grub would turn us in for that kind of payday."

"He wouldn't," Ronnie said. "He's loyal."

The man cracked Ronnie so hard on the back of his head that Ronnie nearly lost his balance.

"Are you stupid? You were doing so well, but here you are being a moron. Loyal means nothing when it comes to money. You better learn that lesson quick. A goddamn Amber Alert? That puts people on notice, and next thing there's a reward, and we're talking about rich people—the dad's a fucking movie star—so it'll be six figures, and that means all bets are off. Money talks. Got that?"

"Yeah," Ronnie said.

Amber Alert. CeCe knew what that meant. She had learned about it in school—"stranger danger"—and she knew how someone might seem nice but could be a kidnapper. When children were taken, the police put their names in Amber, and the whole world learned they were missing. Was CeCe's name in Amber?

She was almost to the door. Her heart was skittering as if it had been dropped and was bouncing and rolling across the floor. She glanced over her shoulder. Two more steps and she'd be there. She flexed her hands to get ready to pull on the knob, and she took a deep breath so she could scream as loud as she could.

But then she heard tires crunching on snow and ice. Both Ronnie and the man turned fast to look out the window.

"Jesus Christ, it's Tom Reid," the man said.

"The Coast Guard dude?" Ronnie asked.

Ronnie's father didn't answer. He jumped toward CeCe, picked her up with one arm, and covered her mouth with his hand. He carried her into the next room, and CeCe squirmed and twisted, trying to get away. He slammed the door behind them.

"Shut up, shut up," the man said. He banged her face down on the floor so hard it hurt her nose and mouth and she tasted blood. A hard piece of broken tooth scraped her tongue. The man pulled her arms behind her and knotted them with something, then did the same with her legs. He shoved dirty socks into her mouth and tied a belt around her face. The socks tasted and smelled like dead things that washed up on the beach. Her chest began to heave, and she knew she was going to throw up.

"Knock that off. You want to choke on your own puke and die?" he asked. "Just breathe through your nose. I don't want to come in here and find you all blue and choked to death. Breathe like I tell you and you'll be okay."

"I want my mommy!" she cried into the dirty socks, but her words were muffled. She wanted her mommy, she wanted her, never mind that she had seen her in the snowbank with the red ribbons and the pink snow and the dark black hole. That had been a bad dream, and she wanted her now. She needed Star; if only she had Star, she would feel better. Star would help her think.

The man opened a wooden chest, tore out a bunch of blankets and sheets, and lowered CeCe inside. She was screaming, but no sounds could get through the socks. He closed the lid on the chest, and it was pitch dark. He left her there, and she heard the room's door open and close behind him.

After a few seconds, her eyes got used to the dark, and she saw light coming through slivers in the chest's wooden slats. She tried to be perfectly still because the cracks also let sound drift in from the other room. She could just barely hear voices talking, and she wanted to know what they were saying.

"Hello, Zane," one voice said. "How are you doing? That was a pretty rough scene out there on the water."

"Damn right, Commander," the man—Zane—said. "Can't thank you and your guys enough for the rescue. Fucking bummed you couldn't save my boat at the same time, but you can't win everything."

"Thanks for saving my dad," Ronnie said.

"Where were you during the blizzard, Ronnie?" another man asked. "While your dad was out there on his boat?"

"Who the fuck are you?" Zane asked.

"This is Conor Reid," the commander said. "He is investigating a murder and kidnapping in Watch Hill."

"Shit, we were just watching that on the news," Zane said. "What a terrible thing."

"It is," the commander said.

"You a cop?" Zane asked. "Another Reid? You two related?"

"I'm a detective with the Connecticut State Police," Conor Reid said.

"Last time I noticed, this isn't Connecticut," Zane said. "So why are you asking us questions?"

"Why are you being defensive?" the commander asked.

"I'm not," Zane said. "Go ahead, ask whatever you want."

"Ronnie, where were you during the blizzard?" Conor Reid asked again.

CeCe so badly wanted to tell Conor Reid exactly where Ronnie had been during the blizzard, but no matter how loud she yelled, no one could hear her. Even though she was tied up, she could kick her legs, so she started to do that, her feet banging against the side of the chest, but they didn't make a lot of sound because there were still blankets lining the wood.

"What's that noise?" the commander asked.

"My furnace," Zane said. "It's on the blink. Been banging night and day since this cold snap began. Why do you want to know where Ronnie was?"

"Because a key chain was found near the murder scene, and from Commander Reid's description, the fob looks a lot like a Garson lobster buoy," Conor Reid said.

"Well, it couldn't be ours, we weren't in Watch Hill, were we, Ronnie?" Zane asked.

"Nope," Ronnie said.

"You sure, Ronnie?" Conor Reid said. "Because how could your father know where you were, since he was out there in the ocean on a sinking boat? Maybe you went to Watch Hill and dropped your key?"

"I didn't drop any key," Ronnie said.

"But you did go to Watch Hill?" Conor Reid asked.

"He was right here the whole time," Zane said. "Tell him, Ronnie."

"I was right here the whole time."

"Weird that it's so cold in here," the commander said. "Even with your furnace not working great, you'd think you could keep the stove going, Ronnie."

"All that firewood stacked outside," Conor Reid said.

"Yeah, seems with all those nice seasoned logs, you could have kept this house toasty warm. But it feels chilly. Like it was cold for a while and hasn't been able to really warm up," the commander said.

"Furnace is messed up," Zane said. "I told you."

"But, Ronnie, didn't you keep that fire going? While your dad was on the boat, getting rescued? Or were you out of the house?" the commander asked.

CeCe kicked the chest harder and harder.

"Is the furnace in that room over there?" Conor Reid asked. "Because that's where the noise is coming from. Mind if I take a look?"

"I do mind," Zane said. "Who the hell are you to walk in here and act like you own the place? I want you to leave now."

"Mr. Garson, a little girl is missing," Conor Reid said. "Cecelia Lafond. Her mother was murdered, and a foam key fob marked like your lobster buoys, with your initial, was found near the scene. I should think you'd want to be helpful."

At the sound of her name, CeCe kicked even harder. She heard words—*her mother was murdered*—but they were just words, they were just words, they were just words.

"That has nothing to do with us," Zane said. "Right, Ronnie?"

"Right, Dad."

"So I want you to leave now," Zane said. "Okay?"

"Okay," the commander said.

CeCe wanted to kick some more so that the commander and Conor Reid would push their way past Ronnie and Zane and rescue her, but suddenly she was paralyzed. Those words—*her mother was murdered*—had stabbed her in the heart, and she couldn't breathe. The socks hadn't choked her, and the closed-off chest hadn't stopped her from breathing, but those words had.

Murdered meant dead. She knew that because her father was sometimes in movies where he was a murderer, or where he was an officer looking for one, and once he was killed, and her parents had explained to her that even though murder sometimes happened in real life, when her father acted, it was only make-believe. The picture of her mother under the snow with the black hole in her head came back into CeCe's mind, and she felt her own life leave her body. If her mother was dead, she would be dead, too.

So when the commander and Conor Reid left the house and said they would be back with cops and a warrant, and when Ronnie and Zane in the other room said these things, she heard them, but she didn't feel them, and they slipped through her mind as if they were water draining into the ground.

"You fucking idiot," Zane said. "Don't tell me you left the key there."

"Dad, I lost it. I don't know where."

"Well, they have it now. Great. Great. You moron."

"Dad, I'm sorry! What can I do—"

"Look out the window—are they still there?" Zane asked.

"They're driving away."

"Okay," Zane said. "Can you find your way to Uncle Grub's?"

"I think so."

"I'm going to put the girl in the car, and you get her there. We need a few more hours to make this whole thing work. We'll let Grub take care of this last detail—thanks to you. Goddamn the weather. We'd be in the clear by now otherwise."

"Okay, Dad."

"I am trying really hard not to knock your head off. The only reason they came here is that you dropped the goddamn key. She's a loose end, and you didn't take care of it. If we wind up in prison, it's on you."

"Dad! We won't. I am really sorry—"

"Yeah, whatever. And her bouncing around in that chest made it worse. Drive slow and safe, and when you get to Grub's, he'll know what to do."

There was a long silence.

"No, Dad. She's nice. She's okay, Dad. Maybe I shouldn't go to Uncle Grub's house. Let's just keep her here."

"Shut up, moron. You brought this on us. Now the Reids are suspicious, and you've got to get her out of here. Whatever you do, don't get pulled over."

"I don't even have a license," Ronnie said in a low voice.

"Yeah, well, you won't go to prison for that. There's plenty else they can get you for. You're the one. It's on you. They only care about the one who done it. My big boy, my brave boy. I could have been so proud, but you dropped the fucking key. Put on your boots and get going," Zane said.

"Okay, Dad. I did a good job, though, right? Except for dropping the key?"

"Who cares? You just undid anything good."

CeCe heard but not really. Sometimes voices go into the ears but not into the brain. She was in the chest, staring into the enclosed darkness of the small box, thinking of her mother and feeling the word *murder*.

Footsteps got closer. The lid opened, and Ronnie helped her to her feet. He didn't loosen the ties, though. He didn't take the socks out of her mouth. His father put a blanket around her and picked her up, then carried her outside into the freezing cold. Ronnie was right beside them, and he opened the back door of the car.

"Whoa!" Zane said. "They're coming back. Get back in the house."

He carried CeCe into the same room where she'd been before. She still had the gag on, and she'd started throwing up; there was no way to stop it. Zane tugged the gag off and shoved her into a small bathroom.

"Do it in the toilet," he said, sounding as if he hated her. She threw up, even though she had nothing much in her stomach, and the taste made her even sicker. Tears poured from her eyes. She wanted her mommy there, to hold her hair back from her face, to pat her back and tell her she was going to be okay.

Outside the bathroom door, she heard Ronnie and Zane talking.

"Forget the car," Zane said. "They're parked out there, by the shed, watching. I'll distract them. You're gonna have to go out the back way and get to Uncle Grub's fleet trucks. Take the black Ford 250. The key's in the left front wheel well. Got that?"

"I got it, Dad."

"And keep her quiet. Don't forget, they've got a goddamn Amber Alert on her. Tell her . . . never mind, I'll tell her myself."

CeCe's stomach clenched because she heard his footsteps, and then Zane opened the door and stared down at her. He handed her a towel.

"Wipe your face," he said.

She did.

"I think you're probably a fine kid," he said with a fake smile on his face. "And I bet you're smart, and I bet you know how to follow directions. We gotta have some rules, to get us all through to the other side. Okay?"

"What other side?" CeCe asked.

"Don't talk back," he said in a snarling way, no more fake smile. "The rules are: No making noise. Like, no yelling or screaming. No running away. Because if you do, I'm gonna have to take action that no one's gonna like. Not you, not me. I saw the news, okay? I know you still got a father and an aunt. I'll have to kill them if you break the rules. You probably don't want that to happen, right? It's up to you."

She squeezed her eyes tight. She'd do anything to make sure he didn't hurt her papa or Aunt Hadley.

"I'm gonna trust you to follow the rules," he said. "Ronnie's your guard; he'll make sure you obey, and then he'll take you somewhere nice. You'll like it. And your father and aunt will be just fine. Now, I'm going into the other room. You behave now."

He left and slammed the door to the outer room.

"You okay?" Ronnie asked when she came out of the bathroom.

She didn't answer.

"We'll go to my uncle's house," Ronnie said. "Just do what my dad said, make it easy on all of us. My uncle's house is a whole lot more comfortable than this place; you'll be warm. Just don't do anything stupid, you'll be fine. You'll be going home soon. Okay?"

CeCe couldn't have answered even if she wanted to. Her broken front tooth had cut her lower lip, and it hurt, and she could taste the blood; she was afraid that if she said anything, or even breathed too deeply, she would throw up again. She clenched her fists and pretended she was holding Star. Star helped her think. If she thought hard enough, she could find a way to escape.

She could warn her father and Aunt Hadley. And she could stop being Amber.

22

When Hadley got back to the Ocean House after seeing Johnny and Donna in the studio, she went straight to sleep. The next morning, when she checked her phone, she found that she had several voice mails. Friends who had heard about Maddie had called, texted, and emailed. One message was from a lawyer named Jeanne Gladding. And there was another from Genevieve Dickinson.

"It can't be true," Genevieve's voice mail said. "Not Maddie. Hadley, I am devastated for you. I know she and I had our issues, but that's in the past. She and I made up. We were friends again, and now I've lost her! We both have. The news says it happened in Watch Hill—Maddie's favorite hotel is there, and I am guessing that's where you're staying. The roads are pretty clear right now, so I am going to drive down. I'll see you soon."

Genevieve and Maddie were friends again? Hadley listened to the message a second time. Genevieve sounded as if she were crying. Hadley knew that many friends would be hearing the news about Maddie and feeling shock, feeling sorrow. But Genevieve? The pure hatred that had poured out of her during the lawsuit had been extreme. How would Genevieve know that the Ocean House was Maddie's favorite hotel?

Surely Maddie would have told Hadley if there had been any sort of rapprochement. Hadley had been her sister's biggest support during the pendency of the suit. Genevieve had hired a Boston lawyer with a reputation for being a "paperhanger" because of all the papers he served. He had flooded her with subpoenas for documents, notebooks, drawings, and correspondence going all the way back to college. He had hired a forensic accountant to examine bank records, statements from her agent, and sales figures from her galleries.

Hadley had accompanied Maddie to several depositions. Each time, she had sat in the lawyers' waiting rooms while Maddie was inside at a conference table being grilled by Genevieve's attorney.

"I feel as if she's after my soul," Maddie had said to Hadley. "Not just money and credit for my ideas and paintings, but my actual being. The deepest part of me."

"Don't let it get to you," Hadley had said. "That's what she wants, to wear you down."

"She's there at every deposition, staring at me across the table," Maddie had said. "I look at her and try to remember when we were friends. Those days on the schooner, studying whales . . . it was so wonderful."

"We see those days as beautiful and inspiring," Hadley had said. "She sees them as the beginning of your success and a mirror of her failure—she measures them differently than we do."

"She's talented, Hadley," Maddie had said. "She can do whatever she wants. Just why can't she leave me alone?"

"Because she's obsessed with you. She always has been, Maddie. It's easier for her to go after you than to dig deep and find her own material," Hadley had said.

Hadley had a secret. She didn't want Maddie to know that she had a fishhook in her own heart, one that had lodged there not long after her sister's career began to take off. She would never tell Maddie that she could relate to Genevieve's envy. As much as Hadley adored her sister and cheered her on, part of her wondered why she couldn't have been the one to create that iconic image of the whale and the swan.

When Hadley was up on a ladder in a port city like New Bedford, shivering in the March chill or sweating in the July heat, doing the equivalent of paint-by-numbers brigantines and sea captains, or in the rotunda of the Drake Aquarium, working off-hours when patrons were home sleeping and she and Johnny could have the place to themselves, to cover a wall with frolicking beluga whales and smiling white-sided dolphins, diving terns and impish harbor seals . . . well, she would find herself thinking of Maddie in her north-facing studio at the edge of Topanga Canyon, overlooking the Pacific Ocean, and she would feel a pang.

Hadley hid those feelings from her sister. She was so proud of her, overjoyed at her accomplishments and the rewards they brought. And Maddie was always so generous. She bought Hadley soft leather boots from Prada, tiny watercolor sets from Sennelier in Paris, a delicate gold chain with their initials entwined on a disk—the back engraved with the words "We'll have many friends in life, but only one sister." Maddie had given her the very first charm depicting the whale and the swan, struck by a Florentine goldsmith. And more than once, Maddie had paid Hadley's mortgage on her condo in Providence.

Maddie had felt so attacked by the lawsuit. Genevieve had brought suit in the Cookes' home state because that was where Maddie had been living when the image had become famous and Maddie had begun making her fortune.

Each time there was a deposition or hearing, Maddie would fly east, and Hadley would pick her up at the airport. Hadley had to juggle her work deadlines, but being with Maddie, being able to support her throughout the long ordeal, had been what mattered to her.

Sometimes Maddie would leave CeCe at home with Bernard and the nanny, but when she brought her along to Connecticut, Hadley would babysit her while Maddie went to the law offices alone. CeCe had been two years old when the lawsuit started. At that time, the family was still spending much of the year in France.

"Aunt Adley," CeCe had said when she was about three, dropping her *H* the way her father did, with his heavy French accent. "What we doin' today?"

"I have to pick up some paint at the hardware store," Hadley had said. "Then a quick trip to the garage because there's a funny noise in the engine."

"Broken?" CeCe had asked, her brow furrowed.

"Maybe," Hadley had said. "But don't worry, sweetheart. They can fix it."

"I fix it for you," CeCe had said.

"You will?" Hadley had asked.

"Yes, I want to 'elp."

"Oh, I love you. Thank you."

"I love you, Auntie."

Hadley had gone about her errands with CeCe, and she felt that spending her days with her niece was the most wonderful thing in the world. CeCe was always great company, curious about everything Hadley was doing, full of fun and humor. Although Hadley had had boyfriends, there had been no one she'd considered having a child with. But being with CeCe had made her wish she had a daughter.

After a while, CeCe lost her semi-French accent, and Hadley missed it. She loved every stage of CeCe's development. She almost wished that the lawsuit would go on for years longer, because as long as it lasted, CeCe would be making frequent trips to the Northeast with Maddie.

When the judge eventually ruled in Maddie's favor, the flights east became less frequent. Maddie, Bernard, and CeCe would occasionally visit for a weekend, a holiday, or a vacation in Newport or on Martha's Vineyard. Occasionally they would stay in Black Hall. But those times when Hadley would have CeCe to herself were different. Babysitting was only for a dinner or a tennis match, not for the long days when Maddie had been tied up in legal hell.

Hadley knew that many women had babies without partners, and she often dreamed of holding a baby, of raising a child. She knew those dreams were signs from the interior that she longed to be a mother. But the problem was, she loved CeCe. How could any love match what she had for her niece? She had even talked about it with Maddie, because her sister was always worried about her, sad that she was so alone.

"Being an aunt is enough for me," Hadley had said.

"It's not the same," Maddie had said.

"Maybe not, but I can't imagine loving anyone as much as I do CeCe."

"Well, and she loves you, too."

That much? Hadley had wondered. Did CeCe know that Hadley's world revolved around her and Maddie? That Hadley would do anything for them? Hadley laughed at herself, knowing how sad it was for a forty-year-old woman to be basing her life around her sister and niece, but she honestly didn't feel deprived. She just felt lucky to have the connection with them. Boyfriends came and went. She sometimes wondered if it could be love, but so far nothing had felt right.

"I just wish you lived closer," Hadley would say to Maddie.

"So do I," Maddie would say.

And then, once Maddie had decided to leave Bernard, that wish came closer to being a reality.

"I'm moving back to New England," Maddie had said after filing for divorce. "I've found an amazing place—a suite in the Ocean House just became available. They almost never do. It's absolutely gorgeous, and I'm going to jump on it. Hadley, it's close to you and far away from him. I can't take it anymore. He doesn't trust me. He is constantly telling me how much he loves me, but you know what? He acts like he owns me. He wants to keep me and CeCe to himself."

"But I know he does love you," Hadley had said. "Isn't there a way for you to let him know you feel constrained?"

"Controlled is more like it."

"Well, however you put it. How can he bear to lose you, Maddie? And CeCe?"

"He won't lose his daughter—I won't keep her from him. But I can't live with him anymore. He is jealous of everyone, even you."

"That's crazy."

"Is it?" Maddie had asked. "Sometimes I think you are a little like him."

"What?" Hadley had asked, stunned.

"Obsessed."

"In what way?"

"With CeCe," Maddie had said. "You're a wonderful aunt, but every so often I think you wish you were her mother."

"Maddie, that is so nuts. I can't believe you would even say it."

"We can tell each other everything, can't we?" Maddie had asked.

"Yes, except that you think I'm a psycho aunt!"

Maddie had laughed, and Hadley had, too, but her heart wasn't in it. Maddie had just said something that cut her to the quick, partly because there was truth in it.

Now those words of Maddie's echoed in her mind: *We can tell each other everything, can't we?* Hadley listened to Genevieve's message again. And again, she wondered if it was possible that Genevieve and Maddie really had found a way back to being friends. And if so, if Maddie could tell Hadley everything, why hadn't she told her that?

Hadley stared at her phone, trying to decide whether to call Genevieve back or not. In the end, she dialed the number, but Genevieve didn't answer. Hadley got her voice mail, and she didn't leave a message.

23

Conor and Tom sat in Tom's truck, heat going, eyes on Zane Garson's house. The morning sun was up, veiled with thin clouds. It was still so cold that none of the snow or ice was melting. Conor had called Joe Harrigan, wanting to alert him about the key's connection to the Garsons, but Joe had been too busy to talk for long. He was meeting with a special agent of the FBI, and later he would head to the office of the medical examiner to attend Maddie's autopsy, something homicide detectives regularly did.

"Do you feel left out?" Tom asked.

"Yeah. I can't help it," Conor said. "It's weird to be on the outside. To be even more invested right off the bat than in most murders, considering Kate and I were right there when Hadley found Maddie's body."

"I mean, you're still involved," Tom said.

"Of course. I can't let it go. This might sound morbid, but I mind not being at the autopsy."

"How would that help?" Tom asked.

"It would give me a better understanding of the way Maddie died."

"Well, gunshot wound, right?" Tom asked.

"Yes, but being there when the coroner does his exam would show me the bullet's trajectory. The wound itself, the damage done. It would help me figure out where the shooter stood, how tall he was in relation to Maddie. Whether there were defensive wounds. Did she try to fight him off?"

"You say 'he,'" Tom said.

"He or she," Conor said. "We don't know yet."

"What else?" Tom asked. The whole time the brothers were talking, they faced forward, toward the Garson house, not looking at each other.

"How close was the shooter? If it was a planned meeting, which it seems to have been, Maddie must have known the person. Was there contact between them? Any injury other than the bullet wound?"

"You saw the bullet wound, right?"

"Yes. In the center of her forehead. Her face was intact . . . which means she was shot from the front. She saw her killer, looked right at him. But the autopsy will reveal more."

"That's one part of the investigation I wouldn't mind skipping," Tom said.

Conor thought of other cases he had worked. How, early in his career, he had hated going to the autopsy suite. But how, over time, he had come to value it, even need it. It was a way of accompanying the victim through this stage of death, of the body being cut open, taken apart, organs removed. He did it for the families, too. No one dreams of such a thing happening to them, or to someone they love. An autopsy is an invasion, an indignity beyond the murder itself.

"If you were Harrigan, would you be trying to get a warrant to search Garson's house?" Tom asked.

"I'd want to, but probable cause is thin. This is mostly a hunch— thanks to you," Conor said. "There is absolutely no real evidence that the flotation key chain belongs to him."

"Except it does," Tom said.

"The *G*?"

"Yes, and the lobster buoys. Check them out," Tom said, pointing toward a shack on the wharf. Lobster traps were stacked high beside it.

Blue bait barrels lined the dock. Gulls perched on the shack's roof, facing into the wind. In spite of the sun, the frigid air kept the snowdrifts from melting. Protruding from a drift were several foam buoys that must have been mounded underneath.

They were red-and-white striped, large versions of the key fob.

"You think they're marked with a *G*?" Conor asked.

"Could be," Tom said. "They might also be imprinted with the number of Garson's lobstering license."

"Let's take a look," Conor said.

The Reid brothers got out of the truck and walked through ice-crusted snow to the dock. Conor glanced at Zane's house, where smoke rose from the chimney, and wondered if father and son were watching.

"Think we're making them nervous?" Tom asked.

"If they're guilty," Conor said.

"I would have said Zane might be, except for the fact he was busy trying not to die in a sinking boat," Tom said. "But I can't see the kid being involved. What is he, fourteen, fifteen?"

"Sounds about right," Conor said. "Are you sure the timeline works out that way for Zane? Could he have killed Maddie, *then* gone out on his boat?"

"Well, he would have left from this dock," Tom said. "It's not far to where he began taking on water, but the conditions would have slowed him considerably. So I don't see how he could have done it. Do you have a time of death?"

"Hard to be precise," Conor said. "Because the air temperature and snow would have slowed decomposition. From talking to Isabel, the desk clerk at the hotel, it seems Maddie went out somewhere between one and two hours before Hadley found her."

"We'd have to know that before saying Zane could or couldn't have done it," Tom said.

"How would Zane even know Maddie?" Conor asked. "She's not local, so she probably wouldn't have known him from before. Something tells me he's not a regular at the Ocean House."

"You never know," Tom said. "We both see a lot of odd couples in our work."

Conor knew that was true. Friendship, attraction, employment, and mutual need brought unlikely people together.

"Could she have hired him to do something for her?" Tom asked.

"Like what? She's staying at the nicest hotel I've ever been in. Seems to me they tend to their guests' every need."

"I don't know," Tom said. "Just thinking out loud."

They stood at the ramshackle building, looking at the pile of lobster buoys. They were mostly covered by the snowbank, but Conor could see the stripes and numbers on a few of them.

"Are we standing on the Garsons' property?" Conor asked. "Because I really want to turn one of those buoys and see if there's an initial on it. Just to prod him, if nothing else. He's definitely watching us."

"The dock belongs to the town, but obviously Garson owns the equipment," Tom said.

"Technically, this is trespassing, but I'm going to relax the standards," Conor said, reaching into the snowbank and pulling out a buoy. It was marked with the letter *G*, just like the key fob.

"Well, that answers that," Tom said.

Conor glanced over at the house. No sign of Zane storming out the door. "I'm a little surprised there's no reaction. He seems like the excitable type."

"You're right," Tom said. "He doesn't take kindly to trespassing, which he considers disrespect. Lobstermen are notoriously territorial. Once the Santos clan dropped some pots in the Garsons' area, and he cut their lines. Seventy-five traps lost on the bottom of the ocean—still catching lobsters, with no way to haul them."

"What did Santos do?" Conor asked.

"Shot up one of the Garsons' trucks."

"That's serious."

"And Zane returned the favor, with a twelve-gauge."

"Lobster wars?" Conor asked.

"Macho wars. They see each other at the Magellan Club and don't speak. Grub Garson's girlfriend's family owns a lobster restaurant down the road from the Coast Guard station. One night the power went out, and the generator didn't switch on, and a hundred pounds of claw and tail meat spoiled. Turns out, the generator had been disabled."

"Santos did it?" Conor said.

"That was the rumor," Tom said. "No proof."

And then the house door opened, and Zane came walking toward them. Conor would have expected him to be scowling with anger at the sight of him and Tom, but instead he had a big smile on his face.

"Guys," he said, "you wanted to look at my buoys, all you had to do was ask."

Conor and Tom watched him approach.

"You like them?" Zane asked. "My father and his father before him used the same red-and-white stripes. In fact, c'mon inside. I'll show you some old Garson buoys. I got 'em hanging on the wall, kind of like a museum of Garson family history." He pulled some keys from his pocket and moved toward the door to the shack.

"Hey, do you mind showing me that?" Conor asked, gesturing at the key ring.

"Hey, anything for the commander and his brother," Zane said, handing Conor his key ring: brass, in the shape of an anchor.

"Don't you use a floating one?" Conor asked. "What if you drop it overboard?"

"Then it would be bye-bye keys," Zane said.

"Because I keep thinking about that foam fob that was found in Watch Hill. It sure looked a lot like these lobster buoys of yours," Conor said.

"Any tourist can buy that shit at the souvenir shops around here. Probably came from one of them. Now, come inside and take a look," Zane said, kicking snow away from the door and sticking the key in the lock.

"Take a look at what?" Tom asked.

"In here," Zane said. "I'll show you the origins. The family secrets to our success. The reason why we rule the fleet. C'mon, Commander. This is my office, ha ha. Did you know one of my great-uncles was in the Coast Guard? Stationed around the corner, right at the lighthouse, like you. I've got his picture. And his sidearm! It's the coolest, a family heirloom."

Conor knew Zane seemed eager to show them some family arti-facts, but that didn't mean he wasn't hiding something. He might have wanted to distract the Reids from whatever his son was doing at the house. If this building was Zane's sanctuary, there would be clues to what motivated him. And that motivation could be connected to Maddie and CeCe.

Tom glanced at Conor, and they followed Zane inside. But Conor stayed by the door, where he could keep an eye on the door to the house and the vehicles parked out front.

24

The suite where Maddie and CeCe had been living was so full of their presence that it felt as if they could come back at any minute. The Ocean House staff had put up a Christmas tree for them, decorated it with sand dollars, scallop shells, a starfish on top, and strands of white lights. Wrapped packages, including the ones Hadley had brought, were strewn beneath the branches. Hadley sat on the love seat by the fire, looking at tiny lights twinkling on the tree, hearing waves crash on the beach, feeling numb.

Someone knocked at the door, and she ran to answer it. Kate stood in the hall, dressed for the outdoors.

"What is it?" Kate asked at the sight of Hadley's face.

"I just thought . . . ," Hadley said, with the sense she was coming out of a dream.

"I think I know," Kate said. She put her arm around Hadley, and they walked into the living room.

"No, it's too crazy," Hadley said.

"You thought it was your sister at the door," Kate said.

Hadley felt startled to hear Kate put it into words.

"I used to think that about Beth," Kate said. "My sister and I were so close, and after she died, I wanted so badly to believe she was coming back that I would hear and see her everywhere. If the doorbell rang, for one incredibly wonderful moment, I would think it was her."

"That's it," Hadley said. "I thought it was Maddie."

"You wanted it to be. When someone rings the bell, or when the phone buzzes, I still want it to be Beth."

"Could you tell me about her?" Hadley asked.

"Of course," Kate said. "Nothing makes me happier than talking about Beth." She paused for a few seconds. "She was my younger sister. We had a secret language—one word, one look, was all it took. We could practically read each other's thoughts. We worked together, running our family's gallery, together all the time."

"Gallery?" Hadley asked.

"Yes, an art gallery—it used to be our grandmother's, and we took it over after she died. That's how I know Maddie's work. And why I want to know more about yours."

"Maddie was so sought after by galleries," Hadley said. "Not me. I paint on walls. It's more commercial." Hadley felt uncomfortable talking about what she did with someone who was obviously so sophisticated about the world of art that she'd always wanted to enter yet felt it was closed to her.

"Think of Banksy. A great artist who hits and runs, mostly on outdoor sites. And Keith Haring—he started in the graffiti subculture."

"They were original," Hadley said. "Brave, defying convention. I am literally the definition of convention. Johnny and I work for municipalities."

"I've seen what you do, in person," Kate said. "And I've looked you up online. Lots of articles out there, Hadley. Your murals are pure art." She smiled. "I see subterfuge in them."

Was it possible she had detected the little clues Hadley left, buried in every mural she did? No one had ever mentioned them to her before. She always incorporated hidden objects, details, or phrases that reflected her beliefs. In one completely sexist and macho scene of a male crew harpooning a whale, she had painted the captain as a woman—not dress-wise but essence-wise—and the words "Watch me save the whales" were woven into the hem of her coat. Until Kate, not one person had ever mentioned those details to her—not even Johnny had noticed.

"Would you ever think of producing work for a gallery show?" Kate asked.

The question made Hadley feel both flattered and uncomfortable. "Yes, of course," she said.

"We'll have to explore that," Kate said.

"Tell me more about Beth," she said. "How you listen for her in every knock at the door. And how she reminds you of Maddie."

"That's easy," Kate said. "Your love for Maddie reminds me of mine for Beth. Both our sisters were murdered."

"Thoughts flood into my mind, and I push them away, over and over. My sister is dead," Hadley said. "I've watched true-crime shows, read the news, know that murder happens to other families. I've thought of how terrible it is, and I've felt their pain—or so I thought."

"But never, really, till now," Kate said.

Hadley nodded. "I would watch the shows and wonder how someone could end another's life. Who would do that? What could possibly drive them to do it? But I never imagined it could happen to Maddie."

"And to you," Kate said. "Because the killer took your life, too. You're still living and breathing, but . . ."

"I'm not the same," Hadley said.

"I know," Kate said.

"I never will be," Hadley said, a question in those words.

"You can't go back to how it was before Maddie's murder, but it will change," Kate said. "It won't always be like this."

"Yet you say you still listen for her to call or knock."

Kate didn't reply to that, and her silence said it all.

"You have a niece, too?" Hadley said.

"Yes, Beth's daughter."

"Also an only child?"

"Yes," Kate said. "Samantha—Sam. Very loved and doted on. But she was a teenager when Beth died. They were fighting a lot."

"That's normal for that age," Hadley said. "Maddie and I were pretty much in a constant state of rebellion till we got to college. Our parents were strict. How is Sam doing now?"

"Well, it was terrible for a long time afterward. Sam felt so guilty for all the fighting, for how distant she'd been—and so critical of Beth. So there was a long spell where she tried to bury the feelings—drinking a lot, pot, other things. Then a crash into bad depression."

"Navigating grief, too," Hadley said.

"Definitely."

"Did she get through it?" Hadley asked.

"She did. It was kind of a miracle. We were going to send her to rehab, or a hospital for depression, but she came out of it on her own."

Hadley was happy for Kate and her niece, that after all Sam had been through, she was somehow okay. But she could only think about CeCe.

"What's going to happen to CeCe?" Hadley asked. "If she's even still alive, how will she live with what she must have seen?"

"She just will," Kate said. "Because you'll be there with her."

25

CeCe sat very still in the house with Ronnie. Zane had told her the rules, and she had thought Ronnie was going to take her somewhere else, but they hadn't left yet. She realized that something was happening outside the house, but she didn't know what. She could tell Ronnie was nervous. He crouched by the window, peeking over the sill. He wasn't paying any attention to the stove. It needed wood, so the fire was going out, and the house was getting cold again.

She heard voices outside, men talking. Were they good people or bad? Was it the commander and his brother? They were good. She had been able to tell by the things they said, but what if it wasn't them out there? If she screamed, would they come to help her, or would they kill her father and Aunt Hadley? Ronnie kept turning to her, putting his finger to his lips: *Be quiet!*

Should she do what he wanted? What if she yelled and tried to run outside and the men were even worse than he was? She was thinking as hard as she could, glancing around for a way to escape so none of them would see her—not Ronnie, not any of the other men—but she didn't see any doors, and the only window was covered by a thick curtain. Who knew what lay outside?

Her stomach was better, but her nose and cheeks hurt from where she had fallen, and she kept touching her broken front tooth with her tongue. The tooth edge was sharp. It kept scraping her tongue and making it bleed. She rubbed her tooth with her finger, and when she saw the blood on it, she wiped it on her knee. Then she did something naughty, and she didn't really know why she did it, but when Ronnie wasn't looking, she dabbed her finger in more blood and wrote on the wall.

CeCe liked to draw. Her mommy was an artist. Sometimes she and CeCe sat in her studio, painting and drawing pictures. CeCe had her own watercolors and charcoal pencils. She had a tall stool at her mother's worktable, and the long-necked lamp cast cozy light on her paper. She would tell stories in what she drew and get lost in the picture. Sitting in the cold room while Ronnie stared out the window, she wished she could disappear into the marks she was making on the wall.

After a few minutes, Ronnie turned toward her. His eyes were wide, as if he were scared. He opened the drawer and took the gun out. He grabbed a tall flashlight from a shelf in the kitchen.

"We've got to get out of here," he said, walking over to her.

She jumped up and kept her back to the wall so he wouldn't see her name.

There was a dirty rug next to the rumpled sofa. He lifted a corner, and beneath it was a door in the floor. He pulled it open. She looked down and saw rough wooden stairs leading into a dark basement.

"Come on," he said, pointing.

"I don't want to go in there," she said.

"You have to," he said. He showed her the gun. Then he pointed it at her. It made her shiver so hard she felt she might topple over. But she had to stay standing because if she fell, he would see that she had written on the wall.

"I don't want to shoot you," he said. "But my dad and I have too much to lose, so I will if you make me. Get going—down the stairs."

She moved away from the wall, toward the opening in the floor.

"There's no light," she said.

"I have this," he said, waving the flashlight. He turned it on, swept the beam into the basement.

The stairs were steep. CeCe stepped slowly from one tread down to the next. The flashlight barely illuminated anything because Ronnie was holding it behind her, so all she could see was her own shadow. She felt silky strands on her face and knew she was walking through spiderwebs. She thought of *Charlotte's Web* so she wouldn't be even more scared.

The basement smelled like wet dirt, like the garden in Malibu after the sprinklers were on. She told herself she was walking on the stone path from her house to the deck, past white roses and purple flowers. She could picture the wall covered with dark-pink blossoms and the orchard trees full of lemons.

"Wait here," Ronnie said, startling her out of her fantasy.

She saw another set of stairs leading up. He climbed them and slid back a bolt, inching open a door to the sky. It was metal, and the hinges creaked. She watched him look around, and then he beckoned her to follow him. They stepped out of a hatchway that must have been on the back side of the cold house.

It was on the opposite side of the dock. Ice-crusted snowdrifts were very high here, but a path had been trampled, so obviously someone had walked here after the storm. Ronnie pushed her ahead of him. The mounds of snow were over her head, and the path was so narrow that her shoulders scraped the sides, making little clouds of snow twinkle down onto the ground.

At the end of the path, they stepped out into a parking lot. It had been plowed, CeCe knew, because she could see the pavement. Slick with ice, it had been sanded, so she didn't slip. She glanced at Ronnie. He was still holding the gun, but instead of watching her, he was looking over his shoulder, back toward his house. She thought of the voices that might have been help or might have been danger. By the look in his eyes, she knew he thought they were danger—to him.

That made her heart pound. Because if Ronnie was scared of those voices, she knew they were there to help her. She was sure they belonged to the commander and his brother. This was the moment she had been waiting for. She flexed and unflexed her fingers.

He had that gun. His father had told her to follow the rules or he would kill her father and Aunt Hadley. But CeCe trusted herself more than anything Ronnie and his father said. She knew what she had to do. They were walking toward a row of big trucks. Painted on the side of each truck door was the same lobster she'd seen on the sign and on Ronnie's jacket.

Ronnie reached into the crevice above the front tire on one of the trucks, and he pulled out a small metal box that contained a key.

"My dad was right—here it is," he said, flashing her a grin, as if finally something was going well for him. "Everything is going to be so good. We're getting out of this shithole, gonna buy a big house where everything works, and a big garage. We'll fix up the boats, and we'll have the best in the fleet. We can afford it now."

He unlocked the driver's-side door, held it open for her.

"Get in," he said.

She took a step back.

"I told you," he said. "Get in. Now."

"No," she said, staring him in the eyes.

"You heard my dad. You want to get your father and aunt killed? And you? He told you the rules. Follow them and you'll be fine."

CeCe didn't believe anything he said, so she blocked out his words. She thought of races on the beach, of how she and her friends tried to beat each other to the finish line, and she crouched so she'd get a good start, then took off like the fastest girl on earth.

She screamed as she ran, words screeching out of her chest, not even knowing what she was saying—they were gibberish, like sounds made by a wild animal. She ran onto the snow path, toward the horrible house, because that was where the voices had come from, the people who were there to help her.

She heard footsteps pounding behind her, so she screamed louder.

"CeCe!" Ronnie called. "Stop!"

Then she felt him bump her back. He pushed her into the snow-bank. She made a snowball and threw it at him. It hit him right in the face, and he looked so surprised that it gave her a few seconds to stand up, make another, and throw it at him. She moved so fast she lost her balance and fell backward, hitting her head on something hard buried under the snow.

Ronnie reached out his hand, then bent down to help her up.

"Come on, CeCe," he said. "You cut your head."

She gulped back tears, but then they all came pouring out.

"CeCe, I don't know what we're doing," Ronnie said. "But I'm not leaving you here with my dad. Let's go, I'll figure it out. My uncle can help us, okay?"

It wasn't okay at all. CeCe wanted her mother. She wanted Star. Ronnie picked her right up out of the snow. He had his arms around her, carrying her. She sobbed into his shoulder.

"Mommy," she wept. "Mommy."

26

Hadley felt nervous, waiting for Genevieve to arrive at the hotel, so when the suite's doorbell rang, she hesitated before answering. Kate, sitting on the sofa, noticed her reluctance and answered the door.

"Genevieve?" Hadley heard Kate ask.

"No," a woman's voice said. "I'm Jeanne Gladding, Maddie's attorney. Hadley, I am so sorry about your sister . . ."

"Double mistaken identity," Kate said, leading the lawyer into the living room. "I'm Kate Woodward. This is Hadley."

Hadley stood to shake the woman's hand. She looked about fifty, with shoulder-length brown hair and low-key makeup. She was dressed in black pants and a double-breasted black blazer over a starched white blouse. On her lapel was a pin, the enamel painted with Maddie's whale-and-swan motif. Her battered brown leather briefcase looked as if she might have had it since law school, and she set it on the coffee table when Hadley gestured for her to sit down.

"Hadley, I can't imagine what you must be feeling. Maddie adored you—we spoke about you often. I know how close you were," Jeanne said.

"We were," Hadley said.

"I wanted to come as soon as I heard. This might sound strange, but when someone dies, the family so often gathers together, and I feel like her family," Jeanne said, her voice breaking. "She was so much more than a client. I waited as long as I could, wanting to give you time for yourself, but then . . . I had to come."

"Thank you," Hadley said.

"I hope you don't mind."

"No, I don't."

"I considered her a dear, dear friend," Jeanne said. "And I think she felt the same about me."

Hadley felt drawn in by Jeanne's warmth and obvious grief, but also a little sorry for her. She knew Maddie had several lawyers that handled various issues in her life, but she had never heard her mention Jeanne's name before. She figured Jeanne was no different from many of Maddie's other fans. Her paintings drew people in, made them feel like she was speaking directly to them through the images. Essays had been written about Maddie's ethereal work, studies done on ways it affected viewers.

One psychiatrist had published an article in the *Hanover Journal of Neuroscience* about how her images had entered the collective unconscious. Strangers often thought they knew Maddie better than her family did—and felt closer to her than she did to her actual friends. Several patients with Cluster B diagnoses grew angry when Maddie didn't respond to their emails, phone calls, and letters. Some threatened suicide when she ignored them; others promised to hurt her or the ones she loved.

Several fans with disorders that manifested in auditory hallucinations believed that Maddie—or the subjects of her paintings, such as the whale—was speaking to them directly, giving them orders that ranged from self-harm to violence against others.

Hadley doubted that Jeanne's wanting to feel close to Maddie approached those levels, but still, she felt that the lawyer was feeling something that Maddie wouldn't have reciprocated.

The midday sun cast silver light on the beach and ocean. The temperature hovered around ten degrees, so Kate got up to turn on the gas fireplace. The flame burst on, instantly throwing heat. Kate stood in front of it, warming herself and gazing at Jeanne with a curious look on her face.

"Did you say your last name is Gladding?" Kate asked.

"Yes," Jeanne said.

"I'm familiar with a law firm in Hartford," Kate said, "with Gladding in the name. Is that yours?"

"It is. My father was a founding partner, and I've been there since I graduated from law school." Jeanne smiled. "I thought I recognized your name, too. Kate Woodward, from the gallery in Black Hall?"

"Yes, Woodward-Lathrop," Kate said.

Jeanne nodded. "Our firm has many clients who collect fine art, much of it acquired from your gallery. American Impressionists, in particular. Woodward-Lathrop is very well known, highly respected."

"I'm glad to hear that," Kate said.

"You've also, on occasion, done appraisals for us. For the estates of clients who have passed away. In one case, you discovered a forgery . . ."

"I remember," Kate said. "A supposed Henry Ward Ranger, moonlight on a pond in Black Hall."

"Valued close to a hundred thousand until you looked at it," Jeanne said.

"Life lesson," Kate said. "Don't buy fine art on eBay."

"Are you serious?" Hadley asked. "Someone bought a Ranger on eBay?"

"You'd be surprised," Kate said. "There are eBay listings full of names you'll find on museum walls. Ranger was one of the earliest American Impressionists. Foolish buyer. We look at eBay and several of the less ethical auction sites—they're full of fakes."

"Have you ever looked there for work by Maddie?" Hadley asked.

"I did last night," Kate said. "There are plenty of paintings and drawings being offered as her originals. At prices you'd expect. It's possible that some are genuine, but they would be the exceptions."

"The forged Ranger was a blow to the family," Jeanne said. "Not only to discover that a painting they had assumed was by him was a fake, but also to realize that their father wasn't as astute an art collector as he—and they—had thought. They had intended to donate it to the Mystic Museum of Art."

"That would hurt," Kate said.

"One of the daughters said she was glad her father had died before knowing the truth," Jeanne said. "That was quite heartbreaking to hear."

Hadley felt the lawyer's compassion for her clients. "What is your specialty at the firm?" she asked.

"Trusts and estates," Jeanne said. "And it literally is trust. I feel honored that people entrust me with their goals—not just after death but during life."

"In what way?" Hadley asked.

"Well, we counsel clients about privately held and family businesses. Safeguarding and managing assets is a big part of our work. In cases where there is litigation, we have an excellent department to take care of that aspect."

"Litigation?" Hadley asked, thinking of Maddie's court fight with Genevieve.

"Yes," Jeanne said. "It's very sad, but sometimes when someone dies, there is dissention within the family regarding distribution of assets. For example, when there is a pending divorce."

"Things can get ugly," Kate said. "I saw that when my sister died. Pete—her estranged husband—showed his true colors."

"Bernard will be difficult," Hadley said. "He was terrible to Maddie in the divorce. All I care about is protecting CeCe."

Jeanne was very still, giving away nothing about Maddie's wishes, and Hadley had no interest in knowing anyway.

"Is Bernard still in the hotel?" Jeanne asked. "I saw him on the news, giving a press conference."

"I think so," Hadley said. "But I haven't seen or heard from him all day. Have you, Kate?"

"No," Kate said. "Maybe he's being questioned again."

"Good," Jeanne said. "He's a nasty guy. I hope they get him."

"'Get him?' You think he killed Maddie?" Hadley asked.

Jeanne tilted her head. "I don't know, Hadley. But Maddie wanted nothing to do with him, and that drove him crazy."

"He needs a good lawyer," Kate said.

"Well, we do criminal defense work, although that's not what we're known for. However, it would be a conflict of interest for anyone at Cross, Gladding, and White to represent him. Because we are Maddie's attorneys."

Kate's phone buzzed, and she answered it. Hadley glanced at her watch. It was nearly five. "I thought Genevieve would be here by now," she said.

"Genevieve Dickinson?" Jeanne asked, sounding shocked. "You're in touch with her?"

"Yes, and I'm surprised, too," Hadley said. "But she called and left a message that she's on her way. She said she and Maddie made up. I had no idea. Did Maddie talk to you about her, about the lawsuit?"

"Of course," Jeanne said. "Obviously the suit was settled a long time ago. Maddie wanted peace, no more animosity. She had such a generous spirit, Hadley. She was able to see goodness and talent in Genevieve."

That did sound like Maddie, Hadley thought. "I'm sorry, but it's impossible for me to imagine Maddie being okay with Genevieve, after what she did. The lawsuit took up years of Maddie's life."

"If there's one thing my law practice teaches me," Jeanne said, "it's that people's attitudes change."

"Did Maddie mention when they last talked?" Hadley asked.

"I believe it was recently," Jeanne said. "They were talking about new work. Maddie said something about showing a painting to Genevieve. She told me that very day, her last day on earth."

"And then she was killed," Hadley said.

Jeanne nodded her head. "It's terrible, beyond belief. I mean, I do the work I do. I deal with death all the time. People always say, 'But I just saw her!' or 'I just talked to her!' As if that contact could have somehow protected their loved one, as if it made death impossible. I should know better, but here I am doing it, too. I just can't believe we've lost her—she was so alive that day, so full of hope and plans."

"I feel the same way," Hadley said.

"Hadley, I want to talk to you about next steps. It might seem insensitive of me to bring them up now, but these are important matters. Did you know that Maddie made you the executor of her estate?"

"No," Hadley said. "I had no idea."

"She did. It will be your responsibility to carry out the wishes she expressed in her will, to settle her financial affairs, to oversee Cecelia's care."

"I don't know anything about financial matters . . ."

"Maddie had sole custody of Cecelia. She named you as her testamentary guardian. In that capacity, if—when—CeCe is found, you will be in charge of seeing to her material needs, as well as making decisions about her education and health care."

If she is found, Hadley thought, hearing how Jeanne had corrected herself.

"Maddie chose you for these roles not only because she loved you so much but also because she knows you share her values. That was incredibly important to her, especially regarding Cecelia. But, Hadley . . . don't underestimate the time and effort all of this will take. If you feel the duties will be too demanding, or too emotionally challenging, you can decline."

"What would happen if I did?"

"She named a contingent executor and an alternate guardian."

"Who is that?" Hadley asked.

"Me, actually. It's common for clients to request that their attorneys serve as executors. Especially with estates as complex as Maddie's." Jeanne paused. "This is a lot for you to take in. Think about it. You and I can be in touch during the next few days, as much or as little as you want."

"Thank you," Hadley said.

"The one thing I believe should be done immediately, or as soon as possible, is an inventory of her storage unit. She kept her paintings there—older ones as well as works in progress. It's a specialized facility, designed specifically to store fine art. Those paintings represent a fortune—I'm sure you're aware of that."

"It's not something I think about," Hadley said.

"If you decide to continue as executor, as she wished—and as I hope you will do—you'll have to think about it. And, on that note, although you haven't asked for my advice, I would be very careful interacting with Genevieve Dickinson. We can discuss that more deeply, but you mentioned she may be on her way here."

"I appreciate your telling me that," Hadley said.

"You have the right to choose an attorney to help you deal with the legal matters connected to Maddie's will and trusts. I would be happy to continue on, but please do feel free to interview other lawyers and hire anyone you like," Jeanne said. "I have the combinations and key to the storage facility. I will meet you there when you're ready."

I'll never be ready, Hadley thought.

Kate had ended the call. Jeanne stood to leave. She put on her coat, shook hands with Hadley and Kate. Hadley walked her to the door, and they said goodbye. When she returned to the living room, she noticed an odd expression on Kate's face.

"What's wrong?" Hadley asked.

"Nothing," Kate said. "Just . . . it was interesting to meet her. There's a story about her firm. About the way they dealt with a certain art collector's estate."

Hadley knew she should ask what Kate had heard, but just then she was too overwhelmed. She gave Kate a hug, as if they'd been friends for a long time instead of just the two days since Maddie's murder and CeCe's disappearance. Then she walked into the bedroom to close her eyes and shut out the fact that her sister had put her in charge of just about everything that had mattered to Maddie in life.

27

When they finished the tour of Zane Garson's lobster shack, Tom and Zane walked out the door where Conor had been standing watch, keeping his eyes on the house and vehicles.

"Spot anything suspicious, Mr. Detective?" Zane asked, with what looked to Conor like a taunting grin.

"Nope," Conor said.

"I tell you what," Zane said. "If it will set your mind at ease, come on into my humble abode. It ain't much, but it's home sweet home. You can look around all you want. I'll put some coffee on. You can tell me all about the foam key thingie."

"We'll take you up on that," Conor said. "But we don't need any coffee."

"My mother always taught me it's not polite to decline hospitality," Zane said. "But suit yourself."

"Let's go in," Tom said.

When they approached the house, Zane initially blocked the way. Conor watched him open the front door a crack. He looked around. Seeming satisfied, he stood aside and allowed Conor and Tom to walk into the cold living room. The first thing Conor noticed was that the place seemed empty, and the banging had stopped. He detected a strong smell of vomit that hadn't been there twenty minutes earlier.

"Where's Ronnie?" he asked.

"Dunno," Zane said. "Must've gone out."

How? Conor wondered. He'd been watching the front door, hadn't seen anyone exit the house. "I didn't see him leave," he said.

"Maybe he's in the bedroom," Zane said. "Make yourself at home. Look around. I'm going to put on a pot of coffee."

Without having to speak about it, the Reid brothers split up. Tom stayed with Zane while Conor walked slowly through the cluttered room. He stepped over a pile of oily machine parts beside an oval maple dining table, marked with hazy white moisture rings and a black burn. The room was L shaped, with a small kitchen at one end and two doors at the other. They were hollow core, and one had a jagged hole, as if someone had punched a fist through it.

Conor opened it. Inside was a small bathroom. It had a rust-stained sink, a toilet, and a shower with a cracked glass door. The vomit smell was much stronger here. Conor saw streaks around the toilet's rim.

He stood there staring. Ronnie hadn't looked or acted sick when he'd seen him, and this was definitely fresh. He took his phone from his pocket and snapped a photo. The hair on the back of his neck stood up the way it always did when he knew he was on the right track. He made a note to tell Joe to get some crime-scene techs to sample it for DNA. If Zane came toward the bathroom, Conor would block him before he could clean the mess.

The second door, the undamaged one, was shut tight. Conor turned the knob, and although it stuck, he pushed it open. It was a bedroom with two unmade twin beds, a bureau, and a straight-backed chair. At the end of one of the beds was an old wooden sea chest.

There were piles of dirty clothes on the floor. Was there another bedroom somewhere that Conor hadn't seen yet, or did Zane and Ronnie share this one? Conor's heart was pounding as he focused on the chest. It was compact but big enough to hold a small child. He wanted but didn't want to see what was inside. He undid the iron latch, lifted the lid.

The chest was lined with sheets and blankets. He knelt beside it and held his hand inside without actually touching anything. Was it his imagination, or was there warmth rising from the oak planks, the kind of retained body heat that would mean someone had very recently been trapped there? He smelled sharp sweat, the kind he had encountered in many crime scenes over the years. It was the smell of fear.

His gaze traveled slowly and carefully over the chest's interior. He looked for anything that seemed out of place. A bit of green fuzz was caught in the edge of one splintered plank. He knew it could have come from a blanket or bedspread or flannel sheet, but none that he saw piled inside were green.

Until it was tested, it was evidence of nothing. There were some dark blotches on one of the blankets. They could be blood or stains from another liquid. Like the fuzz, they would have to be tested. But Conor had to wonder: Would Joe have probable cause to search this house, to take the chest to the lab and examine it for evidence that someone had been held captive inside?

Then Conor spotted a hair snagged on a splinter. It was blond, nothing like the dark hair of the two Garsons. It reminded him of the pictures he'd seen of CeCe, the ones that were now splashed on the front pages of newspapers, on billboards up and down I-95, on television stations across the country.

He glanced at the bedroom door. No sign of Zane coming to check on him; he heard him talking with Tom, his voice droning on as he told a story about fishing Georges Bank with his father when he was a boy, back when the water was so thick with cod you could use them as stepping stones, of how the Garson family had grown prosperous selling their catch at the Boston Fish Pier for top dollar.

Conor took a close-up photo of the blond hair. He stood up, continued his tour around the room. It was a total pigsty, with rumpled clothes everywhere, rubber boots glittering with fish scales, an overflowing wastebasket, and a single braided rug bunched up in the corner.

The pine floor was discolored, black in places, as if from water damage. The roof obviously leaked—there were two pans set in the middle of the room. Conor examined the floorboards. When he got to the section that would have been covered by the braided rug, he saw a rectangular outline and a brass pull set flush with the wood. It was a hatchway, and he knew then that this was how Ronnie had gotten out. Maybe he was hiding down below, or maybe he had escaped through an exit in the basement.

Conor had his finger through the brass ring, ready to open the hatch. He steeled himself, in case Ronnie was waiting for him. Perpetrators were more likely to attack when they were cornered. He took a deep breath, and just as he was about to lift the door, he caught sight of a word written on the bedroom wall. It looked as if it had been scrawled in red crayon.

He walked over to it, bent down because it was just about waist height. There were four letters. They were smudged, hard to read. It began to dawn on him that they had not been written in crayon after all. They had been drawn in blood.

As he stared at them, he texted Joe Harrigan. **Get here NOW**, he wrote, and gave the lobster dock's location. **Bring forensics.**

Why, what's up? Joe texted back.

Conor didn't bother explaining. He just took a photo of the word, but it wasn't a word at all—it was a name. He sent the picture to Joe:

CECE

Then he went out to find Zane.

28

Tom Reid had worked several cases with his brother, and he always enjoyed seeing him question suspects. This time it got a little physical.

"Where is she?" Conor asked, walking over to Zane.

Zane must have realized that he was caught, because he turned to run. Conor grabbed him by the back of his coat, and Zane turned and threw a punch. Conor flinched, and it missed him.

It took both Reid brothers to subdue Zane. Conor braced him, trying to hold him still.

"Where is she?" Conor asked again. "Tell me right now."

Zane didn't answer, other than trying to spit in Conor's face. Conor pushed him through the bedroom door.

"She wrote her name in blood," Conor said, pointing at the wall.

"Who?" Zane asked, trying to yank himself out of Conor's grip.

"Where is she?" Conor asked.

"I don't know what you're talking about."

"Where did he take her?" Conor asked.

"I'm calling the cops; you assaulted me!"

"They're on their way," Conor said. "Your son has CeCe. That's kidnapping. Tell me where they went. He's going away—that's a done deal already—but if you help me save her life, he might see the light of day. And you, too."

Zane stared at Conor with hatred.

"Listen, Zane," Tom said, "I've known you a long time. You've had a tough time these last few years. I'll attest to that."

"Right, Commander. As if you would."

"I want to help you make this right," Tom said. "Your son is just a kid. Just like that little girl. You've got the power right now. You can save her life, give him a chance, too. Do the right thing here."

"I had no idea she was here," Zane said. "Maybe Ronnie hid her himself. Or maybe she wasn't here at all. Maybe he wrote that as a prank." He gestured at CeCe's name. "You think I'd have let you come inside if I knew anything about my kid holding a girl in here? Give me a break."

"You didn't know she'd outsmart your son," Conor said evenly. "You thought you two had it under control."

"I don't know what he's doing half the time," Zane said. "He's a little screwup."

"You're going to throw your son under the bus?" Tom asked.

Zane shrugged. "I'm just saying he goes his own way. I had nothing to do with whatever you're accusing him of."

Zane's phone began to buzz. He took it from his pocket and looked at the screen. The screen lit up with the name Grub. Tom grabbed it from his hand and answered the call. He pressed "Mute" so Grub couldn't hear Zane shouting. Conor held Zane back while Tom went into the other room, holding the phone to his ear and listening.

"Hello? You there?" Grub Garson asked. Tom knew Grub's voice—he was a lobsterman, just like his younger brother, Zane, part of the Garson fishing dynasty. Tom's distrust of them was mixed with a grudging respect for how they survived the hardships they faced—they broke plenty of rules, but he couldn't help rooting for families who made their livings on the water.

Silence from Tom, heavy breathing on the other end.

"Can you hear me?" Grub asked. "Cripes, Zane, I don't need this bad connection right now. Are you on your way here? Fucking Route 1—worst signal in the world. Zane, this whole thing is going to shit. Not at all what we signed on for. But the more I think, having the kid could work. Pretty little one, right?"

Tom tensed up. Having CeCe could work—how?

"Double our money," Grub said. "Maybe triple. Hear me?"

Tom didn't reply.

"I have someone in mind," Grub said. "Should have thought of it before."

Tom unmuted the call. "In mind for what?" he asked, and as soon as he did, he knew he'd made a mistake.

"It's not me. Don't talk to him!" Zane yelled from the other room.

"Zane?" Grub asked. "Who is this?" When he realized that he wasn't talking to his brother, he disconnected the call.

Tom's heart began to pound so hard that he could hear his own blood rushing. He saw the look on Conor's face.

"I screwed up," Tom said.

Conor didn't say anything—he didn't have to. Tom read the alarm in his eyes. What did this mean for CeCe?

"Pretty sure Ronnie is on his way to Grub's," Tom said.

"Get him off me," Zane said, trying to wrench free from Conor.

"Zane," Tom said, "Grub says he's going to double your money. He was talking about CeCe. What did he mean?"

Zane suddenly went slack. He stopped moving. Tom saw panic on his face. He thought of marine mammals, of large ocean predators. When terrified, they sometimes went perfectly still. They'd roll on their backs in the face of an attack, exhibiting tonic immobility: playing dead so the predator would swim away.

Tom knew they weren't getting any answers from Zane. "Let's get going," he said to Conor.

"We've got to hold him here till Joe arrives," Conor said.

"Zane's not going anywhere," Tom said. As a Coast Guard officer, he was law enforcement, and even though he was off duty, he had his gear in the truck. He went outside, grabbed his handcuffs, and returned to snap them on Zane Garson—securing him to the radiator.

Conor stood, brushing himself off. "You know where Grub lives?"

"Yeah, I do," Tom said. "Not far."

"Let's go," Conor said.

"Give me back my phone!" Zane yelled.

"Right," Tom said as he and Conor slammed the door behind them and got into his truck. He didn't know Grub's exact address, but he knew the street in South Kingston. He would recognize the Garson Lobster Company vehicles when he saw them in the driveway.

He had the truck in gear, ready to pull out of the parking lot, when a line of Rhode Island State Police cars came speeding down Galilee Escape Road. He and Conor were itching to get to Grub's; instead, they sat back and waited for Joe Harrigan.

29

Hadley felt restless. Kate had gotten her to leave the suite and sit in the lobby for a while. A harp played, and Isabel, from hotel reception, brought a silver tray of complimentary sparkling water over to the cozy seating area next to the grand piano and sweeping staircase. She placed it on the low table.

"Thank you," Hadley said, expecting Isabel to head back to the front desk, but she hovered close by, as if she had something to say. She seemed to be having an inner dialogue with herself, and Hadley got the sense she was trying to decide whether to speak or not.

"I've been thinking so much about you," Isabel said after a few moments. "I feel so involved . . . I was the last one to see Maddie. I can't get her out of my mind. I liked her so much."

"I appreciate that," Hadley said.

"I wish there was something I could do."

"You told everything to the police, right?" Kate asked.

"Of course. But you know how it is," Isabel said. "You think you've remembered everything, but then other things come back."

"Like what?" Kate asked.

"Just impressions, mostly," Isabel said. "Not really facts. More like feelings woven into the memories."

"Can you tell us?" Hadley asked.

"Would it help?"

"It might," Kate said. "Do you have time now?"

"I'm about to go on break," Isabel said. She glanced around. "I'm really not supposed to take it here in the lobby, though."

"Is there somewhere else we can go?" Hadley asked.

"Yes," Isabel said. She gestured for Hadley and Kate to follow her. They walked down the grand stairway, through the Bemelmans Gallery, into a small anteroom with a sofa and two chairs. They each took a seat, and Hadley watched Isabel, waiting for her to tell her story.

30

ISABEL

Two Nights Ago

I am almost ready to go off shift.

With this blizzard, I am not going home, though. Even though I can't afford this triple Five-Star resort on my own, when the weather is this bad, the manager lets us employees stay. I look forward to my room with its comfy bed, embroidered linens, Italian towels, and marble bathroom.

I really do love my job and want to make life better for our guests. They are all important to me—to the whole staff—but children are especially important. I want them to feel the magic of this place, especially during the holiday season. We have the annual tree-lighting ceremony, with a carol sing and hot chocolate. Santa joins us for brunch every weekend. The children love it.

So I've kept a special eye on CeCe. I don't know everything about what's going on in her life, but I can see how affected she is by her parents' divorce, how protective her mother is of her, and how her mother wants her to feel happy and loved.

Our hotel knows how to be discreet, so I would never even let on to Ms. Morrison—Maddie—that I know who she's married to and so much more. But she uses a pseudonym and has asked for no calls, except from her sister and lawyer, to be put through to the suite. She deserves better than a Hollywood blowhard who has seen better days and is trying to soak her for all she's worth.

When the snow stops, I will borrow my cousin's toboggan and pull CeCe around on the beach. Maybe I'll have a seaside picnic for her and her mom. I'll ask Didier—my pal and the hotel's amazing sommelier—to choose the perfect wine for a blizzard.

He's a sweetheart and is also staying in-house for the duration of the storm. I'll fill a thermos with hot chocolate for CeCe, and we'll heat up some lobster canapés. The Ocean House has one of the best chefs in the world, and needless to say, we get the freshest lobster, straight off the docks in Galilee.

Those are literally my thoughts when CeCe and Maddie walk up to the front desk. I beam, so happy to see them.

"Hello! What a crazy storm, right?" I ask.

"I love it," Maddie says. "After so long in Malibu, I am here for some good New England weather."

"A great night to sit by the fire in your suite and listen to the waves," I say. "I'm sure you can hear them, even through the windows. If you're brave, step out onto the terrace!"

"Oh yes, they're pounding the beach," Maddie says. "And we'll do more than step out onto the terrace."

That's when I notice what they are wearing: They are dressed for the nor'easter. Maddie is wearing a Moncler parka with a watch cap, and CeCe has on a cute little ski jacket. I can tell, from looking at her, that her pockets are stuffed full.

"You're not going out, are you?" I ask.

"Not for long," Maddie says, resting her hand lightly on her belly, as if she has eaten too much. "But we need some air and a little exercise."

"It's dangerous out there, Ms. Morrison," I say.

"Call me Maddie," she says, smiling. She has told me that many times since she and CeCe first checked in. I know she means it, and I want to, but my training won't let me. We are very correct here at the Ocean House, careful not to blur boundaries.

But since I am the only one at the desk, I do what she asks.

"Thank you. Maddie," I say. "But truly, please, don't go out there. There's zero visibility, and the wind will blow you away. We just heard that the highway department is about to close the roads."

"Oh," Maddie says, looking concerned. "But they haven't yet?"

"I don't think so," I say. I see her glance toward the front door. It seems obvious she's expecting someone.

"A lot of the town has lost power. Traffic lights are out," I say.

CeCe has been strolling around the lobby, looking at everything and seemingly telling herself a story, but she gets to the desk in time to hear me mention lights.

"Christmas tree lights," she says. "All over the trees and garlands and whales and swans. How many lights are there?"

"Millions and millions," I say. "We make sure of that, CeCe. There are as many tiny lights on our trees and whales and swans as there are stars in the sky."

"Really?" CeCe asks, her eyes wide.

"Yes," I say. "When the storm stops, by tomorrow night, you can go down to the beach and count the stars, then come back here and count the lights."

"I will do that," she says very seriously. "I know a lot about stars."

"You do?"

She nods and reaches into one of her pockets. I try not to laugh when a collection of six-year-old-girl valuables tumbles out: a pine cone, a small silver bell, and a handful of moonstones.

"Oops," she says, gathering them up. "I don't need these. May I leave them here?"

"Certainly," I say.

"I have other things in my pockets," she says, "including the most important thing. The reason I love stars." She stands on tiptoes to place a rather raggedy square of flannel on the desk in front of me. It has traces of raspberry jam on one side.

"What is this lovely . . . ?" I trail off, not wanting to call it a scrap.

"It's Star," she says. "My best friend."

"Hello, Star," I say.

She beams, so I know I've said the right thing.

"Isabel," Maddie says, checking her watch, "we have to hurry. My sister is on her way, and I want to get back before she arrives. I'm going to leave her a note. Do you have paper? Just in case she gets here before we do."

"If you're not back in ten minutes, I'll send out the ski patrol and a Saint Bernard," I say, joking.

"Papa!" CeCe says. "He's Bernard! That's his name!"

My heart skips—has she spotted her father? He made me promise not to tell them he was in-house. They are supposed to think he's out in Hollywood or on a film set in Europe—anywhere but the Ocean House. I look around, but he's not in the lobby.

"She means a different Bernard, CeCe," Maddie says. "It's a great big dog."

"Ha ha, Papa," CeCe says, and she barks.

I watch Maddie take off her gloves to pick up the fine pen I hand her to start writing on the stationery I've set on the counter. The note is brief; it takes her less than a minute to write. She folds the paper, puts it in the envelope, hands it to me. I turn and insert it into the cubbyhole for Maddie's suite. She zips CeCe's jacket up to her chin, wraps a scarf around her neck. Then she puts her gloves back on.

"I'm worried about you and CeCe going out," I say.

"Isabel, I'm a New Englander like you. When have we let a little storm get in our way? I got my driver's license during a blizzard! This is nothing."

That's what she says—*This is nothing*—but I detect nervousness.

"Come on, CeCe," she says, starting for the door. She turns back for one moment and speaks to me. "Let Hadley into the suite if I'm not back yet, okay?"

"You bet," I say.

I watch them go down the wide, curved front stairs to the circular drive; I assume Dermot is there to see them off, but then he appears in the corridor, carrying another guest's bags.

Tops on the list of rules for employees at the Ocean House is that respecting our guests' privacy is paramount. But I am anxious about Maddie's safety, her state of mind, so as soon as she is out of sight, I break that cardinal rule and reach for the note she left her sister. I take it from the envelope and read:

Hi, H! I'm not going to text because you are driving and I don't want you spinning out in the storm. I have a little errand to run, a very quick meeting on our favorite path. Sorry to be mysterious—I'll explain when I get back. I'm taking CeCe, hoping a walk in the snow will tucker her out so you and I can have a good talk while she sleeps. Lots to tell you. Heading out now, be back in no time. XXXX M.

I reread it several times. I want to tell Maddie that she's fooling no one. I know—or at least think I know—whom she is meeting. It has to be the person who has sent her flowers so often during her stay. Until this week, they were always the same: white roses. But yesterday they were red.

I am relieved when Hadley arrives safely but incredibly uneasy because Maddie and CeCe still aren't back. So rattled by that fact, I make a stupid mistake: I hand Hadley Maddie's note, but I forget to put it back in the envelope. Of course, Hadley doesn't notice. How would she know?

A moment later, giving Hadley that glass of champagne feels wrong. We offer a drink to our guests to welcome them, to celebrate their arrival, to put them in a festive mood. I worry that drinking that champagne will be Hadley's last carefree moment. Because I have a terrible feeling, deep down, that something bad has happened to Maddie.

And to CeCe.

They should have returned by now.

How much does this have to do with Bernard—unwilling to let his wife and daughter know that he's here at the hotel? I am mad at myself for letting him make me his ally. As much as I can't stand him, I've let him think I'm "on his side" by keeping his presence a secret from Maddie.

More to the point, how much of Maddie's failure to return from her walk has to do with her admirer, who sends her roses, both white and red?

Hadley listened carefully to Isabel's account of the last time she saw Maddie and CeCe. She had hung on to every word, wanting to see her sister through Isabel's eyes, to picture Maddie and hear her voice during the last hour of her life, to turn over every detail in her mind. And she did—it was as if Isabel had brought Hadley straight back into those moments before Maddie and CeCe left the hotel.

"I am really sorry I read her note," Isabel said. "And I can't help thinking that if I had told her Bernard was here, things might have been different."

"Because you think he killed her?" Kate asked.

"I don't know," Isabel said. "But what if he did?"

"It's not your fault," Hadley said. "No matter what, you can't blame yourself. I certainly don't."

"Thank you," Isabel said. She sounded grateful, but she looked unconvinced. "I'd better get back to work. Please, if there is anything I can do for you, just call."

"So many secrets," Hadley murmured after Isabel had left to return to the reception desk.

"You mean Isabel not telling Maddie about Bernard?" Kate said. Hadley didn't reply, but that wasn't what she meant.

"Everyone has secrets," Kate continued. "We all have things we want to keep private—thoughts, feelings, actions—but when someone is murdered, every single thing gets examined." She paused, and Hadley knew she was remembering back to Beth's murder. "You heard Isabel—you can tell she blames herself."

"I told her she shouldn't."

"But how can she not? If he did it."

"There are no roses in the suite," Hadley said, as if she hadn't even heard Kate.

"Sounds as if they were delivered pretty regularly," Kate said.

"Why wouldn't Maddie have kept them? Did she like them? Did she throw them out as soon as they were delivered?" Hadley asked.

"We should check with housekeeping," Kate said, "though I'm sure the police already have. Find out who the florist was, whether the order came from Bernard."

"Maddie used to hate when he sent her flowers," Hadley said. "She said he'd send them to apologize. When he'd been jealous, overbearing, controlling toward her, he would burn his anger out, and the next thing she knew, she'd be getting a five-hundred-dollar bouquet from the Empty Vase in West Hollywood."

"That wouldn't do it for me," Kate said.

"No," Hadley said. "Same with people he worked with. He'd throw a tantrum during a scene, blow up at the director or one of the other actors, and storm off the set. The next day he'd wind up having the whole flower shop delivered to the production company."

"Too little, too late," Kate said. "And manipulative."

"I don't think the roses were from Bernard," Hadley said quietly.

"Then who was the secret admirer?" Kate asked.

"The father," Hadley said.

"Bernard is CeCe's father," Kate said, sounding slightly worried, as if Hadley had lost her mind or at least her memory.

"I'm not talking about CeCe," Hadley said.

"Then who?"

"I mean the father of the new baby," Hadley said. She could just hear Isabel describing how Maddie had stood there, her hand on her belly, and all of a sudden she knew what the secret had been. "Maddie was pregnant when she died."

31

Law enforcement swarmed the waterfront outside Zane Garson's house. Rhode Island State Police officers and a team of FBI agents led by Special Agent Patrick O'Rourke arrived within minutes of each other. Conor led Joe Harrigan through Zane's cellar, up the outside hatchway, and into the snow tunnel. The small footprints left no doubt in his mind that they belonged to CeCe Lafond.

"She was here," Conor said. "Not just in that bedroom but right here on the path. While Tom and I stood out on the dock, letting it happen."

"We don't know for sure," Joe said.

"We don't?" Conor asked. "Let's see—she wrote her name in blood on the wall, and check out these little footprints."

"I'm with you, Conor. But I can't assert too hard. The kidnapping case belongs to the Feds. Patrick made that clear, as if I didn't already know—and you know, too. I'm going to keep investigating, but this scene is theirs."

"The Garsons talked about doubling their money, tripling it. What does that mean?" Conor asked.

"It's not good," Joe said.

"They're talking about trafficking her, aren't they?" Conor asked.

Joe didn't answer and didn't have to. The solemn look in his eyes said it all.

Conor knew trafficking went on, all through southeastern New England. On the Major Crime Squad, he had taken part in raids of houses in Connecticut's wealthiest suburbs: a stone mansion in Silver Bay, a rambling colonial in Hawthorne, a shingled cottage near the beach club in Black Hall.

They had rescued individuals brought across various borders by the cartels. Some came all the way from what law enforcement had started calling Pimp City—Tenancingo, in the Mexican state of Tlaxcala—to Connecticut and other northeast states. Most of the trafficked were taken to cities like Las Vegas, Chicago, and New York, but there were customers everywhere, even in the suburbs. This was a world where women and children were commodities, to be sold. The sellers went to where the money was.

Conor's Major Crime Squad had raided nail salons where women were being held against their will, forced to work off the debt they owed to their human smugglers—payment for bringing them into the United States from their countries of origin. Their work didn't stop at the salon doors; it often took them to darker places where they were expected to have sex with whoever would pay.

Many of the women Conor had rescued gave off the impression that their lives had already ended. Dead eyes, an unwillingness to testify, no desire to return home. To go home would be to reveal what they felt about themselves, what they felt they had become. Traffickers most often subdued their victims by creating drug addiction. Heroin, meth, fentanyl. The drugs killed the pain. They also killed the spirit.

Conor hadn't encountered them often, but the worst cases involved trafficked children. Kids whose tearful parents appeared on the news, holding up school photos, begging for whoever had their child to return them.

Police departments had media experts and victim advocates who always advised parents willing to go on air to stress the child's name, to humanize them, mention their Little League prowess, their dreams of college, tell how they loved their puppy or kitten, in the hope that such details would soften the kidnappers' hearts, allow the beloved child to return home.

But to the kidnapper, the trafficker, the child was just merchandise. Someone would buy them, and there would be no going home. Conor knew that Joe was thinking the same thing, that Grub's words about money might mean this could be CeCe's fate.

"What is Zane saying?" Conor asked. "Has he asked for a lawyer?"

"No, he hasn't. He's saying he doesn't know anything. He claims he never heard of Cecelia Lafond before seeing her on the news. That she was never in his house, but if she was, his son must have brought her here."

"Nice equivocation."

"Yeah, I almost feel sorry for his kid. Except the fact he's probably got CeCe with him."

"Look, I don't know the Garsons, but Tom does. He's had lots of experience with both Zane and his brother. Ronnie might take her there, to Grub's."

"We know Grub," Joe said. "If the two of them are in it together, Grub's calling the shots. He's the older one, and we've had plenty of run-ins with him. He's the leader of the duo. He lets Zane think he runs the fishing operation, but actually he just lets him do the grunt work. He sits in the office where it's safe and warm."

"Doing what?" Conor asked. "Selling CeCe? Can you get over there?"

"I've already said the Feds have taken control of that part of things; they're probably already at the house."

"Don't you want to be there?"

"There's plenty else for me to do."

"You're going to test that hair? The blood? Prove that she was here?"

"Jeez, what a good idea! Thanks for suggesting it," Joe said. "What do you think? Of course they'll be tested. And don't worry—I know you found them. You'll get the secret glory."

Secret glory. Conor knew what that meant. The FBI would claim success when the blood on the wall and in the sea chest came back as CeCe's, and so would the Rhode Island State Police. As it should be.

"We're holding Zane, we'll find out how this all started." Joe paused. "The main problem is the fact he was on a sinking ship when CeCe was taken gives him an alibi. Your brother's a witness to that."

"And he's laying the groundwork to blame his son for it," Conor said.

"Ronnie's what, fifteen?" Joe asked.

"What difference does age make? We've both dealt with teenage killers," Conor said. "Or maybe Grub killed Maddie. But then how did Ronnie wind up with CeCe? If the point was to traffic her, Grub would have just taken her with him."

"It's premature to say for sure, but I hear multiple people will alibi Grub."

"What, a blizzard party?"

Joe shrugged. "Not sure it started out that way, but word is he was at the Magellan Club. A lot of fishermen, seafood industry people hang out there. Sailors. Locals. Even cops. I go there for the fish fry on Fridays during Lent. Great bar."

"Okay," Conor said. "Would his buddies lie for him?"

"Some might," Joe said. "We'll find out. But for now it sounds as if he wasn't in Watch Hill."

Conor pictured the beach path where he and Kate had come upon Hadley with Maddie's body. Zane had been on his foundering fishing boat. Grub might have an alibi, too. Yet a Garson key ring had been found at the scene, and Conor had no doubt that CeCe had been in Zane's house not even an hour ago.

"It doesn't track," Conor said. "It wasn't a crime of opportunity—the killer didn't just stumble on a random victim in freezing temperatures and snow blowing sideways. It wasn't a sexual assault. It wasn't a robbery—Maddie was still wearing her Rolex watch. She wasn't related to the Garsons . . ." Conor trailed off. "Was she?"

"Madeleine Morrison related to Zane and Grub Garson? Ronnie?" Joe asked. "Um, no. Well, not that I know of. But we'll check. Maybe they thought they were in line to inherit." He paused, looked into Conor's eyes. "Come on. We are not talking brain trusts here. Whatever happened can't be that complicated. We just have to get one of them to break. It'll all come spilling out. You and I can both feel Zane wanting to throw his son to the wolves."

"And you're the alpha wolf," Conor said.

"Patrick and I are duking that out, but yeah, I am. Quit messing up my crime scene and my case. I'll call you when I know something," Joe said.

"Appreciate that," Conor said.

He stepped over the yellow crime-scene tape and walked toward Tom's truck, parked by the dock.

"How bad is Grub Garson?" Conor asked when he climbed in.

"Depends on what you mean by that. Like I told you, he's poached other lobstermen's pots, cut lines. He fished for SG back in the day, but that was a long time ago, and now pot's legal," Tom said.

"On a large scale? Was he ever convicted for it?" Conor asked. He knew that SG stood for *square grouper*—bales of marijuana or cocaine, wrapped in plastic and thrown overboard or out of planes by smugglers, waiting to be picked up by local contacts. They had been more prevalent in the eighties, and mostly in southern waters. Conor once had a case in which one smuggler had shot and killed another over a shipment. The trade came with violence and a kind of cowboy recklessness.

"He was arrested but never convicted," Tom said. "He insulated himself pretty well, threw the blame at another lobster fisherman who disappeared before trial."

"Was he ever found?" Conor asked.

Tom shook his head. "No. We don't know if he went overboard tied to an anchor or if he managed to start a new life in the islands. Rumors fly, but no proof."

Conor thought about that. The Garsons seemed adept at shifting responsibility, and they didn't shy from violence, even murder.

"Would Grub sell a child?" Conor asked.

Tom was silent for minute.

"Is there a chance he's into trafficking?" Conor asked.

"Jesus," Tom said. "I don't want to believe anyone could do that to CeCe, but with Grub . . ." He paused for a second. "It's possible, Conor."

Then Tom put the truck in gear and drove out of the parking lot. Without him saying anything, and despite Joe's warning, Conor knew that his brother was driving them toward Grub Garson's.

32

"That snowball hurt," Ronnie said.

"Sorry," CeCe said.

"Why are you saying sorry?"

"Because it's not nice to hurt people," she said.

"Yeah, but I hurt you," he said. "You were just fighting back."

It was true—he had hurt her. Her broken tooth, from when his father had shoved her into the box, had cut her lip when she had fallen in the snow. It kept scraping her tongue. She wondered if she would get in trouble for writing on the wall with her blood. She knew she wasn't bad, but things were mixing her up. She thought of the rules, how she was supposed to obey them, and how if she didn't, Ronnie's father would kill her father and aunt.

"Where are we going now?" she asked. She almost didn't care, as long as it was away from Ronnie's father.

"You'll see," Ronnie said.

"To your uncle's?" she asked.

"Thanks for the reminder; I should let him know we're almost there," Ronnie said.

He hadn't had his cell phone when they were trapped in his car during the blizzard, but he must have found it in his house, because he pulled it from his jacket pocket and dialed. He put the call on speaker, and CeCe heard the line ringing.

"Why are you calling me?" the deep voice said when he answered.

"Hi, Uncle Grub. We're on the way. I think Dad's in trouble . . ."

"Yeah, he is. Change of plans. Don't go to my house."

"You're not there?"

"No. And the cops are probably listening to this and tracking the phones. So I'm going to say this just once, and as soon as I'm done, ditch your phone. Go to Coach's house, okay? Do you know who I mean?"

CeCe saw Ronnie's expression change. He went from looking strong and bossy to scared.

"No," he said.

"No, you don't know who I mean, or no, you won't go there?" Uncle Grub asked, his voice deeper and meaner, sounding a lot like Ronnie's father.

Ronnie didn't answer. CeCe wasn't sure whether he even hung up the call—he just rolled down the window and threw the phone as hard as he could. CeCe looked back and saw it skid off the slick pavement into the roadside brush.

"This is bad," Ronnie said.

CeCe nodded because she agreed. It had been bad for two days.

"No, you don't understand," he said, looking across the seat at her. "You're in bad danger."

CeCe was only six, and there was nothing funny about what was happening. But she tilted her head and looked at Ronnie because it sounded as if he were making a joke about something so obvious. She wanted to say, "DUH!!!"

"I mean it, CeCe. I can't let them find you. When Uncle Grub gets with Coach . . . they'll do anything to make money. We have to hide you."

"Haven't we been doing that?" she asked.

"Yeah, but this is different. Before, we were hiding from the cops. Now we're hiding from Uncle Grub and Coach."

"Who is Coach?" she asked.

"Believe me, you don't want to know," he said.

Then he steered the truck off the main road, up a hill lined with pine trees. The night was getting dark; the snow glistened under streetlights, and then they were so deep in the woods that there were no streetlights anymore. The time of day reminded CeCe of the last moments she was with her mother. It made her so sad that she began to whimper.

Ronnie reached over. He patted her hand, and she flinched.

"Don't cry, CeCe. I'll take care of you," he said.

"I want Mommy," she said.

"I know," Ronnie said. "I want mine, too. I am so sorry, CeCe. I did a really bad thing."

Then he began to cry; she looked over at him, saw tears running down his face. What was happening to Ronnie? Suddenly he seemed like a different person than the one who had held the gun, stolen her away from her mother, and not let her go back to the yellow hotel.

He was sniffling, making sobbing noises. His cheeks were wet. For some reason that made her feel worse than anything. She wanted to pat his hand, the way he had done to hers, but instead she closed her eyes and pretended that she was with her mother and Star, that she was safe and surrounded by love.

33

By the time Conor and Tom got to Grub Garson's house, the FBI was swarming, and Grub was gone. His girlfriend, Elise Braga, had just gotten home from working the lunch shift at a Narragansett seafood restaurant owned by her family, and she seemed extremely distraught by all the officers and FBI vehicles.

Conor got a text from Joe that shocked him:

Per ME: Madeleine Cooke Morrison was eight weeks pregnant.

Joe also confirmed that the medical examiner had taken tissue samples that would be compared with DNA swabs from Bernard Lafond, John Morrison, all three Garson men, and any other as yet unnamed suspects. Maddie's toxicology screen had come back negative for drugs and alcohol. The cause of death was homicide. She had been shot at close range. A small-caliber bullet had been recovered. It would be helpful evidence if the murder weapon was eventually found.

Conor knew Joe didn't have to give him this information, and he was grateful for it. Next, he hoped to hear about tests on the blood, hair, and vomit at Zane Garson's. Conor had no doubt they would reveal that CeCe had been locked in the sea chest. That the single hair found inside had come from her head. He pictured the blotches of blood and the scratches in the wood. Conor was sure they had been made by CeCe trying to claw her way out. And he believed she had gotten sick before Ronnie took her away from the house.

Conor read Joe's text while he was in Tom's truck at the end of Grub's driveway, distracted from what was going on at the scene.

"I know Elise," Tom was saying. "She was a good kid. She enlisted in the Coast Guard just out of high school—she was stationed in New London when I first got there. She was promising."

"What happened?" Conor asked.

"She had a bad car accident, hurt her back. She took medical leave but never came back—got addicted to painkillers and ended up being discharged. I was sorry about that."

"Is she still an addict?"

"I don't know," Tom said. "I eat at her family's place once in a while. She works there, and she's always friendly. She asks about the crew, what we're up to. It seems as if she's clean—she's held that job for a long time. But you can never be sure. Opioids are brutal."

"How did she wind up with Grub?" Conor asked.

"It's a small world down here," Tom said. "The Garsons supply the restaurant with lobsters. I'm sure they've known each other most of their lives. Along the way, they got together."

"I know you said Grub dealt, but does he also use?" Conor asked.

"I would say no," Tom said. "He and Zane both run a tight ship. They're sharp; they're not users. They're about profits."

Conor was getting the picture. "Humans, narcotics—as long as it makes them money. I'd really like to talk to Elise," Conor said. "Ask her about where her boyfriend and the kid, Ronnie, might be, where they'd hide CeCe. You think anyone else at the restaurant is close to them?"

"They all are—it's one big extended family. Her aunt is usually at the front desk; her uncle, behind the bar. They own the place. Her sisters and cousins work there."

"Maybe someone will know something," Conor said.

"If they're willing to talk. The Bragas and Almeidas are a loyal, tight-knit group."

"Let's hope someone has a conscience and wants to save CeCe."

"Yep," Tom said. "Let's hope."

It was just a few miles to the Binnacle, and when they arrived, they saw that the parking lot was empty. Tom pulled under the red awning that covered the entryway. There was a white paper taped to the door. Conor got out of the truck and walked over to read it:

DUE TO FROZEN PIPES, WE ARE CLOSED UNTIL TOMORROW AT NOON. WE APOLOGIZE FOR THE INCONVENIENCE.

"Frozen pipes?" Conor asked when he climbed back in. "Timing seems weird."

"Right," Tom said. "They might have frozen during the storm, if the heat went out along with the power."

"But if Elise was here working the lunch hour and the place was in full swing, I don't see why there'd be a problem now," Conor said.

"Especially because there are contractors in the family. Braga Plumbing, Almeida Heating and Cooling—they'd fix it immediately. They wouldn't want to lose an entire night of dinner reservations during the holidays. I'm sure there are Christmas parties booked."

"So, word has gotten out that Elise got picked up. And the Garsons are under suspicion."

"Circle the wagons," Tom said.

34

The next morning dawned with a narrow streak of yellow over Block Island to the east, the sun instantly disappearing into thick white clouds. The ocean was dark gray-green and turbulent, with whitecaps building off Watch Hill Point. The first flakes had started to fall as Hadley got dressed. Christmas was just days away, and the suite felt so empty. She could almost feel Maddie's presence in the other room, almost hear CeCe singing, talking to her mother and aunt and stuffed animals. That was how the holiday was supposed to be, how she had taken for granted that it *would* be. But instead of her sister and niece, there were ghosts.

She remembered Isabel telling her how Maddie had rested a hand on her belly, and how Hadley had known what it meant. Now she knew that she had been right: Maddie's autopsy had revealed she was pregnant. Hadley could only imagine how they would have hugged when Maddie told her. A new baby in the family, a sister or brother for CeCe, a new niece or nephew for Hadley. Who could the father be? Who had sent Maddie all those roses?

She checked her phone again—she had been doing that nonstop, hoping for a call from Joe Harrigan telling her that they'd found CeCe, that she was safe—but nothing. And she hadn't heard from Genevieve again. She felt relieved. Maybe Genevieve had realized how insanely uncomfortable it would be for both of them and changed her mind about coming.

She felt uneasy about the day ahead, the drive to Maddie's unit at Silver Bay Fine Art Transport & Storage, where Jeanne would meet her with the key. Kate knew the storage facility well—her gallery rented space there—and had offered to go with her. Hadley had accepted.

But Hadley didn't want to go. It felt wrong—so final, an inventory of Maddie's possessions. All she could think about was her niece. With CeCe missing, nothing else mattered. Despite that, going to Maddie's storage unit would be doing *something*—and it felt better than just sitting around. She couldn't help but wonder what she would find there, whether there might be something that could help the cops, something that could help find CeCe. Even if it was a long shot, she was willing to look.

Kate was waiting by the high-tech coffee station in the lobby. They filled cups with cappuccino and stopped by the reception desk on the way out. Isabel wasn't there, but Agnes was.

"Good morning," Hadley said.

"Hello, Ms. Cooke," Agnes said. "How may I help you?"

"Could you ring my brother-in-law's room?" Hadley asked. "Bernard Lafond?"

"Of course," Agnes said and dialed the house phone.

Hadley had called and texted him repeatedly but had gotten no reply. With everything else being so uncertain, it threw her off, being unable to get in touch with him.

"He's not answering," Agnes said.

"Have you seen him today?" Kate asked.

"No, I haven't," Agnes said. "Shall I tell him to call, if I do see him?"

"Please," Hadley said. "I have an errand to run and will be gone for a little while. I don't want to leave, in case the police need me, but I can get back here right away. If Detective Harrigan or anyone else comes looking for me, will you please call?"

"Of course. Your cell phone number is in your profile. I'll leave a note for my colleagues, in case I'm not here."

"Thank you," Hadley said.

Outside, the snow was falling. Dermot had Hadley's truck ready—heat on full blast, windshield wipers going. Hadley and Kate climbed in and headed west, through the town of Westerly. They were both Nutmeggers—Connecticut natives—and somehow that felt comforting to Hadley, an additional bond with this woman she'd met only a few days ago.

"Do you think it's odd that you haven't seen Bernard?" Kate said.

"Definitely," Hadley said.

"I know you're wary of each other, but why is he avoiding you?" Kate asked. "In spite of the problems, you're both worried about CeCe. Wouldn't he want to stay close, if only to share info? Could it be Maddie's pregnancy, if he was the father?"

"Or if he wasn't," Hadley said.

"Would she have told him?" Kate asked. "They were in the middle of a divorce, and that makes everything weird. My sister and her husband were about to separate when she was killed. He and I both loved Sam, but by that point, we couldn't stand each other, so we kept away from each other as much as we could. We only spoke when it had to do with Sam."

"She didn't even tell me she was pregnant," Hadley said. "She would never have told him, and there's no way he's the father."

"Maybe he's just so worried about CeCe that he doesn't have the energy to be around other people till she's found," Kate said.

"Bernard has never lacked energy," Hadley said. "Maddie used to say that the more that went wrong—between them, in his career—the more he kicked into high gear. He's always trying to fix things, make people see them his way. He can never understand when the world goes against him. She said he was a narcissist. That word is thrown around so much, but it fits him."

"I get it. My brother-in-law was a classic example. Every single interaction is seen through their eyes—they don't take into account the fact that others have a point of view. It has to be their way," Kate said.

"He's probably trying to keep busy," Hadley said. "Since he came here to 'scout locations,' maybe that's what he's doing."

"I hear sarcasm there," Kate said. "You really do think that's not his real reason for coming to Watch Hill?"

"I think he somehow knew that Maddie would be at the Ocean House. The coincidence is too great. And I do know that he wanted to get her back. He probably thought he could charm her into loving him again, in such a romantic hotel."

They drove in silence for a while. The snow fell thickly and covered the hilly contours of southeastern Connecticut: the fields and granite ledges, the coves and saltwater creeks, the stone walls and marshes, the glacial erratic boulders that lined the roads. It was a beautiful part of the world. Hadley and Maddie had driven this stretch countless times as teenagers on their way to Rhode Island beaches. She tried not to think about how her sister would never see it again.

"I feel strange going to Maddie's storage place," Hadley said. "But Jeanne was so adamant about making sure her paintings are safe and accounted for."

"She's right about that," Kate said. "Maddie's work is her legacy, and it will give CeCe financial security while she's growing up. It's really important, Hadley."

"I get that. But it's so soon after Maddie died."

"All the more reason. Valuable artwork has a way of disappearing soon after an artist's or collector's death," Kate said. "If people have access, there's the risk of it being stolen before the executor has the chance to secure the location."

"Who has access other than Jeanne?" Hadley asked.

"Exactly my point," Kate said.

"My sister obviously trusted her, or she wouldn't have had her as her attorney," Hadley said, remembering a comment Kate had made yesterday. "What were you going to tell me about her?"

"Not about her, specifically," Kate said. "But I had some trouble with her firm over an artist's estate. Our gallery had been representing him for decades—my grandmother had nurtured him as a young artist. We'd gotten close; I'd been to his house many times—for parties, tea by the river, and to see work in progress. I was very familiar with the house and all his furnishings."

"Is it common for gallery owners and artists to have that kind of relationship?" Hadley asked.

"Sometimes," Kate said. "For my family, always. Our role is to encourage and protect our artists. We don't take anyone on unless we love their art. Most often we wind up loving them, too."

"Lucky artists," Hadley said.

"We're the lucky ones," Kate said. "Anyway, Caleb Hart appointed me executor of his estate. He was ninety-three. His wife had died twenty years earlier, and they had no children. He lived in Black Hall—in a 1700s house right on the Connecticut River. It was filled with antiques. He collected eighteenth- and nineteenth-century furniture. Oriental rugs. First editions by Melville, Hawthorne, Frost, Alcott, Millay. Colonial-era silver, including a tea set attributed to Paul Revere."

"That's amazing," Hadley said. She was riveted by the story while concentrating hard on driving through the snow, making sure she didn't skid off the road.

"He also had a cache of his own paintings, as well as a number of works by American Impressionists," Kate said. "Jim Bradley, Jeanne's partner at Cross, Gladding, and White, was his lawyer. He had drawn up the will and trust. Caleb was leaving everything to the Black Hall Museum of Art. He had talked to me about it often over the years. He saw it as his legacy, and it was my job to protect it, to see that his wishes were carried out."

"Like my job to fulfill Maddie's wishes."

"Yes," Kate said. "And very similar to what you are doing today—meeting Jeanne to get the key to Maddie's storage space—I met with Jim at Caleb's house, where he was going to give me the keys and alarm codes and make arrangements for an appraiser to come in and catalog everything in the house."

"Did it go well?" Hadley asked.

"No," Kate said. "When I did the walk-through with Jim, I noticed that things were missing."

"Don't tell me—the Paul Revere silver," Hadley said.

"No, that would have been too obvious. Several other silver pieces, though. Nothing famous but all quite valuable. Some rare rugs that would have fetched a great deal at auction. He had a drawerful of vintage fountain pens, too."

"That's a lot to go missing," Hadley said.

"It sounds like it," Kate said. "But Caleb was a tremendous collector. His house was jammed full of his beloved belongings. He hung his art salon-style—from chair rail to ceiling. His bookshelves were crammed with first editions, as well as modern novels he loved and one of the most impressive groups of art books I've ever seen."

"So it would be hard to spot things that had been taken?" Hadley asked.

"By anyone but me," Kate said. "Probably because I was so close to him and had spent so much time at the house, I could see what wasn't there."

"Someone stole everything?"

"That's the only explanation," Kate said.

"What did you do?"

"I filed a police report—that is, I told Conor. He and detectives on the state police Art Theft Squad investigated the cleaning person, the gardener, various service people who might have gotten into the house.

But it always came back to the fact that the alarm was set, the doors and windows locked."

"Could any of the service people have taken things while Caleb was still alive? Or could he have given belongings away?" Hadley asked.

"That's what Jim and the rest of the firm said when they were questioned. But I knew that wasn't the case. I'd had dinner with Caleb two nights before he died, and everything was in place. I'm positive that Jim and his partners did it. There is no other explanation—they were the only ones with keys and codes."

"That's unsettling, to put it mildly," Hadley said.

"It is, but there's no direct evidence," Kate said. "Conor said that suspicion wasn't enough to arrest them or take them to trial. As executor, I—or the museum, as Caleb's sole beneficiary—could bring a civil suit. That will be up to the museum's trustees."

"Didn't Caleb have security cameras?" Hadley asked. "That would have recorded anyone coming or going?"

"He didn't," Kate said. "He had a very sophisticated alarm system that did provide a record of times it was set and disarmed, but no cameras."

"But if the firm's lawyers were the only ones with the alarm codes . . . ," Hadley said.

"They claimed that Caleb must have given the combinations to other people—including me. I was furious, but there was nothing I could do. Conor says the Art Theft Squad is letting the case go cold."

"Why?"

"Because there is no case," Kate said. "I was the only one who knew what Caleb owned. He hadn't kept an ongoing list or inventory. He'd told his insurance company about items worth more than ten thousand dollars each, but he hadn't kept a running list. He had bought much more than was officially accounted for."

"That's awful," Hadley said.

"It's why it's so important that you take charge of Maddie's paintings right away," Kate said.

"Who cares about them, considering that CeCe is missing?" Hadley asked.

"CeCe will care," Kate said. "Her mother's work will mean the world to her."

"But I won't know what should be there," Hadley said. "I won't know if something is missing. It's not like you, spending time with Caleb and his collections. I've never even been to Maddie's storage space."

"You can start from today," Kate said. "Get the keys from Jeanne and change the locks. In fact, would you like me to call the locksmith I use? He can meet us there."

"Thank you," Hadley said. "That would be great."

Silver Bay Fine Art Transport & Storage was located in the only semi-industrial section of town. Just off the highway, it was in a cul-de-sac with a stonecutting business, a shop that did after-market modifications to high-performance sports cars, and a veterinary hospital.

Hadley noticed that the storage facility was surrounded by a chain-link fence topped with barbed wire. A keypad was stationed just outside the fence and obviously opened a sliding section.

"I don't have the combination," Hadley said.

"I have it to this gate," Kate said. "But we should wait for Jeanne."

They looked toward the building and the surrounding parking area. There were two panel trucks with the Silver Bay Fine Art Transport & Storage logo painted on the side but no cars. Hadley checked her watch. Right on time, when Jeanne had said she'd be there.

"Maybe the snow is holding her up," Kate said.

Hadley nodded. She felt pressure building up inside, a combination of excitement at the prospect of seeing Maddie's work and trepidation because she knew how hard it would hit her—the fact that this was it; there would be no more new paintings.

A car pulled into the cul-de-sac and drew up next to Hadley's truck. The driver rolled down the window and waved. It was Donna Almeida. Hadley was shocked to see her. She hadn't told Johnny she was coming. Even if she had, why would he have sent his girlfriend?

"Hi, Hadley," Donna said.

"What are you doing here?" Hadley asked.

"I think I mentioned to you that I work at Cross, Gladding, and White. I'm a paralegal in Jeanne's department, and I'm here on her behalf."

"You said a firm in Hartford, you didn't tell me the name," Hadley said.

"I'm pretty sure I did," Donna said. "I wouldn't have left that out."

"Why isn't Jeanne here?" Kate asked.

"I'll explain in a minute. Follow me—I've got the combination," Donna said. She pulled ahead, then tapped the code into the keypad, and the gate slid open. Hadley drove right behind her into the enclosure.

"Who's that?" Kate asked.

"Johnny's girlfriend," Hadley said.

"And Johnny is Maddie's ex-husband?"

"Yes," Hadley said. She felt confused. Had Donna mentioned the firm? Hadley had been so upset that night. Was it possible she'd just blocked it out? Or had she heard, and the name just hadn't meant anything to her? Until the next day, she hadn't even known Maddie's lawyer's name or that of Jeanne's law firm.

"Hadley, I am so sorry if you feel I wasn't straight with you," Donna said after they had parked and gotten out of their cars.

"It's weird to me," Hadley said. "That you didn't tell me."

"I should have told you right away that I sometimes work with Maddie's lawyer. It was such a terrible time, having just learned about her death. I couldn't bear to bring it up," Donna said. "Also, please understand—it's a big law firm."

"Largest in Hartford, second largest in Connecticut," Kate said. "I know—some of my artists have used your trusts and estates department. I'm Kate Woodward, Hadley's friend."

"Donna Almeida," Donna said. "Kate, you're right. We have so many clients, and Hadley, I want you to know that I'm not assigned to Jeanne's team, or to Maddie's account."

"I thought you said just now that you work with Jeanne," Hadley said.

"I do, occasionally, but not on a regular basis. Only when she's in a pinch and her usual paralegals are busy with other things."

"Why are you here today, then?" Hadley asked.

"Jeanne is so terribly sorry she couldn't be here—she slipped on the ice leaving her house this morning and had to go to the clinic," Donna said.

"Is she okay?" Hadley asked.

"Her wrist is broken," Donna said. "And because it happened this morning, she didn't have anyone lined up to take over and meet you. I was the only paralegal available. I hope you don't mind."

"No," Hadley said. "It's fine."

But none of it was fine. She steeled herself to enter her sister's storage unit, uncertain of what she would find but knowing that Maddie would never be here again.

"Thanks," Donna said. "Bear with me—I've never been to Maddie's unit before, so I'm seeing it for the first time, just like you. Jeanne gave me some fairly complicated directions on how to get in."

The building's outer door had another keypad, and Donna punched in the code. Once inside, Hadley felt warm. Art needed to be stored in a temperature-controlled environment. The heat couldn't go too high or the cold too low. Extreme fluctuations on either end could be damaging. Equally or more important, there had to be moisture control—humidity could cause mold, which was extremely destructive to works on paper.

The large building was in the shape of an E. Numbered units were located along the corridors. Maddie's took up most of the center section, the middle row of the E. Donna dug into her cross-body satchel for her iPad. She opened the email in which Jeanne had sent instructions.

"Okay," Donna said, reading. "We have to put in a code first, and that gives a twenty-second delay on an alarm. It has to be perfect the first time. If it isn't, the siren sounds, and the signal goes straight to the police. We don't get a second try. Hadley, I'll let you type it in. And Jeanne told me she suggests you change it right away, for extra security."

Hadley glanced at the screen. The combination was the month, date, and year of CeCe's birthday. She entered the number, and three clicks sounded.

"Now, here are the keys," Donna said, handing them to her. "Top and bottom lock. Twenty seconds."

Hadley fumbled, dropped the keys, picked them up, and managed to open the steel door with a few seconds to spare. The unit was dark. Donna turned on her cell phone's flashlight, found the light switch.

"Wow," Kate said when the space was illuminated. "I have units at the other end of the building, and they're nothing like this."

"It's amazing," Donna said. "Beautiful, like a gallery . . . or an apartment."

Hadley shouldn't have been surprised. Her sister had had such style and grace. But who would have expected her to furnish her storage unit like a Paris atelier? Every wall was hung with her paintings. There was a seating area with Victorian furniture—a sofa and two chairs covered in burgundy velvet, with ornately carved rosewood backs and arms.

Racks and sliding shelves lined one wall from floor to ceiling. They looked chock-full of canvases, expandable portfolio cases, drawings stored in archival sheet protectors, and aluminum boxes. Four tall filing cabinets stood at the very back of the space. Hadley spotted a black leather chair pulled in front of an antique rolltop desk made of kingwood with inlaid strips of yew. She knew that desk well; she had been with Maddie when she'd bought it at Les Puces, the Paris flea market at Saint-Ouen.

"It's going to be a daunting job," Donna said, "inventorying the contents. Jeanne wants you to know we will help as much as you'd like us to."

"We can help, too," Kate said to Hadley. "Our gallery uses a very reputable and discreet photographer and assistant. We have them sign a nondisclosure agreement."

"It goes without saying that our law firm is discreet," Donna said sharply.

"I didn't mean to imply you weren't," Kate said.

Bickering done, everyone was silent for a while, walking around as if it really were a gallery and taking in Maddie's work. Hadley stopped in front of a painting that took her breath away. She had never seen it before. Oil on linen, fifty by fifty inches—it was one of Maddie's largest. It still smelled of linseed oil and was obviously a new piece.

Kate stood beside her, and Hadley heard her take a deep breath.

It was a self-portrait of a clearly pregnant Maddie lying on her side, sleeping in the snow. Her hands were clasped, holding a bouquet of red roses. Stars blazed in the midnight-blue sky overhead. In the distance, the constellation Orion rose out of the ocean, riding on the back of a humpback whale. A trickle of red ran from the roses, as if they were dissolving into the snow, or as if they were turning to blood. Sitting on Maddie's shoulder was a tiny girl with cascades of blonde curls. She was holding a star.

"It shows what happened to her," Hadley said. "As if she came back from the dead and painted it."

"Or as if she dreamed it was going to happen," Kate said.

"But she couldn't have, right?" Hadley asked.

"It's almost as if she did this painting, then went out into the blizzard to reenact it," Kate said, leaning closer to examine the brushstrokes.

"Reenact it with the shooter? She knew she was going to be killed?" Hadley asked.

"No," Kate said. "Of course not. But what if she was tricked into it? A sort of performance art?"

Hadley thought about that. Performance art was magical, ephemeral, fleeting. The tableau that was created would last only for the duration of the act, and then it would dissolve into memory. Unless it had been filmed, and that made her heart race. Could someone have documented the murder on video?

"It makes a kind of sense," Kate said. "Conor and I have been wondering what could have driven her out into the storm, especially with CeCe. Could someone have convinced her it was a way to celebrate this incredible painting? Even take it to another level? Because, Hadley, this is her masterpiece. It is beyond anything else she has ever done."

"It is," Hadley said. She pointed to the words *Last Night* in tiny white script at the bottom of the painting, just beneath Maddie's signature.

"The title?" Kate asked.

Hadley nodded.

Donna walked over to gaze at the painting, and Hadley drifted away. She wanted to be alone with her thoughts about Maddie, and whatever had driven her to paint this work, and whoever had lured her to her death. Hadley wondered if Kate was right—that she had gone into the storm to create performance art based on the painting—or if Maddie had met the person for an entirely different reason.

Maddie's rolltop desk was piled high with papers, correspondence, and the small black Moleskine notebooks she favored. Hadley knew she used them as a combination calendar, diary, and phone book. She liked the small size, the elastic closure, and the fine silk ribbon to hold the writer's place. She always kept a pen tucked inside.

Hadley reached for the top notebook on the pile. The pen and the silk ribbon held the place of the last notes Maddie had made. She felt qualms about reading what her sister had written—Maddie had been fierce about privacy—but what did it matter now? She opened to the last page that had been written on.

But instead of writing, there was a receipt stapled to the paper:

$1,000,000 to Genevieve Dickinson, plus past royalties

Public apology

Renunciation of credit—the idea was Genevieve's

On that printed page was a pencil sketch of the original image, the one that had made Maddie's name and fortune: the swan and the whale. The sketch was terrible—not just in technique but in atmosphere, which was pure evil. The whale looked shrunken, almost as if decomposing. And the swan was a stick figure, like a skeleton. It was as though Maddie had done it while drunk, or dying, and gripped by shame.

Hadley shoved the notebook into her pocket. When she turned to look at Kate and Donna, still regarding *Last Night*, she saw Donna catch a glimpse out of the corner of her eye. Hadley was shaking as she left the storage unit and walked outside to feel snow falling on her face.

35

Conor knew that Elise Braga had been questioned by the police, but they hadn't held her. So when he and Tom showed up at the Binnacle to see what they could learn from the family, she was there, suiting up for the lunch shift.

"Hey, Elise," Tom said as they walked into the dining room. "Got a table for two?"

"Sure, Commander," she said, leading them to a good spot by the window.

"This is my brother, Conor," Tom said.

"Nice to meet you," Elise said.

"Hello," Conor said.

He was going to let Tom take the lead on this. Tom knew Elise and the Braga family. They mostly trusted and liked him because he tended to be understanding about small maritime infractions that could cost their fishing captains big fines if the Coast Guard officer wanted to be a hard-ass.

"Hey, it's almost Christmas," Elise said. "Our family would like to buy you a drink. What'll you have?"

"A Coke," Tom said.

"Same for me," Conor said.

"Oh, you're no fun," Elise said.

"It's barely noon," Tom said.

"Well, we'll get you next time you're here for dinner. Meanwhile, your Cokes are on us."

She handed them menus and headed across the room. An older man wearing a navy-blue Binnacle polo shirt stood behind the bar and looked toward Conor and Tom when Elise spoke to him.

"Is that her uncle?" Conor asked. "The owner?"

Tom glanced over. "Yes, Joachim Braga. Big Jack, he's called. Patriarch of the family."

Instead of Elise delivering the Cokes, Big Jack brought them over to the table.

"Merry Christmas, gentlemen," Jack said. "These are on the house. In fact, your lunches are."

"No, Jack," Tom said. "But thanks."

"Stop! You're going to have the lobster pie. You'll love it, Tom. Big hunks of claw and tail meat, enough heavy cream to stop your heart, my wife's pastry—all of it flambéed tableside with cognac."

"How about two fish-and-chips platters but we pay for them?" Conor asked.

"Tom, Tom, Tom," Jack said, his wide smile revealing an upper-right gold molar. "You gotta educate your brother on how we do things around here. We're family, Conor! Not blood, like you and Tom, but saltwater families. We're related through the sea."

"He's right about that," Tom said.

"Damn straight. My cousins and best friends all fish for lobsters, we cook 'em, and Tom saves our lives when something goes wrong out there in the ocean. Like you did for Zane—not a cousin but a lifelong friend, just as close as family." Jack made the sign of the cross, blessed himself. "He almost didn't make it."

"He was lucky," Tom said.

"Damned idiot going out in a blizzard. Copy that, Commander?" Jack asked.

"Copy that," Tom said.

"He'll probably get a nice fine for fuel leakage, right?"

"That's up to the DEM," Tom said.

"Well, hope he can pay it and get out there lobstering again. He keeps our lobster tanks full. I gotta say, screw the Department of Environmental Management. People have to make a living. People love to eat here; we don't want to deprive them."

"It's a popular place," Tom said. "That's for sure."

"We've been at it a long time," Jack said. "It didn't happen overnight. We pull together."

"I can imagine," Conor said. "It must be hard on all of you when one of you has trouble."

"We've had plenty of trouble, but we're from a long line of survivors," Jack said. "Dating back to the Portuguese explorers. There's a monument to us at Breton Point in Newport, right across Narragansett Bay. You'll see our ancestors there—tell their ghosts I say hi."

"The police are probably still holding Zane," Conor said. "And they're looking for his son, Ronnie. Do you know where he is?"

Jack shook his head. "That kid takes after his mother," he said. "Other side of the family. You should ask them."

"It was nice to meet your niece Elise," Conor said.

"She's a sweetheart," Jack said.

"She must be upset about her boyfriend," Conor said.

"Nothing to be upset about," Jack said. "Grub is a great guy. He'll help the police in any way he can."

"Sounds as if he might be harboring Ronnie," Conor said.

"No truth to that," Jack said. "He'd never help a fugitive. Our family supports the police. We abide by the law. Right, Tom?"

"We have a missing child, Jack," Tom said. "Her name is CeCe. You have daughters and nieces, and I know you can imagine what the family is feeling. How worried they are for her. Anything you can tell us that would help . . ."

"Of course, Tom," Jack said. "Now, let me think. I don't know Ronnie at all, but have you checked with his high school buddies?"

Conor looked across the room. He saw Elise standing by the bar talking to two women, one of whom he recognized as Isabel, from the front desk at the Ocean House. She was wearing jeans and a sweater instead of the suit she wore at work. When she saw him, she waved, and he walked over.

"Hi, Isabel," he said.

"Hi, Mr. Reid," she said. "This is my coworker Patricia. We always come here for lunch on our days off. They are so good to us." She leaned into Elise and gave her a hug.

"We give discounts to our friends in the service industry," Elise said. "We love our locals."

"We're grateful," Isabel said. She looked around. "Is Ms. Woodward here?"

"No, she's out with Hadley."

Elise had a worried look on her face. She made eye contact with Conor, and he felt she wanted to speak with him privately.

"Don't let me keep you from your lunch," Conor said to Isabel and Patricia. "Enjoy it."

"You, too," Isabel said, and they went to find seats at the bar.

Elise beckoned him, and he followed her outside and around the corner of the restaurant.

"What is it, Elise?" he asked.

"I'm just so worried," she said.

"About Grub?"

"Yes," she said.

"Do you know where he is?" Conor asked.

"They're going to arrest him, aren't they?" she asked.

"At this point, they just want to ask him about Ronnie and CeCe."

"It's a nightmare," Elise said. "The news says she's only six."

"That's right."

"And now she has no mother."

Conor wanted to ask what she knew about Maddie's murder, but he forced himself to keep those questions inside till he heard what she had to say about Grub and where he might be.

"Don't blame Grub for everything," she said.

"But he ran away when he knew the police wanted to talk to him," Conor said.

"He's protecting someone. The one who did it."

"Ronnie?" Conor asked.

"Yes. His nephew. His godson," Elise said.

"Does Ronnie have CeCe?" Conor asked.

"Ronnie used to be such a good kid," she said, as if she hadn't heard the question. "So sweet and helpful. Before he started lobstering with his dad, he worked here at the restaurant during summer vacation. Shucked littlenecks like a champ, picked lobster, bused tables. But they've ruined him." She sounded angry. "Grub said Zane wanted to make a man out of him!"

"Did they make Ronnie kill Maddie?" Conor asked. "Why did they want her dead?"

Elise's shoulders went up to her ears. "I don't know! Don't ask me!"

Conor knew she was lying, but he didn't want to accuse or push her. "Tell me where to find him so we can save CeCe and help him," he said.

"I shouldn't be talking to you at all," Elise said. "My family will kill me. I mean, not really. I shouldn't even joke about killing, but oh my God."

"Think of CeCe," Conor said.

Elise pressed her hands against her eyes, as if by not seeing him she could avoid facing what was right in front of her.

"Elise, Tom told me you've struggled with addiction. You're clean now, right?" Conor asked.

She nodded, slowly taking her hands down from her face.

"That's huge," Conor said. "I'm a cop in Connecticut, and I see addicts and what they go through. How the disease turns them into people they never wanted to be. I know how hard it is to get straight. It takes a ton of hard work, and from what they tell me, one of the biggest parts of recovery is getting honest."

"'Rigorous honesty,'" Elise said. "That's what we learned in rehab."

Conor listened. He didn't want to push her, possibly cause her to stop talking. But he needed to know where Grub went, where CeCe might be.

"We did the steps of AA. Step five: 'Admitted to God, to ourselves, and to another human being the exact nature of our wrongs.'"

To Conor, it sounded like a confession. He realized she was grappling with whatever she was about to say.

"The exact nature of my wrongs," Elise said, "is that I've hidden things from myself."

"Like what?"

"Can you love someone even though you know they're bad?"

Conor didn't reply, just waited.

"I would have said there is no way he would hurt a little girl. He didn't even know that she'd be there. It was just supposed to be the mother."

"You're talking about Ronnie?" Conor asked.

"No," she said. "Grub."

"How would he hurt her? You mean more than just taking her?"

"Maybe," she said. "He's been hanging out with someone—I can't stand this guy. They call him Coach. It's short for Coachella, where he's from. Coachella Valley, in California. You know, where the music festival is? He moved here a few months ago, and he talks about finding girls, taking them back down there."

"You mean children?" Conor asked.

"No," Elise said. "Of course not. Grub said girls who like to party."

"Okay," Conor said, unsure of whether she really didn't know or whether she was covering for Grub.

"Where is Grub, Elise? And where is Ronnie? Tell me what you know, right now," Conor said.

"Grub is at the Magellan Club," she said. "It's on Route 1, heading west. Just, please, don't tell my uncle. Otherwise, he'll call Grub and warn him."

"Okay," Conor said. "But you won't?"

"No. I want CeCe to get rescued," she said. "That's all that matters now. Bad things could happen to her. And it would be Coach's fault, not Grub's."

"Thanks, Elise," Conor said, not wanting to alienate her by saying the obvious: they already have.

Conor hurried back to the table. Jack was sitting with Tom, and the fish and chips had just been delivered. Conor knew he had to get Tom out of there right away without tipping Jack off. He said he wanted to bring his food home to Kate while it was hot and asked if it could be packed up.

"What's your hurry? Eat here. The batter will get soggy," Jack said.

"It'll be fine. I'll drive fast," Tom said, catching Conor's eye and knowing something was up.

"Great to meet you, Conor," Jack said, slapping Conor on the back. "Bring your girlfriend next time, okay? Tom, your wife, too. We throw a hell of a New Year's Eve party. And we're going to treat you to lobster pie, no arguments!"

"Sounds good," Tom said. "Thanks, Jack."

Conor and Tom went back to the truck. Conor had already opened his phone, looked up the address of the Magellan Club, and punched it into the GPS. He showed the map to his brother.

"I know the club," Tom said. "Some of the guys at the station are members."

"We've got to tell Joe to meet us there," Conor said. "And he needs to have someone pick up Elise for questioning. She knows what happened to Maddie and CeCe, and I think she's ready to tell."

Tom drove out of the parking lot and headed toward Route 1 while Conor called Joe Harrigan. He explained what Elise had told him.

"There's this guy, Coach," Conor began.

"He's on our radar screen," Joe said. "He was on a sex offender registry out in California, but he left without reporting in. The FBI was going to pick him up, but he's gone. No sign of him. His apartment looks lived in, but his dog hadn't been fed, and his mailbox was crammed full. He seems to have fallen off the edge of the world."

Conor thought of the crew member who had disappeared before Grub could go to trial on drug-smuggling charges. Possibly overboard with an anchor chained to his feet? If Grub felt law enforcement closing in, he might have thought Coach was too much of a liability. Conor wondered if anyone who posed a threat to Grub was destined for the anchor treatment.

The club was ten miles away, in a nondescript one-story building set back from the road. American and Portuguese flags flew above the front door. Unmarked police cars arrived at the same time as the Reids. Conor and Tom stood back, letting Joe and his team go inside to take Grub into custody.

But he wasn't there.

His truck was in the parking lot, which meant he had borrowed someone else's vehicle. Club members were closemouthed. No one admitted to loaning him their car or truck. No one even said he'd been there, except for one fisherman who told the police that he had gotten a text and taken off right away. Conor wasn't really surprised. He wondered whether Elise had changed her mind and called to warn him, or whether Jack had figured it out.

Either way, Grub was in the wind, and there was still no trace of Ronnie and CeCe.

"What did Elise say?" Joe asked.

"That Grub will hurt CeCe. She alluded to him working with—or at least talking to—that guy Coach. She didn't like the friendship, said that Zane wanted to make a man out of Ronnie. He got his son to kill Maddie."

"Nice, setting his son up to take the heat," Joe said. "With absolutely no evidence that any of them even knew her."

"We're all thinking the same thing, aren't we?" Conor asked. "That it was murder for hire?"

"Yes," Joe said. "That's the theory."

"Who hired them?" Tom asked.

"That's the question," Joe said.

"What about CeCe?" Conor asked. "Where does she come in?"

"Grub might have seen her as a bonus," Joe said. "Unexpected but to be exploited. An asset, a way to make more money."

"Where is she now?" Tom asked.

Neither Conor nor Joe could answer that. None of them knew. And they had no idea where to start looking.

36

"Where are we?" CeCe asked, looking around. She had slept for a little while, but now she was awake again and saw tall buildings, so she knew it was a city. She had been to lots of cities with her parents: Paris, Los Angeles, and New York. These buildings weren't as tall as the ones in New York, or as beautiful as the ones in Paris, or surrounded by palm trees and flowers like the ones in Los Angeles. But the streets were crowded, the buildings were close together, and there were lots of cars.

"Providence," Ronnie said.

"I don't know where that is," she said.

"That doesn't matter," he said. "I have to figure things out. They won't look for us here."

He drove them around, up and down streets. Her stomach was growling so loudly, and she felt sick again.

"I know you're hungry," he said. "So am I. And we're going to run out of gas soon. I don't have any money, though. They were supposed to pay me, but I can't go home now. And it's not because of the police, CeCe."

"Then why?"

"I have my reasons," he said.

She looked at him while he drove. He had changed in the last day. He seemed different, as if the awful, mean, tough part of him was slipping away. It reminded her of her papa in one of his movies. She wasn't supposed to see it, because her mother said it was scary, but her parents had a screening—that's what they called it when they showed films in the little theater they had in their house—and CeCe snuck in because she wanted popcorn. The room had big, comfortable seats facing a big screen, and there was a popcorn machine in the back, where the control panel was.

In the movie, her father was a bad man. He robbed a bank, and he was awful, like Ronnie was, with a gun, and swear words, and a car that drove too fast because he had to get away. He went to his daughter's school to pick her up and take her to Canada, but she didn't want to go. She wanted to stay with her mommy. She cried.

And it was his daughter's sadness that made him change. He was still a robber, and he still had the gun, but the look on his face was different, just like Ronnie's was now. He took her home and dropped her off in the front yard, where she had a swing set and a pink bicycle. And her mother, who was looking out the window, ran out the door to pick her up and carry her inside, and the father was watching from the road. And then he drove away.

CeCe hadn't even felt like eating popcorn after she saw that. Her papa acted, which meant he pretended to be other people in movies, but even so, he always looked like himself, and CeCe knew that part of him in the movie was real, that it came from part of his heart. And she didn't always like that.

"You like going to the zoo?" Ronnie asked.

She nodded. Her parents had taken her to a big zoo in California with a section called the Petting Kraal, where she had gotten to pet baby goats.

"Roger Williams Zoo is near here," Ronnie said. "It used to be my favorite place, after Drake Aquarium. But that's in Connecticut—it's too far, we'd run out of gas. So I'll take you to the zoo instead."

She gave him a quizzical look. What was going on?

"Why are you being so nice?" she asked.

"I am going to save you," he said, not exactly answering her question.

"Save me?" She frowned.

"If it was night, we could really see the Holiday Lights Spectacular," he said. "They do it every Christmas, and you wouldn't believe how many lights there are. A snowy day is pretty dark, though, so maybe we'll still be able to see them."

CeCe thought of the Ocean House and Isabel, how Isabel had said there were as many Christmas lights inside as there were stars in the sky. Was it possible there were that many at the zoo?

He smiled at her, then drove faster, as if he were excited to get to the zoo. She felt a little excited, too. She would like to see animals and maybe be able to pet goats. The thought of seeing a million lights made her sit up straighter, watch out the window. *Stars,* she thought. *Stars, Star, Star in my pocket.*

But when they got to the zoo, all happiness left the truck.

Ronnie stopped in front of a sign and read it. "I forgot—we have to pay admission to get in," he said, looking at CeCe.

"Oh," she said, her heart falling.

"I'm sorry," he said. "I don't have the money."

"That's okay," she said, but tears popped into her eyes. It seemed weird that this would be the thing to make her cry, after everything else, but she had really wanted to pet a goat and see those stars. She tried to hold her sobs in, but her shoulders began to shake.

They sat in his truck, engine running, outside the zoo entrance.

"Don't cry, CeCe," Ronnie said. "Please."

She couldn't help herself.

"There might be a way," he said. "It's kind of a long shot. But when I worked at the Binnacle, the Almeidas catered an event here. They did a lobster boil for a bunch of board members, and I helped in the kitchen. We got to drive the truck right through the guard gate and park in a back lot."

CeCe knew about catering. Her parents had lots of parties. Chefs and servers came to their house in Malibu with pizza trucks, or taco trucks, or New England–style clambakes with chowder, or steaks for the grill, or fancy dinners with French dishes that reminded her father of home in Bordeaux. And on film sets, they had craft services, where the caterers would set up snacks and drinks under a tent, including bowls of candy, and the young actors her father worked with called it "crafty."

Ronnie rolled down his window and spoke to a guard. The guard looked as if he didn't believe him, but then Ronnie pointed at the lobster embroidered on the patch on his grimy jacket.

"Ever been to the Binnacle?" Ronnie asked.

"Who in Rhode Island hasn't?" the guard asked.

"Well, we supply them with lobsters, and I'm meeting them here for a party."

"I don't have anything on my list about a party," the guard said.

"Christmas party," Ronnie said. "Probably too many to keep track of. Let us in so I can talk to the manager, okay?"

"Dude, you're driving a pickup truck, and I can see you got no lobsters back there."

"I'm helping with the setup," Ronnie said.

The guard gave Ronnie a look, as if he knew he was being lied to, but he wrote down the truck's license plate number and waved them through the gate.

Ronnie laughed like crazy, pounding the steering wheel with his hands.

"Yeah!" he said. "Score! He didn't even ask me for ID."

He seemed to know where he was going and drove around the outside of the zoo buildings. He found the kitchen area, where there were a few parked vans, including one with a lion painted on the side.

He was right about the snowy day. It was dark enough that Christmas lights on the trees and on the rooftops of the buildings were glowing. They didn't really look like stars to CeCe, not as much as she had wanted them to. But she had stopped crying, except for some lingering hiccups, and she still had hopes of petting a goat.

She watched Ronnie open the glove compartment and put the gun inside. Then he locked it.

He looked at her, long and hard.

"Come on," he said to her after a minute. "Let's go see some animals."

She nodded and together they walked into the zoo.

37

After the locksmith arrived and changed the locks and codes, Hadley dialed the number she had for Genevieve. It went straight to voice mail. She felt as if her sister had become a mystery to her in death, and she wanted to talk to Genevieve—as calmly as possible, even though she felt like screaming—and find out what that receipt stapled into Maddie's Moleskine notebook meant:

$1,000,000 to Genevieve Dickinson, plus past royalties

Public apology

Renunciation of credit—the idea was Genevieve's

"Did Maddie even write this?" Kate asked as they drove back to the Ocean House from the storage property.

"It was stapled right onto the page. She kept those notebooks private," Hadley said.

"The receipt was typed. Nothing in her own handwriting. Doesn't that seem suspicious?" Kate asked.

"Yes, totally," Hadley said. "But if she didn't write it, how did it wind up there?"

"Maybe there's something about the agreement in her journals," Kate said.

"I don't want to read them," Hadley said. "They're Maddie's— they're private—but you're right. I need to know about this claim. I just can't believe it, though . . ."

"I feel the same," Kate said. "The whale and swan are so indelibly hers. If the work really is Genevieve's, the news will shake the world."

"Kate, I've believed Maddie all along and still do. I was there when she saw the actual whale, the swan, the moonlight. There's no question that she did the painting—Genevieve had nothing to do with that. So what does this receipt mean?"

"Maddie's talent isn't in question," Kate said. "I can't stop thinking about that painting. *Last Night*. I've never seen anything like it. It reminds me a little of Rousseau's famous work, *The Sleeping Gypsy*. A sense of repose, and magic, and moonlight and danger. It's extraordinary."

"It is," Hadley said. "It has the same power as the original of *The Whale and the Swan*—a myth, done in oil on linen."

"Predictive, though," Kate said. "Insanely so. She foresaw what was going to happen to her, the way her life ended. The rose is her blood. I just can't get over that."

"The two paintings seem cursed," Hadley said. "The whale painting caused years of lawsuits, and now this cryptic receipt. And *Last Night*— you're right, it predicted her death, whether she had a premonition or whether someone saw it and set her up."

"What if it's Genevieve?" Kate asked.

"Behind Maddie's murder?"

"She had a lot to gain," Kate said. "What if she typed that receipt herself? If she went to the storage unit with Maddie, she could have stuck it into the notebook when Maddie's back was turned."

"Why would Maddie have invited her there? It was obviously a sanctuary for her—she never even took me."

"Not that we should believe Genevieve, but that message she left you made it sound as if she and Maddie had had some sort of rapprochement. Maybe Maddie wanted to make peace with her, show her works in progress."

"How would murdering my sister help Genevieve in any way?" Hadley asked.

"The receipt," Kate said.

"But Maddie didn't sign it. It's not an agreement, a legal document," Hadley said.

"If Genevieve planted it, she might have planted other things as well. You'll have to go through everything to see what's there. She might be setting herself up to make a claim for the million dollars and the credit on the whale painting."

"She will never get credit for that," Hadley said, fury rising inside her.

Kate nodded. "I know, Hadley. That work came from Maddie's soul. Her heart. There are head paintings and soul paintings. An external idea is one thing, but when the subject matter comes from deep inside, it's the artist's experience. It's as if they've swallowed it whole; it inhabits them. And it comes out of their fingertips, through the brush, onto the canvas. That is Maddie's way. Without ever having met her, I know from studying her work."

Hadley felt the same way. She could barely breathe. What if Kate was right and Genevieve had come to Rhode Island not to make peace with Maddie but to kill her? Hadley redialed Genevieve, and again the call went straight to her voice mail.

When Hadley and Kate arrived at the Ocean House, Hadley thanked Kate, then left her in the lobby because she just wanted to be alone.

No, that wasn't true: she wanted her sister. She wanted to talk to Maddie, ask her about being pregnant, share her excitement. She wanted to trash Genevieve, badmouth her for trying to con Maddie out of her reputation and a million dollars. And she wanted to sit by the fire, read a book to CeCe, feel the everyday coziness of snuggling up with her sister and niece.

Rounding the corner on her way to the elevator, she spotted a man and a woman conversing at the end of the corridor. It was Bernard talking to Isabel. Isabel held a navy-blue folder and was showing him the contents. Bernard was frowning, shaking his head, and raising his voice in French.

"Bernard!" Hadley called, heading toward them. "Where have you been?"

"Hadley, they are claiming I've not paid my bill! Merde, it is a lie."

"Mr. Lafond, I don't want to embarrass you," Isabel said.

"Worse than embarrassing me," he said, "is calling me a liar. I told you—I paid by company check, in advance, the day I arrived. I want to speak to your manager!"

"We can discuss this in private," Isabel said, backing away. "I'll leave you to talk to your sister-in-law."

"There's nothing to discuss!" Bernard snapped. "Rude allegations!"

Hadley stared at him. He looked as if he hadn't slept or taken a shower in days. His eyes were wild, his skin sagged, and his white hair was dark with grease. His shirt and trousers were rumpled, looking very unlike his usual fastidious wardrobe.

"I haven't even been staying here," Bernard said, raking a hand through his long hair.

"It shows, Bernard. You look as if you've been sleeping in your car," Hadley said.

"How can I stand to be in this hotel, where my love spent her last night?" he asked.

The words were jarring. *Last Night.*

"Do you know about Maddie's last painting?" Hadley asked.

"Her what? I am not thinking about paintings, Hadley. I am thinking about Maddie leaving this hotel to walk through the snow to her death. And to lose our daughter to a monster—I can't bear it. I'll never get either one of them back," Bernard said.

"CeCe's coming back," Hadley said. "We have to believe that."

"The news is all about her. I can't escape. The highway, the little roads—they all have billboards with my baby's face on them," Bernard said.

"That's part of how the FBI plans to get her back. Someone will see her picture, and then they'll see her. Someone knows something, Bernard."

"I want to leave this state and never return," he said. "But I can't—I need to be in Rhode Island until we know for sure about Cecelia. Until they find her. Have you learned anything at all?"

"Something strange has come up," Hadley said. "I don't know what it means, but it seems related. It has to do with a recent painting Maddie did—the one I was asking you about—and with Genevieve Dickinson."

"That bloodsucker?"

"Yes," Hadley said, unable to disagree with his description.

"What about her?"

"Has she tried to contact you?" Hadley asked.

He frowned. "Of course not. Why would she?"

"Did Maddie ever say anything to you about giving Genevieve credit for *The Whale and the Swan*?"

He snorted. "I hope you're kidding. Putain. An art whore trying to get what was never hers."

Hadley nodded. She agreed with what he was saying, but he looked crazy, his expression wild. A couple was coming down the hall toward them. They clearly recognized Bernard but averted their eyes to give him privacy. This was the kind of hotel where guests didn't bother, much less fawn over, famous people.

"Hadley," he said after the strangers disappeared around the corner, "I hate to ask you this, but can I borrow some money?"

"Sure," she said, assuming he meant a little cash till he could get to the ATM.

"That receptionist, she may have been correct. It is possible my check had a small problem."

"You mean you don't have the funds in your bank?"

"You make it sound so ugly," he said. "I paid the first part of my stay, no problem. It's this week and going forward that will be difficult. A simple cash-flow glitch, my agent is working on it. Another issue: I am unhappy with the cops. I tried to hire Conor Reid, but he wouldn't help me."

"He's a cop, too, Bernard," Hadley said.

"Well, nobody is doing anything. I told him I wanted to find a private investigator, the best there is, to locate my daughter!" he said and took a step toward her. "Don't you care?"

"Of course I care! How can you ask me that?"

"Then prove it! What else is money for? If you have it, you should help me hire a detective! I am family; your sister was my wife. She would want us to work together, to do everything we can to find CeCe!" Bernard said. His face, inches from hers, was bright red, the cords on his neck standing out.

Hadley heard his desperation, and she felt it herself. But he seemed unhinged, and his air of violence scared her. Was this the Bernard her sister had seen every time he got angry with her?

He seemed to see the fear in her eyes, and the monster retreated. Suddenly he seemed deflated. His shoulders slumped, and he wiped sweat off his face with his shirt sleeve. "It's not your fault," he said.

"What's not my fault?" she asked.

"The fact she's still missing. And no one is finding her," he said. "Look, I'm not feeling well. Will you help me pay my bill here or won't you? I am sure Madeleine would have."

"Bernard," she said, "first of all, the only reason I am staying here is that Maddie owns the suite—I could never afford it myself."

"Surely you could add my room to her account. She would want me to be nearby, for our daughter."

"Second of all," Hadley said, as if she hadn't heard him, "Maddie was divorcing you. She wouldn't have bailed you out. You've been lying to me about why you're here. It wasn't to scout locations. It was to be near my sister, to spy on her. You said horrible things on the phone to CeCe. You scared her . . ."

"You're just like Madeleine. The high-and-mighty Cooke sisters. No wonder you don't have a man—you don't even have a heart," he said, his eyes blazing with white rage. He raised his arm as if to strike her, then he abruptly turned and stalked away, toward the lobby.

Hadley was shaking. His fury had exploded, diminished, then returned again, and it was terrifying. Maddie had been right about him. He could never take criticism or listen to anything but gushing praise. She had spoken to Hadley about his anger issues, but without seeing them herself till now, Hadley had had no idea what her sister must have faced.

She wondered if Maddie had encountered that rage on the beach path, in the middle of the blizzard, with their daughter watching him shoot her in the head.

38

Conor got the call.

The body of an unidentified female had been discovered behind a pile of road sand and salt at the Stonington Park & Ride. None of the vehicles there seemed to be hers. She was wearing a gold ring on the index finger of her left hand. A fine gold chain with a blue-enameled gold pendant had most likely been around her neck, but the chain had broken and was found in the folds of her jacket.

She was five foot eight, 150 pounds, with short dark hair and brown eyes. The medical examiner estimated her to be in her midthirties. She was wearing dark-red nail polish. Her right forearm was slashed almost to the bone through the sleeve of her white wool coat. Several of her fingernails were broken, indicating defensive wounds.

The cause of death was determined to be homicide. The method of death was asphyxia by strangulation and stabbing. She had been stabbed twenty-eight times. There was no identification or cell phone on or near the body.

Stonington was just over the border in Connecticut. This was Conor's territory. Amanda Birkhall, another detective on the Major Crime Squad, had caught the case, and at first she assured him that she had it handled. He had taken two weeks off, expecting to propose to Kate and spend the rest of their vacation celebrating, and Amanda didn't want him to cut that short. But a development changed all that. Amanda filled Conor in, emailing him images, and he called Joe.

"The Park & Ride murder victim had an old photograph in her coat pocket," Conor told him. "It's obviously of Maddie, from a long time ago. I'm guessing she was in her late teens."

"Okay, that's interesting," Joe said. "I'm glad to have an insider. We work together on this, right? With those photos, it's clearly connected to my case."

"I'd say so," Conor said. "Two dead women, the unidentified victim with Maddie's picture in her pocket."

"So tell me what you know," Joe said.

"A van driver pulled off I-95 and stopped in the parking lot to take a leak. When he went behind the sandpile, he found the body. He called 911, and Vicky Nisbit, one of our troopers, caught the call. She asked for a supervisor, and Amanda, my colleague, was dispatched."

"And Amanda called you," Joe said.

"Yeah. She knows I've been working with you, and as soon as she realized that it was Maddie in the picture, she got in touch. It took time because Maddie was so young in the picture that she looked different from her press photos. By then, the scene had already been processed."

"And no identification on the body?" Joe asked.

"No," Conor said.

"How about in her vehicle?"

"None of the vehicles in the lot were hers," Conor said.

"She could have been in someone else's car. They could have parked, and he could have attacked her there," Joe said. "But are you sure that was the murder site?"

"We're thinking it wasn't," Conor said. "She had twenty-eight stab wounds, zero blood at the scene. She was killed and bled out somewhere else."

"She knew him," Joe said, obviously making the same assumption Conor had, based on the number of times she'd been stabbed.

"Yep, and he drove her body to the parking lot and dumped her behind the sandpile. He probably brought a shovel or another tool to cause a little avalanche to bury her. He thought she wouldn't be found till spring."

"And then someone had to relieve himself and spoiled that plan," Joe said.

"Here's another thing," Conor said. "She was wearing a necklace—gold with blue enamel." He started scrolling through his phone, looking for the photos Amanda had sent him.

"What about the necklace?" Joe asked.

"Blue background and an engraved design, with color filling in the etching. Recognize it?" Conor asked.

"Huh," Joe said. "That famous painting by Maddie—MC. The one you see everywhere. My daughter has a poster of it in her dorm room. The whale and the swan."

"The thing about the photo," Conor said, "is that it had an address written on the back. Amanda checked it out, and it's a fine-art storage facility. You know where Kate and Hadley were yesterday?"

"The place Maddie stores her artwork. Same address?" Joe asked.

"Yes," Conor said. "I think we'd better find out if Genevieve Dickinson is five foot nine and has short brown hair. She was supposedly on her way here, but she hasn't shown up."

"Her name has come up repeatedly, and I know she and Maddie were involved in a long lawsuit," Joe said. "But it was settled."

"I should have given you this right away, but Hadley only showed it to me last night," Conor said. He scrolled to a photo of the receipt found in Maddie's storage unit.

"Okay, this is bizarre," Joe said, reading it. "Maddie is acknowledging that Genevieve has rights to the whale-and-swan business? Where is the actual document?"

"Hadley has it."

"I'll get it from her," Joe said.

"And I'll work on getting Genevieve Dickinson's description," Conor said.

39

Ronnie found some food for them to eat, but CeCe was past being hungry. He knew where the snack bar was, and he grabbed some half-eaten pizza and french fries off a table. He gobbled it down, but CeCe didn't care about food. She was floating above her body, and all she wanted was to see animals and pet them, put her arms around their necks, feel their warm fur.

"This is crazy," he said as they walked through a crowd.

"What?"

"People are supposed to be recognizing you," he said.

"They don't know me," she said.

"You're famous because of me," he said.

CeCe looked at him as if he had no idea what he was talking about. Her papa was famous, and so were some of his friends. Her mommy was famous because of her art. They kept CeCe hidden from photographers to protect her.

"It's true," he said. "You're on the news. Your picture is all over the place."

She didn't believe him.

"It's brave of me to be doing this, you know. I'm a fugitive. I could be shot on sight. So why do you think I brought you here?" he asked.

"To see the lights," she said.

"Uh-uh," he said. "To get you rescued. Why aren't you screaming for help?"

CeCe didn't know. She had wanted to shout and yell at the beginning, and she had made so much noise when she was in the wooden box at Ronnie's house. But none of that had worked; no one had come to help her. Her head hurt from being banged, and she had broken her tooth. Her tongue was cut and swollen from the sharp edge. Mommy was gone. Star was gone. The only thing that seemed to matter now was petting baby goats.

"Scream, CeCe," he said.

When she was little, a year ago, she'd had pain in her tummy. It hadn't gone away, so her mommy had taken her to Dr. Maguire. She didn't like to go to the doctor, especially that time, because he pushed on the sore spot, and it got worse. They had rushed her to the hospital, where the doctors did an operation on her hernia.

Before the operation, they'd given her medicine that made her feel as if she were in a dream, not alive, a ghost, like when her kitty, Tim, had gotten sick and the vet had come to put him to sleep. She'd been so sad that she'd thought she would die with him. CeCe felt that way now, in the zoo, everything in her body and mind feeling numb, as if she were dead. Ronnie told her to scream, but she didn't want to. She just wanted animals.

"You're not gonna do it?" he asked. "I could push you down, and you'd make noise then. But fuck it." She watched him look around. There were people coming and going, walking right past them, not paying any attention. Now he stopped looking at the strangers and bent down to look into CeCe's eyes.

"I'm sorry for what I did," he said.

She stared back at him. Maybe she was dead, and maybe he was, too. Like Mommy and Tim.

"I shouldn't have done it," he said. "It was a mistake. I mean, I knew what I was doing, I can't say I didn't. But it was all in my head, like a TV show, until I got there. I liked holding the gun. I liked that my dad had taught me how to shoot and said we were a team, we were partners. He said I was gonna help save the boats and the fleet, that we'd have money."

"I need animals," CeCe whispered. She didn't want to hear this.

"I wish I knew her name," Ronnie said. Suddenly he started to cry.

"Madeleine," CeCe said. "That's my mommy's name."

"Not your mommy," Ronnie said. "I mean the lady who paid us to kill her. I would tell the police if I knew."

He began walking away. Her mind buzzed with the word *kill*. She should have been glad to see him go, but she was scared to be left alone. She hurried to keep up. He walked over to a family—parents and two girls older than CeCe.

"Hey," he said to the mother. "See this girl? Know who she is?"

"Oh my God," the mother said, putting her hand over her mouth.

"It's Cecelia!" one of the girls said. "She's alive!"

"Call 911, Don," the mother said. She knelt down, stared into CeCe's eyes. "Sweetheart, we're getting help right now."

The father was dialing on his cell phone, talking into it, but then Ronnie pointed.

"Security guard," he said to CeCe. "He can handle it."

Ronnie walked over to a man wearing a uniform. He pointed at CeCe, and the security guard spoke into a walkie-talkie. Everything happened very fast after that. Another guard came. He pushed Ronnie up against the wall. He had handcuffs, and he put them on Ronnie. CeCe watched as if it were a movie. But then Ronnie turned to look at her, and because he was still crying, she began to cry, too.

Then the police came and took Ronnie away, and CeCe sat down on the floor. A crowd of people circled around, and she heard them talking and saying her name. She drew her knees up to her chin, put her arms around her legs, made herself as small as possible. A policeman knelt down beside her.

"You're safe, CeCe," he said. "We're going to take care of you."

"I just want to see the baby goats," she said. "I need them."

But then the policeman picked her up, and all the officers surrounded them as he carried her out into the snow and into a police car. She wasn't arrested, but the sirens were loud, and the flashing white-blue lights hurt her eyes as they drove away.

40

Toward the end of the day, the snow stopped. Tom drove to Duffy's Marina, where the *Anna G* had been towed and hauled. She had pretty lines, like the many forty-five-foot Novi lobster boats in the Port of Galilee, but it was clear she needed a lot of work. Not just because of the substantial damage done when she had gone aground during the blizzard, but because she hadn't been well maintained for a while now.

The Novi was up on jack stands, and Tom could see how galvanic corrosion had gotten to the hull. Not only that, but the bottom, rudder, and propeller were covered with layers of algae, barnacles, and seaweed. The paint was peeling, the windows cloudy. Ice from the storm had broken the mast, knocked the radar askew, and stoved in the port rail.

Not that long ago, Zane had been a proud and responsible lobster fisherman and, thus, boat owner. Every July, for years, the Garsons had taken part in the annual Blessing of the Fleet. Point Judith lobster boats and trawlers, Coast Guard vessels, the Block Island ferries, pleasure yachts, runabouts, and all kinds of watercrafts would pass through the Galilee Breachway to receive a benediction from a local priest.

Zane would always have the *Anna G* in perfect condition. When his wife was still alive, she would be on the deck of her namesake vessel, wearing a straw hat and her best summer dress; young Ronnie would stand at the rail, beaming and waving an American flag at the crowd of spectators cheering from Salty Brine State Beach.

The Blessing of the Fleet in Point Judith had been going on for over fifty years, but it came from a centuries-old tradition that had begun in Europe. The priest would make the sign of the cross and say a prayer as each boat passed. It was a solemn occasion. At noon, the lead fishing boat, sometimes the *Anna G*, would drop wreaths in memory of fishermen who had died at sea.

But it was also a joyful day. Families would decorate the boats, and prizes would be given for the top three, as chosen by the judges. Some boat owners would go all out, choosing a theme like *Jaws*, or *Finding Nemo*, or even Harry Potter. Zane hadn't allowed his wife and son to do anything that cute. He considered fishing a serious business, and he didn't want to trivialize that. But he let them hang red-white-and-blue bunting and flags, and to sound the air horn when passing the beach.

Tom wondered when everything had changed for Zane. He'd gone from being a friendly guy, a pillar of the Point Judith fishing community, to being moody and reclusive. Grub was a different story. He had always been nasty—getting into bar fights, leading the charge on the buoy-cutting incidents.

He'd been suspected of, but never apprehended for, smuggling marijuana. When he was young, he bought into the Coyote Den in New Bedford, a "gentlemen's club" that was later raided for prostitution. Grub sold out just before his business partner was arrested for tax evasion and money laundering. Tom still wasn't sure how Grub had managed to avoid being indicted, too.

So Tom wasn't completely shocked that Grub would be involved in what was looking like murder for hire. But Zane? He hadn't seen that coming, not by a long shot. When he thought about Zane's downward spiral, he honestly believed it had begun when Anna died. She had loved Zane and kept him on track, steered him away from Grub's influence.

He wasn't perfect, but with Anna he was okay. A decent enough husband and father, a good fisherman and boss.

Those days were over.

Zane had been taken into custody; there was a manhunt for Grub and Ronnie. Tom determined that he needed to inspect the damaged fishing vessel. So he climbed the ladder and stepped onto the deck. Here he saw the blizzard's destruction up close. The sheet ice had cracked fiberglass, destroyed the portside winch supports, tangled stainless-steel stanchions and stays.

The cabin door had splintered in the storm. Tom stepped inside, felt the cold breath of damp and freezing December air. He glanced around, looking for any sign that the hull was compromised. But his attention was immediately grabbed by a design modification that he had never seen in any fishing boat before.

The cabin's table and settees had been removed, and shelves—or racks—had been installed. They were crudely made out of unvarnished pine, as if they were temporary installations. Tom took a closer look. There was a large frame, about the length and width of a twin bed, with boards set up vertically, six inches apart, like dividers in an oversize file cabinet.

He had been wondering why Zane went out in that storm. The lobsterman had been heading toward Watch Hill, where Maddie had been shot—most likely by his son. But what purpose would the boat have served? Presumably, Ronnie had a vehicle and wouldn't have needed transportation on a lobster boat in treacherous seas. Had the plan been to pick up cargo? Were these racks intended to hold drugs? Or, if Zane was working with Grub, were they supposed to imprison people? CeCe? The thought was horrific.

Tom took some photos of the structure from different angles and texted them to Conor with the message What do these look like?

Art storage racks, Conor texted back. Kate has them at the gallery. Where are you?

Now that Conor had put the idea in Tom's head, he saw it perfectly. That's exactly what they were. But for what art? Maddie's, he assumed, but there had been no paintings found at the Ocean House and certainly not on the beach path. He felt there was still a missing step: If Zane had been taking the *Anna G* to Watch Hill to pick up art, who was supposed to deliver it to him?

His phone buzzed. It was Conor.

"Hey," Tom said. "Thanks for the info—I think you're right. Zane was planning to transport paintings. I'm on his boat, and . . ."

"Have you checked your news app?" Conor asked, interrupting him.

"No, why?" Tom asked. "Did you identify the body at the Park & Ride?"

"It's about CeCe," Conor said. "Tom, she's been found."

Tom let the words sink in. He felt choked up; he heard it in his brother's voice, too.

"Come to the hotel," Conor said. "The police are bringing her here now."

"On my way," Tom said.

41

Hadley stood outside, in front of the Ocean House, waiting. Joe Harrigan had called her right away, told her that they would be there in twenty minutes. He had phoned and texted Bernard, too, but Bernard hadn't responded.

She wore her parka. The wind was bitter and blew up the hill, off the harbor on one side and the ocean on the other, but she didn't feel it. She faced north, in the direction the police car would come. She listened as hard as she could, wondering if they would speed up with sirens going. She felt they should. To announce this moment, to commemorate it, to clear the way of slow traffic so they could get here faster.

Her arms ached because of who she hadn't been able to hold. She tensed them now, hugging the air. She stared at the hotel's grand portico, the white columns and graceful porch railings, the holiday greenery and red ribbons, the little white lights starting to come on as darkness fell. She looked at the shingled houses where Bluff Avenue met Plimpton Road and curved northward into Westerly Road. Her gaze ranged back and forth from one road to the other, knowing that any minute she would see the car.

She strained to hear, was distracted by the howl of the wind, so much so that she almost missed it: the dark-blue car coming fast and silently, headlights on, no flashing strobes, no sirens. She walked straight into the road, pulled to it like a magnet, before realizing she was in its way. She stepped aside, then ran alongside it until it pulled into the Ocean House's circular drive.

Dermot, the bellman, stood ready. The front desk staff had stepped outside and were ranged in a half circle at the top of the stairs. Hadley didn't see any of them. She was lost in this moment, with the darkening sky and the tiny white lights and the car stopping, its brake lights glowing red and CeCe inside.

Joe Harrigan got out of the driver's seat. A policewoman Hadley didn't recognize opened the back door and climbed out. She held the door open, and the little girl slid across the seat. The policewoman held out her hand to help CeCe out of the car, but it was as if she wasn't even there.

CeCe just launched herself out of the back seat as if she could fly, straight into Hadley's arms. Hadley lifted her up, held her and rocked her, whispered her name over and over.

"Aunt Hadley," CeCe said, her breath warm against Hadley's ear.

"It's me," Hadley said. "And you're here."

"The yellow hotel," CeCe said. "I've been trying to get back here for so long, for days and days and nights. I don't know how many."

"Too many," Hadley said. She reached into her pocket, pressed the little piece of flannel into CeCe's hand.

"Oh, Star," CeCe whispered, holding it to her cheek. She tilted her head back, just enough to look up toward the porch and front door, at the greenery, the garlands, the wreaths, the Christmas lights.

"Millions of lights," CeCe said.

"Yes," Hadley said.

"Can we go to our room?" CeCe asked, clutching Star.

Hadley nodded. She put CeCe down. CeCe took her hand, and together they walked up the stairs. The hotel staff surrounded them, but at first no one said a word. They just stepped aside so Hadley and

CeCe could walk through. The silence felt holy. But then they began to clap and cheer.

When CeCe saw Isabel, she stopped to give her a long look. "Mommy's friend," CeCe said.

"I'm your friend, too," Isabel said. "I'm so glad you're home." Then she leaned down to kiss the top of CeCe's head.

Hadley felt CeCe tug her hand, and they kept going—through the lobby, past the Christmas trees decorated with lights and starfish, to the elevator. CeCe pushed the button. When they got to their floor, she ran ahead of Hadley to the suite's door, danced in place while Hadley pulled out the key card and touched it to the sensor.

CeCe shoved the door open and burst inside. She tore down the short corridor into the living room, then into all the bedrooms, calling at the top of her lungs: "Mommy, Mommy! Where are you? I'm home! Mommy, I'm home!"

42

Conor had come to realize that crime created unlikely, even impossible, families. There were the victims' blood relatives, of course, but the dead also acquired another branch of the family tree: the investigators, the people who came to know them without ever having met them, and to care about their lives, their deaths, their hopes and dreams that would never come true. Conor felt that way about all the victims whose murders he had investigated.

When he and Kate had knelt beside Maddie's body, they had signed on. Her death had made him care about the life of Madeleine Cooke Morrison and her daughter, Cecelia, just as if they were members of his own family. He saw CeCe as Maddie's greatest hope personified, and he knew he would do everything he could to care for and nurture all the dreams CeCe would have that Maddie no longer could.

The morning after CeCe came back, he and Kate sat in the suite with her and Hadley. Since CeCe had returned last night, she was inseparable from her aunt. She clung to Hadley, not letting go for a moment. When Conor and Kate stopped in to see her after breakfast, he heard her slip up and call Hadley Mommy twice before correcting herself and saying "Aunt Hadley."

Conor knew it was a trauma reaction. Victims of violent crime internalized and expressed their experiences in different ways. Some remembered the entire thing, every sense on high alert. Others blocked out what they had gone through, unable to bring up any aspect of it. He suspected that CeCe's loss of her mother was too horrible to accept, and that Hadley's resemblance to Maddie comforted her and allowed her to have moments of respite.

Through it all, Bernard was missing in action. Hadley had told Conor that her brother-in-law had been out of control, his anger so frightening that she was actually glad he hadn't come back. Law enforcement was looking for him—and not because he had disappeared without paying his hotel bill. He was still high on the list of suspects who might have hired Ronnie to kill Maddie.

Kate stayed with Hadley and CeCe while Conor walked to the beach path to think about the case. Joe met him there and told him that Zane wasn't saying anything, but Ronnie had said he was a hired killer and immediately confessed to shooting Maddie.

"Why did Ronnie do it?" Conor asked.

"His father told him to."

"Isn't that taking being an obedient son a little too far?"

"His father told him it would make him proud. He said they were going to get rich, that Ronnie would get all the credit for that. They'd have a decent house. They could fix up the boat, the dock. They could pay their crew. He said Grub would be proud of Ronnie, too. Ronnie thought he'd be the family hero."

"Where was the money coming from?"

"That, Ronnie didn't know," Joe said. "He said some lady was paying it."

"Ronnie didn't know the lady?" Conor asked.

"That part is unclear, even to Ronnie. He said his father told him she was 'a friend' and that she and Grub had made the deal. But Zane never told Ronnie her name."

"How much money?"

"Ronnie says he doesn't know, just that it's 'a lot,'" Joe said. "I can't decide what makes more sense. That the person who paid for Maddie to be murdered was a Garson friend or acquaintance, or whether she was a semi-stranger who zeroed in on the Garsons because of their reputations. Anyone local would know that they're not exactly the most law-abiding folks around."

"I think the first scenario is more likely," Conor said. "That whoever set this up knew exactly who she was dealing with."

"So someone from the Garsons' inner circle," Joe said.

"Yes. Have you gone back to Elise?"

"Yeah," Joe said. "She still claims to know nothing—can't even help us find Grub."

"She sounded pretty done with him," Conor said.

"Someone called to warn him, though," Joe said. "He left the Magellan Club fast, disappeared after he got the call. My money is on her."

Conor nodded. Love and denial in the world of murder. "Does this mean Lafond is off the list?"

"Of course not—he could have used a woman as a go-between. We're still curious about Genevieve and her relationship with him. Any word on the parking lot victim's dental records?" Joe asked.

"Not yet," Conor said. "Waiting to hear."

"Okay. Anyway, Lafond's not using his credit cards. We pinged his phone, and nothing. It's off. Either he lost it or ditched it. Or someone got to him, and he's a victim, too. LAPD is sending a detective to question his assistant—not just to find out what she knows about his whereabouts but also because she's a woman. Maybe she did the hiring."

"That's good," Conor said. "What about the Garsons' crowd? What other women are there besides Elise?"

"Endless possibilities," Joe said. "There is a big network of extended family and friends—the Garsons' lobster fleet at the center, spreading out to the Binnacle, and who knows from there. But who would want

Maddie killed and would benefit from her death? Who would even know her?"

"Worlds collide," Conor said. Murder never made sense. But in some cases, connections seemed logical, at least in retrospect, and the intersection between the victim and the killer was easy to trace. Then there were other cases in which everything seemed random, and previous meetings didn't exist.

"Could this whole thing have snowballed since she and CeCe moved to Watch Hill?" Joe asked. "She pissed off the wrong person? Is this about the pregnancy?"

"I think it's about her art," Conor said. Given what Tom had discovered on Zane Garson's boat, Conor believed that they held the key to her murder.

"Why kill her? Why not just rob the storage unit?" Joe asked.

Conor didn't have the answer. He had looked at the photos Kate had taken of Maddie's painting *Last Night*. Now, standing on the beach path on a sunny morning, it was still possible to conjure up a vision of Maddie in the blizzard. Kate had been right—the painting had been predictive. It was as if Maddie had dreamed her own death, right down to the bloom of red, the gush of her lifeblood.

A phone buzzed. They both checked their devices, but it was a message for Conor.

"Wow," he said, staring at his screen.

"What?" Joe asked.

"It's from my office. They just got an ID on our Park & Ride victim."

"Genevieve Dickinson?" Joe asked.

"No, Donna Almeida. The paralegal who worked with Maddie's lawyer," Conor said.

43

When Conor spoke with Hadley about Donna, she told him that
Johnny sounded wild with grief and rage. She said she felt it over the
phone when she called him. She wanted to drive straight to Providence
to help him through the shock of losing Donna, but she couldn't bear
to leave her niece. CeCe wouldn't let her out of her sight.

Conor and Kate waited in the Sea Garden suite's living room until
CeCe finally drifted off to sleep in the bedroom. Hadley joined them,
and they talked quietly, so as not to disturb CeCe.

"Will you go up to Providence?" Hadley asked Conor. "Johnny
shouldn't be alone, and even though you two don't know each other,
you're so invested in the case. I know he'll be grateful to talk to you. The
murders have to be related, don't you think?"

"It seems as if Maddie is the connection," Conor said, "considering
Donna worked on her estate." He didn't add that of course he would be
going to see Johnny, and not as a family friend.

"And she was seeing Maddie's ex-husband," Kate said.

"I haven't said anything about this," Hadley said. "But that day
in the storage unit, Donna was watching me when I opened Maddie's
desk. I almost felt like she knew I was going to find that receipt from
Genevieve. Kate, she told us she'd never been there before, but what if
she had?"

"She could have planted it," Kate said.

"That occurred to me," Hadley said.

"Everything about that receipt feels fake," Kate said. "It's printed, not handwritten, no signature. If I didn't know from experience that Donna's law firm has engaged in shady business practices, I wouldn't be so suspicious."

"Stealing valuables from a client's house or failing to include them in the inventory the way they did with your artist is bad," Conor said. "But it's a leap from that to forging a document assigning a seven-figure amount to be paid to Genevieve Dickinson. Is your theory that Donna—or others at the law firm—and Genevieve are working together?"

"Why not?" Kate asked. "Makes sense to me."

"How would they have connected? How would Maddie's lawyers have known to get in touch with someone out of her past?" Hadley asked.

"Because of the lawsuit," Kate said. "When the law firm took on Maddie as a client, they would have investigated her whole financial profile, as well as past legal actions. If they were inclined to steal from Maddie, what better way than to require her estate to pay out a million dollars? Besides, didn't Donna act surprised when you said Genevieve had reached out to you? She had heard about her."

Hadley nodded. "That's right, she did."

"If Maddie were still alive," Conor said, "she would figure it all out—she'd know they forged a document."

"So she had to be killed," Kate said. "The thing is, how did they rope Ronnie into it? How did they even get to him?"

Obviously through his father, Conor thought. But what was Donna's connection to Zane? To the Garsons? He pictured Zane's boat, tricked out with shelves to hold artwork. Was the plan that part of the payment would be made in Maddie's artwork?

"Hadley," Conor said, "when you went through Maddie's storage space, were there any missing paintings?"

"I have no idea," she said. "I don't know what was there before."

Conor wondered if Donna could have stolen works before she opened the unit to Hadley and Kate. Because who would miss them? Even if there was an inventory list, Donna could have destroyed it. Zane might have already received paintings as partial payment for killing Maddie.

"Oh my God," Hadley said. "You asked about how they got to Ronnie. That night at my studio, when I first met Donna, she told me her family owns the Binnacle."

"Where Zane and Grub sell their lobsters and hang out," Conor said, the connection falling into place. "And where Grub's girlfriend works. Donna obviously knows the Garsons—she's related to Elise."

"Even if that is the case, how did they approach Genevieve?" Hadley asked. "It seems crazy that they would suggest to a total stranger that they become partners in stealing from Maddie Morrison."

"What if Genevieve went to them?" Kate asked.

"How would she know they represented Maddie?" Hadley asked.

"Because she's obsessed with Maddie," Kate said. "Remember how Bernard said she showed up to work on his film set? She engineered that—to be near Maddie, to torment her. Maybe she's gotten good at hacking, or maybe she has other ways . . ."

As a cop, Conor had access to databases that provided details about a person's private banking, legal dealings, employment information. Certain versions were available to the general public. It just took money; anyone could subscribe to the services, including Genevieve.

"Why was she coming here?" Hadley asked. "If she was involved, I'd think she would want to stay as far away as possible. To keep from being suspected. Why would she call me?"

"Because of her obsession," Kate said. "She wouldn't have been able to stop herself from being close to the action surrounding Maddie's death."

Conor watched the reality hit Hadley. She closed her eyes, and he thought he saw her shiver. He didn't blame her. Obsession could be deadly. He had seen it in cases before, including in the murder of Kate's sister.

"Genevieve didn't just want to take everything from Maddie in that lawsuit," Hadley said. "She wanted to *be* Maddie."

"I think we should go look at *Last Night* again," Kate said. "Maddie's last painting."

"Why?" Hadley asked, but Kate didn't answer. She had a thoughtful, faraway look in her eyes.

"Something else," Conor said. "We know that Maddie's safe-deposit box is at the BSNE office in Hartford, and I'm pretty sure Joe's gotten a court order to have it opened by now. He's got the key. We should find out what was in there. I'll check with him. Maybe there's something that will help with all this."

"Thanks," Hadley said. Conor watched her turn away and knew how overwhelmed she must be.

He left the Ocean House to head up to Providence. Hadley had given him the addresses for both Johnny's home and the warehouse where she and he shared a studio. Conor found him at the studio. The freight elevator creaked its way upstairs, and when Conor stepped into the vast space, he was greeted by Johnny. Conor introduced himself as a Connecticut State Police detective who was investigating Donna's death.

"Hadley told me you were coming," Johnny said. "I just can't believe this. Donna's dead. She's the nicest, best, most caring person. No enemies, just people who love her."

"When did you last see her?" Conor asked.

"Last week," Johnny said.

"And the last time you talked?"

"A few days ago."

"Was that unusual?" Conor asked. "To go days without talking?"

"No," Johnny said. "She lived in West Hartford, Connecticut, a town away from her office. I've been working on a project that's taking all my time. Hadley and I have a commission to do a large mural in Charleston, and she's just not available—for good reason."

"She has a lot going on," Conor said.

"I know. I've been sleeping here, up almost every night, trying to hit the deadline. Donna understood the pressure I've been under, so she left me alone. I was going to finish before Christmas, and we'd spend time together then."

After years with Kate, getting to know the artists she represented, he understood that creative people could keep unusual hours, and often needed to safeguard their space, limiting contact with others.

"I'm assuming Donna heard that Ronnie Garson killed Maddie," Conor said. "How did she react?"

"Total disbelief," Johnny said. "She knew him from the restaurant, said he worked there one summer, then delivered lobsters with his dad. She said he was a sweetheart. There was some prank he got in trouble for one Fourth of July, but it was an aberration."

Conor thought of what Joe had said about "the prank" being deliberately aimed fireworks, but he let Johnny talk.

"It upset her," Johnny said. "She was worried that somehow she had brought danger to Maddie—that because she worked at Cross, Gladding, and White, she'd opened a door to Zane and Grub wanting a piece of her wealthy clients. But I don't see that."

"Why?" Conor asked.

"Because she was very discreet about client matters, as well as sensitive to her family."

"Sensitive in what way?"

"She didn't flaunt her success. She had more education than anyone in her family, wanted a different kind of life than serving seafood on the waterfront. She thought what they do is interesting and honorable—she just didn't want it for herself."

"And she thought they resented her?"

"Yeah," Johnny said. He was visibly distraught, red faced, as if he'd been crying. "She never wanted them to feel she'd left them, abandoned them, for a wealthier crowd. But you know something? She loved Ronnie like a nephew, and he murdered Maddie. Now I'm thinking he could have killed Donna, too."

"Resentment?" Conor asked, wondering about the timeline and whether it was possible that were true.

"Money," Johnny said. "Donna didn't have kids of her own. Yet. She wanted them, very much. We talked about the future."

"Getting married?"

"Yes," Johnny said, his red eyes filling with tears. "We both wanted to be married."

"You said 'money'—what did you mean?"

"Ronnie is in Donna's will," Johnny said. "So are some Almeidas and Ronnie's father, Zane. Not that she was rich, but she wanted to make sure to take care of her family."

"She showed it to you?"

"I was one of the witnesses to her signing it. Could it have been the will, her generosity to those people, that got her killed?"

"Who was the other witness?" Conor asked, wondering if that person—inadvertently or not—might have revealed the will's contents to Donna's murderer. At the same time, he still wondered if Donna had stolen Maddie's paintings, if they had been meant to be transported away aboard the *Anna G.*

But Johnny didn't answer. He laughed wryly. "Guess I am destined to witness people signing wills. I did it for Maddie, too. She handwrote a brand new one for herself while she was at the Ocean House, and she had me witness her signature, right there in the lobby. Crazy, right?"

"Handwritten instead of properly done by Jeanne Gladding?" Conor asked. He had investigated deaths where the deceased had left holographic wills. They weren't valid in certain states unless witnessed and notarized.

"It's better she did it herself, instead of having that scammer do it," Johnny said.

He walked away from Conor, braced himself against his work-table, his head down and shoulders shaking. Conor had seen plenty of fake emotion during his career, but he sensed that this was true anguish—not unlike Bernard's when he first learned that Maddie had been murdered.

Conor knew it didn't mean that they weren't involved in the respective crimes—their strong feelings could be about "having" to kill the victims, for whatever reasons, or for losses as yet undisclosed. But, as with Bernard, Conor was inclined to believe that Johnny's grief was truly over losing the woman he loved.

"Johnny, why did you call Jeanne a scammer? What did Donna say about her law firm?" Conor asked after a while.

"She wasn't thrilled with their ethics," Johnny said.

"In what way?" Conor asked.

"She didn't go into it much. I just know she didn't like Jeanne. She said that if she were a client, she wouldn't turn her back on her, because Jeanne would stab it. I chalked it up to greed. Anything to make money."

"It's a pretty well-known and respected firm. I'd think they would have high standards," Conor said, not letting on to what Kate had told him or mentioning his theory about a possible theft of Maddie's paintings.

Johnny shrugged. "Who knows? Who cares? Donna was thinking of leaving. It bothered her that Jeanne sent her to Maddie's storage unit, along with Hadley. Made her feel used. And she thought it was a conflict of interest. Our relationship plus her working for Maddie's attorneys. And she didn't like not being open with Hadley. But she didn't have a choice. Jeanne made her go."

"I wonder why," Conor said.

"To keep her under their thumbs, she said. The more they dragged her in, the harder it would be for her to leave."

"Did she ever say anything about planting a fake document?" Conor asked.

"Of course not," Johnny said.

"How about people from her firm stealing art?" he asked, not directly accusing her.

"Hell no. She would never stand for that."

His hard tone left no doubt that there was no room for discussion, and Conor decided to leave it at that for now.

Conor looked around the studio. The extensive brick wall space was covered with mock-ups of the murals Johnny and Hadley would paint on the sides of buildings in waterfront towns. A large bookcase was filled with volumes dedicated to New England lore, fishing histories, the natural world, and the whaling industry. Some of the books looked very old, probably valuable.

He looked through the shelves. Antiquarian books pulled him in. They held so much truth and mystery. One of Kate's favorite things to do was visit used bookstores, spend hours there. While she scoured the art section, Conor would wander around looking for something new to read. She had gotten him hooked. In the beginning, he'd focused on crime titles—police or military investigations. But as time had gone on, he'd started getting lost in the history sections. And even—the longer he'd been with Kate—in books about art history, especially art theft.

He noticed that a shelf in Johnny and Hadley's studio was filled with art books, including one about the Isabella Stewart Gardner Museum heist. Tucked in—shoved, actually—behind a row of other books was a very slim leather-bound volume titled *Last Night*.

That got his attention. Wasn't that the name of the painting Kate had mentioned earlier?

He pulled it out. The book was so old it was almost falling apart. He glanced at the copyright page—it had been published by Crawford House in 1898. Every other page contained a poem, each by a different poet, all having to do with night.

Poems by Robert Burns, William Blake, Elizabeth Barrett Browning, John Keats, and Emily Dickinson, among others, writing about stars, the moon, darkness, secrets, romance. On the page opposite each poem was a very fine and delicate pen-and-ink drawing, done by shading and crosshatching, an image of night.

He turned to the bookmarked page. On it was a poem by Emily Dickinson titled "The Last Night That She Lived." The words were haunting, about a woman dying, the poet envying the fact she was escaping the pain and difficulties of life.

The poem sent a shiver down Conor's spine. He wondered why it was significant to the person who had marked the page. Inside the front cover was a bookplate and, in her own handwriting, the owner's name: Madeleine Cooke. The name she was born with, before two marriages.

"What are you looking at?" Johnny asked.

Conor held up the book, and Johnny gave the cover a quick glance.

"I don't recognize that one," Johnny said. "I've never seen it before."

"It was Maddie's," Conor said.

"Oh, wow," Johnny said, suddenly perking up. "Boy, that dates back. She left some of her things with me when we split up. Guess that was one of them." He paused, frowning. "Or maybe Hadley brought it. Maddie used to give her stuff she didn't want or care for anymore."

Conor turned that over in his mind. Why wouldn't Hadley have mentioned that she had an old book of Maddie's with the same title as the shocking painting they'd discovered in the storage unit?

"May I take it?" Conor asked.

"You're a poetry fan?" Johnny asked.

"I thought I'd show it to my girlfriend," Conor said. "She'll enjoy seeing the illustrations."

"Another artist?"

"She owns a gallery," Conor said.

"The gatekeeper," Johnny said, a note of bitterness in his voice. But then, as if he'd heard himself, he smiled. "Galleries have a lot of power. And we artists are lucky when we get chosen by one."

"Well, she feels she's the lucky one, to have artists trust her with their work," Conor said.

"Maybe someday she'll take a look at mine. And Hadley's."

"Yes," Conor said.

"I'm sure she would have rather represented MC—Maddie. I mean, who wouldn't? Maddie was brilliant, and her work is basically money in the bank for anyone who touches it. Plus, endless fame."

Was that envy in his voice?

"Don't listen to me," Johnny said. "I'm all over the place today. Anything to keep me from thinking about what Donna must have gone through. And, Jesus—Maddie, too. I loved them both, ten years apart, but still. I can't help but think, *Why them?*"

"I get that," Conor said. "Did you and Maddie wind up having that drink?"

"What drink?" Johnny asked.

"Hadley said Maddie told her you two were going to get together and talk."

Johnny hesitated, then sat down at his drafting table. "Yeah, we did," he said. "I felt guilty about it because I know Donna would have felt threatened."

"Did she have a reason to feel that way?"

"It's a big mess," he said, letting out a huge breath. "They're both gone, so what's the difference now?"

Conor listened, watching his face.

"I loved Donna," Johnny said.

"You said you talked about marriage and kids with her."

"No," he said. "I said I wanted to be married." He put his head in his hands.

Conor suddenly understood. "But not to her."

"No," Johnny said.

"To Maddie," Conor said.

Johnny looked up. "I didn't realize, until she came back."

"That you still loved her?"

He nodded. "The feelings were always there. But what could I do? She left me, became MC, married a movie star. It was over."

"But?"

"It wasn't over. I had no idea she felt the same way I did all these years. We were too young when we got married—we couldn't handle it. I was a pretentious art student, and she was about to become MC."

"You didn't see any of that coming?" Conor asked.

"I saw none of it coming—the breakup, her fast track to, well, you know, fame and fortune. And I'm not blaming her for leaving," Johnny said. "I wasn't ready for her. I had to be a selfish jerk for a while. She was smart and couldn't take it, so she took off."

"And then she came back," Conor said. "Did you play a part in that? The reason why she chose Rhode Island?"

"Yes," he said. "We were in touch before she moved out of Malibu. It started over a year ago. I saw an article about her in the *New Yorker*. I could have asked Hadley for her contact info, but instead I found her on social media. I wasn't even sure she did her own posting—lots of famous people have a publicist for that, but turns out it was all her. No shield. So I messaged her, and it started from there. But it was tricky."

"Why is that?"

"Her divorce. It was so vicious; she didn't want anyone to know about what was happening with us."

"Which was?"

"Falling back in love, both of us. Full speed. If Bernard found out, he could have used it against her. She didn't even tell Hadley."

"But the sisters were close."

"Yes. Maddie adored Hadley, but she always said there was sisterly rivalry. She knew that Hadley loved her, would have done anything for her, but even so . . . Hadley was jealous. Deep down, she thought Hadley was glad she was getting divorced—that she liked the fact there was at least one area Maddie was failing in. Marriage."

"Johnny, are you the reason Maddie was splitting with Bernard?" Conor asked.

"To some extent," he said.

"What extent?"

"Shit," Johnny said. "I wasn't the reason—he was an asshole. She would have left him anyway. But us falling in love—that pushed her into it. Gave her a reason to get out. Separating from him, then moving back here."

Conor watched him closely for a reaction. "You know she was pregnant?"

"Yes, I know."

"Were you the father?" Conor asked.

It took Johnny a minute to reply. "Yes. She told me, the last night I saw her. She was pregnant—I went to the Ocean House, and we had dinner in her suite. She had a bottle of champagne, chilled in a silver ice bucket. Veuve Clicquot rosé. I had no idea until then."

"The champagne gave you a clue?"

"I said to her, 'This is how you live, Maddie. Veuve in the Ocean House. I'm more like Gansett in an old warehouse.' She told me that beer in a studio was more her speed and that that would be her last glass of champagne for nine months." He paused. "She didn't even drink it. It was just a symbol of us celebrating a new life together."

Conor took it all in. What were the layers of truth and lies here? How had he juggled the two women he said he loved?

"Did Donna know?" he asked.

"One hundred percent no," Johnny said. "And if you're saying that Donna paid Ronnie, you're fucking wrong." He looked angry, but Conor detected a hint of doubt. "She had no clue about Maddie. Certainly not that she was pregnant."

"Okay," Conor said. "And what about Hadley? Any chance you or Maddie let it slip to her? About the pregnancy."

"No way."

"Back to Genevieve for a minute," Conor said. "Are you sure you haven't heard from her?"

"I haven't heard from her. You know what? I think the law firm is behind all of it. I believe they did something fucked up with Maddie's estate, and Donna either knew or they thought she did. Go after Jeanne—she knows it all, I'll bet anything. They killed both Maddie and Donna. What else can I say?"

"What gives you that idea?" Conor asked.

"I told you before. Donna had a problem with their ethics. Ask Jeanne."

Conor watched him pace, then stop and stare with a blank look in his eyes.

"Look, this is a bad day," Johnny said. "And I'm sick of this. Do you mind?"

"I'm leaving," Conor said. "Thanks for your cooperation."

"Yeah."

"Is it okay if I take the poetry book? To show Kate?"

"Sure," Johnny said. "But it belonged to Maddie, so I want it back. I don't have much of her left."

44

Hadley finally heard from Bernard. He called with what he obviously considered to be great news. He told her that after all of Maddie's encouragement, even nagging, he had finally decided to do a four-episode arc on *Border Saints*, a hit series on Prime Video. It focused on a United States senator bribed by a cartel boss to ease regulations. Bernard would portray a crooked judge pitting the politician against the drug lord. The job paid very well. It shot in San Diego and the Anza-Borrego Desert, and Bernard was already on set at the time CeCe was rescued.

He told Hadley that the producers were thrilled to have him. They had rushed him into wardrobe. He was running lines, and he could tell that the crew was in awe at having Bernard Lafond in the cast. He was excited because, in the fourth episode, his character got to kick the bucket in a spectacular way—strung up on the border wall by narco-saints. Shooting had already begun, his first scene was tomorrow, and if he returned to Rhode Island, the producers would replace him.

He was overwhelmed with joy at CeCe's rescue, full of gratitude for the Rhode Island State Police. Since CeCe was safe, he would trust Hadley with her, and reunite with his daughter as soon as he could.

"There's no life for me with Cecelia unless I do this show," he told Hadley. "I am ashamed that I begged you for money. That will never happen again. I need to pay my bills, don't I?"

"You do," she said. "But, Bernard, CeCe lost her mother. She needs her father now."

"Hadley, you have no idea how important this show is. Yes, it is popular, but its value is social commentary. The story is so important; it needs to be told."

"Goodbye, Bernard," Hadley said.

She looked at her cell phone and considered blocking him. On the one hand, any father who could be so selfish, who could put himself ahead of his child, deserved to be permanently ignored. On the other hand, she had to admit she was relieved that they wouldn't have to deal with him—having seen his rage that day in the hotel, knowing that Maddie had lived with it, she knew that she would do anything to protect CeCe from it.

Conor needed to talk with her, so she set CeCe up with a puzzle on the suite's dining table and sat with him in the living room, overlooking the ocean.

"How is she doing?" Conor asked in a low voice.

"She had nightmares last night. She slept in my bed and woke up crying for Maddie."

"Has she said anything more about what happened?" Conor asked.

"A little," Hadley said, thinking about how creative and allegorical her niece was. She knew it came from having an artist for a mother and an actor for a father—how they wove stories into their lives. "Nothing too direct, but impressions. She talked about the red ribbons streaming from her mother's head."

"Blood?" Conor asked.

Hadley nodded. "She told about hearing voices—her mother's and someone else's. I asked her if it was Ronnie, and she said no, it was a woman's voice."

"There wasn't evidence of anyone else at the scene," Conor said.

"She might have heard wrong," Hadley said. "The wind was so strong, and she must have been terrified." Hadley paused, thinking of what CeCe had said—not only to Hadley but in interviews with an FBI agent, trained to question children. "She told me she wasn't even scared at first. Only cold. Maddie had hidden her in a little snow fort in that thicket. CeCe thought it was a game."

"Until Ronnie took her," Conor said.

"Yes. That changed everything," Hadley said. "She's told all this to the Rhode Island police, to the FBI."

"I know," Conor said. "She's great. Everyone says she's been so brave. It's just that details and memories might come back long after the questions stop—she might tell you something she hasn't mentioned before."

"It's amazing how things come back," Hadley said. It was the same for her. As hard as she tried to push away that moment of finding Maddie's body, images forced their way into her mind, waking her up in the middle of the night. She saw her sister's blue lips, the way ice crystals had formed around that terrible black hole in her forehead. She heard the sound of her own shriek rising into the brutal wind.

Conor slid a book across the coffee table. It looked very old, with the spine cracked and the title in gold lettering on the dark-blue leather cover. The gold foil was flaking off, and the print was faint, but she could see the words *Last Night*.

"The title," Hadley said. "It's the same as Maddie's painting. Where did you get this?"

"It doesn't belong to you?" Conor asked.

"No," Hadley said. She picked it up and began looking through the pages. It was full of poems and beautiful, mysterious black-and-white illustrations. She turned to the front cover and saw the bookplate where her sister had written her name. "It was Maddie's? Where did you find it?"

"In your studio," Conor said, and she saw that he was watching her intently.

"How did it get there?" she asked.

"Maddie didn't give it to you?"

"No, I've never seen it before."

"Could she have slid it into your bookcase when she visited your studio?" Conor asked.

"Why would she do that?" Hadley asked. "If she wanted me to have it, why wouldn't she just give it to me?"

Conor shrugged. It was weird, but Hadley felt he was accusing her of something. He was acting suspicious of her. He was treating her as if she had stolen a book from her sister, and she didn't like it.

"What's wrong?" she asked.

"Nothing," he said. "I was just wondering about the book. Johnny assumed that you had brought it to the studio."

"Well, he's wrong about that," she said.

"Maybe Maddie left it there when she went to see him," Conor said.

Hadley stared at him. Why would he say that? "She never stopped at the studio except that time with me."

"They saw each other quite a bit, Hadley," Conor said.

"I don't believe that," Hadley said. "Maybe that one drink, but otherwise, no."

"Well," Conor said, and now he was making her uncomfortable. He was watching her as if judging her reactions. "It was more than that. They were getting back together. They saw each other whenever they could."

"Conor, I don't know why you're saying these things," Hadley said. "Maddie wasn't interested in him. She would have told me if she was. Besides, Johnny wouldn't cheat on Donna."

"Okay," Conor said. He smiled as if to reassure her, but he'd left Hadley feeling bad and confused. This wasn't a conversation—it was an interrogation. She thought of him as a friend, but right now he was just a cop, treating her like a suspect.

"I have to go now," she said coldly. She had a plan, and she didn't feel like telling him what it was.

"Sure," Conor said. "It's just that the book is such a mystery. Everything from the title to how it got into your studio." He smiled again, and she saw concern in his eyes. "I'm just trying to figure out what happened. The book and the painting. How do they go together?"

"I'd like to know that, too," she said.

"I know this is hard on you, and I'm really sorry," he said. "I want to solve this—for you and CeCe. And for Maddie and Donna."

She believed him. She felt him wanting to soften the interview, letting her know they were still friends. "Thanks, Conor," she said.

When he left, she shut the door behind him and went into the closet to get warm clothes for CeCe to wear on the drive. Her mind went back to what Conor had said. Was it possible that her sister and Johnny had been seeing each other?

Her emotions bothered her, and she realized the idea made her feel jealous and betrayed. She had liked Johnny seeing Donna. It had seemed safe in some way; it didn't intrude on Hadley's own feelings. She had formed an opinion about Donna: that she was too practical, too conventional, too provincial for Johnny.

Maddie had been perfect for him. Wild, passionate, brilliant, full of magic. But Johnny and Maddie together again would hurt too much. It would take each of them away from Hadley. They would belong to each other, and she would be left out. She wasn't proud of these feelings. In so many ways, she had always been in Maddie's shadow. Working with Johnny on the murals had made her feel as if she could shine without her sister.

Hadley helped CeCe into her jacket. She felt overcome with love for her niece. She remembered when CeCe was born, how Hadley had flown out to California to stay with Maddie and help her with the baby, help her adjust to being a mother. It hurt so much, right now, to know that Maddie would never hold CeCe again—or the baby she had been carrying, who would never be born.

"You're my girl," Hadley said, hugging CeCe.

"But mostly I'm Mommy's girl," CeCe said.

"That is true, and you always will be," Hadley said.

"Where are we going?" CeCe said.

"A secret errand," Hadley said.

Riding down in the elevator, she kept thinking of Conor's questions and the look in his eyes. He had told her that Maddie and Johnny were getting back together, but he was also telling her something else, without words.

Johnny was the father of Maddie's baby.

Hadley should have known. Who else could it have been?

45

CeCe woke up very early, just as the sky was turning light. Aunt Hadley told her to get dressed because they were going on a drive. The hotel restaurant wasn't even open for breakfast yet.

When CeCe and her mommy had first come to Rhode Island, she had loved riding in Aunt Hadley's truck. They were up high, above the cars on the highway, and there were lots of pretty lights on the dashboard. But today, CeCe didn't like it. Being in a truck reminded her of Ronnie's. That one was cold, and he was mean, and this one was warm, and she loved Aunt Hadley, but even so, CeCe felt sick to her stomach. She clutched Star.

"Auntie, can we go back to the yellow hotel?" she asked.

"We're just doing this one errand," her aunt said. "It won't take long, and we can go out for pancakes right afterward."

"I think I'm going to throw up."

Her aunt steered to the side of the road, jumped out of the truck, hurried around to open CeCe's door. As soon as fresh air flooded in, the bad feeling got better. Still, CeCe got out of the truck. There was a field of snow, and she ran into it, making big, wide circles with her arms open, as if she were an airplane. Zooming, flying, diving. She held Star like a flag that was streaming in the wind. She flopped into the snow, rolled onto her back, and looked up at the sky.

"Are you having fun?" Aunt Hadley asked.

"I can be free," CeCe said, thinking of how it had felt to be trapped with Ronnie, how he had put her in that box, how she could never get out of the truck, not even to go to the bathroom. She liked this, being able to run and jump and not be caught.

"You sure can," Aunt Hadley said and sat beside CeCe in the snow. CeCe still lay on her back. The ground was cold, but she didn't care.

"Do you know how to make snow angels?" her aunt asked.

"What are they?"

"You do this," Aunt Hadley said, lying on her back and sweeping her arms over her head and then down again, swishing her legs back and forth, making patterns in the snow. Then they both stood up, and CeCe saw the angel her aunt had made: the arm swooshes were wings, and the leg sweeps were a beautiful long white skirt.

So CeCe lay backward and made the same arm-and-leg movements as her aunt. She stirred up the snow, and a fine dusting of it landed on her face; she felt as if it came from heaven, from her mother.

Maybe Mommy was a snow angel now.

She and Aunt Hadley got back into the truck and started to drive. Since CeCe knew they could stop anytime she wanted, she didn't feel like getting sick anymore. They went a long way on the highway, then into a city, where they parked next to a building with glass walls that shimmered gold in the sun. They waited in the truck for a few minutes, and then they saw a man in a uniform opening the big front door.

"Where are we?" CeCe asked.

"In Hartford. The bank just opened, and we're going to go into a special room full of treasure."

"Rubies and diamonds and crowns from pirate ships?" she asked.

Aunt Hadley laughed. "Probably not," she said.

They went inside, and CeCe was quiet while Aunt Hadley talked to a man at a desk.

"I'm Madeleine's executor, and I'd like you to open her safe-deposit box," Aunt Hadley said. She handed the man a paper. He read it carefully.

"This seems to be in order," he said.

"Has anyone else been here to open it?" she asked.

He glanced at a white card. "Not since Madeleine herself, in November."

"Thank you," Aunt Hadley said, and CeCe thought she sounded relieved.

"Do you have the key?" the man asked.

"No, I'm afraid I don't," Aunt Hadley said.

"Well, we can drill the box," he said. "Just wait here for a few minutes." He smiled at CeCe and asked if she would like a lollipop. She said yes and chose an orange one from the tray. He said to have two, so she took a lime one and gave it to Aunt Hadley because she should have a treat, too.

It seemed like a long time to CeCe, but the man finally came back and told Aunt Hadley they were ready. She and her aunt followed him down a corridor.

The treasure room was not what CeCe had expected. It was just a big square room with no windows and rows and rows of tiny metal doors in the wall. The man explained how they had used a special tool to pop out the lock on one of the doors. Then he opened it and pulled a long gray metal box from the wall.

CeCe and Aunt Hadley went into a little cubicle that had a shelf, a chair, and a very bright light. Aunt Hadley shut the door behind them. At first, CeCe's chest hurt because it was a very small space—bigger than the wooden chest, but still, the door was closed tight, so she might not be able to get out. She put her hand on the doorknob, eyes on her aunt, seeing what would happen.

Aunt Hadley smiled. "You can open it if you want."

CeCe did, but she didn't leave the cubicle. She just opened and closed the door a few times.

"I don't want it to be locked," CeCe said.

"We won't lock it," Aunt Hadley said. "And we won't stay long."

"Good," CeCe said. She was glad the door wasn't locked, but she still didn't like the small room. It wasn't a wooden chest at the end of a bed, but it was still stuffy, and it would be easy to feel trapped in here. What if someone outside the room locked them in?

Aunt Hadley looked through the gray metal box, taking things out one by one and putting them into a canvas bag she had brought. From what CeCe could see, there was no pirate treasure. Just papers. Letters, maybe. A notebook. A sketchbook like the ones Mommy had at home in Malibu. And then some folded papers in a pale-blue folder.

Just as CeCe thought they were ready to leave, Aunt Hadley opened the blue folder and looked through the papers. She stopped and stared when she got to the last page.

"Hmm," Aunt Hadley said.

"What's the matter?" CeCe asked.

"Nothing."

"Yes, something is, I can tell," CeCe said, feeling anxious. She didn't want anything to be wrong; that would scare her.

"No, sweetheart, it's just that I'm surprised by the witnesses to your mother's . . . Oh, never mind. Let's leave now. I'll have to tell Conor about this; it's odd."

"Odd, even, odd, even," CeCe said, thinking of a game she had played back in Malibu with her nanny. She wasn't so anxious anymore—well, maybe a little. Aunt Hadley looked confused, that was all. Then they left the room, and Aunt Hadley thanked the man, and they walked out of the bank.

Aunt Hadley kept her promise, and they stopped at a coffee shop for pancakes. CeCe's were full of blueberries. She ate them while her aunt drank coffee and texted someone on her phone.

46

Kate read the text Hadley had sent to her and Conor, telling them about Maddie's will and who had witnessed her signature. The police hadn't opened the box yet, so as Maddie's executor, Hadley was able to get it drilled open. Her initiative in going to the bank to get it, uncovering information that could be helpful to the case, made Kate feel as if everyone was doing something except her. She wanted to contribute.

She had gone on social media and tracked down Genevieve Dickinson. She learned that Genevieve was nowhere close to Watch Hill: according to photos posted just that morning, Genevieve was in Wiscasset, Maine, getting ready to leave to work on another film. It turned out she really was a freelance continuity editor, and her assignment on Bernard's film about Paul Éluard was truly work related. By next week, she would be on a set in Nova Scotia.

Kate wasn't accustomed to feeling useless. She was tired of waiting around while Conor and Joe—and now Hadley—worked on the case. She had always been independent, and her education and training as an art historian had made her a good detective—focused not on crime but on the lives of artists and their subjects.

Genevieve was an artist, and Kate wanted to dig into what inspired her, what made her tick. It was the winter solstice, cold and clear, and she decided to fuel up her Cessna and fly to Maine.

"Wait till I can go with you," Conor said.

"You've got plenty to do here," she said. "That's the point."

He didn't even look hurt, because he knew her well enough. Her escapes had become less frequent, but she still needed them.

"Kate, at this point Genevieve is a suspect. You can't question her."

"I won't," she said. "I know artists, Conor. I want to hear what she has to say about her work. Her art. That will tell us a lot."

He just stared at her. She could read it in his eyes: worry she might be encountering a killer—or at least a woman who had hired one.

"You know I'm good at that, right?" Kate pressed.

"Of course I do," he said.

"You might not realize how much you can tell about an artist by visiting their studio, listening to them tell about their work." She put her arms around him. "You don't have to worry. I'm always careful."

"I can't stop you from going, and you can't stop me from worrying," he said.

She kissed him goodbye and had the valet bring their car around. If Conor had places to go, she knew Tom could drive. Westerly State Airport was just ten minutes away from the Ocean House. She fueled up, ran through her safety checks, and got clearance for takeoff. The sky was perfectly blue, there was no wind, and the flight was smooth.

It had been easy for Kate to find Genevieve's address on the internet. She took a local taxi from Wiscasset Municipal Airport into town. Genevieve's apartment was in an old house that had seen better days. The front steps were sagging, and the railing was broken. It had a row of buzzers next to the door. "Dickinson" was the top name, with the number 3A beside it. Kate pressed the button and waited. There was no answer. She tried again, but just then a man walking a black Lab came out, and she slipped in before the door could close.

She walked up three flights. The banister was loose, and she felt cold air coming through cracks in the wall. Clearly the house needed some insulation. On the second floor, she heard a conversation going on in 2B—a woman admonishing someone to finish her sandwich: "It cost money; don't waste food."

There was only one apartment on the third floor. Kate knocked hard on the door. After a minute she knocked again. Maybe Genevieve was out, or had gone away for the holidays, or was already up on the film set in Nova Scotia.

But Kate knew she was there—she smelled oil paint. The fumes were drifting through the keyhole. It felt as if the house had been made cheaply a hundred years ago, probably for shipyard workers. The walls were as thin and porous as cardboard.

"Hey, Genevieve," Kate called. "May I talk to you for a minute?"

Silence, then the sound of footsteps. "I'm busy," a voice said from the other side of the door.

"I won't take long," Kate said.

An exasperated sigh, and then the door opened. A woman stood there wearing a paint-stained sweatshirt and jeans. She had short dark hair and sun lines around her eyes and mouth, as if she spent lots of time outdoors.

"Genevieve?" Kate asked.

"Yes. Who are you?"

"Kate Woodward."

"Didn't you realize that when I didn't answer the buzzer, it meant I didn't feel like having company? Why are you here, anyway?" Genevieve asked.

"I'm a gallery owner," Kate said.

That perked Genevieve up. "Oh?" she asked.

"I've heard about you from Hadley Cooke."

"Maddie's sister," Genevieve said. "They were so close. I started to go see her after I heard about Maddie, but I just couldn't bear how sad it would have been. I read that Maddie's daughter was found. Thank God for that."

Genevieve led Kate into the living room. It was cluttered, books tilting everywhere—on shelves, tables, the floor. Framed photographs were jammed onto the mantel. Two of them were of Maddie.

"Guess you like to read," Kate said.

"My parents were professors. I inherited their library."

Kate followed her into another room that was set up as a studio. It had north light, and there was a canvas on a tall wooden easel, turned away from the door. A worktable was piled high with tubes of paint, some crimped and almost empty. Brushes stood soaking in a murky glass jar of linseed oil.

"A work in progress," Kate said, starting toward the easel, always eager to see what an artist was painting.

"No!" Genevieve said forcefully, blocking Kate's way.

"I'm sorry, I didn't mean to . . ."

"It's fine," Genevieve said, relaxing slightly. "I just don't let anyone see until I'm finished. It's a superstition of mine."

"Of course," Kate said. She backed away, to ease Genevieve's mind, and glanced around the studio.

"You can look at anything else," Genevieve said. "I should let you know, though—I already have a gallery. I'm represented by L. P. Nason, in town."

"Oh," Kate said, adding a note of disappointment, glad that Genevieve assumed she was here to offer representation. "Well, I'm not surprised. You're very talented," she said, and meant it.

Genevieve led her around the studio, watching Kate's reactions as she examined various landscapes and still lifes. They stopped in front of a framed image of Maddie's famous painting of the whale and swan hanging on the wall opposite Genevieve's easel. Kate wondered why Genevieve would want that picture here—wouldn't it remind her of losing the lawsuit? Or was it incentive to follow through on the receipt?

At first Kate thought the image was a print, but as she drifted over, she saw that it was an original painting. Leaning closer, she saw a detail missing from Maddie's version.

"A watercolor," she said, turning to Genevieve. "It's beautiful."

"The subject matter is," Genevieve said. "I paint it over and over, once every few months. I probably have a hundred."

"Because it means so much to you," Kate said.

"Yes," Genevieve said, arms folded across her chest, her lips tight. "Why have you come? Not to see my art, I'm guessing."

"That's not true. I am always interested in artists and their work. Hadley told me about you, and I was curious to see your work," Kate said. "Tell me about this one." She pointed at the watercolor.

"What about it?"

"It's similar to the famous one that Maddie did. But it has its own grace—you've made it all yours."

"You mean MC?" Genevieve asked, then snorted. "She cheapened the inspiration."

"How?" Kate asked. "By commercializing it?"

"She sold out. The original was beautiful—truly enchanted—but she ruined that. Sold it to advertisers, manufacturers, whoever would pay—she turned it into a visual cliché, and it lost its magic."

"Is that why you paint the scene over and over?" Kate asked. "To bring back the magic?"

Genevieve nodded. She ducked her head, as if not wanting Kate to see her tears.

"And the magic you feel for Maddie?" Kate asked.

"She used to be my best friend," Genevieve said. "But she ruined that, too. And now she's dead, so there's no chance . . ."

To Kate, it sounded as if Genevieve had been in love with Maddie. Had the feelings ever been returned?

"No chance of reconciling? Of fixing your friendship after the lawsuit?" Kate pressed.

"We did fix it," Genevieve said. "I am sorry I ever sued her. It caused more grief than anything. But I was mad . . ."

"Because she stole your idea?" Kate said, not believing it but thinking of the receipt and wanting to hear how Genevieve would answer.

"Partly."

"It really was your idea?" Kate asked. "You saw that happen, with the whale? Up north on the schooner?"

"I saw the North Star," Genevieve said.

"Polaris?" Kate said.

Genevieve nodded. "See, we loved the stars—Maddie, Hadley, and I. We were inspired by the Summer Triangle. Maddie was Deneb, Hadley was Vega, and I was Altair. The triangle points away from Polaris, so Maddie didn't really notice it that night."

"But you did," Kate said.

"Yes. And I told her the North Star was for guidance—safety, especially inspiration. I told her that she was my North Star. So that's why I put Polaris in the paintings I do, instead of the other stars. To remind me of Maddie."

"You loved her?" Kate asked.

"Yes, and still do. Unrequited, to this day, and now forever."

"Did she know?" Kate asked.

"Of course. I never hid it. It wasn't that she didn't like me—it was that she didn't *mind* me. She tolerated me, like a puppy dog."

"That must have hurt," Kate said.

"It did. But I've made peace with it. And she forgave me for the lawsuit. She told me it felt like a divorce. She said I was creating havoc and ugliness as a way to hate her, to give her up and get her out of my life for good. You know what? She was right."

"But at least you got to make up, before she died," Kate said.

"Yes."

"I still don't get it," Kate said. "You thought the idea was partly yours because of seeing the star?"

"Not just that," Genevieve said. "But it's over now. I told you—I'm at peace. I have a cool job that I love. I get to travel, work on interesting films, and come home to paint between projects. And Maddie and I were good with each other before she died. We came to an agreement, and that makes everything okay."

Kate felt prickles on the top of her head, a sign from inside that she wasn't buying Genevieve's story.

"I brought something I'd like to show you," Kate said, taking her phone from her jacket pocket. "I'd like to email it to you so you can read it on a larger screen. The print is rather small."

Genevieve gave Kate her email address, and Kate hit "Send." While Genevieve opened her laptop and waited for the email to land, Kate glanced around the room. She saw how absorbed Genevieve was in reading the document. It gave her the chance to peek at the work on the easel.

Kate had no idea what she would see, but nothing in the world prepared her for this. She was shocked and had to compose herself. She lifted her phone, took a quick photo, and walked over to the desk where Genevieve sat, hoping she hadn't been seen looking at the painting, hoping Genevieve couldn't hear her heart pounding. Genevieve bent forward, peering at the screen.

"Our agreement," Genevieve said, reading the receipt Hadley had found in Maddie's desk.

"What does it mean?" Kate asked.

"Exactly what it says," Genevieve said. "She was going to pay me a million dollars and give me credit, publicly, for *The Whale and the Swan*."

"But now she's dead, so . . ."

"That's what an estate plan is for," Genevieve said. "She put these terms into her will and trust."

"Why would she do it?" Kate asked, making herself sound stunned.

"Because she had so much. All I really wanted was her, but this was an okay second best. It was her way of showing she loved me. Not the way I wished for, but something that would show the world I mattered to her."

"Wow," Kate said. And the prickling on the top of her head was now spreading all over. She had the photo of Genevieve's work in progress, and she knew she had to get out of there.

"Listen," Genevieve said, "I hope I've answered your questions. Because that's why you came, right?"

"Like I said, I was curious about your connection to *The Whale and the Swan*."

"So, now you know."

"Thank you very much," Kate said. "I really appreciate your time."

Genevieve walked Kate to the door. Kate felt an air of impatience coming from her, as if she were in a rush for her to leave. Kate said goodbye and walked down to the second-floor landing. As much as she wanted to run out of there as fast as she could, she thought she had stirred Genevieve up, and she needed to know what would come of that. She tiptoed back up to the third floor, leaned close to Genevieve's door.

Genevieve's voice came through the cracked wood loud and clear, talking to someone on the phone. Although Kate didn't know who she was talking to, she heard the words:

"She pretended she was here as a gallery owner, like she wanted me to think she might represent me. But that was bullshit—she came all the way to show me the receipt and catch my reaction," Genevieve was saying. She paused, as if listening to the person on the other end. "It wound up being perfect. I got to tell her my side of things, and she bought it. We are almost there. Just a little longer, my love. It's all happening . . ."

When the conversation ended, Kate hurried down to street level. She caught a cab and told the driver to take her to the airport. The whole way there, she stared at the photo she had taken of the painting on Genevieve's easel.

She climbed into her plane, and just before taxiing, she texted Conor and said she'd see him at the Ocean House in just a few hours. The flight back to Rhode Island was as calm as the one up to Maine, but inside, Kate felt nothing but turbulence.

47

It was midafternoon on the winter solstice, and Conor felt nervous, wanting Kate to get back from Maine. He hadn't wanted her to go at all, but she had made up her mind, said she knew how to talk to artists, and that was how she planned to approach Genevieve. She'd texted him to say she was on the way back, and he couldn't wait to see her.

Meanwhile, he and Tom returned to the *Anna G*, still high off the ground in a cradle at the boatyard. The sun glowed white in a snow sky, throwing no warmth into the day. The brothers climbed the ladder from the sandy, ice-slicked lot up to the deck and entered the cabin. Tom had told Conor about the racks, but seeing them for himself confirmed that they had been built to transport paintings.

"I take it this isn't the average lobster-boat interior," Conor said.

"Far from it," Tom said. "Zane went to town on these racks."

Conor examined the construction. The pine planks were crude, but the frame was solid. Whoever had built it knew what he was doing but hadn't the funds to use wood—like mahogany or walnut—that wouldn't splinter and potentially damage any stored canvases.

"Check this out," Tom said, pointing at a blurry purple ink stamp on one of the boards.

Conor saw the insignia—stylized ocean waves in the shape of a W, inside an oval. It was about three inches long, two inches high.

"What is it from?" Conor asked.

"Wickenden Lumber, a yard in Providence," Tom said. "On Fox Point."

"I passed Wickenden Street on the way to Hadley and Johnny's studio," Conor said.

"Yeah, that's where it is. It's part of the Providence Arts District, just across the bridge from the old Davol Square."

"What's the significance?"

"This isn't typical wood for fishing boats," Tom said. "It's soft, doesn't hold up. Zane didn't have it lying around his dock, waiting for the next project. He went to Wickenden Lumber specifically to buy these slats. Or someone bought them for him. I think he probably had them custom cut, too."

"Or the frame prebuilt somewhere else, then installed here?" Conor asked.

"Possibly," Tom said, looking at the frame's footings. "They're not bolted to the deck. Zane attached them by these brackets." He pointed at flimsy metal plates that lined up with the hull and looked as if they had been twisted off. "Obviously they were less than effective."

"The blizzard?"

"Yes. The wind and wave action tossed this boat so violently that the screws tore out. Lucky for Zane, whatever art he'd been planning to transport wasn't aboard. It would have gotten slashed." Tom gestured at fishing gear in the corner and bolts protruding from a wooden beam. Conor could imagine the job they would have done on an oil painting's canvas. *Amateur,* he thought. Zane should have built a reinforced crate, especially if the artwork was valuable.

The lighting was dim, so Conor had to squint as he explored his way around the boat. Tom handed him a pocket flashlight, and that helped. He made his way from the main cabin to the forward section, where there was a V-berth for the captain to sleep.

The police would have gone through everything, but Conor moved carefully, trusting his impressions. There was nothing fancy about this boat. The bow was V shaped, with thin mattresses, fitting the V. The bedding was musty, soaked over the years with salt air. Shelves were guarded by slats, built to protect books and toiletries from flying around the cabin in rough seas.

Conor had always been curious about the books at a crime scene, or in a place connected to a suspect. He sat on the edge of the berth, leaned forward to examine the books. They looked to be a combination of saltwater titles, like *Surfcasting Around the Block* by Dennis Zambrotta, and a selection of John D. MacDonald mysteries.

He noticed carving on the side of the bookcase. There were a few dates, a rough-looking lobster, and several sets of initials. Some were obvious—ZG was Zane, RG was Ronnie. The ones that caught his attention were DA and, especially, IA.

Hadley had texted both him and Kate after she'd read Maddie's will. Maybe it didn't mean anything, but IA were the initials of one of the two witnesses: Isabel, from the Ocean House.

Tom edged into the bow to lean over Conor's shoulder and see what he was so entranced by. Conor pointed at the initials.

"It's not uncommon for captains to have their families, especially the kids, carve initials somewhere on the boats," Tom said. "It's a type of blessing."

"Only family members?" Conor asked.

"Pretty much," Tom said.

"So Isabel is related to the Garsons," Conor said.

"One way or the other," Tom said. "By blood, or by fishing."

"Or by the service industry," Conor said, thinking of how he'd seen Isabel and her sister talking to Elise at the Binnacle, how Elise had said they always gave discounts to workers.

And family.

Conor stared at the carved initials, thinking of the witnesses' signatures on Maddie's will, and he knew they had to get back to the Ocean House right away.

48

CeCe didn't want to be alone, but when she and Aunt Hadley returned to the yellow hotel from the bank, her aunt was very tired. They had gotten up so early that morning. Aunt Hadley said she was going to take a little nap. She fell asleep on the couch in their Sea Garden home. CeCe finished the puzzle, and she colored for a while, but then she felt bored. She thought about waking up her aunt, to feed her, but that wouldn't be nice.

Being with Aunt Hadley, doing things with her, had made CeCe start to feel brave again. Not as much as when Mommy was here, but she was getting better. CeCe wanted to show her aunt that she could be like she used to be. The lobby was fun, full of music, so she would go there. It was safe. She had a friend. She smiled. She would surprise her friend because she had a secret about her. And she would make her aunt proud because she could get something to eat for herself.

She kissed Aunt Hadley while she slept, and she opened the suite door and walked into the hallway. They were close to the beautiful old elevator, and she pressed the button to call it to her floor. When it came, she stepped inside and pushed the button to go to the lobby.

The Christmas trees were twinkling, just like the starry sky. The pretty blonde lady was playing the harp, just the way she did every afternoon. It was almost dinnertime, and people were talking and laughing, waiting to go into the dining room. CeCe walked past everyone and went to the reception desk, where her friend worked.

Even though there were some people waiting for their turn, Isabel saw CeCe and waved.

"Hi, Isabel," CeCe said. "I want to tell you something."

"Be there in a minute, CeCe," Isabel said. She smiled, then turned back to the people she was helping. CeCe waited for a while. She didn't want to bother her friend, but she also had something so funny to tell her. And she'd started to feel a little nervous about being down here without Aunt Hadley. Some of the guests were staring at her and whispering.

"You're that little girl!" one lady said. "Thank God you're safe. But where's your adult? You're not down here alone, are you?"

"Isabel," CeCe said, standing as close to the desk as she could without feeling she was too close and being rude.

"Just a second, sweetheart," Isabel said, showing some people a map and telling them how to get to their restaurant.

"Odd and even, odd and even," CeCe began to whisper. She was thinking of being at the bank with her aunt, and how her aunt had said it was odd, so odd. Somehow, thinking of Aunt Hadley and what she had said comforted CeCe. She was just about to run to the elevator and go back upstairs when Isabel stepped out from behind the desk and crouched beside her.

"Where's your aunt?" Isabel asked.

"Sleeping," CeCe said. "So I came to see you."

"That's so sweet! What did you want to tell me?" Isabel asked.

"My auntie said it was odd," CeCe said. Isabel was a friend, and being so close to her made CeCe feel better. "Odd even, odd even." She laughed, waiting for Isabel to see how funny it was.

"Hmm," Isabel said, and CeCe could see she didn't get it.

"Because we went to the treasure room, and Aunt Hadley said you're a witness, and it was odd, so odd!" CeCe said, smiling up at her, but Isabel wasn't smiling.

"What did you just say?" Isabel asked.

"That you are a witness," CeCe said, her shoulders slumping, suddenly feeling that she'd said something wrong. "You signed the paper for Mommy."

"Where did you see the paper?"

"At the bank. In the little tiny treasure box."

Isabel didn't smile, but she pasted a nonsmile smile on her face, and her voice was pretending to be nice, and CeCe knew the difference.

"Let's go have an ice cream," she said to CeCe.

"I don't want one," CeCe said, starting to back away.

Isabel's face was red and angry as her hand shot out and tried to grab CeCe. But CeCe wasn't going to let her. She had seen that same terrible look on Ronnie's father's face, so she knew what to do. She bit Isabel's hand very hard.

And then CeCe ran away as fast as she could.

49

Hadley woke up feeling groggy. The temperature outside had dropped as darkness fell. She pushed up the suite's thermostat and turned on the gas fire. It blazed brightly, throwing warmth. She realized she must have dozed off before sunset, so she switched on table lamps, then sat back down on the sofa where she had slept.

"CeCe," she called softly, in case her niece had gone to her bed and fallen asleep.

Her gaze fell upon *Last Night*, the book of eighteenth- and nine-teenth-century poetry that Conor had brought her, sitting on the coffee table. She and Maddie loved books and had shared favorites. They'd sometimes quoted from them to each other, as a type of secret lan-guage—phrases that meant nothing to those around them but sent waves of delight through the sisters.

Hadley had never seen this book before. She opened the front cover, gazed at Maddie's handwriting on the bookplate. How old had her sister been when she'd inscribed her name?

Hadley paged through the book. One page was marked—a poem by Emily Dickinson. "The Last Night That She Lived." She read it and felt disturbed. The poem had obviously meant something to Maddie. It talked about how the day, the night, that a person died was the same as any other, except for the moment of death. Hadley had never heard her sister ponder life and death. Maddie had lived with joy and passion. She had sometimes paid the price, but it never stopped her.

Opposite the poem was an intricate pen-and-ink drawing. It appeared to depict a full moon shining through a thicket of brambles, the moonlight creating twisted shadows. Hadley assumed the illustration was original to the book, which had been published in 1898, but the closer she looked, the more she realized that it had been inserted more recently.

It had been drawn by Maddie.

The gnarled branches spelled out a message. Etched into the blank spaces of moonlight were the faces of angels. Hadley stared, letting the words sift through her vision, into her brain.

> He is my love
> Once and again
> And forever
> We will meet in the snow
> Roses will bloom
> When I die
> For love
> For art

Hadley read and reread the lines. They echoed—or anticipated—the imagery in Maddie's last painting. She felt unsettled, reading them.

"CeCe!" Hadley called again, wanting to hug her niece and drive the uneasy thoughts from her mind. She had felt bothered ever since being at the bank, finding Maddie's documents, seeing the unexpected signature on the last page. She had texted Kate and Conor to let them know—not that it meant anything. After all, Isabel worked right here at the hotel, and it shouldn't really be that weird that she had agreed to be a witness to the signing of Maddie's will.

CeCe didn't answer, so Hadley went looking for her. She searched the suite, but CeCe wasn't there. Hadley felt panic building. She texted Kate to ask if she had seen CeCe. When Kate wrote back to say no, she hadn't, she had just landed at the airport, Hadley knew she had to check the lobby, the porch, the rest of the hotel, anywhere CeCe might be. She ran down the stairs, not willing to wait for the elevator.

50

Conor looked for Isabel at the front desk, but she wasn't there. Her colleague Agnes said she was on a break and would be back in fifteen minutes. He texted Joe to hurry. He stepped outside onto the verandah and reread the text Hadley had sent from the bank. He had asked her to let him know who had witnessed the signing of Maddie's will, and she had sent a photo of the document's last page. He looked at the two names, one line above the other.

John Morrison
Isabel Almeida

Isabel's last name was another clue, helping him to put it together. So many cases were built on the thinnest threads of circumstantial evidence. But as the investigation continued, the threads wove together into a story that started to make sense, eventually revealing motive, intent, the mental twists that had led to murder.

There was the book Johnny had denied knowing about, the lie he had lived with Donna, and the one he had lived with Maddie. Was it fun for them to put this over on her? Had Maddie figured it out? Johnny and Isabel. Conor looked inside the hotel again, checking to see if Isabel had come back to the desk. She hadn't. He hoped Joe would get there soon because questioning her would be up to him.

Conor returned to his spot on the verandah, where he breathed the sea air and waited for Joe. But instead of seeing the detective's unmarked police car pulling into the turnaround, he saw something he hadn't expected.

A Subaru drove in. When Dermot went to open the door, the driver waved him away. It was Johnny. He parked there, engine idling, obviously waiting for someone to run out and meet him, jump into the car so he could drive her away. That wasn't going to happen. Conor walked down the wide, curved steps.

"You won't be seeing her. Not today," Conor said, climbing into the passenger side of Johnny's Subaru. Johnny looked startled, but he got right back on track.

"Maddie, my love, I know . . . ," Johnny said.

"Not Maddie," Conor said.

"Then who are you talking about?" he asked, sounding nervous.

"Isabel Almeida."

Johnny was silent for a long moment. Then he slid a sharp smile across the seat toward Conor.

"What's that look for?" Conor asked.

"You know her last name. Good for you," Johnny said.

"Let's see," Conor said. "Donna Almeida. How are they related?"

"Isabel's her younger sister," Johnny said.

"You and sisters," Conor said. "Maddie and Hadley, Donna and Isabel. And, let me guess, you love them all."

"I do," Johnny said. "In different ways."

"But Isabel the most?" Conor asked.

Johnny didn't reply. He stared straight ahead. His cell phone was on the console between him and Conor, and it buzzed. Conor glanced down and saw the screen light up with the name "Belle."

"Let me guess—Isabel?" Conor asked. "Go ahead, pick up."

Johnny made no attempt to answer the call.

"Almeida," Conor said. "One of those names you mentioned, of people Donna included in her will. Relatives. And I take it there's a connection with the Garson family, too?"

"So what? It's one big fishing community. They support each other."

"And kill for each other?"

Johnny gave him a dirty look. "You have a good imagination. Tell me how you think that worked?"

"You set Maddie up," Conor said. "You loved her, and she broke your heart; you never forgot it."

"I forgave her," Johnny said.

"Not enough," Conor said. "She had too much that you wanted. Her money, her paintings. You saw that she was vulnerable with Bernard . . ."

"That piece of shit," Johnny said. "He can't even be bothered to come back here, to be with his daughter. After everything CeCe has been through."

"Yeah," Conor said. "But a little ironic, considering you set it in motion—the trauma CeCe has had to endure."

"Get out of my car," Johnny said.

"You know your mistake? How I figured it out?" Conor asked. "You're a smart guy. I bet you can guess."

"I don't care, and no one else will, because you're wrong," Johnny said.

"You did so many things right," Conor said. "You contacted Maddie on Facebook, started it all up again. She was unhappy; you reminded her of being young artists together. Before she was MC. Before the world owned her."

Johnny had both hands on the steering wheel, as if he were driving, but the car was in park, and they weren't going anywhere.

"That little leather book in your studio," Conor said. "I asked if you'd ever seen it, and you said no. You said Hadley must have put it there. But when I said I wanted to take it, you asked if I was a poetry fan."

"So what?"

"How would you have known it was a book of poems if you'd never seen it before?" Conor asked.

Johnny took that in.

"You got Maddie to come back here, to Rhode Island," Conor said. "Was Isabel already working at the Ocean House? Or did she take the job once you knew Maddie was buying the Sea Garden suite?"

"Aren't you sick of hearing yourself talk yet?" Johnny asked. But Conor saw that Johnny looked pale. He knew he was hitting home.

"How did Isabel feel when you got Maddie pregnant?" Conor asked.

That's when Johnny couldn't hide it anymore. He cleared his throat, looked out the driver's-side window. Conor saw him swallowing hard, trying to keep feelings inside. It showed Conor something he hadn't known until this moment.

"You didn't anticipate that, did you?" Conor asked. "Maddie getting pregnant?"

Johnny shook his head. "It was a surprise to both of us," he said in a low voice.

"And even more so to Isabel. I'm sure she thought you were playing Maddie, reeling her in. She had no clue that you were sleeping with her. That you had fallen back in love with her," Conor said, the truth unfolding to him as he talked to Johnny.

"She didn't expect that," Johnny said.

"And neither did you."

"No." Johnny glared at Conor. "I didn't want anything bad to happen to Maddie. I did love her. And she knew it. She died knowing I wanted to be with her—we were going to get married as soon as her divorce was finished."

"But you had two women to break up with," Conor said. "Both Donna and Isabel. The two sisters. You are quite a player."

"None of it was malicious," Johnny said. "Love is love. It goes where it goes."

"Yeah, but yours went more places than most," Conor said.

"Lucky you, having a conventional life," Johnny said. "Enjoy being bored. I told you already—get out of my car."

"One last thing," Conor said. "Genevieve."

"What?" Johnny asked.

"Genevieve Dickinson. It's pretty clear she was involved. The fake receipt?"

"I have no idea what you're talking about," Johnny said.

"I think you do," Conor said, showing Johnny the photo Kate had texted him—of the painting on Genevieve's easel. It was a copy of the one in Maddie's storage unit: the woman lying in the snow with roses.

"*Last Night*," Johnny said, staring at the screen. "Where did you get that picture?"

"The painting was on Genevieve's easel. Is she the one who wrote the story of Maddie's death, before it happened? A painting that predicted the way she would die?"

"No," Johnny said. "Maddie wrote that story. It was her idea to enact it. It just . . . wasn't supposed to come true. She wasn't supposed to die."

"No?"

Johnny shook his head. "It was performance art. Maddie and I planned it. *The Whale and the Swan* was such a wild hit, decades ago. We kidded around, dared each other to create something even bigger. Something that would captivate the world."

"A dead woman in the snow?" Conor asked.

"Yes. A painting of that image by MC would be seen as magical—Jungian, tapping into the collective unconscious. Snow, roses, death. So we set it up. We were planning to stage it—right there, on the path to East Beach. But we needed snow."

"So you waited?"

"Yes," Johnny said. "We outlined the sequence in October. The idea was, Maddie would have the painting ready. It would be as mystical as the whale one. And we would do a short film to go along with it."

"So you would do a video of Maddie pretending to be the character in the painting?" Conor asked.

"Not pretending. *Being.* You saw the painting, right?"

"A photo of it."

"It's a self-portrait. Maddie painted her own face, her own wildness, the poetry she has always had inside her," Johnny said.

A self-portrait of her dead body, Conor thought.

"So we watched the weather reports, and we decided we'd go for it on the first real snow of the year. We were picturing a light covering— turning everything white but not a serious accumulation. But then the blizzard hit . . . it was so intense, too dangerous for me to drive down from Providence, and crazy to think of Maddie going out in it." He paused. "I never thought she would. I didn't want her to get hurt."

"Just murdered," Conor said.

"No!" Johnny said. "That wasn't the plan! I told you—she and I were going to go out on a snowy night, shoot a video based on her painting. That was all."

"But someone saw her sketch? Or you told them the basics?"

"Donna went into Maddie's storage unit when she wasn't there. She was just going to look around, see what Maddie had in there. Then she saw the painting. I swear I didn't know—she only told me afterward," Johnny said.

"But she told someone else first," Conor said. "So when the blizzard hit . . ."

"Isabel was ready," Johnny said. "She lured Maddie there. I swear, I didn't know she was going to do it. I had no idea. She must have figured out that Maddie and I were real. And it was her way of getting back at me."

"By killing her."

"Having her killed," Johnny said.

Conor heard the rasp in his voice.

"Look," Johnny said, "I'm telling you this so you'll know I wasn't involved. You're a cop, I'm taking a chance. But you've got to help me, okay?"

"You're doing the right thing by coming clean," Conor said.

"So you won't arrest me? And the Rhode Island detective won't?"

Conor could have lied to him, assured him that he was out of the woods, but he didn't. "It's going to depend, Johnny," Conor said.

Johnny looked pale. He took a deep breath, exhaled.

"What about the fake receipt from Genevieve?" Conor asked. "You've told me this much."

Johnny shook his head. "Isabel got a kick out of manipulating Donna. They got to Genevieve—it was easy because of the lawsuit; all her information is in the legal databases. It was easy for Isabel to find her on a dating app and pretend to fall in love with her."

"And Genevieve fell in love back?" Conor asked.

"Yes. She fell hard, crazy in love. She would have done anything for Isabel. It took a while, but Isabel reeled her in. Talked about how Maddie had screwed her out of what should have been hers. She really revved Genevieve up."

"Worked on her resentment," Conor said. "That's a powerful motivator."

"Yes, Isabel got her red hot. She put her in touch with Donna, and Donna's law firm was ready and waiting to exploit her."

"A way to get to Maddie's fortune," Conor said. "Who came up with the fake receipt?"

"The Almeida sisters," Johnny said.

"And they were going to split the million dollars with each other and Genevieve," Conor said. "Three ways? Or did they tell you about it, too? Were they going to cut you in?"

Johnny had the grace to look ashamed. "I didn't know, didn't even guess, at first. But after Maddie died, when Isabel believed they were home free in terms of collecting on the proceeds, she told me everything. She was proud of it."

"Now Donna's dead," Conor said. "Isabel killed her?"

Johnny didn't answer. He didn't have to.

"I want to hear it from you. Isabel murdered Donna? And together they paid the Garsons to kill Maddie?"

"I swear, Conor, I didn't know Isabel was going to hurt either of them."

"How did she get to Maddie?" Conor asked.

"The night of the blizzard, I was home in Providence. It never even occurred to me to text Maddie and tell her our video project was off. I figured she would have known—considering how crazy the weather was out there. Way too dangerous."

"Okay," Conor said.

"Isabel told me that CeCe invited her to the suite for tea. It's frowned on, for staff to mingle with the guests, but Maddie was so cool, she was friendly with everyone. Isabel went to the suite, and Maddie served tea and scones. Isabel just enjoyed it all."

"Knowing she was going to kill Maddie?"

"No. She and Donna had brought in the Garsons. It was going to be a lot of money for them. Cash, plus they would split the profits from selling the artwork," Johnny said.

"How would that work?" Conor asked.

"I found out later that Zane came to Fox Point to buy the same kind of lumber I use to build painting crates. He was ready to take them on the boat. He and his brother had contacts who would buy Maddie's paintings—a black market. Donna and Isabel wouldn't have to unload them—they wouldn't have had a way to do that without word getting out. News travels fast in art circles."

That was true. Conor knew from watching Kate do business at the gallery. Provenance was so important to legitimate collectors. If stolen paintings were being shopped around, Kate would have heard about it through the gallery grapevine.

"So Maddie's paintings would be partial payment for killing her?" Conor asked.

"Yes."

"How much were they paying?" Conor asked. "The total?"

"A hundred thousand," Johnny said. "Isabel said it would be worth it, considering that they had a fortune to gain."

"They got Ronnie to pull the trigger," Conor said. "A kid."

"Yeah," Johnny said, looking down.

"Tell me what happened after tea," Conor said. "In the suite."

"What do you think?" Johnny asked.

"Tell me," Conor said, his voice getting harsher.

"Isabel knew everything. Donna had given her a photo of *Last Night*—Maddie's painting. And she knew the plan Maddie and I had—to turn the whole thing into a performance, to create a living tableau that would be a media sensation, to make it all as big as the North Star."

"And then?"

"As far as Isabel was concerned, the money was going to pour in after Maddie died. Donna had the Genevieve agreement and receipt—that part was easy. All Isabel had to do was play on Genevieve's obsession with Maddie . . . and gently shift it to herself. Genevieve saw it as a win-win."

"'Gently,'" Conor said with disgust.

"Donna had the combination to Maddie's storage unit. She planted the receipt in Maddie's notebook. She inventoried the art, estimated its value. Her law firm wouldn't have blinked if she had emptied the whole thing, as long as she cut them in," Johnny said. "But that was never going to happen."

"Because Isabel didn't want to share. She killed her sister," Conor said. "Was Genevieve going to be next?"

Johnny just stared straight ahead, eyes wide as if he were sleepwalking.

"So, back to the night of the blizzard. Maddie thought she was meeting you on the beach path?" Conor asked. "To shoot the video that would go with her painting? Your big creative collaboration."

Johnny didn't reply. It seemed he was beyond answering.

"Okay, then, Johnny. I need to know where Isabel is. You obviously came to pick her up," Conor said. His pulse was pounding. He was sitting inches away from a man who had hurt so many people, and no one had known. Now his actions had turned on him. Conor saw the sorrow in his face—but it was too late to take anything back.

"I swear, I didn't know she was going to do it," he said. "I thought—"

"Isabel didn't just have Maddie killed," Conor said, interrupting him harshly. He didn't feel one bit bad for him. In spite of everything he knew about Isabel and what she had done, he was right here waiting for her. "Your baby died, too. Tell me what I need to know so I can get her. You want to make things right? That's a start."

"Yes," Johnny said, turning his head slowly, looking into Conor's eyes. "I do want that."

51

CeCe ran through the big yellow hotel with Isabel behind her. There were corridors and stairways, more than she could count. They went down to the spa, where the pool was, where CeCe loved to swim with Mommy. Out the door, across a wide deck that curved out toward the beach. Then into a different door, through the ballroom, through the gallery with the blue walls, past the paintings by the artist who wrote the Madeline books. CeCe kept running, looking over her shoulder for Isabel.

Mommy had taken CeCe all through the hotel, telling her that this was their home now, with wonderful rooms and restaurants and nooks and crannies to explore. Nicholas, who wore a blue blazer and was always nice, had given them a tour one time, showing them secret places. CeCe remembered everything. There was the tower, up a spiral staircase into the very peak of the Ocean House, with round windows like portholes on every side looking out forever.

There were other suites like Sea Garden, with magical names. Each one was different, and Mommy said someday they would make friends with the people who stayed in them so they could see what the rooms looked like. CeCe darted up and down the halls, around corners, staying ahead of Isabel. She figured that if anyone knew the hotel as well as she did, it would be Isabel, because she worked there.

She tried to remember what Isabel had said, all the times CeCe and her mommy had talked. Isabel loved hotels; she had gone to school to study the best ways to make guests happy. She had sounded so friendly, as if all she wanted was to take care of the people who stayed here. CeCe remembered that she said she wanted to study wine, go to France and Italy and California.

And she had taken Mommy and CeCe down to the hotel's wine cellar. It was downstairs, near the room with the pool table, next to the small kitchen where the hotel's chef taught cooking classes, in a glass enclosure with shelves up to the ceiling, full of dark wine bottles. The lights were golden but shaded, and the room was both dim and cozy. It reminded CeCe of visiting châteaus and wine caves in Bordeaux, where her grandmother lived.

That is where she would go to hide. Isabel would never guess, because she would think CeCe was too smart to go back to the part of the hotel Isabel had said she loved most. Besides, CeCe had seen something there, something that would help her, give her power. She ran into the underground garage, darted through a door that led to the soft-pink hallway. It was lined with watercolors by Sem, the artist Papa loved, and for just a moment, CeCe's heart hurt, because she wondered where he was.

There was nobody in the corridor, the little kitchen, or the wine cellar. CeCe looked behind her. She had run very fast, and there was no sign of Isabel. So she tugged open the heavy door and slipped into the glass enclosure with the massive wooden shelves full of wine bottles. There was a ledge full of glasses. The crystal sparkled in the light. They were fragile looking, waiting to be filled with wine, and CeCe passed very carefully, not wanting to bump into them and break them.

At the very end of the room, there was a narrow space between the tall shelf and the wall. No grown-up could get in there; it was the perfect size for a little girl.

CeCe stood sideways and wriggled in, then wedged herself behind the rack of wine bottles. Ever since being kidnapped, she didn't like feeling trapped in closed places, but it felt safe and quiet here. She liked that it reminded her of France, a place where her family had been happy.

No one would find her here. She could look out through the rows of wine bottles stacked on top of each other, but if someone came in, they wouldn't see her. She just had to stay here long enough for Aunt Hadley or Conor Reid to come looking for her. She was a little out of breath from running, but she was calming down now. Hand in her pocket, holding Star. Everything was going to be okay.

But then she heard her name.

"CeCe," Isabel called very softly. "Dear little CeCe, I don't know what I said to upset you. Where are you? Everything is okay. Let me take you upstairs to your aunt. You know how worried she must be?"

CeCe stayed perfectly still. She peered out between the wine bottles and saw Isabel moving slowly and surely, like a snake in the garden. Isabel was looking from side to side, bending down to see under the big table, poking her head into the kitchen, opening cupboards. She was holding the hand CeCe had bitten, as if it hurt.

"Come on now," Isabel said. "Isn't it so silly to be hiding? I'm your friend; you know that. Your mommy would want you to come out. I'm not mad that you bit me; I'm not at all mad. I know you didn't mean it."

The little kitchen was only a few feet away from the wine cellar. Isabel turned around, began walking very slowly past the shelves full of wine. She must have thought there was nowhere to hide in there because the room was glass; anyone could look inside. But then she stopped. Her eyes seemed to bore straight through the tiny space between the bottles.

CeCe watched an actual smile come to Isabel's face.

"Hello there, CeCe," Isabel said.

52

It turned out that Johnny had lied once more. He'd told Conor he wanted to make it right and help Conor catch Isabel, but he'd just filled the air with more self-pity, blaming Isabel and the Garsons and everyone but himself. He had come here to pick her up, but Isabel must have seen Conor and changed her mind. When she didn't come out, Johnny said she'd probably called one of her friends or cousins. Gotten away.

When Joe pulled up to the Ocean House, Conor was happy to watch him handcuff Johnny and turn him over to uniformed Rhode Island State Troopers. They stood on the Ocean House's verandah, watching one of the troopers open the back door of a police car and put Johnny inside.

"Conspiracy to commit murder," Joe said.

"He claims it wasn't him," Conor said.

"He can claim it all he wants," Joe said. "But he sure knows an awful lot about what everyone else did. Especially Isabel Almeida. And he has expensive taste in flowers."

"Flowers?" Conor asked.

"Yeah. We checked with the florist. Johnny's the one who sent all the roses—mostly to Maddie, but plenty to Isabel, too. And charged them on Maddie's account."

Conor nodded. He figured that no matter what, Joe could use Johnny to leverage Isabel, once they caught her. She hadn't been at the desk when he went looking for her—Agnes had said she was on break, but she never came back.

"Court orders take forever," Joe said. "If we'd gotten into Maddie's safe-deposit box right away, we would have had Maddie's will and found Isabel's name. At least known to question her."

"Well, we know now," Conor said, glad Hadley had gone to the bank.

It was clear that Isabel had either left the hotel or was hiding inside. Joe had his officers set up a perimeter. One group was dispatched to search the building, another to canvass the grounds. The lights and activity were reminiscent of the hours after Maddie had been murdered and CeCe had gone missing.

"She's going to get away," Conor said. "Like the rest of them."

"No," Joe said. "Not everyone. Ronnie and Zane are in custody; now Johnny is, and Pat O'Rourke's team caught Grub and Elise at Logan Airport with false passports."

"Where were they heading?" Conor asked. While talking to Joe, he kept his eyes on the turnaround, hoping Kate would drive in at any minute.

"Mexico City," Joe said. "Pat said their passports were first rate. The airline clerk didn't make them as fake. The only reason they got caught is that some passenger recognized Grub from the news."

"It isn't easy getting false papers," Conor said. "They must have had a connection."

Tom pulled up in his truck, parked it on the side of the circle.

"Hey," he called as he walked up the wide steps. "Did you hear they picked up Grub?"

"We were just talking about it," Conor said. "Where do you think a wayward lobsterman would get first-rate forged passports?"

"Cartel," Tom said. "Grub did a good job of seeming small time, but too many signs are pointing to him getting into trafficking."

"The FBI thinks so," Joe said.

"We'll work with them," Tom said. "We'll board Grub's boats; the other agency will look closer at the Binnacle. And Zane, too."

"Trafficking's the growing industry around here," Joe said.

"Grub had CeCe," Conor said. "If he was in with the cartels, who knows what he told them about her. What he promised them. What about Coach, whatever his real name is? Where is he?" Conor asked.

"Still missing," Joe said.

"Like Isabel," Conor said.

"For now," Joe said.

There was a flurry at the door, and Conor turned to see Hadley running toward them.

"Have you seen CeCe?" she asked, sounding frantic.

"No," Conor said. "What's going on?"

"I fell asleep, and when I woke up, she wasn't in the suite," Hadley said. "I've asked everyone at reception, in the restaurant—no one has seen her."

"Isabel," Conor said, feeling a kick in his gut.

"She's not at the desk," Hadley said. "Agnes just told me the police are looking for her. But she's a friend, isn't she? I told you—she witnessed Maddie's signature. Maddie wouldn't have had her do that if she hadn't trusted her, right?"

"She's not a friend," Conor said.

No one asked any more questions; they simply joined the search. It wasn't just Isabel now—it was CeCe. Joe radioed his team to tell them that CeCe was missing, and that Isabel very likely had her.

Conor and Tom worked together. They started on the main floor, then checked the stairwells. The stairs were covered in blue carpet, so their footsteps were muffled. But then, Isabel's would be, too, if they were on her trail. Doors led from the stairway to various levels. They walked down the beach-level corridor, wound around and up to the movie theater, where a few guests were watching *It's a Wonderful Life*.

They descended another stairway to the lowest level, and they walked into the garage. Various hotel vehicles were parked here, as well as cars belonging to the suite owners. Conor knew that Maddie's Volvo wagon was among them.

On the far side of the garage, they walked through a door that led to a salmon-pink hallway marked with a sign that said CENTER FOR WINE & CULINARY ARTS. Conor had been down here with Kate the first day they'd arrived, for a cooking demonstration. The chef had shown a small group how to properly prepare filet of sole.

Then the sommelier had served glasses of French white wine—Conor had had no clue what it was, but Kate had been impressed. They'd learned that the Ocean House had an eight-thousand-bottle collection, stored in their library wine cellar adjacent to the cooking-class station. Kate had pointed through the wine cellar's glass door and said, "I wonder how many of those eight thousand bottles cost a thousand dollars or more."

"Are you serious?" Conor had asked.

"Sure," she'd said. "Some of my art clients collect wine, too."

"A thousand dollars for some wine that will be gone an hour after it's opened?"

"Should we have one for dinner?" Kate had asked.

"Why not two?" Conor had asked back, and they'd laughed.

Now, entering the space with Tom, Conor wondered how likely it was that they would find CeCe and Isabel here.

They stopped and listened. The Center for Wine & Culinary Arts was apparently empty, but Conor heard a small scuffling sound, then some mewing, almost like a kitten. That's when he knew: they were here.

He nodded to Tom, who had his hand on his holstered sidearm. Conor went first, walking slowly down the wide corridor toward the intimate kitchen and the doorway to the wine cellar. The mewing sound stopped. Had he imagined it? He paused to listen again, and everything exploded.

He heard a rumble first, then the sound of shattering glass. It seemed to go on forever, punctuated by a woman screaming: "Look what you've done, look what you've done!"

Conor and Tom tore around the corner, into the wine cellar, and saw Isabel lying in a pile of broken glass, bleeding from cuts on her arms and face. CeCe stood with her back to a wall of wine bottles.

"I didn't break any wine," she said, looking up at Conor. "I just tipped over the glasses, that's all."

"It's okay, sweetheart," Conor said, scooping her up. He held her tight. His heart was racing. He knew how close they had come to losing her.

"She's bad," CeCe said, pointing at Isabel.

"What a little liar you are," Isabel said. "All I was doing was trying to find you. Everyone was worried. I was trying to help you." She stood up, bleeding from her cuts, then stalked toward the door.

"Tom?" Conor said, gesturing at her. His brother nodded and held Isabel's wrist to stop her from leaving. She screamed and began to hit him, but he reached for his handcuffs and snapped them on.

"She was going to kidnap me, like Ronnie did," CeCe said.

"But you stopped her," Conor said. "You are brave, CeCe."

"Take her to Hadley," Tom said. He nodded at Isabel. "I got this one."

"I'll send Joe down."

"Yep," Tom said, not taking his eyes off Isabel Almeida. She kept struggling, even though she was cuffed, saying that CeCe was a liar, that the little girl was just trying to get attention, that she would report Conor and Tom for abuse, for brutality. She'd get a lawyer from her sister's firm to sue them.

"Am I in trouble?" CeCe asked, frowning, her arm slung around Conor's neck.

"Not one bit," Conor said. "You're a hero. And you're going to get a medal."

"I want Aunt Hadley," CeCe said as Conor carried her away from the broken glass, away from Isabel.

"We're going to go find her right now," Conor said.

He carried her up a flight of stairs and down a long hallway to the beautiful old elevator, where she loved to push the buttons. And when they got there, they met Kate, just arriving back from Maine.

While holding CeCe as tightly as he could with one arm, Conor pulled Kate to him with the other.

"We got them," he whispered into her ear.

"I knew you would," Kate whispered into his.

Then CeCe pushed the arrow pointing up, and together the three of them rode the elevator to Hadley in Sea Garden.

53

And CeCe *was* a hero.

Hadley knew that more than anyone.

When everything had calmed down, Conor explained the whole thing to her and Kate. Joe and his team took Isabel Almeida away. Conor called his counterpart in the Maine State Police, and they picked up Genevieve Dickinson. When they got to her apartment, the painting based on Maddie's *Last Night* was gone, but the photo Kate had snapped of it was evidence that it had existed. Hadley realized the risk Kate had taken, going to Genevieve's. She watched Conor put his arms around Kate.

"I didn't want you to go up there," Conor said. "And that was before I knew how involved she was. She was in on the murder plot, and you were alone with her. If she had seen you take that photo . . ."

"But she didn't," Kate said. "I told you—I'm always careful."

Hadley could see that Conor was full of emotion, as Hadley herself was. Genevieve could have killed Kate. They might have never seen her again.

"She probably destroyed the painting after I left," Kate said. "Once she figured out their whole plan was falling apart. I stood outside the door and heard her talking on the phone. I assume it was Isabel."

"I think you're right," Conor said.

The day after the winter solstice, when Isabel and Johnny were arrested and the Garsons caught at Logan, Joe told them that Johnny had agreed to take a plea bargain in return for testifying against Isabel and the Garsons.

Hadley felt raw from his betrayal. He was her business partner. Even more, he had once been her brother-in-law, and he was the father of Maddie's baby. He hadn't killed her, or steered the plot, but there had been so many opportunities for him to stop the Almeidas. To protect Maddie.

No one had been there for Maddie. She had trusted, even loved, the people who had conspired against her. Johnny, her lawyer Jeanne, and Isabel—a woman who had pretended to be her friend, who had convinced her she would protect her from the outside world.

On the day before Christmas Eve, Hadley learned that the state's attorney would be filing charges against Jeanne Gladding and others at Cross, Gladding, and White. She tried to call Bernard, but he didn't answer. She figured he was still shooting his TV show and making excuses. Hadley kept waiting for CeCe to ask if she would see him at Christmas, but she didn't. It was as if CeCe had the inner wisdom of someone much older, as if she already knew her father wasn't coming.

Instead, she asked about Ronnie.

"Where is Ronnie?" she asked that afternoon, when they were in the suite, making cookies for their friends who would be coming over the next night to celebrate Christmas Eve.

"He's in jail," Hadley said, watching CeCe's face. Her niece seemed to be concentrating on cutting out dough with a Santa cookie cutter. CeCe didn't speak for a few moments, but then she looked up with a very serious expression.

"Is he okay?" CeCe asked.

Hadley wasn't sure how to answer that. She knew that Ronnie, like the others, was being held without bail at a correctional facility. And Hadley wanted it that way. The plan might not have been his idea, but he had pulled the trigger and ended Maddie's life. He was only fifteen, but he had killed her sister and terrified CeCe.

"He's in trouble for what he did," Hadley said. "He did some really terrible things."

"I know," CeCe said. "He cried, though."

"He did?"

"He said he was sorry," CeCe said. "That's what he told me. 'CeCe, I'm sorry,' he said. He was crying."

Hadley waited for her to say more. CeCe had told the police many details about her experience, but how many more was she holding inside? As Conor had said, traumatic memories could stay locked inside a person for days, for years, or forever.

"His father was bad to him," CeCe said, picking up the Santa-shaped cookie dough and, with vigor, squishing it into a shapeless blob between her two palms. She rolled it into a ball and held it. "Zane, that was his name. He was very mean."

"I know," Hadley said. "The police caught him, too."

"He's in jail, too?"

"Yes," Hadley said. "He's not going to hurt you anymore, CeCe."

"Or Ronnie?" CeCe asked.

"No, he's not going to hurt Ronnie anymore, either," Hadley said.

CeCe nodded, her expression neutral as she pressed the dough down on the marble counter, patting it flat, getting it just the way she wanted it, then using the cookie cutter to turn it back into Santa.

Hadley had invited the Reids to join them for Christmas Eve, so the next night, CeCe's people gathered around the tree in the Sea Garden suite. Signs of Maddie were everywhere. Her black coat was still in the hall closet; her velvet slippers were tucked under the table in the foyer; her notes and sketches were scattered on the desk. The snow had stopped, so the night was clear. There was no wind. The sound of the waves came through the closed windows, gentle and peaceful, a reminder that the ocean was forever.

Other things were, too.

Hadley stood with her back to the fireplace, gazing at her niece. CeCe sat on the floor, drawing pictures on the low table in front of the sofa. Hadley couldn't help but see that CeCe took after Maddie when it came to line and color. She drew with a suggestion of magic behind the images on the paper.

Tom had invited his wife, Jackie, and they sat in chairs flanking the sofa where Conor and Kate leaned against each other. The Ocean House had sent up trays of cheese, charcuterie, and desserts. The sommelier treated them to bottles of champagne and a pot of hot chocolate for CeCe.

Hadley had arranged for Maddie's last painting to be delivered. Kate was an expert at hanging large canvases, so she had measured the wall, determined the proper height, and directed Conor on where to place the hooks.

Last Night now hung in Maddie's beloved suite. At first, Hadley had worried that it would be too terrible to face every day: a tableau illustrating Maddie's death. She wasn't sure if she could stand it, and she was even more concerned that it would trouble CeCe.

But it turned out to be the opposite. CeCe seemed to take comfort in the painting—the peaceful image of her mother asleep in the snowy night. And it wasn't blood. It wasn't a stream of red ribbons. It was a garden of red roses. Low over the ocean, the stars glowed, telling stories in the night sky.

"She's a snow angel," CeCe had said the moment she first saw the painting.

"She is," Hadley had said.

Now, with people who loved CeCe surrounding her, talking, drawing, Hadley felt it was a celebration. Maddie hadn't wanted a funeral. She had wanted to be remembered for her art. Someday down the road, Hadley and CeCe would take her ashes to museums. They would dance in front of her favorite paintings.

Maybe they would do that in the spring.

"Okay, everyone," Kate said, standing up and raising her champagne glass, "are we ready?"

"Yes," everyone except CeCe said.

"Ready for what?" CeCe asked.

"For your medal," Conor said. "Remember?"

A huge smile filled CeCe's face. "When you picked me up and carried me away from Isabel," she said.

"That's right," Conor said. "I said you were a hero. I also said—",

"You were going to give me a medal," she said, smiling even wider.

"And here it is," Kate said.

Hadley knew that Kate had gone foraging in local antique shops until she found the perfect plain silver disk. It had originally been a pendant on someone's necklace, suspended by a leather cord. But she'd found a length of red-white-and-blue-striped satin ribbon at the same vintage store, slid it through the ring atop the silver disk.

Hadley had imposed on an artist friend in Charlestown, who made jewelry out of metal and precious gems, to do the engraving as quickly as possible.

Conor slid the ribbon over CeCe's head.

CeCe looked down, held the disk in her hand, tried to read the inscription.

"It's upside down," she said. "What does it say?"

"CeCe the Hero," Conor said.

"Look on the back," Hadley said.

CeCe turned it over, and there, etched in the silver, was the image of a snow angel.

"Mommy," CeCe said.

"Yep," Hadley said.

"Forever," CeCe said.

"She is," Hadley said, looking around the room, feeling all that love for CeCe pouring from their friends. Then she looked at the painting on the wall, the one that her sister had done of the last night of her life, and she knew that the love was for Maddie, too.

They all sat by the fire, drinking champagne and hot chocolate, admiring CeCe's drawings, telling her how proud her mother would be of her. They put on music, and CeCe pulled Hadley to her feet so they could dance.

CeCe had gotten everyone dancing, and Conor felt the heat rising. He held Kate in his arms, doing a slower dance than the music called for. She was his best friend, his true love. She stood on tiptoes, arms around his neck, gazing up at him with an odd smile.

"I'm a terrible dancer," he said.

"No, you're not," she said.

"I've never been good at it," he said.

"You're wonderful at it."

"I get nervous."

"Maybe you just need some fresh air," she said.

She crossed the room ahead of him and opened the french doors. While everyone else stayed inside by the fire, Conor and Kate walked onto the terrace. There was no wind. He heard the waves breaking— gently, not crashing. He noticed how dark and still the beach looked. The police had left, taken their lights with them. It was a scene of perfect peace. He took a deep breath and realized it was the first he'd taken since that night when they had found Hadley kneeling beside Maddie's body.

They could see the five windmills, miles across the water, on the far side of Block Island. Their red lights flashed in the distance, landmarks that would always remind him of this night. He and Kate would look back and remember how their lives had changed on Christmas Eve.

"This is what I've always wanted," he said to Kate.

"Me, too," she said.

"I brought you here to the Ocean House because . . . ," he began, the words he'd planned to say for so long running through his mind. He reached into his pocket, and that's when the panic hit him. He'd had the ring with him every minute since arriving at the hotel. And now it wasn't there.

He patted his pockets again. Could he have dropped it on the terrace floor? Or inside, while they were dancing? When had he last felt it? He knew for sure he'd had it when he was standing on the verandah with Tom and Joe.

It was a beautiful ring, a sapphire, Kate's favorite stone, flanked by two diamonds because Conor felt that Kate deserved all the diamonds in the world.

"Kate," he said, "I can't believe this. I have something. I can't find it, though . . ."

"You dropped it," she said, "when you put the medal around CeCe's neck."

She opened her hand, and he saw the ring glinting in her outstretched palm. He took it from her, and then he held her hand, and they both laughed. The laughter didn't last too long before he noticed that her eyes were wet. So were his.

This was their night, his and Kate's, but it was CeCe's, too. From the moment they had come upon Maddie murdered in the snow, their families had become entwined. It had happened in an instant. In other cases, solving the crimes had eased the strong bonds between him and the victims. He would always care, but he might not ever see the victims' families again. That hadn't happened here, and it wouldn't. CeCe and Hadley were in his and Kate's lives now, and that wasn't going to change.

"I hadn't expected to do this on a terrace with a bunch of people just inside," Conor said, gesturing at the french doors.

"I wouldn't have it any other way," Kate said.

Conor glanced over. Through the glass, he saw his brother and Jackie, Hadley and CeCe, all dancing by the fire. Above them, Maddie seemed to be watching them, looking out from the canvas of *Last Night*. He felt the challenge: there were promises to be made.

"Kate, will you?" he asked.

"I will," she said.

He slid the ring onto her finger. She stood on her toes and kissed him, and they were surrounded by the sounds of the waves coming from the beach and the soft voices of the people they loved coming from inside the suite. He thought of the promises demanded by the moment, by the painting: life had to be lived, and love had to be held on to, as tightly as possible.

So he held Kate tighter and tighter. They stood there on the terrace of the Ocean House for a long time, in the cold, still night, until one last kiss, when it was time to go inside and tell everyone what he was pretty sure they already knew.

"Hey," Conor said, holding the door open for Kate as they stepped back into the warm suite, arms around each other, smiling at the family. "We're getting married."

ACKNOWLEDGMENTS

The Ocean House is one of my favorite places in the world, and it is my home away from home. I've written parts of many novels there, including this one. It captures my imagination, so forgive me if storytelling has occasionally swept past reality throughout these pages. Every grand hotel deserves a fictional murder tale, so I offer this one to the dear Ocean House.

I am so grateful to my friend Deborah Goodrich Royce. She is a bestselling author and the founder and host of the Ocean House Author Series. She brings writers and readers together in this literary haven by the sea and has created a great community for all of us. Thank you to the booksellers at Savoy Bookshop and Café for their tremendous energy and support.

I have deep gratitude for everyone who works at the Ocean House. They make it feel like home. There are too many to name, but every single person means a lot to me and is forever in my heart.

All my love and thanks to Maureen, Olivier, and Amelia Onorato.

Endless thanks to my lifelong friend William Twigg Crawford.

Much gratitude to Susan Fisher, Amelia Onorato, Cara Lopilato, and everyone at the Mystic Museum of Art.

Big thanks to Matt Cavaco for sharing stories of his experience in the United States Coast Guard. Thank you for your service, Matt.

Once again, I thank Rob Derry for generously answering my questions about law enforcement in Connecticut.

Thank you to Patrick Carson, my very talented social media manager.

I am incredibly lucky to work with my editor, Liz Pearsons; my developmental editor, Charlotte Herscher; and my whole team at Thomas & Mercer. Gracie Doyle, thank you for believing in me.

Andrea Cirillo has been my agent forever. I am so grateful to her, Jane Berkey, Jessica Errera, and everyone at the Jane Rotrosen Agency for all our years together, for making everything possible.

ABOUT THE AUTHOR

Photo © by Kristina Loggia

Luanne Rice is the Amazon Charts and *New York Times* bestselling author of thirty-eight novels, including *The Shadow Box* and *Last Day*. Several have been adapted for television, including *Crazy in Love* and *Blue Moon*, as well as *Follow the Stars Home* and *Silver Bells* for Hallmark Hall of Fame and *Beach Girls* as a Lifetime miniseries. For more information, visit www.luannerice.com.